THE PALADI

Whistle Blower

KAY COVE

Whistleblower © 2023 by Kay Cove LLC

Editing by Caitlin Lengerich
Proofing by C. Ross and Caitlin Lengerich

eBook ISBN: 978-1-961071-96-4
Paperback Print ISBN: 979-8-9863043-9-7
Hardback Print ISBN: 978-1-961071-95-7

www.kaycove.com

This one is for all the kind, loving, tender souls who choose to take the high road, but secretly fantasize about getting even.

Grace isn't a weakness. ***You're so much stronger than you realize.***

"You've seen my descent, now watch my rising."

-RUMI

PLAYLIST

"SILENCE" - MARSHMELLO, KHALID
"AIMED TO KILL" - JADE LEMAC
"MET HIM LAST NIGHT" - DEMI LOVATO, ARIANA GRANDE
"CLOSE" - NICK JONAS, TOVE LO
"GANGSTA" - KEHLANI
"CONTROL" - BRYCE SAVAGE
"CHILLS - DARK VERSION" - MICKEY VALEN, JOEY MYRON
"CHAINS" - NICK JONAS
"SKIN" - RIHANNA
"THE BEST I EVER HAD" - LIMI
"YEAH, I SAID IT" - RIHANNA
"MIDNIGHT SWIM" - VANESSA ELISHA
"YOU PUT A SPELL ON ME" - AUSTIN GIORGIO
"WICKED GAME" - DAISY GRAY
"OCEAN" - MARTIN GARRIX, KHALID
"INFINITY" - JAYMES YOUNG

CONTENT NOTES

This romance story contains violence and explicit sexual content that may be considered disturbing for some readers. For a full list of triggers please click here, or scan the code below.

www.kaycove.com/content-warnings

PROLOGUE
CHANDLER

12 YEARS AGO

IS sixteen old enough to be a man?

I don't feel like one, even with this pistol in my hand.

"Suz?" I whisper, but I know she won't respond. She's face down on the tile, her long, thick hair sprawled out, saturating in the growing puddle of blood. She was my last friend in the world.

It may seem odd that my only friend was a forty-nine-year-old bar owner who chain-smokes and takes her whiskey neat, but she has been more of a mother to me than mine ever was.

"Suzanne, please?" I don't really know what I'm asking for. *Please rise from the dead. Please let this be a nightmare.*

It's my fault. I could've saved her if the damn safe didn't lock me out. Suzanne told me to stay low and run when the armed men shot through the glass, hoping they hadn't spotted me. She promised me all they wanted was to rob her. "Hide in the kitchen, Chandler," she instructed. When I hesitated, she assured me, "It's just money, honey. Better broke than dead."

I heard the cash register open and close. There was shouting and Suzanne telling everyone to just calm down. I heard a few bottles breaking on the ground. Then it was silent. I thought the worst was over until I heard the sharp *pop*. With my heart racing so fast I thought it'd explode, I ran to the hidden safe to get to the emergency pistol. It locked on me when I transposed the stupid numbers. Every single time I switched the two and the one, I had to wait an *entire* fucking minute. By the time I burst through the kitchen, arms outstretched, gun in my hand, the only person left was Suzanne…

And she wasn't moving.

The sudden crunch of glass makes me look up at the front door. Straining my arms, I point the gun, still in my hand, at the woman who has crawled through the shattered window.

"Easy now," she says, her voice calm, soothing, and surprisingly deep for her slight frame. She's dressed head to toe in black, including her work boots. It looks like some sort of uniform, but I've never seen a cop wear this much leather. She holds up her palms in surrender but continues to advance, the glass crunching under each of her steps.

"Stop," I hiss. "I'll shoot."

"Well, relax your shoulders first," she says, taking another step forward. "You won't hit the broad side of a barn tensed up like that."

The gun begins to slip against my sweaty palms, so I grip it tighter. "What?"

Her footsteps are silent now as she's past the shattered glass from the window and almost within my reach. "Have you ever fired a gun before, Chandler?"

My heart stops at the mention of my name. Taking a closer look, this woman is younger than I'd thought. Her lipstick is bright red, but she wears no other makeup to accentuate her angular features. Her jet-black hair is pulled into a low ponytail. She's graceful, poised, and seemingly unbothered by the dead body lying next to us.

I don't know why, but relief floods through me as she

reaches out, palm facing the ceiling, intent on relieving me of the gun. She's a stranger. I shouldn't trust her but somehow my instincts tell me I'm safe now. I hand her the gun, surrendering my very last defense.

"There you go," she mumbles, as she switches on the safety and tucks it in her coat pocket.

"No," I mumble.

"Hm?" she asks, already having moved on from her question. She examines me head to toe.

"I've never fired a gun before. I didn't do this," I say, looking at my friend, hot tears beginning to blur my vision. "I didn't hurt her. I wouldn't."

"I know you didn't. Did you see it happen?"

I look at my raggedy tennis shoes in shame as I shake my head side to side. "I was hiding," I admit. "I couldn't get to the gun in time." I wipe my face with both palms, attempting to remove the evidence of my unmanly hysterics. "I left her out here all alone."

"Chandler," the woman says, her dark eyes looking wary. "Gun or not, there was nothing you could do. The men who came through here are part of Dom Peroli's gang. They're ruthless, merciless, and don't blink twice at hurting women"—she raises her brows at me—"or children. It's good you hid, or you'd be lying next to your friend right now."

"Are you a cop?" I ask.

"No."

"FBI?" I ask, looking her up and down.

"Used to be," she offers.

Who did I just give a gun to?

"Grab a seat," she says, nodding to the stools at the bar behind us. "We don't have too long. The cops will be on their way soon, and Chandler, it'd be easier to pin this on you than to provoke Peroli by going after his men."

"*What?*" The nightmare of this evening won't end. I'm innocent. "But I didn't—"

3

"Take a seat." She pats my shoulder before she steps behind the bar. "We have a lot to talk about and not a lot of time."

As my thudding heartbeat begins to slow and my adrenaline calms, the reality of this bizarre encounter really hits me. *Who is she? Why does she know my name? Why aren't we calling for help? Why am I the only person uncomfortable with a dead person in the room?*

"Who are you?" I growl, trying to sound more threatening.

"My name is Vesper," she mutters absentmindedly as she scans the bottles on the glass bar shelves. She settles on one of Suzanne's most expensive whiskeys. No one ever orders it because it's sixty dollars for a single drink. And considering our customers were bikers, seedy poker players, and cheap drunks, that limited edition Macallan was more of a souvenir than anything. Suzanne always said we'd open it on my eighteenth birthday if I stuck around.

Of course I was going to stick around. She needed a barkeep she could pay peanuts under the table, and I needed a family. We were a good pair.

Pop. Vesper uncorks the bottle after fetching two glasses. "Do you drink?"

I pull out a stool, now eager to sit. My legs feel heavy, but also like jelly. It feels like I'm trying to run in a dream. "I'm underage."

She snorts and pours two drinks anyway. "Good answer, but at sixteen you should also be in school, sleeping in a bed instead of an air mattress in a shitty studio above a dive bar, and certainly not bartending sixty hours a week for far less than minimum wage." She slides the glass over to me. Planting her elbows on the bar, she leans closer to peer at me. "Funny…" she mumbles. "Your eyes are blue."

I take a small sip of the whiskey, enjoying the burn on my tongue. "So?"

4

"I put green eyes in your file. I don't normally miss the little details."

"Why do you know so much about me? What file?"

"I know your father, in a way. He was involved with a case I worked a few years ago."

"So you lied—you are a cop."

She shakes her head. "*Former* FBI."

I throw back the entire glass and wince as the whiskey sets my throat on fire. "I hope you're the one who threw that piece of shit in jail."

"I helped," she says. "I was worried about what would happen to you and your mother when your dad was sentenced. So, I've been watching."

My dad was an abuser, rapist, and murderer. Life in prison, without the possibility of parole wasn't enough. My mother, on the other hand, was a trickier subject. Can you throw someone in jail for giving up on themselves, and their kid? Is that *actually* a crime?

"My mother has had pills to keep her company for the past four years. She didn't even notice when I dropped out of school and ran away six months ago."

"It's a shame. You're smart. Good grades, great test scores. You only had two more years in school and probably would've gotten a scholarship. A decent college could've gotten you out of here. Why'd you quit so close to graduation?"

"A scholarship won't pay room and board." I purse my lips, not sure if I should be honest. Why spill secrets to this stranger who emerged minutes after a murder? Then again, who else in the world do I have to talk to? "And also, because my stepdad threw even more punches than my dad."

She nods like she already knows my sordid family history. "You're a strong-looking guy. Why didn't you hit him back?"

I wanted to. Every single time. I wanted to wrap my hand around my stepdad's throat and watch the light go out in his eyes. But I couldn't. "Because when he really felt threatened, he took it out on my mom."

The drugs made Mom so weak, she couldn't take any more hits. I was terrified I'd watch him beat her to death. I begged her to leave for years, for us to just run away and start over somewhere new. It took me a while to learn she'd already left without me... The pills, the needles, the smoke... They took her away.

"Let me tell you something right now. Something very important. Women are not weak. But the men who lay hands on them *are*."

I bite the inside of my cheek. "Except my mom *is* weak."

"Your mom is an addict who needs help."

"She won't take it. I've tried but I can't figure out—"

"You're a kid. You were robbed of your childhood, Chandler. It's not your job to save her."

I press against my temples with my palms as the memories from as early back as I can remember flash through my head. How many times did I find her passed out, thinking she was dead? If I ever thought I'd see a cold body on the ground, it wasn't Suzanne. It suddenly dawns on me that we're conversing as if my murdered friend isn't lying three feet away.

"Can we cover her, at least?" I ask, pulling at the hem of my thin hoodie.

She shakes her head solemnly. "I'm sorry. Don't touch her. We don't need to give the cops any more evidence against you."

"Why would they blame me? This makes *no* sense. Tell me what's going on. Who are you, really?"

She slams back her drink. "You want to dip a toe, or dive right into the deep end?"

"Dive."

"I run a team of *insurgents* so to speak. We're not cops, not military, not FBI, CIA, DIA. But we help them from time to time. You see, law enforcement and government agencies have some limitations, and that's why they call upon us."

"Limitations? Such as?" Looking closer, I see Vesper has not one gun, not two…but three. One in a holster around her hips. One strapped around her thigh. The last is Suzanne's, still in her coat pocket. That's a lot of bullets at her mercy.

"Civil rights. The Constitution. Sometimes, just outright stupidity." She shuts her eyes, inhales, and then slowly exhales like she's breathing away a bad memory. "In about twenty minutes, the police are going to dust this place top to bottom, put your friend in a body bag, and report this as a robbery gone bad, instead of what it is—a gang slaying. They know who's behind it, but they won't pursue Peroli or his dogs because he's wanted for much higher crimes. Pulling mass quantities of cocaine across the border is one of his more redeeming qualities, it's the human trafficking that the feds are most concerned about. But they don't have enough infor-mation and pursuing his gang will only spook him. He'll go back into hiding. The best way to get Peroli is to let him oper-ate, unleashed, hoping he'll get too greedy, too cocky, slip up, and make a mistake that they can use to put him away for good."

I clench my jaw, thinking about the scared look in Suzanne's eyes. She confidently told me to hide and every-thing was going to be okay, but now that I'm reflecting on it—her fearful expression didn't match her words.

"How many innocent people have to die before he makes a mistake?"

"I wish I knew." She tips the whiskey bottle, filling her glass again. "But here's what I do know—this is a well-known bar in a small town. People won't like the idea that one of their own can be murdered in cold blood and the killer walks free. The cops will be highly motivated to close this case. What's one more angry delinquent, who is bound to fall into a life of crime anyway, behind bars?"

7

"Fuck you," I growl. "Like I said, I didn't do this. I would never hurt Suzanne. My mother. Any woman."

"Would you kill to protect them?"

"What?" I croak, surprised at her candid question.

"Chandler, my team is comprised of hired assassins. But I am very careful about the jobs we agree to. Peroli and his men don't need justice. They need to meet death—swiftly. *That's* what we do."

I inhale and exhale in silence. The nerves prickle through my forearms, up my shoulder, and then around my neck. I wish it was just nerves, but I'll admit there's a sprinkle of intrigue. I just don't know how to respond.

She takes another sip from her glass, her eyes locked on me. "I know you're not old enough to really know about whiskey, but this is *superb.*"

"It's looting," I grumble. "We're drinking a dead woman's prize possession."

"I'd pay her for the drink, if I could." She swivels the glass in her hand causing the amber liquid to swirl furiously. There's something ethereal about Vesper. Something power- ful. I envy her confident demeanor at the moment.

"If you've been watching me because you think the apple doesn't fall far from the tree... I'm nothing like my dad. Suzanne took me in when she found me sleeping by the dumpsters out back. I needed a job, and somewhere to stay. That's it. I don't get into trouble. And I've definitely never killed anyone."

"I know, Chandler. Which is why I think I can trust you." She pulls Suzanne's gun out of her pocket and sets it on the bar between us. "If you knew how to operate this properly, would you have stepped in? Would you be willing to take a criminal's life, to save an innocent one?"

I glance at the gun, then Vesper's steady gaze. "I think so. Your team is good guys...who kill bad guys?" I really need her to be *good.*

8

"It's a little bit more complicated than that."

I take a deep breath as I glance at my hands and see that they are finally still and steady. "Are you offering me a job?"

"I'm offering you a life," she says. "But I can't guarantee it's better than this one."

"What can you guarantee?"

"You'll never be hungry again. You'll always have a roof over your head. You'll have a family, *of sorts*, but most importantly, my protection. And I promise, Chandler, I take really good care of my own."

"Sounds too good to be true," I mumble.

"There are requirements. This life I'm giving you, won't be yours. You'll be part of my team. When I say chase—you run. When I say jump—you fly. You never take a life unless I give the command."

"So, you'd basically own my ass?" I let out a short laugh.

Her gaze grows cold, and I have the sudden urge to cower. It's as if I just taunted a lethal lioness. "I'll protect you from making the painfully hard decisions I have to make every day, Chandler. It's not as simple as good versus evil in this world. The good guys do bad things, and sometimes bad guys help others. The world is gray and muddled, but that's my bullshit to sift through. And you should know—"

"I'm in." The words are out before I really register them.

"Let me finish," she warns. "If you're going to help me police this world, you can't be part of it. We're ghosts. We operate in the shadows. We don't have homes, just places we stay. We don't get married. We don't have kids. No blood ties. We stay as detached as we can. Do you really understand what that means?" Her expression is strained. Her forehead crinkles and she looks at me piteously, like she's debating whether to send a small puppy into a vicious dog fight.

I'm silent as I ponder it for a moment, just to show her I'm taking her seriously. "You can't miss what you've never known."

9

"Okay," she says. "Then it's time to go. Do you have a wallet on you?" I nod in reply and she continues. "Throw it on the bar, opened, but keep your cash." I do as she says while she pulls a pocketknife out of an obscure compartment on the inside of her coat. "Are you squeamish about blood?"

My stomach twists as I question my sanity. "Not particularly."

Vesper extends the blade, then holds it out to me, handle first. "I just need a few drops. Enough for forensics to pick up on." She taps the heel of her palm to show me where I should cut.

I don't give myself a chance to think twice. What are my other options here? I can't go home. Suzanne's gone. I have no one in the world who'd help me... Except apparently this woman. Taking the knife, I poke the heel of my palm, feeling the sharp sting. I watch the dot of blood grow into a thick drop.

She finishes her drink and tucks the cup into her pocket. "Touch your wallet and then wave your hand around a bit."

I wipe a red stain on the front of my wallet, before sending blood droplets flying across the bar as I shake my hand violently.

"Perfect," Vesper says. "Now it looks like there were two victims tonight."

She pulls a wipe out of her pocket along with a little bottle that has a strong chemical smell. At first, I think it's to clean my hand, but instead she grabs Suzanne's gun, collects the bullets, and then proceeds to wipe it down with the solution.

"You're getting rid of the evidence that you were here?" I ask.

"Yes."

"Do you want my glass too?" I nudge it toward her with the back of my hand.

"Not necessary. *You* were here, Chandler. *I* was not." Grabbing the bottle of whiskey, she slides out from behind the bar.

Vesper clasps her free hand against my shoulder and squeezes. Her grasp is firm, but there's something tender in her touch. It's reassuring. It's the only reason I'm willing to hand my life over to a complete stranger.

"I already knew you were something special, but I'm impressed. You are incredibly brave. Far braver than you should have to be." She smiles at me, but there's sorrow in her eyes. I wipe the last remnants of blood against my jeans and my hand looks good as new. Vesper knew exactly where to cut, so the wound would close quickly.

"Are you ready?"

Glancing down at the ground, I look at Suzanne one last time. I close my eyes and try to shake the visual. I don't want to remember her this way. Instead, I picture her in the metal chair in the alleyway, smoking a pack, a stiff drink in her hand, telling me some story or another about how she broke up a bar fight between two bikers twice her size. Suzanne was tough. That's how I want to remember her... Not like this.

Bye, my friend. I'm so sorry I couldn't save you. Thank you for everything.

Letting out a deep breath, I nod. "I'm ready. Where are we going?"

"Home," Vesper says with the warmest tenor—like a mother calling her kid in for dinner, the way mine never did. I like the way it sounds. *Home.* Vesper moves for the front door and I fall in line behind her. Suddenly, she spins around, stopping me in my tracks.

"By the way," she says, extending a hand, "welcome, officially, to operation PALADIN."

ONE

EDEN

"SO WHAT EXACTLY DID YOU do at your most recent position?"

Ronnie, the Chief of Human Resources at Redd Tech, questions me with a shit-eating grin. I hate the way he sits on the edge of his desk, one knee hiked up, and the sole of his sneaker scuffing his modern white desk.

"Is this really necessary?" I ask, glancing around the office. "You know what I do." Or more accurately, what I *used* to do.

I swear… If he follows up this question with, "Where do you see yourself in five years…"

This interview—hell, this entire office—screams Silicon Valley. It's meant to be energetic and casual. The embedded message is: *we're young, we're fun, we're tech badasses, and we care more about the invention than the presentation.* Except, I know the truth. Ronnie's anarchy t-shirt only looks casual, but it retails for over two hundred dollars. The sneakers, which he purposely left untied, are from a designer line that isn't even available to the public. They have to be custom-ordered and cost about the same as a down payment on a brand-new Ford F-150.

Ronnie is wearing ripped denim blue jeans while conducting an interview for the Director of Personnel—a position with a salary in the low six-figures.

I think.

It's been a while since I've had to negotiate my annual salary. I'll ask for two hundred thousand, but the truth is, with my baggage, I'll settle for one twenty, which is peanuts in this city.

Ronnie scoots an inch forward toward the edge of the desk, his left leg dangling. I shift in the weird, turquoise egg-shaped office chair I'm sitting in, and try to divert my gaze away from his crotch, which is uncomfortably close to my face

"Eden, play along. Please. It's a formality."

Filling my lungs to the brim, I let out an exaggerated sigh before I give the speech I've given hundreds of times before. "As you know, my doctorate is in organizational leadership and development. My role as a consultant has been to help data-centric companies scale their workforce without imploding from rapid growth."

"Can you elaborate a bit?" Ronnie asks with a teasing smile. I want to slap him right now. He knows exactly what my expertise is because we went to school together. I pursued my doctorate, while Ronnie finished his master's, but we shared a few classes. Not to mention, at one brief point, I was his boss. This entire interview is borderline demeaning.

"How so?" I ask curtly, forcing a clipped smile.

"The company you worked for most recently—Empress—what did they do? What did you do there?"

Now, I'm pissed.

What's his endgame, bringing up Empress? This was supposed to be a job *offer*. Ronnie is a friend. I'm overqualified for the position I'm interviewing for. In fact, I'm overqualified for *his* position.

Still, I'm desperate. So, I bite back my irritation and

answer his ridiculous questions. "As you're *well* aware, Empress developed a ground-breaking app that secured half a billion dollars in its first round of fundraising. The algorithms they developed were like nothing else on the market.

"Empress would allow users to compile all of their social media platforms into one control hub. The technology was built to continuously evaluate all platforms, and compare them against the user's content performance, engagement, and target audience to essentially create a tailored rapid-growth approach depending on the user's specific goals. Their algorithm changed social media virality from a lottery system into a predictable pattern."

"One algorithm to rule them all," Ronnie jokes. *What an ass.* He knows what Empress did better than anyone. Redd Tech was their competitor—if you could call them that. Their developments paled in comparison. Empress's tech cracked the code on all the other social media platform's sneaky algorithms, but instead of hoarding it, they shared it, wanting to level the influencer and creator playing field.

Everyone deserves recognition. Everyone deserves a chance to be seen.

"Right. Something along those lines. As a user you could just create content and the app would predict the success of that content on various platforms based on your following, current trends, optimal posting time, etcetera. The predictions were unbelievably accurate. Empress could tell you almost down to a single digit what you could expect in likes, reach, and follows. It was basically a cheat sheet for the intricacies of content strategy. All you'd have to do is create content, and the Empress algorithm would monetize it for you."

"Beautiful elevator pitch."

"Thank you," I sass. "Empress was wildly successful right out of the gate, they needed to scale—*quickly*. I was their lead consultant on growth strategy for personnel."

Empress's tech division went from five employees to nearly eighty within the span of a month. They built a U.S.-based customer service team from scratch. They needed analysts, legal, accounting, human resources—you name it. The founders of the company were in so far over their heads. Their genius was in tech, but they had no idea how to build a healthy corporation. That's where I came in.

Ronnie nods along enthusiastically. "And you were success-ful. So successful, Empress offered you a full-time role as Chief of Operations?"

"Right."

"Which you accepted."

"Correct."

"And were fired three days later?" Ronnie asks.

I suck in a sharp breath, surprised at his candidness. "Unlawfully."

"Why?" Ronnie raises his eyebrows at me.

Why is he being so inquisitive? Empress's demise was publi-cized. He knows exactly why I was terminated, but he wants to hear me say it. *Again, what an asshole.*

"I stumbled across some incriminating information about Empress during my first day as Chief of Operations. I reported it to the authorities. Empress terminated me and filed a frivolous lawsuit against me for corporate espionage, which never came to fruition. The company was dissolved and charged on several felony counts."

"What counts?"

Shielding my face with my hands so Ronnie can't see my eyes roll, I grumble. "Ronnie, you know what counts. The corporation, along with the founders, were found guilty of conspiracy as well as aiding and abetting. It's public record."

It was a highly publicized case. From the moment I reported my findings to the feds, almost a year ago to the day, it was a media shitstorm.

"I know what they were charged with, but between you and I…" He leans in closer and I can almost feel his warm breath against my face. It makes my stomach twist with discomfort. "What did you find?"

What did I find? Evidence that Empress was attempting to start a civil war—which I can't say. I'm also not allowed to say that, in addition to charges that were broadcasted publicly, they were also charged with the felony of domestic terrorism. I'm buried so deep under NDAs, that if I were to even say the words *civil* and *war* in the same sentence, I'd have FBI agents breaking down my door so fast.

"Legally, I can't say."

"Come on, Eden. Give me something. Help me help you." Ronnie leans backward to my great relief. I relish the space between us.

Redd Tech is my final option. It was bad enough I had to beg Ronnie for this interview, but now I have the sneaking suspicion that I don't actually have the job, and this interview is far more than a formality.

"Help me?"

"I had to pull some serious strings to even make this interview happen. We have concerns. My boss has *big concerns.*"

"About what?"

"We don't want to go through what Empress went through. Every company has some skeletons in the closet—"

"Are you dabbling in felonies?"

"Eden, between the IRS and SEC, it doesn't matter if you're trying to do everything by the book, you're bound to accidentally screw up one way or another. All companies get nervous around a—"

He stops himself, with a pained expression, like he just ate something sour. But I know the word that's on the tip of his tongue.

"Just say it."

I watch his eyes, but he's suddenly very interested in his shoes.

"Whistleblower," he says reluctantly.

We whisper it like it's a dirty word, because in the corporate business world, it is. When I exposed Empress's illicit activity, I thought I was doing the right thing—saving lives. Preventing a lot of pandemonium and suffering. And perhaps that's still the FBI's narrative, except they've buried that narrative from the public in an attempt to "mitigate mass panic." I believe that was the verbiage they used. What they were really saying is that they didn't want the public to know that the only thing that kept any major tech or data collection company from exploiting a user's social security number, home address, bank account information, or personal internet searches was adherence to the law.

So what happens when a company decides to be unlawful?

Scary...isn't it? That our personal safety is heavily reliant on the ethical behavior of money-driven strangers. Of course, that's not a tidbit that the CIA, FBI, or DOJ necessarily want to shout through a bullhorn.

So, I told the truth...

Then I was told to shut up.

The entire world thinks I destroyed a beloved company and app because of a little bribery and coercion, when the reality is far grimmer.

"You can't offer me this job, can you, Ronnie?"

He shakes his head slowly.

"Then why even entertain this interview?" I finally ask.

Using his top teeth, he tugs on his bottom lip. "Because I wanted to see you. To know how you're doing. You wouldn't respond to any of my calls or texts. I was worried, I know it's been a rough year."

No, you don't know. It's been hell.

It was bad enough I lost my job, my credibility. I thought I had friends but it turns out I had colleagues, and after the

18

ordeal with Empress they disappeared so fast you would've thought I had leprosy.

If that wasn't enough, all the employees who were enjoying generous salaries, retirements, and company stock had a bone to pick with me for ruining their lives. It came out in the form of menacing letters and phone calls, graffitied profanity on my house and driveway, and a witch hunt on the internet. I couldn't defend myself and tell them that maybe I saved their lives…their children's lives. That minor detail probably would've helped calm their rage.

But thanks to the gag order the FBI put on me, as far as the laid-off employees knew, Dr. Eden Abbott, self-righteous snitch-bitch, single-handedly brought down Empress—the very company I busted my ass to help build. Their futures were ruined, and I was to blame.

I'm tired… I'm wary. The burden of doing the right thing is too damn heavy, and I'm about ready to give up. My dad would want me to fight. He'd tell me to pretend I'm brave until I actually am. I can almost hear the words in my head, exactly how he'd say them, *"Fuck this guy, fuck this interview, fuck this city. Hold your head high because the righteous people always prevail in the end."*

But it's been a year and it's only getting harder.

Either Dad was wrong or I'm not as righteous as I think.

I suck in a deep breath, then blow out all the hope I had left. I really thought Ronnie might come through for me. "Well, thanks for your time." I begin to rise, but he grabs my hand. I freeze out of pure discomfort.

"Have dinner with me."

"Excuse me?" I ask in a dangerously low tone. "You're married." I glance at his left hand still holding mine. There's a tan line, but no ring.

"Annie and I got divorced a few months ago. Look Eden… I had the biggest crush on you in grad school. Did you know that?"

KAY COVE

Actually, I didn't. Ronnie's cute and sweet. He has chocolate-colored curls and soft brown eyes. I never found him *sexy*, but I would've obliged a date had he asked. Ronnie is intelligent and we talk the same language—have the same interests, similar goals. But he had ample opportunity while we were both single, yet never made a move. He's only brave enough to ask me now because he's no longer intimidated by me or my career.

Narrowing my eyes, I say, "You should've asked me out, then."

He raises his brows. "Oh?"

"Yes, you should've asked me out, *back then*, instead of waiting until I was at the lowest point in my life and career. Did you really think you could lure me into a date, or whatever else is going through your mind, by taking advantage of my current desperation?"

Ronnie balks in surprise at my frankness. I force myself to smile so much that oftentimes, people forget I'm fully capable of being angry.

"Eden, I—"

"No, listen to me," I say, snatching my hand back. "I don't deserve this. Any of it. I did the honorable thing, and I was punished for it. Everything I've worked for? *Gone.* My reputation? *Brutalized.* I'm not even known as a martyr—just a traitor. I have nothing left except my own self-respect and it's cruel that you'd try to strip me of that too."

He opens his mouth then clamps it shut, unable to formulate a worthy response. I collect my handbag and rise, then point to the funky, modern chair.

"And by the way, this is a *ridiculous* chair for a HR professional's office," I say matter-of-factly. I release the angry breath I was holding and add, "Thank you for at least meeting with me. Up until I realized you were just baiting me with this interview to go out with you, it was actually nice to see you

20

again." I make my way to the door but spin around when Ronnie speaks.

"I'm sorry, Eden. I really am. Hang in there, I hope…"

"Hope what?" Tucking my hair behind my ear, I wait patiently for his response. I'm in dire need of some kind of profound message from the universe, even if Ronnie is the mouthpiece.

"That you get…I don't know…revenge."

"I don't want revenge."

"What do you want?"

Peace.

Rest.

It's been the longest year of my life, and I am so fucking tired.

I pop my shoulders as if it's no big deal. "Nothing. I'll be okay," I lie, then make my way through the office door, careful not to slam it behind me. I fly down the hallway past the rows of community desks and Bosu balls in lieu of office chairs, praying no one recognizes me, or worse, attempts to start a conversation. I've run out of fake smiles for the day.

I'm able to keep my composure until I see my car. Feeling the tears forming and the uncomfortable prickly heat in my cheeks, I hustle the last few steps to my SUV. My hurried foot-steps echo loudly off the walls of the parking garage. Sliding into the driver's seat, I mentally call out "safe."

Despite a year of emotional torture, I make sure that no one ever sees me cry. Tears make a person look guilty. I'm not.

I'm not, I'm not.

But I sure as hell do a lot of crying these days. It's to the point that I have a ritual. I fish through my purse, to find a small visual timer.

I used to teach this strategy to the leadership teams I worked with. Commanding groups of unmotivated and disgruntled entry-level customer service agents is no easy feat. It's like trying to appease the chronically dissatisfied, but I always teach the companies I work with that good leadership is poised—quick to listen, slow to speak, and always gracious.

But let's be honest…that shit can really wear you down.

I'd gather the entire leadership team and give everyone a visual timer and tell them to make room for their emotions. The more they bottled up, the bigger the explosion, and that's how people end up jumping off building rooftops. So, I instructed them to always *make time* to feel angry, sad, frustrated, and vengeful. *In private.* Then when the timer goes off…

Let it go.

Getting comfortable in my driver's seat, I turn the dial to ten minutes and it begins to tick… *No, that was a really big blow. That interview was your last hope. You deserve a little more time…* I twist the dial so the pointer rests on fifteen minutes.

Glancing around, I ensure there are no other cars or passersby on this side of the parking garage. I'm alone and I have exactly fifteen minutes to cry, melt, and completely fall apart. Afterward, I'll put myself back together and trudge forward like I've been doing for an entire year now.

Thirteen minutes left. I picture the cold, callous courtroom and staring into the eyes of the founders at Empress while I confessed to the judge about what I had found. It was a very private hearing, but it felt like I was naked, on stage, at the Super Bowl halftime show. I forced myself to speak clearly, but I wanted to hide and disappear.

Eleven minutes left. I close my eyes and see the late payment notifications for the family home Dad left me. The home my mother wanted to come back to. This home is my history, the only remnants of my family remaining, and I'm about to lose it to the bank.

Eight minutes left. I shiver at the memory of a brick being thrown through my living room window. The note attached read: *Die tattletale bitch.* They set my garden on fire too. Luckily, my sprinklers are on the evening cycle or the little flames might've set my entire house on fire before the bank could snatch it back.

Six minutes—

The sound of a knuckle tapping against my driver-side window nearly sends me into cardiac arrest. I'm caught— blotchy-faced, huffing...pathetic. I glance at the man standing outside my window. He's wearing dark-washed blue jeans with a neat black belt. His dress shirt is tucked in, covered by a black suit jacket.

He peers through the window and squints, reminding me how darkly tinted all my car windows are. Actually, they are well past the legal allowance for vehicle window tints. It was a small security measure I had to take. A brick through my living room window scared the shit out of me. A properly timed brick through the driver's side window of my car could kill me.

Every fiber in my being is telling me not to engage with this stranger, who is wearing dark sunglasses in a parking lot enclosure. My hand creeps towards my car's start button and I have every intention of peeling out of this spot, *Tokyo Drift* style, until he knocks again. This time, he subtly moves his suit jacket to the side, flashing me his shiny gold badge.

Dammit. I know that badge. I've had enough encounters with the FBI over the past year to recognize it.

"Dr. Abbott," he calls out, then points his finger down repeatedly. Hesitantly, I roll down my window.

"Yes?"

His features are unremarkable. Not in an unattractive way, it's just that the combination of his slim face, tan complexion, and neatly combed, dark hair makes him...quite forgettable. He blends. I don't think I could pick him out of a crowd. It's a perfect look for a secret agent.

"You saw my badge?"

"Yes." Even if I didn't, the fact that he called me Doctor

23

Abbott is an easy tip-off that he's an agent. They like titles. But *Doctor* sounds better for M.D.s. I prefer Eden.

"Can you unlock the door?" He points to the passenger side while examining my perplexed expression. "Let's chat." Circling the car, he makes his way to the passenger side. The very second he tugs on the door latch, my timer rings, screeching at the top of its lungs.

Ring, ring! It's time, Eden!

It's time to be okay.

Linc

TWO

LINC

"THIS IS A FUCKING TERRIBLE IDEA. Look at the foot traffic," I snarl under my breath. It doesn't matter how low I whisper, Vesper always hears me.

I scour the massive lobby of one of the largest luxury business buildings in the middle of Washington D.C.'s metropolitan. The entirety of its thirty-two floors is overkill. In this city, architecture is a pissing contest. The bigger your building, the bigger your cock.

"Is it? How many people have looked our way?"

Hm, fair point. Vesper and I don't look out of place in neat suits in this crowd. Everyone is far too busy hustling to their corporate day jobs to notice that the killers in the room are armed.

"Who owns the building?" I ask.

"The Rigett Group. But they turn a blind eye to the basement lessees."

I follow Vesper to the row of elevators. She presses the "Down" arrow and the doors of the center elevator part immediately. I step forward, but she holds out her arm.

"Wait," she whispers, "to the left."

At the end of the row, there's one elevator that's clearly

27

marked—*Private Access to Penthouse.* Vesper sees my disapproving expression.

"You're asking for trouble putting us on the top floor." I've thrown a man from a forty-story building and have since long regretted it. Did he deserve death? *Absolutely.* Did he deserve the horror of falling before inevitably meeting his end? *Debatable.* My philosophy is to put a bad dog down if you must, but be quick about it. Don't torture the damn thing.

"There is no penthouse," she assures me in a hushed tone. "Only our fingerprints can call this elevator. This is one of three entrances to the compound. We'll need to rotate between the three of them for subtlety."

"Clever." But my tone is unconvincing.

I trail behind her into the steel box, like a shadow. She moves, and I'm right behind her. That's our dynamic.

The doors are barely shut when I ask, "Who are the basement lessees?"

Vesper clears her throat. "As of now, us."

She pushes the only black button on the panel. It's unmarked—obviously for our use only. "Close your eyes," she commands, but I'm a half-second too slow. After a piercing *ding*, a blinding flash of light disorients me.

"Fuck," I growl, trying to blink away the white specs in my eyes. "Body scans?"

"In the case of drones or AI," Vesper explains. "Technology's finest. Compliments of the FBI."

"Overdramatic," I spit out in agitation.

"It's a smart precaution," she says as we descend to our destination, the opposite direction of the so-called penthouse that this elevator should be ascending to.

When the door peels open, Vesper banks an immediate left down a dimly lit hallway towards a metal door. She pulls a badge out of her coat pocket and scans it against the white wall—an area that you'd never find unless you already knew where to look. The sound is almost inaudible, but I hear the faint clicking that indicates a door has unlocked.

"Lance is going to struggle with this." I let out a humorless laugh, picturing my comrade running his badge across the entire hallway to no avail.

"He'll figure it out. He always does."

Vesper opens the door and ushers me through. I was expecting this bunker to look like Hannibal's lair, but I'm sorely mistaken. Our new headquarters looks uncomfortably civil. We walk through what must be a lounge or break room of some sort. There are a few oversized leather loveseats and recliners pointed at a large flat-screen television. A couple of side tables hold board games—chess, checkers, and Jenga. Who the hell pictured a bunch of assassins kicking back and enjoying a game of Jenga…?

We pass a few closed doors as we make our way through, what can only be accurately described as, a giant mole tunnel.

"Gym, and data," Vesper says as she points down the hallway to our right. "Medical is down that way, along with interrogation rooms"—she points left then juts her thumb over her shoulder—"and the kitchen is back toward the entry." She finally slows when we approach a large meeting room. Upon entering, I find whiteboards lining one wall and corkboards lining the other. In the center of the generously-sized room is a large, black, laminate table with at least twenty ergonomic office chairs surrounding it.

"What the fuck is this?" I glower at Vesper to convey my sentiment.

"This is our meeting room," she answers. "We'll have weekly team meetings moving forward…"

"Vesper," I say, looking down to find her eyes, seeing something that's not usually present in our fearless leader. *Desperation? Defeat?* "What is going on?"

"This is the new PALADIN, Linc. This compound is a generous, welcome gift. It's a way to bring us all together.

Moving PALADIN under the FBI's command will be a good thing. Callen has a solid plan to get us more support and resources. We've been sloppy and scattered and it's time to make a change. Callen can help." She breaks our deadlock stare and takes a seat at the head of the table.

"Since when are you so chummy with Callen?"

Vesper has a healthy distrust of governing agencies—she's seen too much corruption. So her sudden revere of Jeffrey Callen is unsettling.

Callen is the director of the particular division of the FBI that funds our activity. I think they call it, "Emergency Contractor Services." More accurately known as the group the FBI throws serious money at for us to *just handle it*. We've taken down targets for the majority of the governing agencies, but lately, the FBI has gotten greedy with our time. They've been sending us files left and right. I've killed more men in the past two weeks than I have in the past six months combined. As of late, Callen seems to think PALADIN is at his disposal. He's confused. There can only be one in command, and right now I am baffled as to why she's bending over for a sniveling fed.

Vesper groans, resting her hand against the bridge of her nose like she's reluctant to say what's next. "Linc, I'm now officially a field operative—just like you. Callen is the new commanding officer of PALADIN."

Instinctually, my fists ball up. "Vesper, *what the fuck?* Why would you—"

"Frankie—"

"One rogue operative, and you spiral? There's always a risk with people who are willing to kill for a living. You know this. You're going to roll over and drown in a pity party just because—"

Whack.

Her fist lands with a thud on the table in anger. I must've gone a step too far. "I brought in Frankie. I missed the signs.

30

So every single mistake he made is mine." Her eyes fall to the table and she twirls her thumbs slowly. "You know, I never asked..."

It's Vesper's only weakness. She's a superb leader—smart, capable, focused, whips our asses in shape whenever we need it, but her empathy... It's either her biggest weakness or her greatest strength. I don't know. Vesper trained me, she taught *me* to be cold and detached, however, *she* cries for the world and all her recruits. Frankie was the most recent addition to our team. He turned out to be a bad apple. He started taking lives on his own accord and acting like a midnight vigilante, except not all of his targets deserved death, and he certainly didn't have Vesper's approval. He was out of control, so Vesper told me to put him down.

"He didn't fight or flinch. He smiled as he watched me pull the trigger."

He knew the consequences...and he paid them. Vesper blamed herself, calling it a bad recruit, but on paper, Frankie was a perfect fit for PALADIN—former specialized military, no family—but he grew angry.

I understand that part at least.

The more terrorists, murderers, abusers, and traffickers you encounter, the more you lose faith in humanity. We're all angry, depressed...worn down. PALADIN takes down a target and then ten more pop up in its wake. Evil in this world knows no ends and the good people are outnumbered. It's soul-crushing. At the end, I think Frankie *wanted* me to end him— he wanted to be put out of his misery.

She nods her head solemnly. "My point is, maybe there's a need for checks and balances. I can't keep playing God."

"Why not? You're better at it than Callen."

She scoffs, burying her face in her hands. "Linc, we're scattered, we're divided, we're being picked off left and right. I thought Morely went off the grid..." She shakes her head. "It took me three weeks to figure out his brains were splattered

31

on a wall in Dubai. Jooney and Brady—dead. Fenway—dead. I just found out that Cricket's in Morocco when she's supposed to be in Prague. Did you know that?"

"No. Why?"

Her dark eyes bulge. "I don't fucking know. My operatives are spread across the globe, doing God knows what right under my nose. I can't reach them. I can't control them... I can't protect them. We need—"

"Discipline?"

"Structure," she offers instead.

She closes her eyes, maybe an attempt to hide her vulnerability. I hate seeing her like this. When Vesper feels weak, I feel weak. She's my leader, my friend, and the closest thing I have to a mother. She should know by now that we bear the burden of PALADIN's shortcomings, together.

She should've talked to me before running to the FBI.

"I won't put down another one of mine, Linc. Hear me? Frankie was the first and last." Her tone is low and menacing. It's a solemn vow. I didn't realize how much it was tormenting her. I know Vesper takes responsibility for all her operatives, but this pain is from a maternal place. And judging by the look in her eyes, there's no point in arguing—she's made up her mind.

I now answer to motherfucking Jeff Callen which kind of makes me want to choose early retirement.

"All right," I murmur, leaning against the wall of whiteboards. "Whatever you want. But no matter where you're sitting at the table, our loyalty is to you, not Callen. Clear?"

She doesn't lift her head and instead glares at me from the corner of her eyes. "Then show your loyalty now and do what I say is best. Don't give Callen, or his new management, trouble. We're safe under his command and I *need* my family safe."

"Fine, I—wait...what is 'new management?'"

A mischievous smile creeps across Vesper's face. At least

she's smiling. "PALADIN is now legitimate. Callen says we're getting a human resources department."

Pinching the bridge of my nose, I exhale making my irritation clear. "Human resources, Vesper? For a bunch of fucking assassins?"

Vesper stands, clasping my shoulder before making her way out of the meeting room. "Behave. And call what's left of our family home. *Now.*"

"Awfully bossy for someone who is taking a step down." Vesper simply shrugs on her way out of the door. "Where are you going?" I call after her.

"Break room, Linc. We have a break room now, and it has snacks."

Eden

THREE

EDEN

I THOUGHT Agent Jeffrey Callen simply wanted to talk in the car. The FBI agents used to check in on me often before the trial against Empress was over. After the case closed, they disappeared. Unfortunately, the threats and harassment did not. They abandoned me when I needed them the most.

Therefore, I was surprised to find Callen popping in on me in the parking garage. I was even more surprised by his request to take me to a late breakfast. He insisted we drive to a quaint little diner about forty-five minutes outside of city limits.

Leaning back in the red-tufted booth of the sixties-styled diner, I stare at Callen— bewildered—as he inhales a tall stack of syrup-drenched pancakes. His aggressive chewing is making my stomach churn. I have to remind myself it's probably a felony to reach across this booth and smack a federal agent.

"You've barely touched your food." He eyes my plate, his obvious remark sounding more like a question.

Here's what I've learned about agents over the past year: they turn simple statements into questions, and the questions they ask are never what they're actually asking. At this point, I'm good at reading between the lines.

"I haven't been doing well after the trial. I can't find a job. I can't even leave this city because I have no money, and my reputation would follow me across state lines anyway. I'm in severe debt from legal fees. I'm about to lose my home. I hoped the interview this morning might turn things around, but not even my old friends are able to help me. I'm stuck, and honestly, if it means I can get out of this purgatory, I'm ready to drop right down to hell."

Slowing his chewing, Callen lifts his eyes to meet my stare.

"Oh, I'm sorry. Too much honesty?" I ask with sass before fake-coughing into my fist. "I meant I'm just not that hungry."

He drops his fork which bounces off his plate, causing a couple of sticky droplets to land on the glass tabletop. "I can't imagine any of this has been easy."

"You were—"

I'm interrupted when the waitress, dressed in full costume —a pale pink zip-up dress, with a white apron—stops at our booth to refill our mugs of coffee. She flashes a sweet smile and I thank her. Even at the peak of my frustration, I make room for manners. It's not this waitress's fault my life is in shambles. Winking, she nods once and then retreats from the table. The minute she's out of earshot, I continue my verbal assault.

"The FBI was supposed to see me through every step of the way. Isn't that what you all told me?" It's not exactly fair, Callen is a new-to-me agent. I think it was Fisher and Marks that I communicated with the most. "You guys said no matter what, you'd make sure I was taken care of. You guys called me a…" I trail off, cringing at how pathetic I sound at the moment. Taking a deep breath, I let the urge to cry calm down. "*You called me a hero.* You told me I did the right thing. You said I stopped a civil war, even. And now look at me. Everyone else got consequences or was able to move on, but not me. *Look. At. Me.* I can't go forward, I can't go back."

Callen holds both palms up in surrender, and even I'm surprised by my accusing tone. "I understand, Dr. Abbott. That's why I'm here."

"Eden, please," I remind him. "Why are you here?"

He pulls a pen out of his pocket, then lifts his mug and retrieves the cardboard coaster it was resting on. After scribbling something down on the outside margin of the diner's logo, he slides the coaster over to me.

"I'm here to offer you a job. This is your starting salary. In addition, we'll take care of corporate housing, allowance for meals, a company car"—he rolls his wrist—"etcetera."

I balk at the number scribbled in black ink. At the moment it looks like a get-out-of-jail-free card, but I force myself to keep my composure. "What's the job?"

Something in his expression changes. His cool demeanor slowly dissolves as he mentally scrambles for what no doubt will be a lie. "It's something along the lines of your expertise."

Okay, here we go.

"And what exactly do you think my expertise is?" Explaining what I do is about thirty percent of my job.

"You help keep people in line—compliant. Human resources, right?" Callen squints at me, his bushy dark eyebrows furrowing.

I shut my eyes and rub against my closed lids as I prepare myself to deliver the speech I have hundreds of times before. "I'm a consultant. I work with companies for a few months at a time. I take organizations in their adolescent phases and help them scale by focusing on human capital. My job is to study companies from the inside out and create a strategy to incentivize employees for maximum productivity. Happy employees mean minimal turnover. Turnover is expensive."

"I agree with you there," Callen huffs out.

"The bottom line is I work hand-in-hand with Human

Resources—I *train* HR employees—but I'm not technically HR."

"Potato, po-tah-to. In my opinion, you have a doctorate in goddamn common sense, and you've proven yourself to be upright and trustworthy."

According to you. The founders at Empress would strongly disagree.

"Well, I don't think organizational leadership and compliance is exactly a new concept to the FBI. What could you possibly need my help with?"

Let's just get to the point. I have no room to be picky or choosy, plus Callen just offered me a salary that is comparable to what I was making at the peak of my career. I didn't realize federal agencies even had that kind of budget. It's more than enough to save my home from the bank.

"I need help with a division we call PALADIN, or what's left of it anyway."

Callen scans the diner with his peripherals. We're tucked into the corner, out of earshot and almost out of eyeshot. When he's satisfied that we're attracting no attention, he pulls his wallet from the inside of his suit jacket.

"Let's talk about developing leadership." He throws a couple of pocket-sized laminated pictures on the center of the table. "These are the most talented operatives in the business." Callen proceeds to line them up neatly like he's excited for me to check out his baseball card collection.

"What business?" I ask.

He dodges my question and taps the picture furthest to the left.

"This is Vesper," he mumbles, pointing to a striking woman with dark hair. She has a regal elegance to her. Her jet-black hair barely touches her shoulders and is neatly tucked behind her ears. "She's what you'd probably refer to as 'management.' She's collected a group of off-the-record operatives who help with the FBI's…uh…let's call them '*side projects.*'"

"Side projects?" I ask, picking up the picture and examining it more thoroughly. Judging by her all-black attire and the gun holster around her thigh, I suddenly understand what Callen means by "side projects." My stomach twists in discomfort.

Vesper's lips in the picture are unnaturally red—ruby red. I have lipstick in exactly that shade in my makeup drawer, but I never use it. It's far too bold for my taste.

"Cricket. Lance." Callen names the others as I pick up the remaining photos.

I squint at him. "Is Cricket a name?"

"Hell if I know," he says. "I'm not sure if these fuckers ever had real names. If they did, they've long since forgotten them. Lance is short for Lancelot. I have no clue why they call her Cricket."

I stare at the jaw-droppingly stunning blonde in the picture who's looking over her shoulder at the camera with a cheeky smile. She makes a terrible undercover agent. There's nothing subtle about her. Every man with a pulse would notice a woman who looks like that.

Lance is much the same—clean-shaven, flirty smile, and looks like a frat boy. The kind of frat boy who misses a lot of class because he's spending all day on his back with one of his classmates straddled across his hips.

"I don't understand. Doesn't the FBI do thorough investigations of their recruits? If they are field operatives, they must at least have a top-secret clearance, meaning you should know, not only their birth names, but the color of their piss this morning."

Callen cocks his head to the side. He smiles at me in a way that tells me he's surprised, and impressed. "What do you know about TS clearances?"

"I know that top-secret is barely scratching the surface."

Callen blinks at me, wordlessly, a silent command to explain myself. "My dad was Delta Force," I continue, "he never told me a damn thing, but I could see it in his eyes. He took a lot of secrets to his grave."

"Delta Force," he repeats. "Nice. Killed in combat?"

I reel from his frankness. "No. It was his heart," I respond curtly, trying to cover up my wounded reaction. I get it, it's the obvious assumption. Dad was part of an elite military force that did very dangerous things behind the scenes, but his life was tame toward the end. He smiled a lot…but he felt weak. I soften my tone and elaborate. "He was on the transplant list for a while, but we ran out of time. He went peacefully, in his sleep."

I scoop up my mug with both hands just to have something to do. The steam is still dancing on top of the dark liquid from when the waitress refreshed our mugs.

"Shit," Callen says, looking ashamed. "My job desensitizes me too much sometimes. I'm very sorry for your loss."

Giving him a small shrug, and an even smaller smile, I let him off the hook and say, "It's okay. Me too."

"And I'm no stranger to the difficulties of military life. I was a Navy SEAL. I don't have kids, but some of my buddies did. I'm assuming you guys moved a lot?"

"Not really. Delta Force stays put at Fort Bragg. My dad would have to leave a lot, but we didn't move much."

"If you had roots in North Carolina, how'd you end up in California?"

I fight the urge to roll my eyes. Agents and their questions —everything is an interrogation, even a simple conversation.

"My mom was from San Francisco. My dad met her on vacation."

My parents had a whirlwind military romance. They met, two weeks later they were married. Two years later I came along. "They bought a nice house on the outskirts of the city when they were really young, long before the market blew up.

Their plan was to rent it out so when my Dad retired, it'd basically be paid off."

We almost made it. I took over the mortgage when Dad got sick. I only have four more years to pay it off… But I fell short, right before the finish line.

"And where's your mom?" he asks.

I take a small sip of my coffee, tasting the scorched brew. It's not good coffee by any stretch of the imagination, but there's something comforting about shitty diner coffee. It reminds me of old Saturdays when I'd actually leave the house to eat. For the past year, all I do is cook at home. All I do is *hide* at home.

"She passed away while I was still in diapers. Ovarian cancer."

"Shit, Eden, I'm sorry." Running his hands through his hair he grumbles, "Do you have any family left?"

"I have one aunt who is still alive. But her Alzheimer's is so severe, she doesn't recognize me anymore. I used to visit her at the care facility, but it started to scare her, so I stopped."

"Friends? A pet?"

My cheeks puff before I blow out a big breath. I'm reluctant to admit, out loud, what's extremely apparent. Sure, I've prioritized my education and my career, but I'm only twenty-nine. I thought I had plenty of time for everything else. My dad taught me to work hard and I never imagined that could be a bad thing…until now.

I'm at the most difficult point of my life, and there's no one here standing beside me.

"I'm missing one photo," Callen says, changing the subject. Perhaps my depressing origin story is making him uncomfortable. *Well, Callen, be careful what you ask then.*

"Pardon?"

He taps an empty space on the table with his pointer finger. "There's one more. Vesper's guard dog—Lincoln."

There's something in the way Callen says his name that

causes goosebumps to rise on the back of my neck. "Why don't you have a picture?"

"Because he nearly broke my hand when I tried to take one for his file. Vesper, Lance, and Cricket all act like normal human beings for the most part. But Linc is a ghost on his best day, and on his worst—a cold-blooded killer."

I swallow down the lump in my throat. "A cold-blooded killer that you *employ*?"

"Sort of. But that's the problem. That's why I need you."

Nodding, I finally meet Callen's eyes. Good. Let's get to it. "Help me make sense of this. You want me to help you do *what* with these people? Do performance reviews? Formulate a team mission statement?" I ask sarcastically.

"Operation PALADIN was originally commissioned by…" He trails off, trying to strategically hold back information. "Let's just say there are probably secret files in the Oval Office that explain everything. Get what I'm saying?" He cocks one eyebrow.

"Sure." So clearly PALADIN can't get in trouble with the authorities if they were created by the authorities.

"Vesper has recruited, developed, and managed this team for over a decade. She's incredible—far wiser than she should be at her age, but she's struggling right now. It's hard to find good recruits, and some of her operatives have been going rogue. They're accepting jobs that aren't approved, or just using their skills and resources to exact personal revenge—"

"Are you saying that you have a bunch of armed agents on the loose?" I screw up my face in confusion. *Why are you telling me this?*

"*I* have agents. Vesper has what we like to call…*operatives.*"

"Why?"

He levels a stare. "Because we don't like using words like assassins, hitmen, or killers in everyday conversation. It draws too much attention."

I'm frozen as I blink at him, absorbing the blunt truth.

"Over the past year PALADIN has gone from eighteen operatives to *four*."

"What? How?"

"They went rogue, got cocky, pissed off the wrong people and made easy targets of themselves. Most of them are dead. Even more concerning, a few of them are unaccounted for. There was one misbehaving in our own backyard. Vesper had to put him down. Or more accurately, had Linc put him down."

"Put him down as in—"

"A bullet in his brain," Callen says matter-of-factly.

I push my plate aside and begin to scoot out of the booth. "End of discussion, Callen. I don't do guns. I don't do bullets in brains. I don't do killers. I'm desperate, but not *this* desperate. I don't want to peek behind any more curtains. Been there, done that, and it ruined my life—"

"Eden. *Eden, wait.*" Callen shuffles on his side of the booth, intent on intercepting my retreat. "Hear me out. They aren't just killers," he pleads, looking around the diner to reconfirm we haven't drawn attention to ourselves. "They're the good guys, I promise you. They are just a little rough around the edges. *Please sit back down.*"

I settle back into the booth but keep one knee pointed out, prepared for a quick exit.

"Thank you," Callen says.

"So, what do you want from me?"

"The past three companies you consulted for are now business powerhouses. You took startups and turned them into corporations, fast. *How?* Recruiting? Funding? How did you get these companies in fighting shape?"

"It's simple. Happy people do good work. All I do is spend time with a company, see what they're lacking by *listening* to the employees, finding like-minded individuals to recruit, giving leadership tangible short-term and long-term goals, and incentivizing everyone with something other than money.

43

People spend most of their waking hours at work, it shouldn't be spent in hell. Growth, success, ROI…it's all about human capital."

"How long does that usually take?" Callen picks his fork back up, cutting into his stack of pancakes with the side of his fork.

"Most companies—six months. Empress took longer. I was with them for a little over a year and a half in a consultant role before I was brought on board full-time"

"Okay, so split the difference. Give me a year."

"To do what?"

"The world needs PALADIN. The FBI needs PALADIN. Luckily, for the first time since they were established, they need us. We have an opportunity to replenish their ranks and—"

"Close some cases?" I ask with an accusing look on my face.

"Exactly." Stabbing his fork into the stack of pancakes, he continues, "The people they go after can hardly be considered human beings. Believe me when I say PALADIN operates for the greater good."

I hate that phrase: *the greater good*. It's usually how things like genocide and slavery are justified in an evil man's mind. I've studied societal norms and group behavior for years at one of the most prestigious schools on the West Coast, and what I've learned about leadership is that you don't always need a worthy cause to raise hell… You just need a convincing mouthpiece.

"What *exactly* is the problem you're trying to solve?"

"I've got FBI agents who are afraid of the operatives, thinking they are loose cannons. And I've got the operatives who think the FBI is a joke. Nobody wants to work together. My only saving grace is that Vesper's on my side. Without her cooperation, this whole thing falls apart. I have a lot of higher-ups with their eyes on me, making sure I see this project through, and I can't afford for everything to fall apart. I secured a giant compound for everyone to come together and start acting like a team, but how do I mix oil and water?"

I study Callen's pleading eyes and actually feel bad for him. "You need everyone to play nice in the sandbox together?"

"Exactly. Isn't that what you're great at?"

"Yes," I say honestly. "But I work with tech geniuses, customer service representatives, and business managers. Not kill—" I stop myself. "*Operatives.*"

"They're still people, Eden. They have jobs and responsibilities like everyone else. Ignoring what they do in the field, how would you approach this if it was a normal organization?"

Callen sticks his fork back into his mouth, now managing to chew slowly. His determined eyes are fixed on me, and I'm starting to wonder if I actually have a choice in taking this job.

"Research is the first phase. I need to understand the state of the company, but not from you. From the employee's perspective. I'd set up interviews with every single agent and operative and would encourage them to speak freely about the issues at hand."

"Okay, that sounds good. What then?"

"Part of research is understanding the group dynamic. You'd call a meeting and I'd come in and force everyone to do a little get-to-know-you icebreaker activity."

Callen laughs, his eyes crinkling at the sides. "You think a bunch of operatives are going to tell you what their favorite movie and color is? Who cares?"

"I do. Never underestimate the power of building a good rapport, Callen. Taking an interest in your employees is a smart way to earn their trust. But truthfully, the icebreaker activity has nothing to do with the actual information, it's to identify leadership. Employees who participate with enthusiasm, and are honest and vulnerable, have the most potential.

Identify your potential quickly—promote them, reward them, get them on your side and aligned with your vision. Lead from the middle of the pack, not from the front."

Callen stares at me, jaw dropped. "You should be a motherfucking TED talk."

"I've done a few, actually." Except they've probably been removed seeing as the comment sections on my seminars are now filled with hate speech and threats on my life.

"So, is that a yes?"

I can't tell if the intrigue is coming from the excitement of a little controlled danger, or just actual hope that maybe the match isn't over. Maybe I have one more round in me and can still bounce back from the disaster that is my life.

"Just a year?"

"One year. Help me build this team to its full potential and I guarantee you can *retire* after one year. You'll never worry about money again."

"Where's the job?"

"D.C."

Of course. "I don't want to sell my home...my parent's home," I admit.

"Don't. We'll get you set up with housing in D.C. No problem."

"Would you be willing to discuss an advance on my salary?" I duck my head, embarrassed to taste the words. "I'm delinquent on my mortgage. I need to get caught up on a few payments or I'm facing foreclosure."

"Eden, you agree to help me with PALADIN, and the FBI will pay off the rest of your mortgage...*today*."

Glancing down at the coaster, I tug on my bottom lip with my top teeth. Even the military needs leadership strategy consultations. Is this really any different than working with the armed forces?

"Would I be a federal employee?" I ask.

Callen teeters his head. "Contractor. But if benefits are an issue—"

"They are," I say. I haven't had medical or dental insurance in over a year. I've had no company to provide it and couldn't afford the cost on my own.

"I can make those arrangements too," Callen says in a smooth baritone. "We will take care of absolutely everything you need."

"And I wouldn't be expected to…" I eye his holster, trying to convey my question without actually asking.

"What?" Callen asks, looking at me like I'm stupid.

I don't want to sound as squeamish as I feel. This all still sounds like a movie. Agents, operatives, assassins… It's like something from a very cliché action movie. I prefer to picture this as fiction, the reality is too off-putting. When I was little, I used to pretend Dad was a construction worker. The cuts and bruises he'd return home with after his jobs were simply run-of-the-mill construction hazards.

"Carry a gun. I don't… I don't do guns. They have always made me uncomfortable." Not to mention, after the death threats I received when Empress went under, discomfort turned into unbridled fear.

"It's a desk job, Eden. What would you need a gun for?" he asks with a tone full of sarcasm

My chest expands as I inhale until it hurts. "Okay." I breathe out dramatically. "I'll take it."

"Really?" Callen's face pulls in surprise.

"You thought I'd turn down my only job option?"

"No." He lets out a cocky laugh. "I just figured you'd be a tougher negotiator." He taps the coaster in front of me. "I would've paid off your mortgage and offered you double that," Callen says with a smirk.

Fuck.

What the hell did I just get into with PALADIN if Callen would've been willing to offer me a literal fortune for a desk job?

FOUR

LINC

MY SHOWER IS DRAFTY. The giant glass box is too big for the single shower head above me. The water pressure is powerful. I feel like I'm caught in the prelude of a hurricane, but the amount of space in here could accommodate a small orgy. That's not my taste. Lance, however, would make good use of this oversized shower…although it'd have nothing to do with getting clean.

Come to think of it, my whole house is too big, uncomfortable, and drafty. Four-thousand-square-feet is way too much space for one person, but what else was I doing with my money? Until a couple months ago, I'd never owned a home.

This is too much change, too fast.

I normally don't spend more than two weeks in one place, and now I need to purchase a lawn mower to tend to my backyard. *Backyard.* I have a deed and a title, a mailbox, and a place of work that I'm expected to report to Monday through Friday…

Way too much, far too fast.

I wouldn't be going along with all this change if I wasn't witnessing the mental demise of Vesper. She saved me twelve years ago, giving me a life and a reason to wake up in the

49

morning. It's my turn to help her and *shit*, does she need help right now. Heavy is the crown. Every day she wakes up and makes impossible decisions—who lives, who dies, who pulls the trigger. Those are heavy puppet strings to pull. And, not that I'd say it out loud, but lately she looks tired.

We're all tired.

I wonder if she closes her lids and sees ghosts too. I wonder if she lies awake at night counting the number of bodies like I do, wondering how high I have to count until the world is at peace.

I just want some motherfucking rest.

But it's midnight, and even in the comfort of my home, I can't sleep. The hot shower didn't help. My head is still spinning and my legs are restless.

I need to get out of here.

After twisting the shower handle to "Off" and wrapping a towel around my waist, I find my phone. I call the only other person I'm certain is up this late.

"What's up?" Lance answers, sounding winded, like he's on the treadmill.

"Are you back in town, yet?"

"No," he says breathily, "are you?"

"I've *been* in town…with Vesper."

"How is she holding up after Frankie?"

"Fine. She just needs time—"

I stop talking when I notice the loud rhythmic banging in the background of his line.

"Are you busy?" I ask.

"No… I mean, yeah. But I have a minute." He blows out a sharp breath. "So, what time do we have to be there for this meeting on Monday? Have you talked to Cricket?"

I hear a woman moaning in the background as the rhythmic banging picks up, and I realize what he's busy with.

"*Jesus.* Eight," I grumble right before I end the call.

I debate calling Cricket, but I know she's probably still on a flight. She was out of the country, lingering too long after a job. When I called her two days ago and told her PALADIN officially had a home base and her ass needed to be in an office chair on Monday, she panicked. No one likes to piss off Vesper. She's mostly maternal but absolutely ruthless when she needs to be…like when Cricket lies to her about where she is and what she's doing.

Pausing in front of my dresser, I drop my towel. Standing in the dark, alone and naked, I momentarily debate heading to a bar and getting into the same kind of trouble as Lance. But if I'm being honest with myself, I'm not craving a fuck at the moment… Just a conversation.

Once I've thrown on a pair of sweatpants, I grab my keys and head out the door. I have no clue where I'm going, but anywhere is better than here…

Alone with all the ghosts.

After driving around aimlessly for an hour, I end up at the new compound. Vesper showed me around yesterday, but I still don't feel acquainted. It's bizarre. The closest PALADIN has ever had to headquarters was a seedy dive bar in the slums of D.C. I miss that place. It reminds me of Suzanne's. I even ordered a round of Macallan last time Vesper, Cricket, Lance and I were together, in honor of my old friend.

The lobby entry is locked at this time of night, so I have to enter through the emergency stairwell. It's a little less complicated than the elevator entry. At the emergency exit door that clearly says: Do Not Enter, I scan my badge, let the retina scanner all but blind my left eye, and in we go.

The compound is spacious and there are more offices than we know what to do with. I'm worried that Callen has plans to fill them all. PALADIN is best as a lean team. Admittedly, with only four operatives we're leaner than desirable at the moment, but I don't know why he thinks his weak-willed special agents can keep up with us. Vesper and I recruit. *We train.* We just need some time.

Walking past the main entry, the first thing I notice is the smell of coffee. *That's odd.* Overnight security for the compound is completed through surveillance. There should be no one here at this time of night. If someone broke in, Callen would've been alerted and I probably would've gotten a call to go handle it.

No one is supposed to be here, and yet I see a light spilling through an open office door at the end of the main hallway. I'm suddenly tired as I pace down the hall, fingers in the pocket of my athletic sweats, tapping my finger against the trigger guard of my .22.

I'm really not in the mood to kill anyone tonight, but when duty calls…

Except when I get to the doorway, I halt in place. Standing frozen in the doorway, I examine someone that I am certain, without a doubt, that I will never pull a gun on.

Not now.

Not ever.

Not only because she's a woman, but because she's…

I don't quite know how to put my finger on it. *Innocent looking? Vulnerable?* Very pretty indeed, but that's not the word I'm looking for…

Precious. That's the one.

She's sitting cross-legged on the floor of the office, surrounded by at least a dozen blue folders, sprawled into a tidy rainbow arch in front of her. I've been standing here for at least a minute now, and she still hasn't noticed me. The white earbuds wedged in her ears tell me her music must be too loud to hear me approach. She's sucking on a pen cap and reading a document, a pained expression on her face which is half shielded by her long dark hair.

There's a steaming mug on her desk, the culprit of the smell of coffee.

It's another thirty seconds at least before she finally looks up and notices me hovering in the doorway. She yanks her headphones out, then freezes. Her expression is one I recognize well—unmasked fear.

I can literally hear her try to swallow the lump in her throat. All I want to do is put her mind at ease, so I force myself to speak.

"Good evening," I say, immediately regretting the words that sound like a vampire's greeting. "I mean, hi."

"Good evening...*and hi.*" Her steady tone is a contradiction to the panicked expression on her face. "Are you—"

"Building maintenance." I lie with ease. "Sorry to disturb you. I saw your light on."

"Oh?" She looks me up and down, examining my casual attire, full of skepticism.

"Can you keep a secret?" I ask. She scrunches her face, almost wincing at my words for some reason but I continue without her reply. "I sneak in here sometimes for the gym. Technically, I'm not working at the moment."

"*Oh,*" she says, satisfied with the elaboration of my lie. She rises, tucking the pen behind her ear. "Well, you are in good company because *technically,* I should've left a while ago too." Her cheeks bunch as she smiles, making perfect half-spheres. She's elegant, even in her yoga pants and plain white t-shirt, but her cheeks are round, like a child's, making her an odd contradiction.

With her hand outreached, she closes the space between us and takes my hand in hers. Her handshake is surprisingly firm for such a little thing.

"I'm Eden Abbott," she says, looking straight into my eyes, the worry lines on her face slowly dissolving. "I'm the new resident of this office and I feel like I need to apologize ahead of time."

"For what?"

"I'm a sticky note user." She grimaces.

"Oh no."

"Yeah." She nods, her face growing serious. "It's an addiction. When I've doodled on at least twenty, I scrunch them into little balls and play recycling bin basketball. I am *not* good. My aim is terrible. You're going to hate cleaning this office." Her chuckle is warm.

I can't help but smile in return.

"What are you doing here so late? Are you an agent?" I ask, but I already know the answer.

"No," she scoffs in laughter. "I'm not that cool. I'm a civilian. A contractor…like you, I'm assuming?"

I don't respond and let her draw her own conclusions. I'm not even sure if we have maintenance in this building.

"My official first day is Monday, but my boss let me sneak in early. I'm trying to prepare."

I nod to the folders behind her. "Doing research?"

"Personnel files for every agent in the compound," she says, then lets out a heavy sigh. "But I don't think I'm allowed to say more than that. I still don't understand what's a secret around here and what's not. Have you been doing maintenance here long? My boss said agents have been in and out for a couple of weeks now?"

"Something like that," I mumble. I only saw the compound yesterday, but from what I gather, Callen's FBI agents have already been crawling all over the place.

"Hm." She nods pensively, some odd thought filling her head.

"Why?"

"I just…if people are working here already…it should be livelier. This place feels"—she rolls her wrist—"a little like the haunted house on the hill."

My lips twitch into a half smile. "Well, you're in an underground bunker, well past midnight, so—"

"*What?*" She checks her wrist, but there's no watch. I show her mine that reads one-thirty in the morning. "Oh my God, I got here at six! I didn't even realize. I should…"

She immediately begins stacking folders on the ground, and I instinctively fall to my knees to help her.

"Time flies when you're reading something really interesting," I offer as I gather stacks of papers and push them in her direction.

"I'm not usually one to confess my secrets to strangers, but seeing as you're the only other civilian I've talked to in…God, I don't even know how long…"

"Your secret's safe with me," I assure her, my curiosity rising.

"Good, because I'll totally rat you out about the gym." She winks. "Honestly, I'm in so far over my head. I'm trying to prepare myself by reading up on the agents and their case files. A huge part of my job is finding a way to relate and connect…" She lets out a deep sigh. "But I don't know what the hell I'm doing here. I'm so far out of my element. The stuff these agents encounter daily is basically all source material for the Oxygen channel." She finds my eyes again and tilts her head. "That's a broadcasting station that mostly has—"

"True crime. Serial killer documentaries."

"Exactly." She shudders.

"So you're uncomfortable around that stuff?"

"Downright disturbed. Guns in particular. I hate guns."

At the moment, I'm grateful for my loose sweats and deep pockets, so she can't see I'm armed. *I'm always armed.*

"Which is why it's pretty apparent I took the wrong job," she continues.

"What job?"

"I have no idea what Callen is telling people, but I'm basically here to identify organizational issues, help with recruiting, pacify some interoffice animosity…and other obscure business initiatives that you probably don't care about."

55

My stomach sinks like lead when I realize who I just lied to. I thought she was simply a paperwork girl I wouldn't see again. "You're the new HR person?"

"*Dammit.*" Tossing her head back, she half grumbles, half laughs. "I hate that title, but I suppose. Oh hey, I think HR applies to contractors too—so, I will be setting up a comment box outside of my office. Feel free to complain if my sticky-note basketballs ever become a major nuisance."

"You're already forgiven." My lips continue to curl, I can't help it.

"Is it also a good time to mention that I spilled the coffee grounds in the break room?" She cringes, showing me her teeth as she curls her hands and cups them together. "I made a little pile but I couldn't find a broom. I'm sorry."

My face is a little uncomfortable at the moment, I don't usually smile this much. "You're good at this." I rise, turning my hips to ensure my gun stays unnoticeable.

"Good at what?"

"Conversation."

"Thank you," she says with a curious smile. "That's an odd compliment...but a nice one."

"I just mean, when you first saw me you looked scared, I felt like you were going to try and run or something."

She lets out a deep breath. "Well for a moment I thought you were an operative." She taps the pile of folders. I flinch, wondering if I have a file she's reviewed. Whatever the FBI has claimed I've done probably isn't even the half of it.

I lick my lips as I glance at hers—cherry-colored. Bright and full, but she's not wearing any makeup. "Would that have been bad?"

"How much do you know about PALADIN?"

"Outside of the fact that it's comprised of secret assassins that are now commissioned by the FBI, not much." I shoot her a knowing look.

"Some of the things these people have seen and done…" She shakes her head solemnly. "It's hard to stomach."

"You were scared because you thought I was one of those murderous monsters?"

Her face flattens and it's obvious I offended her. "I don't see them as murderous monsters."

"Well, that's what they do, right? Kill people."

"It seems more complicated than that." She taps the stack of folders again. "Callen says there's a rhyme and reason for PALADIN. I just need a little extra time to *digest* all of this." She waves her hand around the room. "When I meet the operatives next week, I don't want to look so much like a fish out of water."

"I'm sure you'll do fine. You have a presence. They'll like you." The words fall right out of my mouth like someone else spoke them for me.

"That's two." She holds up two fingers.

"Two what?"

"Two odd compliments that have nothing to do with looks, it's quite refreshing." Her eyes crinkle as her cheeks bunch again.

"Would you like a compliment about your looks?" I have a few at the forefront of my mind.

She flushes instantly. "That's not what I meant. It's just…" She shakes her head a little, deciding against whatever she was about to say. "It's been a little while since I've talked to someone normal. It's nice."

Normal? Maybe it's good I lied about who I am. I'm a lot of things…normal is not one of them.

She buries her hands in her face. "I'm sorry," she adds when I don't respond. "I meant that as a compliment."

"Well, two to one. You owe me one more."

She laughs. "Fair enough," she says, but she doesn't offer one. Instead, she continues, "Um, do you usually work in the evenings?"

"Most of the time." Technically, that's not a lie.

"I'm sort of notorious for working late. And my office door is always open. Maybe we could have another conversation."

Shit... Except she'll know exactly who I am by Monday.

"Definitely," I say.

"Oh hey, I didn't get your name."

Dammit. What to say next? I don't want to lie to her anymore, but I'm pretty sure Linc is one of the names in those files. I'm not sure how I'd explain myself right now...

"Chandler."

"Ah, well, it's very nice to meet you, Chandler." Eden collects her purse off of the desk, then brushes by me as she exits through the door. I catch a whiff of her light perfume and it heightens my senses. I spin around, wanting to chase that scent a while longer. "I look forward to seeing you...soon?"

I nod. "Soon."

I try not to watch her walk away, but I can't help it. Attraction has taken over now, and I really like the way her hips sway with each step.

Little does she know, when she sees me again, she probably won't be so eager to chat. She doesn't seem like the kind of person who wants to have a conversation with a killer.

FIVE
EDEN

ON MONDAY MORNING, Callen helps me set out a medley of fancy breakfast pastries on the long meeting table that can seat at least thirty people. We arrange three large platters with glazed donuts, chocolate-dipped croissants, muffins, and a variety of Danish pastries.

When I'm satisfied with the abundant-looking platters, I begin unpacking my supplies. I place a pocket-sized note sheet and miniature pen in front of each chair at the table.

"What are we doing?" Callen asks with his mouth full. I glance at one of the platters, which is now missing a donut. "You think feeding everyone will make them get along?"

I swivel around to face him, and eye his outfit up and down. He's wearing jeans, but a button-down dress shirt and a light sports jacket on top—no tie. He looks neat, but casual. "What's your workplace dress code? Doesn't the FBI require a suit and tie at headquarters?"

"Are you calling me out?"

"Well, you're telling everyone I'm HR, so I'm assuming dress code enforcement is part of my responsibility."

"What's your issue with being called HR?" Callen asks, taking another large bite of donut.

"People hate HR. No one wants to talk to HR. It's impossible to get people to open up when all they think you're going to do is use their words against them. These days, most companies are going out of their way to call it something else —talent management or employee support for example. 'Human Resources' has a negative connotation."

Callen nods in understanding. "That makes sense. And to answer your question, suit and tie at Pennsylvania Avenue, but this is a very private facility, so I guess it's up for discussion."

I point to Callen, surveying him head to toe. "May I suggest *this* for the compound?"

"What?"

"Business casual—collared shirt, sports jacket, no tie. Slacks or jeans—neat, no rips or holes. I'm assuming you guys have work boots or tennis shoes?" I quickly shake the image of blood-stained white sneakers from my mind. "Let's say dark-colored, closed-toe shoes."

"Sure…but, why?"

"It just sends a message. Propriety *without* rigidity. I've seen that work well for organizations in the past," I say as Callen nods along. "You won't even need to make a big announcement. Just lead by example and they'll do what you do. How many female agents do you have? I've only gone through about fifteen of the personnel files you left on my desk."

"Three. Vesper, Cricket, and now you."

That's it?

"Technically, I'm not an agent. Just a civilian."

"True," Callen says, popping the rest of the donut in his mouth. He holds his hand up while he chews and swallows. "But you're now privy to a lot of top-secret information. You have an off-the-record clearance at this point, so for all intents and purposes, you are a part of Operation PALADIN."

"Well, then I'll be happy to discuss the ladies dress code with Vesper and Cricket when I conduct their interviews. Did you get my email about that?"

"Yup," Callen says. "The sign-up sheet is almost full. I sent an email saying it's mandatory and missing their interview will result in serious consequences."

"*Dammit, Callen!*"

"What?" he says, reaching for a pastry this time. It's remarkable to me that Callen is so fit. I've seen how he eats on multiple occasions and, based on his diet, he should not be so athletic, especially as he nears his forties.

"Do not use words like *mandatory* and *consequences* when it pertains to me, okay? I'm here to welcome open conversations, not swoop in like the iron hammer. A hammer shatters things. From now on, let me send my own emails. Please."

He rotates his finger as he points at me. "*This*, Eden. This is why I knew we needed you. My brain doesn't work like that. It's the retired military in me."

"Mhm," I respond, unconvinced.

It's an excuse a lot of military service members use, but it wasn't my experience. My dad knew how to leave it at work. To Delta Forces he was Major Abbott. At home he was just "Daddy Duck," which I called him all the way up until I was fifteen.

Grumbling, I begin to rearrange the platters that Callen stole his breakfast from, trying to cover the bare spots. "Are you finished looting?"

"Probably not. These are delicious, where'd you get them?"

"A fantastic little bakery up the street."

I point to the boxes with the purple logos by the tall wastebasket. Immediately my mind lands on Chandler and our brief encounter the other evening. Funny, I never thought seeing a trash can would give me butterflies, but then again, I never thought I'd be so instantly attracted to a stranger. I went back to the compound on Sunday to continue research, and I'll admit, I lingered late into the evening. I was really hoping to see him again. Yes, he's hot

—beautiful even—but that's not what had my head spinning.

I felt comfortable, strangely enough. I haven't felt comfortable around people in over a year. I'm suspicious, my guard is always up, and it's been hard to converse with new people. I'm always afraid that I'll slip—about my real identity, the burden of information I'm holding that weighs a thousand pounds—or most dangerously…how the trauma of unbridled fear has changed me.

But Chandler…

Chandler had me at ease almost instantly. It wasn't anything he said in particular, it was his *presence*. For fifteen blissful minutes, I didn't feel like a whistleblower who ruined her entire career. I just felt like a normal girl…

With a little crush.

"Okay," I say, glancing at the clock on the wall, "we're ten minutes out, can you do me a favor?"

"What's up?" Callen asks distractedly, eyeing the muffins. *Good grief. He's a bottomless pit.*

"I'm going to tuck into the back corner and just monitor things for a while. Don't introduce me right away. I want some time to observe how everyone interacts with each other to see the best way to approach the situation. Believe it or not, the quickest way to read people is to observe them during a communal meal."

"Ah," he says. "So, breakfast is bait for your experiment?" I tap my nose twice and point to Callen. "You're a mastermind, Eden. I think, with your help, I might be able to pull this off."

Taking a seat in a chair in the far back of the room, I inspect the muffins on the platter closest to me. They look divine. The aroma of the bakery was like if heaven met Christmas—rich, vanilla, sweet, but with a touch of spice. I settled on a gourmet coffee but should've made time for one of those delicious cranberry orange muffins.

As I hear footsteps outside of the door, I know it's too late. I need laser focus and not that delightful little bakery distraction.

"Showtime," Callen undertones before he winks at me.

I draw in a deep breath and blow all my jitters away. They are just people. *Just people.* Not police, not agents…not killers. *Just people.*

The door handle turns and I see a shadow through the frosted door as the nerves prickle into my skin.

Showtime, indeed.

Linc

SIX

LINC

IT'S BEEN a while since Vesper, Cricket, Lance, and I have been together in the same room. A few months to be more specific—in Italy. We don't normally work as a team, but it took all four of us to infiltrate Moretti's lair. We left a hell of a lot of dead bodies behind. Moretti had more security than a U.S. President, and his henchmen were willing to die for him.

So they did.

They died for an arrogant terrorist and rapist who thought he was invincible. *Shameful.*

At any rate, it's odd enough for us all to be together, like sitting ducks, and in a break room no less. It's almost comical.

Cricket finds a seat next to Lance at the small break room table and rolls her eyes. She points accusingly at Lance. "It's the best way to get caught—*get us all caught*—dumbass."

When Vesper enters the room, I point to the pot of coffee that's brewing next to me. "Five more minutes," I say, leaning back against the kitchen counter.

She nods and stands right beside me. She's a little antsy today. We all are. We're meeting Callen's team today and it's uncomfortable, to say the least. I'm still not certain if he's trying to turn his agents into PALADIN operatives, or he's trying to turn me, Cricket, Lance, and Vesper into agents. Honestly, I'm not sure which of those two scenarios infuriates me more.

"Does someone want to tell me what's the best way to get caught?" Vesper asks, looking between Cricket and Lance, who look startled. *See? Ears like a bat. She's always listening.*

"Dumb fuck over here has secured a reputation as 'The Pancake Killer,'" Cricket snarks.

Vesper's brows cinch in utter confusion. "What?"

I chime in, "Lance keeps taking out targets in the exact same manner. One bullet between the eyes, then he flips them over and plants another bullet in the back of the head. It's very...*distinctive.*"

Vesper's eyes narrow at Lance, causing him to shrink in his chair. "Tell me you're not that stupid," she seethes.

"It was three dudes," Lance squalls. "*Three.* Everybody calm the fuck down."

"Seriously Vesper, google 'Pancake Killer.' There are people convinced he's the next Batman—a secret vigilante taking out gangbangers and mob bosses. He's a goddamn hashtag." Cricket slides her phone over to Vesper, but it's pointless. There's next to no cellular service in this basement bunker.

"No one saw me," Lance says, rolling his eyes. "Let it be a rumor."

"We've talked about this," Vesper says through a clenched jaw. "It's not just the lack of subtlety. You can't provoke the public. That's not what we do. We don't exist. We don't leave behind footprints...or *rumors*. Do not make me explain this to you again, Lancelot, because it will not be a pleasant conversation."

Lance shrugs her threat off like a rebellious teenager, but it's obvious he's intimidated by Vesper's menacing tone. "Fine, sorry," he concedes, *wisely*. "No one appreciates a professional anymore. It's a brilliantly fresh take on a double-tap, but if you want me to make hits seem like a fucking sloppy gang retaliation, from now on, I'll blow through these fuckers like a target board. Happy?"

"Thank you," Vesper replies. "And stop pouting. Where's your tie?"

"Where the hell do you think?" Lance sasses. But I see him bite his lip before he can add, "*Up your ass.*" Vesper has slapped him a time or two for his snarky remarks. I'd be lying if I said I didn't thoroughly enjoy it. It's like watching your mischievous little brother getting in trouble with Mom. "Since when do I need to own a fucking tie?"

"Okay, let me be clear everyone," Vesper growls. She makes eye contact with us one by one as her eyes go glacial. "We're all that's left of the old team—the four of us. I'm done saying goodbye to my family, and this is how I'm keeping us safe. We're fighting for the same cause anyway, the only difference now is Callen is providing the resources. So, dress up in the monkey suits, show up where you're supposed to, *on time*, find a way to work with the other agents, and keep your fucking noses clean. End of discussion."

We may not like Callen, but Vesper has saved all of our lives, and we're in her debt, so we collectively duck our heads and nod in agreement.

Because that's what you do when the *real commander* gives an order.

I almost missed her at first.

I figured Eden would be at this *oh-so-important* mandatory team meeting Callen called for, but when I didn't see her at the table as Lance, Cricket, Vesper, and I shuffled into the empty seats at the far end of the table, I was relieved. It gives me a little more time to figure out how to explain myself.

But while I'm watching in disgust as Lance takes down a

donut like a starved boar, I feel eyes on me. Not agent eyes—those are always on me when I'm anywhere near the FBI. I can almost hear the whispers: *He's a sociopath. I heard he keeps their teeth as souvenirs. He's cold-blooded, with eyes like the devil. Is he really on our side?*

Most of that is rumors... *Most.* Am I on the FBI's side? I don't know... I'm on Vesper's side.

Looking past the squirmy agents who refuse to make eye contact, I see her in the back corner, staring right at me. She waits for me to look at her, and raises her brows, conveying her message with just a look, *"What the fuck?"* Then, she goes back to scribbling on the notepad in her lap.

Shit. I could've handled surprise, anger, fear, but the look she just gave me is the same one people get when they've been betrayed. Why do I get the impression that Eden doesn't forgive liars very easily?

The meeting was supposed to start at eight o'clock, but it's well past 8:15 a.m. when Eden finally rises from her covert seat in the corner of the room and begins introducing herself to everyone, individually. Callen shadows her like an eager puppy, adding his unnecessary commentary. I tap my fingers nervously against the table as she nears. Cricket, sitting right next to me, notices and shoots me an odd look.

"What's wrong with you?" she asks in a hushed whisper.

"Nothing, I—"

"Guys, thanks for coming," Callen says, clasping Eden's shoulders with both hands from behind. My jaw clenches in jealousy...but not because of the obvious. They are clearly chummy—she looks relaxed around him, which is probably a way she'll never feel around me. "I want to introduce you to Doctor Eden Abbott."

"Ph.D.," she clarifies. *"Doctor* makes me sound way more sophisticated than I am."

Impossible. I don't ever think I've seen a more graceful creature. Even in yoga pants the other day, she looked regal. But now, dressed in flattering gray slacks, and a form fitting, navy button-down blouse, it's extremely apparent she's way out of our league. Her hair is twisted neatly at the nape of her neck, and her makeup is clean and minimal. She looks like she should be running meetings at Merrill Lynch or Goldman Sachs. What the hell is she doing slumming it with a bunch of hitmen?

"I have a few friends who got their Ph.D.'s," Vesper says and we all shoot her a quizzical look. Vesper doesn't have friends. *Does she?* "It's a lot of work, a lot of school, and takes a lot of drive. It's very impressive, please don't sell yourself short."

Eden blushes, just slightly, but I see it. "Thank you. I appreciate that," she says, a sheepish smile claiming her face as her shoulders relax.

Now, it's obvious. Vesper doesn't have friends who have Ph.D.'s, but she did just find a way to connect with Eden. *Clever.*

"This is Vesper, Cricket, Lance, and that tall, cold drink of water over there is Linc." Callen makes a finger gun and points it at me with a stupid grin. I want to reach across this table and smack the shit out of him. I think he's still pissy about the time I nearly broke his hand off, but don't fucking sneak up on a man who could kill you with his thumb and forefinger. That's just goddamn common sense.

"It's a pleasure to meet you all." She makes a point to shake everyone's hand, making eye contact as she does. She pauses when she gets to my chair, almost like she's savoring the moment.

"It's nice to meet you, Linc. Or do you prefer Lincoln?" Her gaze fixes tightly on mine, but it's like the doors have shut. I can't make sense of the look she's giving me.

I take her small hand in mine, feeling the same little jolt from when I shook her hand the other night. "Whatever you prefer."

She gestures over her shoulder at the half-empty tray of breakfast foods. "You didn't try anything?"

"I'm not hungry."

She grabs a muffin from the platter and holds it out to me. "This bakery is incredible. It's the kind of stuff you eat, even when you're *not* hungry."

Reluctantly, I hold out my palm. I don't like breakfast foods of any type. I'm less enthused about taking food from a community platter. It's an easy way to poison someone. That's not paranoia… I've seen it.

I've done it.

"That good, huh?" I mumble as I grudgingly peel back the paper wrapping and take a large bite out of pure masochism.

"Of course," she says, her eyes flickering with contempt. *"I wouldn't lie to you."*

My chewing slows, then stops, but before I can say anything in reply, she turns on her heel to take her place at the front of the table. Immediately, the chatter settles and she peers down the long meeting table, a composed smile on her face.

"Okay, now that there is some food in your stomachs, how about a game?"

Without a doubt, this woman has worked at a corporate company. Probably in a fancy office on the top floor. She has a presenter's voice and a boss's bravado. I force my eyes to rest on my half-eaten muffin so I don't look like I'm leering.

"I like games," Lance says through a mouthful of food, crumbs flying everywhere, making him look like a mannerless Neanderthal. But Eden smiles anyway.

"Glad to hear it. Everyone if you would grab your pen and the paper in front of you. I think we should start by getting to know each other a little better."

SEVEN

EDEN

HE GOT ME GOOD.

When I saw Chandler—actually Linc—at first, I was pleasantly surprised. I didn't realize this was an *all-hands* meeting. I was already preparing a quippy remark about another conversation so soon… Until it hit me.

There was something about the way the agents in the room didn't want to look at him. Even Callen seemed a bit more tense when Linc entered the room. He isn't a maintenance man who changes light bulbs and empties waste baskets, he's the pictureless man that Callen seemed a little afraid of. But why am I so surprised? Why do I even care?

Because you instantly liked him.

I ignore my internal musing and refocus as I uncap the hot pink Expo marker in my hand and begin to draw on the enormous whiteboard. A burst of strawberry scent fills my nose and I chuckle to myself as a memory comes to mind.

I think of the very first time I gave this presentation. I was only twenty-two, still in grad school, and building my portfolio as a consultant. I was so damn nervous. The net worth of that company was in the ballpark of billions. The executives in the room made more money in a year than I would ever see in my lifetime. Their smart suits and dress shoes probably cost more than my car and yet, they were looking at me like I had the solution to the severe morale problem within their company. I was shaking as I drew the triangle on the whiteboard until I smelled something fruity.

It took me a minute to realize the smell was coming from the marker in my hand. *Grape*. A girly grape whiteboard marker. A bunch of rich, middle-aged white men, full of scowls and skepticism, used a sickeningly sweet, grape-scented marker to conduct their meetings.

For some reason it made me feel better. *So much better*.

I knocked that presentation out of the park. Morris and Hauser Inc. still recommend my consulting services to this day. Or at least they did—until last year.

I breathe in as the memory fades and I'm brought back to reality by the scent of strawberries this time. It's far more tolerable than the grape.

I feel his eyes on me as I draw a triangle on the white-board. His gaze is scorching. Not Callen. Not the goofball playboy, Lance. Not any of the FBI agents in the room whom I've secretly nicknamed Agent Smith one through seven. No… *Him*.

Lincoln.

I resist the urge to turn around and peek, and instead write the power words on each side of the triangle.

Okay, yes—you were attracted to him. Honestly, any woman would be.

He's incredibly handsome—broodingly sexy. He has sandy-blond hair, with just a touch of scruff on his cheeks that's neatly trimmed. All the angles of his face are perfectly chiseled, like his maker spent extra time on this prize creation. He's like a GQ model in a suit, but far more athletic-looking.

But I don't do liars.

He didn't even flinch as he looked right into my eyes and skillfully misled me about who he was. Speaking of his eyes—

his light eyes—the faintest hue of baby blue, and a charcoal rim surrounding them. I can picture them with perfect accuracy because they are ingrained in my brain.

And I certainly don't do killers.

I purposely avoid Linc's gaze when I spin around.

"Okay, everyone, I promise this isn't a lesson in rudimentary shapes." There's a low murmur of chuckles. *Okay... That joke usually does a bit better, but let's move on.* "As you know by now, I'm Eden Abbott. I'm going to skip the introduction about my education and experience because while *I* don't find it particularly boring, *you all will.*" There's a louder rumble of chuckles. *There we go. Much better.* "Callen asked me to come here and help with PALADIN because obviously this team is going through a big...let's say, merger?" I glance Callen's way and he shrugs. *Unhelpful.* But "merger" is the closest business term I can think of for this bizarre situation. "Essentially, I work as a liaison. You guys tell me what you need, then I tell the people who sign your paychecks how to fulfill that need, *within reason.* I've tried in the past, and I've only once been able to secure one margarita machine for a company's break room, so please don't hold your breath on that." That earns me a full round of laughter and I'm officially satisfied that the crowd is warm.

"I've studied quite a few companies and what I can say with confidence is that, while every business functions a little differently, the motor is the same. Successful companies have happy employees. It's as simple as that. So, I'm here to figure out a way to make everyone happy. In my experience, it boils down to three different core needs." I point to the words on the board, one by one. I drew such a large triangle that I have to rise to my tippy toes to touch the top point.

"Fun. Communication. Safety," I recite the words on the board. "It's a well-known fact that architecturally speaking, triangles are the strongest shape. They are able to withstand a tremendous amount of pressure without shifting. My personal philosophy is that every team should build its strategy with a triangle approach."

I glance at Vesper, who seems far more invested in my little speech than I was expecting. Her eyes are on the board, studying my words.

"A job should be entertaining, a team member should feel heard, and a team member should feel safe. *Fun. Communication. Safety*," I repeat again.

Finally, I give myself permission to glance Linc's way. His eyes are down, focused on the little piece of note paper in front of him, and definitely not on me. *Stupid little fantasy.* It's ridiculous to even think about a romantic life right now...but the truth is, I've been lonely. I just wanted to connect with someone.

"In front of each of you is a piece of paper and a pen. I want us to play a game for some team building. I'm sure you've heard of the remote island icebreaker?"

I glance around the table to only see blank stares.

"Really?" I look at Callen who just shrugs unhelpfully, *once again*. I'm starting to question his purpose at this meeting. "You know...where you're stranded on a desolate island and you can only bring a few things...for survival..." I trail off as I see more puzzled expressions looking at me.

"That actually happened to me once," Cricket says. "I was stranded for three days and two nights on a shore in Bermuda with a boat captain when his vessel broke down."

"Wow," I reply, just grateful Cricket's engaging. *That's promising.* "That sounds scary."

"Eh, it was all right. We had some nonperishables on the boat. Plus, time flew by because he had an eight-inch cock. We kept ourselves busy if you know what I mean."

My jaw drops as snickers fill the room. I'm at a loss for words, but only a little bit about the eight-inch cock part. Mostly it's because I do not know the workplace appropriate response to that statement, so I completely sidestep it. "Cricket, is that an Irish accent you have?"

"You hear it, love? Dammit. I've really been trying to tone it down. Everyone remembers an Irish assassin, that's why I don't talk much on the job."

Lance snorts loudly. "Yeah, that's what they remember, Cricket." He glances at her cleavage, visible from her low-cut blouse. *"Your accent."*

Vesper lets out an exasperated sigh. "Since you're here, Dr. Abbott—"

"Eden, please"

"My apologies, *Eden.* Since you're here, maybe you can shed some light on *this* situation." She points between Cricket and Lance. "Please tell these two that, in your ample experience, interoffice relationships are not good for a team and never end well."

I glance between Cricket and Lance and don't understand what Vesper is insinuating. I'm usually pretty good at reading people and relationships. Crude humor aside, all I'm sensing is a brother-sistership. But I ask to confirm.

"Are you two..."

"Nah," Cricket says.

"Nope," Lance adds. "Everyone thinks we are though."

It's because they're both uncomfortably good-looking. People just assume hot people have sex with other hot people, which is ridiculous because it is quite possible for there to be more depth to people's attraction than looks.

"He's gone a few rounds with a couple of women I know though, if you need a reference," Cricket says winking at me. "Word is Lance knows how to work with a vibrator, instead of competing with it."

Lance chortles before pointing at Cricket. "My girl." He then sends a flirty wink my way.

"Okay, you see that?" Vesper says, her brows arched. "Very inappropriate."

"*Jesus*," Callen mumbles under his breath from the other side of the table.

I hold up my palms, trying to calm the chatter. "Listen, I'm not here to police you guys, but if you're asking my opinion, I strongly advise the companies I work with *not* to implement no-dating policies, and here's why…"

I glance to my left and Linc's piercing stare has returned, sending a glorious shiver up my spine. I pray the heat in my cheeks isn't visible. Clearing my throat, I reluctantly peel my eyes away from his icy blue gems.

"The moment you make something forbidden, you only make it more enticing. There are very few things people will lie, steal, cheat and…kill for. Love is at the top of that list. I don't recommend companies try to combat that. In addition, people spend an enormous amount of their waking hours at their day jobs, so how can we expect them not to connect with their coworkers? Now, I'm aware that retaliation after break-ups and even quid pro quo are real problems, but those are case-by-case issues to address, not a mass assumption that should be made. If you treat adults like adults, they'll behave accordingly."

I'm met with more blank stares. Sometimes I forget the amount of business expertise I have doesn't necessarily match my age…or appearance. They are staring at me like I'm a child playing dress up, and yet, I just delivered the presidential inaugural address.

I mentally roll my eyes. *Please don't underestimate me.* Yes, I've been quiet for a while, but this is my element. *This* is what I'm good at—*people.*

"Anyway, back to your papers. I'd like everyone to imagine you're going to be stranded—indefinitely—on a remote island. I'd like you to write down three things you'd bring along." I hold up one finger. "Something fun to entertain you." Then another. "Something that makes you feel safe." Then, a third. "And someone you'd really like to talk to."

Jutting my thumb behind my shoulder, I refer to the triangle on the board again. "Something fun, something safe, and someone great. Don't overthink it guys. Just make it personal, okay?" After clapping my hands together, I make a shooing motion, asking everyone to get to it. I ignore the sea of grumbles. This part is expected. Whenever I was working with giant conglomerates, full of employees begrudgingly yanked from their cubicles, everyone always resists...*at first*. I tend to have a magic touch, so let's see if I can get these robot agents to be a little more cooperative.

Surprisingly, Linc is finished first. He sets his pen down, folds his hands, and sits stoically in his seat. Vesper's eyes hit the ceiling multiple times. *Okay, she's an overthinker, that's for certain.* Judging by the expression on Cricket's face, I imagine her note is going to read something along the lines of, "Seymore Butts," or "Hugh Girection."

Lance looks like there is smoke coming out of his ears... but at least he's thinking. That's a win, I suppose.

This activity is supposed to identify leaders and I have a feeling Callen and I have our work cut out for us.

"Aren't you going to do one?" Linc asks me in a low undertone, as he swivels in his chair to face me at the board.

"Me?"

He nods as his lips twitch with *almost* a smile. *Is he teasing me?* Linc reaches toward the middle of the table where there are extra papers and pens, and he collects one of each for me. In the dozens of times that I've conducted this activity in the past, never once have I been asked to participate.

"Okay, sure." Taking two steps forward, I close the space between Linc and I. I'm standing, and he's seated, so when my eyes drop to his belt area, it most definitely looks like I'm staring at his crotch. Much to my horror, he notices. His eyes go from mine to his lap, and when they return, his smile isn't a twitch. It's a wide mocking smirk that says, *"Caught."*

Clasping both hands over my face, I groan. "I am so sorry, that wasn't—"

"Mhm, sure," he says with a chuckle. For such a scary, cold-blooded killer, he's definitely playful when he wants to be.

I part my hands, letting my palms press against my cheek. I'm beyond humiliated but I can't go unexplained. "When I'm around agents, I find myself always looking for where their guns are hidden. I wasn't checking out your..." I roll my wrist, unable to even verbalize the words. "Guns just make me—"

"Nervous," he finishes for me. Linc glances down to where his holstered pistol is in clear view, hanging beneath his belt.

I don't know what possesses me to respond with vulnerable honesty to this stranger, who already proved himself to be dishonest, but before I can stop myself the words spill out, "I tend to be afraid of people who *aren't* afraid of guns."

Rising, Linc removes his pistol from his holster. I'm not sure of the mechanics, but based on the clicking I hear, I'm assuming he's disarming it. He exits the meeting room without another word and is back just as fast. Settling back in his seat in front of me, he gives me a soft smile as he taps his empty holster.

"There. Better?"

Looking over Linc's shoulder, I see Cricket and Lance with their jaws dropped. Even Vesper is gawking in utter surprise.

I hold out my hand and Linc hands over the pen and piece of paper he gathered for me. When my fingers graze his, I lose my breath. My heart beat jumps like a skipping stone. I'm catapulted back to grade school, when the nervous butterflies from a new crush were the most energizing feeling in the world. Girl likes boy—boy likes girl. It was so straightforward, even in the messy midst of raging hormones and puberty. People weren't so layered. Right wasn't so muddled with wrong. Back when things were so much simpler...

I glance at Linc's empty holster one more time.

"Thank you. Much better."

Linc

EIGHT

LINC

I MIGHT AS WELL unzip and put my cock on display. That's how naked I feel without my gun. The last time I was unarmed was at Mom's funeral. The time before that was the night Suzanne was murdered.

I try to ignore my extreme discomfort and focus on the piece of paper in front of me.

Something fun? I don't think I've had fun in a while…but I'd sound like an ass if I said that, so I write down model ships. I liked building those as a kid whenever I could get my hands on them.

Someone I want to talk to? Mom, of course. But I'm not getting that personal. So, I wrote down Ted Bundy—but mostly just to bring him back so *I* could kill him this time. I don't think the electric chair was painful enough. Usually, I'm apathetic about my assignments. There's nothing glamorous about what I do. Sometimes bad people, who can't stop tormenting others, need to move on from this life, but women abusers boil my blood like nothing else. I normally like to keep my jobs clean—one bullet is all I need—but I'll admit, the last serial rapist I killed was begging me for death by the time I was done with him.

KAY COVE

Something that makes me feel safe? I regret writing down my .22 pistol for two reasons—one, now I know Eden has a distaste for guns, it seems insensitive. Two, it's another lie. There's not a goddamn thing in this world that makes me feel safe. But I wrote in pen, and I refuse to scribble anything out.

"Is everyone done?" Eden asks, smiling and looking around the room at everyone, except me. "Great! So, here's the twist." She flashes a wicked smile. "Push your papers, face down, into the middle of the table, please. Then choose one that's not your own."

She's met with some complaining and gripes, but everyone obliges. Once we all have a new piece of paper in front of us, Eden continues with her instructions.

"We tend to make a lot of assumptions about people based on first impressions, but more often than not, our first impressions are wildly incorrect. So, the purpose of this little activity is to test that theory. Read the paper in front of you and take one guess as to whose it is. Let's see if you're right. Any volunteers to go first?"

Lance reaches for another donut, but otherwise, the room is still. Flipping my paper over, I see only two answers in neat penmanship that match the words on the whiteboard. *War and Peace. Jorey Abbott.*

"Okay, I'll go first." Eden takes a seat at the head of the table and gracefully crosses her legs. "Deserae Pinar, Cricket, and Millie Mae," she reads. Balling up her fist, she lightly taps her knuckle against her plush top lip. Her face twists in confusion. "All right, I give," she finally says. "I am almost certain this is Lance's, but I can't make sense of these answers."

Lance laughs. "You want me to walk you through it?"

"Would that be putting you on the spot?"

"Not at all. I am *not* shy." Lance brushes the crumbs from his fingers and leans into the table. "Deserae is my something fun—she's an OnlyFans model with double D's. Millie Mae is my pistol and the only thing that makes me feel safe. And if I

86

was stuck in some shithole and could only bring one person to talk to and pass the time, *eh*—Cricket ain't bad company."

Cricket clicks her jaw and winks at Lance. Vesper purses her lips in disapproval, but she has nothing to worry about. These two would die for each other before they'd fuck. With our lifestyle, hookups are easy, but friendship is far more difficult to come by. Cricket and Lance wouldn't risk that for a little physical gratification.

"You know what, Lance?" Eden asks with a smirk on her face. "That was far tamer than I was expecting it to be. I would've suggested something along the lines of movies or video games for your 'something fun,' but I did ask for honesty so I guess... Good job."

The whole room, filled with angsty killers and uptight suits, *laughs*. I'll be damned. She really does have a way with people.

Going around the table, we make it through a few more note sheets. I watch the gentle ribbing, the teasing, and the arguing about everyone's preferred assault weapon, in utter surprise. PALADIN blending with the FBI is like the Hatfields and McCoys sitting down to break bread, but surprisingly, we all seem very civilized at the moment.

Eden looks far more relaxed. She leans back in her chair and wears a warm smile as she watches her work unfold. I like the current expression she's wearing. For a moment, I imagine what it'd be like to be a normal man who sees a beautiful woman and doesn't immediately feel the need to hide his identity.

I'd ask her out for a drink tonight. If the conversation flowed, a drink would turn into a late dinner, and I'd buy her the most expensive things on the menu. Maybe I'd even bring her home and cook for her. And after, all she'd have to do is let her pretty, dark-brown hair down, bite her bottom lip, and give me that look. I'd whisper in her ear that what's in my pants would put Cricket's boat captain to shame, and she could use me however she wanted. I'd lick every single inch of her, starting with those sweet cheeks—

Knock, knock.

Two quick rasps on the door yank me from my fantasy as a squirrelly-looking agent bursts into the room. "There you guys fucking are!" he squalls, looking panicked as all hell.

Who are you? Geez, this compound is officially crawling with suits.

The agent tosses a few manilla folders onto the table, causing the contents to spill out. He walks up to Callen and begins to speak in a low, urgent tone, making it impossible to hear what he's saying from across the room.

"Are you okay?" Vesper asks with growing concern in her eyes. When I follow her gaze, I realize she's staring at Eden who looks pale and frozen all of a sudden. I finally see the gory visual in front of Eden. From what I can make out from the photographs, the men are tied to chairs and sitting in a bloodbath. At least two are beheaded—definitely the mark of a terrorist execution.

"*What the fuck?*" I roar at the top of my lungs, causing everyone to look my way. I point at the pictures and then at Eden's face.

"Shit, sorry miss," the agent says, scrambling to stuff the photographs back into the folder.

Eden covers her mouth with both hands and mumbles something that sounds like, "I'm sorry," and, "please excuse me," but she doesn't dare pull her hands away from her mouth because she knows it...I know it...the entire room knows it—she's going to be ill. I see the tears gleaning in her eyes as she rushes out of the room, slamming the door behind her.

I kick out my chair as I rise, fully intent on following her, but Callen stops me.

"Linc. No time." He nods toward the folder. "Get your gun. It's time to go to work—right now."

NINE

EDEN

I LOST ALL the coffee in my stomach. But it wasn't enough for my stomach to be completely empty, I dry-heaved for another ten minutes. By the time it's over, I'm sweaty and nauseous, reveling in the cool relief of the cold tile on my hands and knees as I crawl to the opposite wall of the toilet. Never have I been more appreciative of private bathrooms with a lock.

How the hell am I going to recover from this?

How do I save face and go back to that meeting room?

Do I even want to?

Leaning against the wall, I tuck my knees to my chest. I wish I had my timer. I'd give myself an entire hour to fall apart. I've never seen something so gruesome in my life. Blood is one thing…but…those were headless bodies.

It's not real, Eden.

I shake my head at my subconscious which is trying to protect me. "Shut up," I shoot back in a whisper to my own thoughts. "I saw it. It's very real."

The gore was enough to twist up my stomach and make me damn well lose consciousness, but it was the prisoner in the photo that was still alive who will give me nightmares for the rest of my life. He was looking up at the camera, his eyes full of fear. He had it worst of all. He witnessed the deplorable brutality unleashed upon the first two victims and knew exactly what was coming for him.

People are monsters.

And I'm starting to understand the need for monster slayers.

There's a soft knock on the door but before I can answer, the lock turns. Someone has keys. Please, please for the love of God don't let it be—

"Hey," Cricket says, poking her head through the door.

Thank God. Just Cricket.

"Sorry for the privacy invasion but I had to make sure you were safe."

I paw at my face, trying to mop up the evidence of my meltdown. "Oh, I'm fine. Thank you. I think it's just…food poisoning."

Cricket raises her brows and nods her head. She doesn't believe a word I'm saying, but she doesn't call me out. Instead, she sinks onto the floor, her back resting on the opposite wall from where I'm sitting. She tucks in her legs as well, letting her forearm dangle off her knee. We're in almost identical sitting positions except Cricket looks collected and cool, and I know I must look like a withered mess.

"It freaks me out when bathroom floors are dark like this." She pats the dark green tile next to her. "It's gross because you can't see what's on them. We could be sitting in jizz, and you'd never know."

Small talk—lovely.

"Everything you say sounds like a song because of your accent. It's pretty…even when you say stuff like 'jizz.'"

She snorts in laughter and I chuckle along with her for a brief moment before the gruesome image slips back into the forefront of my mind.

"Can you please leave?" I ask suddenly.

She yanks a fastener off her wrist and pulls her thick long blonde hair into a ponytail. "Why, love?"

"Because I don't like when people see me cry and I don't think I can hold it in right now."

"Aw, come on now."

Cricket scoots across the bathroom floor and wraps her arm around my shoulder. Stroking my hair, she all but forces me to lean my head against her shoulder. She may look feminine, but every inch of her body outside of her breasts is hard and toned. Her embrace is a little uncomfortable, like trying to hug a punching bag, but I lean in anyway.

"I'm not *people*, I'm just Cricket," she says soothingly. "Go ahead and cry, I won't tell anyone. I promise."

I'm not sure if it's timing or her gentle encouragement, but the floodgates break right back open. I cry for the victims and their families. I wail because of the horrid brutality. I sob because this is reality, and I've had the privilege of being blind to it…until now. Are these the secrets Dad was holding on to? How do you see this kind of thing and not break into a million pieces? Is this what Empress could've caused if I didn't stop them?

Cricket holds me for a long time. Her arms must be tired, but she doesn't move. She just continues to stroke my hair and coo in my ear. In less than three hours of meeting her, this beautiful, far-too-forward stranger has become my sounding board—keeping me sane.

Finally straightening up, I wiggle out of her grip. Everything is a little damp—from my tears and sweat. I pull myself off the ground and wet a few paper towels in the sink before pressing them against my forehead. I'm still too hot so I resort to splashing the sink water all over my face.

"There you go, love. Feel better?" Cricket asks from the floor.

"I hope no one is waiting on me." I have no idea how long

I've been locked in the bathroom, but it's definitely long enough to indicate I'm not okay.

"No. Linc and Lance are already gone, and Vesper is ripping Callen a new one for putting you in that situation."

"It wasn't Callen's fault—"

"Ah," Cricket interrupts. "Rule of thumb around here— one way or the other, it's *always* Callen's fault." She winks playfully, but when I don't match her humor, she continues more seriously. "You're a civilian. You shouldn't have to see all that."

My throat is scratchy and sore, partly from the sobbing, but mostly from the retching. I collect a small pool of sink water in my hand and drink. The cool liquid immediately calms my throat. *Sweet relief.* At the moment, I don't even care that it's from a bathroom faucet, I'm desperate.

"Thank you," I mumble. "Is that what you guys deal with daily?"

She shakes her head but doesn't explicitly answer. "I take it you've never worked with the FBI before?" Cricket asks, tilting her head.

"I'm not technically with the FBI."

"Law enforcement? Military?"

Gripping the ledge of the sink, I look at myself in the mirror. My hair is in disarray—frayed, and frizzy. My mascara and eyeliner are smudged to the point I look like Harley Quinn on a bad day. There's no salvaging this. I need a makeup wipe and to start over.

In fact, that's a profound statement. *I need to start all the way the fuck over.*

"Never. I used to work in Silicon Valley, mostly for tech companies. The most serious crimes I've ever dealt with are sexual harassment accusations and fudging numbers on company reimbursement claims. Bottom line"—I turn to face Cricket—"where I come from, nobody bleeds." *Or loses their head.*

"Not to sound rude, love, but what the fuck are you doing here? Does Callen know all this?"

Glancing around the bathroom, I can't help but notice how new everything looks. The fixture lights are fresh and bright. The dark tile floor hasn't had a chance to become grimy. Even the toilet looked sparkly clean when my head was half-ducked into it. Come to think of it, the faint musky smell of piss and rusty pipes is nonexistent. This place smells lemony-fresh.

"I did the FBI a pretty big favor a little over a year ago. In helping them, I basically ruined my life. I guess… Maybe they felt they owed me a favor. They offered me this job for some financial stability."

"Okay." Cricket's eyes are filled with lots of questions, but she settles for only one. "Am I supposed to call you 'boss' now?"

"Only if you want me not to answer."

She chuckles. "I think we're going to be fast friends, Bambi."

My face twists. "Bambi?"

"Oh, yes. Everyone gets an ops name. Vesper loves a good James Bond movie. Lance is because he's Linc's first recruit— he's the Lancelot to Linc's King Arthur. One day Linc will give you his annoyingly dramatic speech on Abraham Lincoln and accidental heroism. And last but not least—"

"Yeah…why do they call you Cricket?"

"I used to keep pet crickets." Her light green eyes glaze over and for the briefest moment, they look eerily dark and cold. But she composes herself just as fast. "They were the closest thing I had to companionship for a long time… Until Vesper found me."

"Oh, well that's sweet."

"Well, that's my version anyway," Cricket says as she rises, brushing off her hands against her hips. "Lance will tell you it's because I'm chirpy in the sack."

Huh? "Wait, so are you guys?"

"Nah." She shakes her head, but she winks playfully, casting doubt on my prior philosophy. "Come on, love, let's get out of here. Maybe replace some of the breakfast you lost."

I wait until her hand is on the bathroom door handle before I'm brave enough to ask. "Cricket, why did you guys all freak out when Linc took off his gun earlier?"

Planting her hand on her hip, she pinches one eye shut and gives me an impish smile. "Why?"

"No reason," I mutter.

"The last time Linc put his gun away was for his mother… at her funeral. That's the only time in my life I've seen Linc unarmed."

"Oh." The nervous butterflies return to my stomach, but it's not nausea this time. I close my eyes briefly and am relieved when it's Linc's light blue eyes and that piercing stare that takes center stage over that awful image. "Well then, that was awfully considerate of him this morning."

"Sure was," Cricket says with a smirk on her face. "You know, I'm sure Callen has already filled your head with stories, but I promise you, Linc is more man than beast. He's the angriest out of all of us because he has the biggest heart. It's just been broken by this world…a lot."

"Oh, Callen didn't…" I trail off, shaking my head—mortified that Cricket can read me so easily.

"Course not." She shrugs with an innocent smile. "Well come on, Bambi, let's get you some water at least. There are cold bottles in the break room."

I actually already feel better. *Is this friendship?* It's been a while since I've had a friend. This is nice. I walked in here in ruins, and now I'm leaving the bathroom with only two thoughts in my head…

Big, bad, beautiful wolf, Linc, has been broken by this world… *A lot.*

And also, I really hope the nickname Bambi doesn't stick.

TEN

LINC

IT TOOK us less than two hours to get to Kansas on a chartered jet. The drive back is significantly longer, due to some *cargo* we had to return. This is why I hate Callen calling the shots. He always takes what should be simple and complicates the hell out of it.

"How's your shoulder?"

Lance winces from the passenger seat as he pokes his wound. The left arm of his suit jacket is soaked. "Still bleeding, obviously."

"There's a safe house forty minutes East. Do you want to stop?"

"With fuckwad in the trunk? No. I can make it."

Callen needed information, so we had to bring home some work with us. We gave our *guest* a very strong sedative so he'd be quiet in the trunk for the remaining eight hours we had to go.

"I'd prefer you don't bleed out in here. I promised Vesper I'd try to bring you home alive," I say with as much sarcasm as I can muster with the little energy I have left. I flip on my turn signal, moving to the right lane.

"No, Linc. I said I'll wait until we get back."

"The fuck is your problem?" I growl as I tighten my grip around the wheel. My hand is sore, possibly fractured. It would not kill us to take a breather. It's been twenty-nine hours since we've slept, twelve targets down and one tied up in the trunk. We've more than earned the reward of rest.

"It's the medics at the safe house. They'll want to stitch this up." He taps his shoulder.

"Yeah genius, stitches might help with the bleeding," I snark.

We were outgunned but it was nothing we couldn't handle. Lance tripped and was exposed for half a second too long. A bullet grazed his left shoulder, slicing him open like a roast chicken.

"If I get stitches from one more field medic, I will officially look like Frankenstein. I need an actual surgeon who understands scarring. Even Cricket says I'm starting to look like I just walked off the set of *The Nightmare Before Christmas*."

"You're worried about scars?"

He scoffs. "Some of us like to look good naked."

"Fair point. Maybe we can get an in-house doctor to stitch you up and do your annual pap smear too."

"You prick," he gripes. "You're just jealous because, after me, Ellie referred to you as the baby carrot."

"You did not fuck Ellie."

"Wanna bet?"

I have never, nor will I ever share a woman with Lance, but he likes to taunt me. Not to mention, Ellie is a fake name. I don't tell Lance about my actual dalliances, although sometimes I lie to him just to keep his wheels spinning. Ellie is a fictitious stripper from Clemmons—a well-known gentleman's club on the West side of town. Lance proudly informed me that he took Ellie for a spin after I raved about her flexibility and athleticism. The only problem with his story is she doesn't exist.

"All right, have it your way." I push down on the gas pedal, accelerating. If we're headed straight home, let's at least get there quickly.

"Hey, what was with you yesterday by the way?" Lance asks as he turns down the radio. I'm not sure why it's even on, it's just static.

"What do you mean?"

"With the new HR chick."

"You're twenty-seven. Grow up," I grumble. "Quit saying 'chick.' She's a woman."

"Yeah, see?" Lance points his finger at me. "*Woman*," he mocks. "What's up with Prince Lincoln over here? You put your gun away."

"She doesn't like guns."

"And you ate a muffin."

"I was being polite." I try to feign nonchalance.

"Linc."

"What?"

"Don't go there, man."

We sit in silence as I watch the headlights dance off the reflective lane lines. It's so dark that if it wasn't for the glowing tape, I wouldn't be able to see the road fully alert, let alone amidst my sleep exhaustion.

Curiosity finally claims me. "Humor me. What's the warning for?" *What could possibly be concerning about Eden?*

"Callen brought her in."

"Obviously."

"No, I mean—what do you know about Dr. Eden Abbott?"

Outside of the fact that she has the cutest pouty smile, the most lickable cheeks I've ever seen in my life, and she's squeamish around violence—nothing. "What do you know?"

"Remember the enormous tech company that went under a little while back—Empress?"

"The one that was selling data to terrorist organizations?"

"Mhm," Lance mumbles as he opens the glove box and

pulls out a few napkins. He presses against his arm and the napkins quickly turn red. "She's the one who went to the feds with proof. She took a lot of shit for it, too. The company sued her and she went bankrupt. She was jobless and nearly homeless. She filed eight police reports for harassment and stalking in the past year."

My jaw instinctively clenches. "The fuck? From who?" I bite out.

"From what I understand, former Empress employees who were pissed about losing their jobs. I think that's why Callen eventually scooped her up and got her out of there."

So this is why she's so skittish. It doesn't matter how righteous the cause is, informants always end up marked. It explains why she flinches like a puppy that's been kicked one too many times.

"How do you know all of this? You looked her up?"

"Fuck yeah I did. There's someone new suddenly all up in our business...of course I looked her up."

"You still haven't answered my question. What's your concern?"

"Her loyalty is to Callen. It'll only be a matter of time before Vesper sees the light of day and we're moving on from the FBI. How long do you really think we can all get along for? This is temporary. She's fun to look at, and hell, even I want to know what her tits look like, but it's not smart, Linc. We don't belong to the FBI, the CIA, or DIA. We're free agents and Vesper will remember that soon. Do whatever you want with your dick, but don't get attached. At the end of the day, she's Callen's girl."

I don't think she's Callen's girl. She's just a girl. Just a normal girl...

I'm still picturing the look on her face when she saw those photos—shock and terror. There isn't an evil bone in her body. She was genuinely scared, and I can't explain it, but I have this urge to make her feel safe. I don't ever want to see that look of dread in her eyes again.

I haven't stopped wondering how she's doing. I'll admit that half of my eagerness to get home isn't just to dump this prisoner off into custody. It's to see her again—her smile. Just to know she's okay.

I realize I still need to explain myself.

I just need to see her first…

I also need to figure out why all my thoughts are suddenly so occupied with Eden. I'm not sure why I'm so quickly drawn to this woman. It's *never* happened to me before. There's a lot I don't understand at the moment, but one thing rings clear…

"Lance," I say, tightening both hands around the wheel.

"What?"

"You will never get to know what Eden Abbott's tits look like." I peel my eyes off the road to glance at him menacingly. "Got it?"

ELEVEN

EDEN

AFTER TWO WEEKS WITH PALADIN, my brain is a puddle.

Callen warned me to slow down—I should've listened. I've done the interview approach at every company I've consulted for. At one point, I conducted fifty employee interviews in a week's span and didn't fatigue. Then again, most of the complaints were about favoritism, lunches and breaks, and promotion opportunities.

All PALADIN wants to talk about is targets. And by targets, I mean human beings. The agents want more high-profile cases and they hate the hoops they have to jump through to pull the trigger. I thought they feared the assassins—turns out they envy them. Apparently there are a lot of evil criminals in this world who deserve to die, and they want to operate as lawlessly as Vesper's operatives do. That's why these agents volunteered to join PALADIN.

The only, somewhat valid, requests I've received so far are a few recommendations for better snacks for the break room and for flat-screen TVs in every office, equipped with HBO.

I'll only be obliging one of those requests. I am happy to have Callen order both Nacho Cheese *and* Cool Ranch

Doritos for the break room. HBO, however, is not a hill I'm willing to climb.

Knock, knock.

Looking up from my dual monitors, I see Callen in the doorway of my office with a big smile on his face.

"Hey." I roll away from my desk. "Come on in."

He enters my office and closes the door behind him. After taking in a panoramic view of my space, Callen looks at me curiously. "Do you need anything, Eden?"

"Pardon?"

"This office looks a little bland."

He's not wrong. It's a smaller office than I'm used to, with one large oak desk in the center of the room, and then a small sitting area crammed into the opposite corner. All the furniture is pleather and generic—which is honestly preferable in case of spills. I eat most of my lunches here, sometimes on the floor, legs tucked under the coffee table. My metal wastebasket is probably the shiniest item in my entire office. My office looks more like the inside of a police precinct than anything else, but what do you expect when your workplace is literally underground?

"It's fine," I say, leaning against my desk and stretching my legs. I've been sitting for way too long.

"You sure? You're welcome to order some stuff on the FBI's dime if you want to spruce this place up."

I point to the left side of my desk where there is a mini sandbox and an itty-bitty rake. "I brought my Zen Garden."

"What is this?" Callen saunters over to my little box of stress relief. "A tiny cat box?"

"No… It's for…" I scrunch up my face, trying to figure out how to explain how arranging mini rocks, trees, and bushes, and drawing words in a miniature sandbox can be very therapeutic. "It's just for fun. Anyway, what's up Callen? Something I can help you with?"

He drops the small Zen Garden rake and makes his way

over to the pleather sofa. It squeaks then wheezes when he slumps down.

"Two things. One—the new doctor is officially here, per your request."

"Ah, good. I'll need to make a personnel file for her." I've taken on the administrative burden of PALADIN as well, but I don't mind too much. Honestly, I am more than relieved that there is a dedicated doctor for the compound now. After the third time, in two weeks, that Lance busted into my office, asking me to please check out something that was itchy on his ass or ball sack, and then me kindly explaining I am *not* that kind of doctor, I insisted Callen bring a general doctor on board. The team needs easy access to medical attention. It seems these people only see doctors if they are near death. I had to explain the importance of preventative medicine and routine physicals.

"And what's the other thing?" I ask.

"Right," Callen says, clasping his hands together and pointing them at me. "A very intelligent organizational leadership consultant once told me that it is important to tell team members when they are doing a stellar job. So, this is me… following orders." He winks.

I blink at him, confused. He responds by rolling his eyes.

"*You*, Eden. You are doing a great job. Oddly enough, this place is running smoothly. Lance called me 'Sir' the other day. Cricket is doing her paperwork. Even Linc greeted me in the hallway today. He said, 'Good morning.'" Callen holds up two fingers and widens his eyes for dramatic effect. "That's two words," he reiterates.

"Linc's back?" I ask. I haven't seen him since my embarrassing meltdown during the team meeting two weeks ago when I ran out, ready to puke. The same one where I found out that my little janitor crush was actually a killer. He missed his scheduled interview but Callen informed me he was still out on yet another job.

"He got back this morning."

"Oh, okay. Well, overall, it's an easy team to work with." As long as I ignore what they really do for work. "My prior leadership theory is defunct though."

"What do you mean?"

"You don't need to develop *new* leadership, Callen. There's only one leader the operatives will listen to, and luckily for you, she has the agents' respect too."

"Vesper," Callen says.

"Yes—none of this works without Vesper. But in my opinion, it *can* work. Everyone just needs to start working *together* on projects. Maybe start sending the operatives on jobs with a… buddy? Is that the term you use?"

"Like battle buddies?"

"Yeah."

Callen laughs. "You really were an Army brat."

"Through and through. But what I'm saying is the agents want to get their hands dirty. They want to feel like contributors, not props. From what I've gathered, they're just as frustrated with the FBI's policies as the operatives are."

"I'll think about it. But I say let's ride the wave while it's at its peak. What other team-building magic tricks do you have up your sleeve?"

I lean back against my desk and feel the hard ledge digging into my ass. "Well, I'm assuming company picnics or carnivals are out of the question, so all I can think of is happy hour, but are you guys even allowed to be seen in public together?"

Callen scoffs. "You watch too many movies, Eden. The agents all have very normal lives, and the operatives, well, most of the people who'd recognize them are all in prison or…" He trails off, but I can finish his sentence for him. *Dead.*

"Okay, then I'd recommend taking everyone out for a happy hour now and again. Nothing too rowdy, try a restaurant or lounge—not a club. And as the boss, only stay for one round, which you'll need to pay for, and then excuse yourself for the evening. That's a perfect balance—participate but don't linger. Give them space to let loose and talk a little shit about you." I smirk at Callen.

Callen's laugh is muffled at best. "Okay, happy hour—I like it. How about next Friday? I'm busy this weekend." He rises.

I shrug noncommittally. "If that works for you."

He must sense my dismissal. "Oh no, no—you're coming, Eden."

I shake my head fervently. The only reason I've been somewhat able to function in this role, especially since that awful picture landed in front of my face, is that I've kept my work life and personal life separate. When I leave this compound, I leave all of my worried, gruesome thoughts *here.* I only ask for details that I specifically need—I don't want to get too close. Hanging out with a bunch of killers and risking a panic attack when they casually start talking about the gory manner in which they end people's lives doesn't sound like a party I want to attend.

"No, Callen. I don't think that's a good idea. Plus, nobody wants to hang out with HR after hours. Come on," I say, trying to sound casual, but it comes out pleading.

Callen flattens his stare. "You're coming. End of story. And I thought you said you weren't HR. I'm sure everyone would love to hang out with an organizational blah, blah, blah," he teases as he rolls his wrist and exits my office.

"Yeah, yeah," I grumble under my breath. "Leave the door open," I call after him.

Callen's barely out of sight before Linc appears in the doorway, as if he was patiently waiting for the coast to be clear.

"Hi," I say, feeling how wide my eyes are. I blink a few times. *Shit.* It's like the nerves from our last encounter went dormant...until exactly now.

"Good afternoon," he says so quietly it's barely audible. "Am I disturbing you?"

"Not at all. Come on in." I wave him into my office and gesture toward the couch.

When he enters, a gust of the most pleasant fragrance fills my nose—it's not cologne, it's clean and simple, like generic bar soap. When he pauses just a few inches in front of me my knees go weak, so I plant my ass further against the desk ledge.

Linc taps his holster, showing me it's empty. Again, he's unarmed...*for me.*

"You don't always have to do that for my benefit," I say as I meet his eyes. I'm relieved when he breaks our gaze and moves toward the couch, releasing me from his spell. His crystal-blue eyes are a vacuum, capable of sucking me right into the unknown.

"It's fine if it makes you more comfortable," he says, settling into the pleather couch. It doesn't wheeze as it did with Callen. Linc doesn't plop—every single one of his movements is graceful and calculated.

"How was your trip?" I ask.

"Rainy."

"Is that a good thing or bad?" Linc eyes the empty chair across from him as a subtle request, but I don't budge. He's settled deep into the seat and his legs are spread in a wide V. I stay planted by my desk. If his eyes are a vacuum, what's in his pants might as well be a black hole, ready to swallow me whole. It's best I keep a safe distance.

"I don't mind the rain," Linc says.

Why does everything that comes out of his mouth seem to have a double meaning? *What are you actually saying?* I allow the quiet moment between us to soak up the jolts of energy caused not only by my attraction to Linc but also by my intuition that's raising every single red flag.

I've been around Cricket and Lance for the past couple of weeks and I never feel this jumpy. Even Vesper, who is far more on the serious side, comes off as comforting and maternal—maybe because she's about a decade older than I am. But even still, Linc has an air about him, one that is captivating and unnerving at the same time.

When I've decided the silence has gone on too long I ask, "Is there something I can help you with?"

"I missed my interview. I was working. Is now a good time?"

"*Oh.*" I was not expecting that. "You know I've gotten the majority of information I need. Unless there's something in particular you want to tell me, you don't have to do all that."

"I don't mind." He squints in my direction, seeming a little offended. "Lance said he did one."

"Well, yes, but that's because Lance loves to talk about himself. I didn't actually write anything down. He basically just used me as a shrink for an hour."

To my great surprise, Linc snorts in laughter—genuine laughter. So much so that I notice he has dimples. I thought Linc was good-looking before, but after seeing his wide smile for the first time…

This man is fucking gorgeous.

His eyes dance up and down my body in the most shameless way, as he cradles his chin, his forefinger hooking above his upper lip. He's studying me again. I cross one leg over the other as if I can shield myself from his hungry stare.

"Feel free to close the door and interview me," he says, causing a chill to come over me at the idea of Linc and I, *alone*, behind a closed door. "I'm feeling generous today. I'll tell you whatever you want to know."

TWELVE

LINC

WHAT THE FUCK just came out of my mouth?

I'll tell you whatever you want to know?

What is wrong with me? I promised myself I wouldn't lie again, but now... I might *have to*, because there are some things Eden absolutely cannot know about me.

She'd run...then, hide.

Eden does as instructed and closes her office door. Her breathing is loud and shallow. We're being professional and coy, but I can't imagine she's forgotten my deceptive first introduction. It'd be nice if we could side-step it. I'd rather focus on the way she blushes every time I look at her.

After grabbing a pad of paper and a pen, she settles in the chair across from me. Eden looks near me, but not *at* me. It's when we make eye contact that she seems the most disoriented. Apparently, she's avoiding the distraction.

Eden clears her throat as she tucks a loose strand of her hair behind her ear—the only piece that's come free of the twisted bun sitting on the nape of her neck. If she thinks I'm not watching...studying...learning, she's sorely mistaken. At the moment, I'm letting myself get lost in this new obsession.

"I used to conduct these interviews mostly as a way to give

employees an opportunity to explain their grievances and to come up with solutions. Do you remember the triangle?" She pauses and waits for me to nod. "This is a way to let team members know they're heard."

"You say 'team members' a lot."

"I do," she says. "It sounds less condescending than 'employee' or 'subordinate.' Who wants to feel like property? 'Team member' says that they matter, that they are part of something bigger."

"Is this what you studied for your doctorate? How to get people to feel good about wasting away in offices?"

"Something like that." She chuckles softly but I don't think she finds it funny. "But hey, I'm supposed to be asking *you* questions."

"Okay." I hold up my palms. "Ask away."

A clever smile crosses her face. "How in the world do you balance a full-time career as an assassin, and still moonlight as a janitor?" Her eyebrows arch.

Fuck. Okay, I'm not off the hook.

"I'm sorry, I sort of *misled* you—"

"Lied," she interrupts. "*Lied* is the word you're looking for." Her tone isn't exactly calm, but she doesn't seem too angry, so I try to explain.

I blow out a short breath. "You seemed startled when you saw me that night. I wasn't sure what you already knew, but I didn't want you to be scared of me."

"Why would I be scared of you?"

"You were alone, in the middle of the night, with a stranger. You said you hated guns and the people who carried them. Look at how you reacted when you saw that photo. You're..." I want to say precious, but that sounds too forward, too fast, so I settle for, "jumpy," and immediately regret it.

"Jumpy?" She drops her jaw, clearly offended.

"Sorry, I mean...sensitive?"

Her open palm finds her forehead with an audible smack.

"You're not supposed to say that to a woman in the workplace —it's a microaggression."

I groan. "See? That's why I lied. Talking was easier when I was a janitor."

She throws her head back in laughter. "Fair point. All right, I'll stop giving you a hard time now, I'll ask you the actual questions." She clicks her pen against the pad and gives me an earnest smile. "If you need to pass on any of these, that's fine. No pressure."

I nod. *Just ask.*

"What's your real name?"

Fuck, that was fast. It'd be nice to tell her that I didn't lie about my name the first time we met, but I really don't want her poking around the name Chandler Janey. According to the obituaries, he died at sixteen. "Pass. I'm sorry—"

"It's okay—"

"It's not personal. I've been Lincoln for so long that in every way that matters, it's my real name."

"That's fine. As I said, there's no pressure—"

"Ask me another, *please.*"

"Okay, how old are you?"

"Twenty-eight. You?"

"How old do I look?"

I scoot forward to the edge of the couch. Just another inch or so and our knees would touch. "I'm not an idiot. I am not answering that question. That's a trap if I've ever seen one."

Her cheeks bunch in my favorite way and her lips curl into an unguarded smile that reminds me of the first night we met. "You're smart, Linc. I'm twenty-nine."

"That's a little young for a doctor with all your accolades."

"For a medical doctor, perhaps. But not necessarily for a Ph.D. I went right from my undergrad to a doctoral program. I kept my grades up so they allowed me to fast track."

She's driven—smart—and should not be cooped in this dungeon that the rest of us now call headquarters.

"So, what exactly is—"

She holds up her palm and closes her eyes briefly. "Who is interviewing whom here, Linc?"

Snickering, I offer her a compromise. "How about a question for a question?"

"Hm," she says, trying to reel in her wide smile. "Okay, but let's make it more interesting. Two passes each—max. But I'll forgive the first one you gave."

"Deal."

"Ladies first."

She draws in a deep breath. "The prisoner who was still alive in that photo... Did you make it in time? Did you save his life?"

I see the painful trepidation in her eyes. *Ah fuck.*

"Pass." Her hopeful expression falls, replacing her sweet smile with a half-hearted scowl. "Eden, I know what it must look like, but those men weren't exactly innocent. The brutality they faced... They'd done much of the same to others. These are insurgents fighting against each other—they deserved what was coming. The FBI's main concern was the fact that it happened on U.S. soil." Among other things...but Eden is on a need-to-know basis and I've already said too much.

"Linc, let me make this clear." Her soft, kind eyes narrow. She almost looks intimidating. "No human being should be treated that way. I don't care if they've done worse, rightful consequence is different from cruel vengeance. They didn't deserve anything. Someone has to break the cycle. The most intelligent philosophers in history already warned us that fighting fire with fire means the entire world will burn."

My heartbeat slows to the point I can inhale and exhale between the beats. A flood of adrenaline washes through me, but it decelerates everything instead of quickening it. What is this?

Is this...*shame?*

I've killed so many men who deserved to die, and yet this, almost, stranger sits in front of me, rocking the entire foundation of my existence. Am I helping or merely contributing to the fire?

"My turn," I say with an exhale. "Who is Jorey?"

"Pardon?"

"Jorey Abbott. He, or she, was on your answer sheet for the icebreaker game."

"You drew mine?" I nod in response and she continues, "Jorey is my dad."

"You only wrote down two answers. The assignment required three." I hold up my pinky, ring, and middle finger together.

She rolls her eyes so quickly, I almost miss it. "If I could talk to anyone, especially about the past year of my life, it'd be my dad, who passed away. And I put down *War and Peace* for my 'something fun,' because it's the book I promised him I'd read, but never got around to. If I'm being completely honest, I mostly like Chick Lit in my free time, but now that Dad's gone, I really wish I would've made time to read the damn thing. He would've loved to talk about it together. Now, we can't."

I have the urge to reach out and touch her, to comfort her, but I stuff it down. Instead, I scoot back into the couch, letting the plastic-feeling cushion mold to my back. "What is Chick Lit?"

She cocks her head to the side. "You know...like women's fiction...for women. It's...uh... books for women...about women." She's flustered as she tries to explain herself and I think I know why.

"Ah, you mean romance books."

"Sometimes."

"Girl on girl?"

"What?" She balks and I widen my eyes in surprise.

"You just said books for women, *about women*."

She's blushing wildly, lighting up her entire face. I'm almost hoping for a flirty shriek, or a suggestive joke, but instead, Eden lobs her pen at my head. I dodge just in the nick of time.

"That almost hit me," I say, laughing.

"I realize," she says, giggling right back. "I meant fiction along the lines of women's coming-of-age stories. Stories about adolescence to adulthood, learning life lessons, overcoming impossible situations, and learning to stand on their own two feet. Not lesbian porn, if that's what you were insinuating."

"I wasn't." *I absolutely was.* "But, anyway, you didn't complete the assignment. What makes you feel safe?"

Her humorous expression sobers and her eyes drop to her lap. "Jorey for both. The person I want to talk to *and* the person who makes me feel safe."

"But you said he passed away?"

She nods curtly but then turns her head to the door as if she hears someone knocking. It's just for show, no one's there, but her eyes are starting to glisten. I'm quickly learning Eden likes to hide her vulnerability. When she's satisfied that she's composed, she turns her head and locks onto my stare.

"I haven't felt safe for years, Linc. Not since he died, and especially not in the past year."

"Why?" I ask as if I don't already know the answer, thanks to Lance and his snooping.

"It's my turn for a question. You just asked three in a row."

"Fine."

She waits so long that I'm tempted to fill the silence myself, but right as I open my mouth, she says, "Did you think less of me because of how I reacted to those photos?"

Twice now, she's caught me off guard with these pointed questions. "Did I think less of you because you were disturbed by a *very disturbing* scene that wasn't meant for your eyes?"

"I could forgive my initial shock, but it's been weeks...I still see it when I close my eyes." She clamps her lids shut like she's testing the theory, then quickly opens them again. "A *picture* shook me. How do you sleep at night seeing that in person?"

Truthfully...it's getting harder to. "I've seen it for over a decade, not much surprises me anymore."

She inhales deeply then lets out a hurried sentence with her breath. "You were right. I was scared when I saw you that night. Had I known who you were, I would've bolted. I'm glad you lied."

"Really?"

"Yes. Because we were able to have a *conversation*. Now..." She cocks her head to the side and her lips relax into a soft smile. "I'm not as intimidated to talk to you."

Good. Relax. You're safe with me. "I *am* sorry though. I'm a lot of things, but not usually a liar. And I promise I won't lie to you again so..."

"So, what?" she asks in a whisper, her eyes still transfixed on mine.

"Be careful what you ask me."

"Okay," she says, her eyes dropping to my lips. I know she doesn't see me noticing—Eden seems to be caught in a little daze, her eyes glazing over. It's obvious what happens next when a woman looks at you like this...

I'm curious enough to test the waters.

I scoot forward again on the couch then reach out and touch her knee. She flinches before she stills and sucks in her lips.

"You owe me an odd compliment by the way. It's still two to one."

"That I do," she says, her voice cracking.

"But nothing physical." I pump my brows at her once.

She's quiet, so I let my hand trail just an inch higher. The material of her pants is so thin, I can feel the warmth of her leg.

"I like that…" She clears her throat to no avail. Her words still come out raspy. "It's just, you seem to feel bad about what you do."

Her statement takes me off guard. "I didn't say that."

"I know," she says. "But you have this…*presence.*" She borrows my word from the other night. "Like you don't enjoy killing. It's nice."

I watch her big, brown eyes grow wide again, like she's worried she overstepped, but I'm not offended. It's just uncomfortable when someone stares right into your soul. "An odd compliment indeed. Now we're even."

"Not quite," she says. "I owe you a lie too."

I let out a breathy laugh as I stare at her plump lips. If only I could taste them. I move in a little closer, my hand inches up her thigh…I'm so fucking tempted.

"Okay. Lie to me."

"I don't think about you. I'd very much like you to remove your hand from my leg, and I most definitely don't want you to kiss me."

Her eyes are steady. She's not smiling, but her lips are slightly parted as she breathes through her mouth. If there was ever a green light—this was it. I could kiss her right now. I could do more…right behind this office door. I would ruin her for every other man after me. But the dangerous thing is I don't just want to fuck her…

I want to kiss her.

And not just as a means to an end…

I really want to kiss her.

Suddenly, I'm extremely uncomfortable. Every warning flag is waving. Every alarm is ringing in my mind. This feels very out of control and I don't like it.

Using her leg as leverage, I rise. "I'm sorry. I should get back to work," I force out, reluctantly. This is new. I need some time to get my bearings. I knew I was attracted to Eden. I didn't know I wanted…

I don't know. What is this? *More?*

Her light brown eyes are wide and startled. The wounded expression on her face tells me she's interpreting this as rejection.

If only she knew.

"Okay. Um…" She blows out a shaky breath. "I'll see you around."

THIRTEEN
EDEN

I'VE HAD my fair share of dating mishaps. I've been embarrassed before…but not like this. I have never so wildly misjudged a situation in my life. Two days ago, I basically begged Linc to kiss me and he literally ran out of my office.

I still don't understand what I missed. I haven't dated in the past year—perhaps I'm out of touch with romantic signals. Is squeezing a woman's knee and slowly trailing your hand up her thigh the new universal sign for *not interested?*

To make matters more confusing, this morning, when I walked into my office, lying on my desk was a brand-new copy of *War and Peace*. Linc left a simple note—

For when you make time.

He didn't even sign it. He didn't have to. I haven't talked to anyone else about Dad and my heaping pile of regrets.

"Holy hell," Cricket groans as she barges into my office, nearly making me jump out of my skin before toppling out of my desk chair. "What a fucking night."

I am very seriously considering changing my open-door policy to a please-fucking-knock-first policy. One thing I didn't take into account is how goddamn sneaky the operatives of PALADIN are. Half of their job is to move around undetected and quite frankly it's like working in a compound full of lurking cats. You never know when one is going to jump out at you.

"Hi Cricket," I huff, pressing my palm against my still pounding chest.

"Why are you holed up in here reading a textbook?"

Such a pretty face and a beautiful thick head of hair, but as far as what's rattling around in her head... I have no clue if Cricket truly has a few screws loose, or if she just prefers for people to underestimate her. Maybe this way it makes it easier for her to strike them down, like a lioness toying with her prey.

"It's fiction. A novel..."

She scoffs. "I'm kidding, love. I know Tolstoy. Why you're reading it still remains a mystery."

"I'm not...yet, anyway. It was a gift from Linc. I mentioned something about my dad and he remembered, that's all."

Cricket tiptoes over to my couch and curls up, pulling the afghan I brought from home over her. She likes to hide in here for naps from time to time. She says her office is chilly, but I think she likes the company. I don't mind, especially because Cricket sleeps like the dead. I've worked for hours in total silence while Cricket's drooled on my couch in a deep slumber.

I cross the room and straighten the blanket over Cricket before settling into the chair across from her. The same chair where Linc almost put his lips on mine.

"May I ask you something?"

Cricket lifts her face to look at me, her green eyes looking especially bloodshot today. I want to ask if it's a hangover, or from a late night at work, but again—it's best not to ask for the details I don't want.

"What's up?"

"Do you guys...date?"

"You mean Linc?" she asks with a smirk.

"Not just Linc—any of you guys. Do you have personal lives outside of PALADIN?"

She's quiet for an uncomfortably long time. *I'm sorry, forget it,* is almost on my lips when she finally responds.

"PALADIN isn't just our job, it's our only family, our entire life. We don't have anything outside of it which is why most of our relationships are short-lived." She clamps one eye shut, like there's something sour on the tip of her tongue. "Do you understand what I mean?"

"Yeah, of course. It makes sense. My dad was much the same. He never remarried after my mom died. He just focused on work...and me."

"Oh, Bambi," she tuts. "I'm sorry. He must've been lonely."

"He had me, he said that was enough. Plus, I'm sure he *dated,* he was just discreet about it. He never brought another woman into our lives. I think my mom was just...kind of incredible, you know? I don't think he thought love existed outside of her."

"That's beautiful," Cricket says with a lazy smile. I can sense her exhaustion and I feel a little guilty for keeping her awake with this conversation. "I want a man like that. I want to be someone's one true love."

"I find it hard to believe *you* can't get a man."

"Oh, I can get a man," she assures me. "But I said *true love.* That's trickier." She winks. "But by the way, Linc isn't your dad."

"What?" I scrunch my brows in response to her awkward inference.

"Linc doesn't have some long, lost love he can't replace. I've known him for a long time. He's never been in love."

"Oh, well, that's neither here nor there."

She purses her lips and her forehead crinkles as she examines me. "I didn't say he couldn't fall in love, I'm just saying he hasn't before."

"Cricket..." I try my best to act indifferent. "It was just a question. Just my nosey curiosity."

"Okay, *nosey*," she says, then blows me a kiss. "Go away. Let me nap."

I roll my eyes and leave *my* office, so Cricket can nap.

Here's the funny thing about being the unofficial HR for a secret band of assassins who work above the law...

I am not above the law.

I still have to abide by the parking rules of the business complex.

I still get a boot clamped on my tire for leaving work at nine o'clock at night when the sign clearly says, "Free Parking Until 6:00 p.m."

Glaring at the gray, company-issued SUV, I mentally scream, *"Fuck my life!"* I'm stuck. This is the last thing I want to deal with on a Friday evening.

I'm tired.

I'm so tired.

I should've paced myself at work, but I ignored good sense and blew well past my limits. My eyes are dry and aching. My back is stiff. My legs are jelly. I just want my bed.

The silver lining is that nowadays I actually have a friend I can call. Sure, I could Uber, but I much prefer Cricket's company if she's around.

ME

Are you around by chance? I'm stuck at work.
tire emoji *boot emoji*

I'll give it twenty minutes. If she doesn't text back by then, I'll call for an Ub—

"Eden."

The voice comes from right behind me and my phone goes flying. The glass shatters as it collides with the concrete.

"*Dammit!*" I shriek and throw an accusing stare at Linc. "Why don't you guys make noise when you walk? It's freaking supernatural."

He steps backward, eyes wide. "Sorry. I didn't mean to startle you."

Collecting my shattered phone—it's clear it's a goner—I press the power button anyway. Nothing. Just a blank, black screen.

I glance at Linc again, he looks worn. I haven't seen him since Monday in the office. I went to find him twice since then, to thank him for the book and to apologize for basically trying to seduce him, but he's been out of the compound all week.

His black button-down shirt is untucked and his pants are creased in the upper thighs. It looks like he's been sitting for a while. Even his normally neat stubble is borderline scruffy. "Are you okay?"

"Yeah, I just got back into town. Callen's supposed to meet me here."

"I think I'm the last to leave. You might have to call him."

He nods. "Car trouble?"

"Boot trouble," I complain. He looks at my feet first, then realizes I'm talking about the orange metal contraption around my back driver's side wheel.

"Turn around and cover your ears," he commands in a mumble before reaching for his holster. "I'll take it off."

"Linc! No!" I place my hands against his arms in protest and then immediately rip them back as if I touched a hot stove. I almost forgot for a moment that our last encounter was what could only be interpreted as rejection. He probably doesn't want me touching him. "You'll put a hole through my tire."

"You underestimate me," he says with a smirk. "I'm a fantastic shot."

"Well just in case you're having an off night, I don't think I have a spare or a jack."

He raises one brow. "You can change a tire?"

"Of course."

"Can you change your own oil?"

I scowl at him. "I can add windshield wiper fluid so that counts for something, right?"

Good grief he's handsome, especially when he laughs. His smile lights up his eyes and I'm mesmerized every time.

"I'd offer you a ride, but my car is incapacitated at the moment."

"How'd you get here?" I ask, looking around.

He doesn't offer an answer, instead, he asks, "Can you pop your trunk?"

As I open the trunk of my spacious SUV, momentarily, I'm appreciative of the size. When Callen first showed me the vehicle, I asked him if he thought I was a soccer mom with four kids. That's the only way I could justify the bus they issued me. I would've much preferred a little sedan in the D.C. traffic. Callen said he'd work on a swap but it's been weeks, and I'm still stuck with my bus.

However, right now, the trunk of the SUV transforms into a makeshift fort. I push the button to flatten the third row and Linc hops in.

"Are you tired?" I ask.

"Exhausted." He groans in appreciation as he sits, his legs knocking against the bumper. He's so tall his feet almost touch the ground. He pats the space right next to him. "Join me?"

"You sure?" I cross my arms, trying to be playful, but the question is genuine.

"Yes?" he asks, looking confused.

"Last time we were that close, you bolted from my office. I don't want to spook you again, especially because you don't look like you're in running condition." *What have you been up to Lincoln?*

He sighs as he tilts his head to the side. His blue eyes meet mine. "You want another lie?"

Damn, he's cute. The killer is cute.

"Sure."

"I haven't spent the entire week kicking myself for not kissing you. I don't regret leaving your office like that at all."

My heart thuds loudly. I'm too old for these butterfly-infused, childish games, but *God* does it feel good to have a little hope. "Why'd you leave?"

He pats the space next to him again. It's a clear trade—I sit, he talks. Of course, I oblige, hopping up to sit next to him, I leave a generous chunk of space between us. He's not satisfied. Jerking his head to the side, Linc invites me to get closer. I feel a little foolish as I shimmy to his side, but I'm rewarded with his large, warm hand on my thigh. The air is brisk tonight, but between my thick denim jeans and Linc touching me, I think I could break a sweat.

"I wanted to get it right," he says.

"Get what right?"

"Try not to take this the wrong way, but no matter how I say this, you're going to judge me."

"I won't—"

"You will, but I'm going to tell you anyway." He squeezes my thigh and the sensation that runs up my spine is nearly debilitating. I could melt into him right now. Linc sucks in a deep breath and blurts out, "In the spirit of being honest, I've never been with the same woman twice." He rushes his words like he's afraid if he waits, he might not say them.

It takes a minute for me to understand what he's saying. Then, I can't help it, my jaw drops. "Wait…you mean you've only ever had one-night stands?"

"Yes."

"So, you didn't kiss me because you thought I wouldn't be

into a one-night stand?" Accurate assumption. I've had exactly two hookups like that in my life. I hated it both times —hated *myself* after.

He turns his head to the side and locks his gaze on me. "No, not at all. The opposite. I was just hyperaware that *how* I kissed you for the first time might determine if, and when, I got to do it again…and I knew I'd really want to do it again."

I try—and fail—to keep my breathing steady.

"I uh…" He rubs the back of his neck like he's in discomfort. "I choked. Even monsters get nervous from time to time."

"You choked?" Leaning away, I show him my bewildered expression.

He presses his lips together and gives me an unamused expression. "Are you enjoying this?"

I can't help but giggle. "Thoroughly."

His hand trails a little further up my leg and I lean in closer, trying to invite his hand to go as far as it pleases. "Eden, I've never cared about a first kiss." His scorching gaze lingers on my lips. "But I do now."

My mouth waters and for some reason, my nerves dissipate. All I feel is sheer determination. I want this to happen… *Right now.*

"Okay," I say, hopping out of the trunk. "I'll walk you through it."

He slides down from his perched position as well, eyes and ears piqued with curiosity. "Walk me through it?"

"Sure. There's nothing to be nervous about if I tell you exactly what to do, right?"

"Bossy, I like it." Shooting me an innocent look, he holds out his hands like he's surrendering. "What should I do with these?"

"Wrap them around my waist."

He immediately follows orders. His hands are so large, it's like I'm being wrapped in a warm blanket. "How's this?"

I teeter my head. "A little lower is fine."

He trails his hands down my lower back, past my hips, and when his hands land on my ass, he yanks me into his body. "Too low?"

"No, perfect."

"What now?"

Tilting my chin up, I tap the side of my neck. "Start here."

My knees nearly give out when I feel his soft lips against my neck. All the intrigue, nerves, and questions about Linc have pooled together in a cauldron, making me a witch's brew of desire.

He plants a sweet kiss on my earlobe and my legs really do go boneless. Feeling me falter, he wraps one arm around my lower back to steady me as he holds me against his body.

I'm pressed so tight against him I can feel his heart beating. It's almost pounding as fast as mine. Placing my fingertips on his cheek, I turn his head so he's staring right into my eyes again. The steely gray-blue gems are whispering secrets... *He wants me as much as I want him.*

"Now what?" he asks.

I flash him a wicked smile. "How about an odd compliment to set the mood?"

His dimples deepen and I'm glad he likes the games. This is the best part—*my favorite part.* I love the anticipation, the tickles, the nerves...of falling for someone.

He presses his lips against my forehead. Then my cheek... my other cheek...the tip of my nose. When his lips graze my earlobe, he whispers, "Eden, I like you so much, I think I could *make love* to you." I snort in laughter and his eyes pop in surprise. "Was that lame?" he asks.

"*No,* not at all." In fact, that might be my favorite sentence of all time now. "I just find it ironic, because I think I like *you* so much, I'd let you fuck me." I like the way the words shock him, so I add, "*Hard.*"

He brushes my hair out my face and secures it behind my ear and then his cool, soft lips are on mine. He's tender, kissing me like I'm delicate. I nearly lose my head as he trails his tongue over mine and he moans into my mouth like I'm quenching his thirst. He presses his hand against my lower back and wedges it below my jeans, past the waistband of my thong. I feel the bulge in his pants growing as he squeezes my bare ass.

"Let's get out of here."

"Okay. Where?" he mumbles into my mouth.

"What if—"

Wait. I feel something cool against my stomach like my shirt has dampened, and I'm horrified when I look down.

My white blouse is smeared with blood. I step back to examine myself. There are red spots and streaks rubbed all across my chest and my stomach.

"Linc, you're bleeding. Are you hurt?"

He eyes me up and down, his face slowly growing pale.

"Linc!" I clap in his face, concerned that maybe he's bleeding out and is about to faint. There's no way I can support his size. Maybe just his head? *Don't let it hit the concrete.* "Are you okay?" I ask again.

He shakes his head. "It's not mine."

Like a plump grape reduced instantly to a raisin, I shrivel inside when I realize what he's saying. *It's not his blood.* I scour his dark shirt. It's nearly impossible to make out, but now that I'm searching for it, the damp spots are there.

"*Fuck,*" he says in a hiss. "Eden." I take another step back, feeling woozy. "It just happened. I didn't realize—"

Blinding headlights flash in our direction. At first, I think it's building security, but then Cricket rolls down her driver's side window.

"You guys okay?" she calls out from a few yards away.

"What're you doing here, Cricket?" Linc asks, his eyes still fixed on me.

"Bambi texted me, said she was stuck. Her phone has been going to voicemail."

They continue to talk but my mind is occupied, deducing the situation. *The blood still hadn't dried, that's why it seeped into my clothes.* That means the amount of time between Linc killing someone to Linc kissing me wasn't even enough time for the blood on his clothes to dry.

What am I doing? I have a hard time killing spiders. *What the fuck am I doing?*

"Eden, go straight home and take a long, hot shower. Don't just rinse. Use soap. I'm...sorry."

I try to force a smile as I shake my head. "It's fine. Sorry for what?"

He eyes me up and down. "You look fucking terrified." *Okay, so I'm not fooling anyone.*

I try to tell him I'm okay, but I start to feel a little woozy as that image from weeks ago pops back into my head. The pool of blood. The headless bodies. The fear in the prisoner's eyes. *What if... Is Linc capable of decapitating someone?* I have to focus on breathing and blinking so the entire parking garage stops spinning.

Just move your feet, Eden.

Just get in Cricket's car.

I collect my purse and the pieces of my phone before closing my trunk door and locking the vehicle.

"I'm going to go home and get cleaned up and...um...you have to meet Callen, right?"

He nods, accepting our moment is ruined. I wish I could tell him it's okay, but it's not. *It's not okay.* I don't want to be wondering who died while I'm kissing a man.

Linc looks so wounded. His eyes hit the ground like he's guilty, and I feel terrible that I'm the source. I'm not this man's judge and jury. This is who he is. I know what he does and why he does it. He's not the problem—*I am.*

I'm weak. I'm sensitive. I'm whatever word means that I will never get used to the reality that killing is his job... That killing is *anybody's* job.

"Linc… I… I just…"

He glances at Cricket in the car and then back to me. He closes his eyes as he runs his hand through his hair. "Go. It's okay. But…" He shrugs, lost for words again. "Again…sorry."

I nod and take a step towards Cricket's car, but then turn around. *I can't leave it—him—like this.*

"Linc?"

"Yeah?"

"You did perfectly. It was a *really* good first kiss." *The best I've ever had, by far.* He lets out a humorless laugh—both our minds are too preoccupied to enjoy the inside joke. "But I don't think there can be a second."

"I know." He nods solemnly. "Goodnight, Eden."

FOURTEEN

EDEN

I'VE BEEN LOOKING FORWARD to Vesper's interview the most, so I purposely saved her for last. Of all the operatives, she's been the most amenable to this change, but I'm still surprised when she shows up on Wednesday morning, *on time*, with a smile on her face and two takeout coffees in her hands.

"Good morning," I say, gesturing to the sitting area of my office as I grab my clipboard.

"I'm hoping you haven't already had coffee," she says as she sits. She offers me the cup in her left hand. "This is from the bakery you recommended. They also make delicious lattes."

I've had my morning coffee. Two cups in fact. But I was a doctoral student, I worked in Silicon Valley, and I was a young woman trying to become a pioneer in a man's world. It's not blood that runs through my veins…it's coffee. I drink so much of it, at this point, I'm sure I'm immune.

"That was really kind. Thank you."

I take the cup and sit down in my usual interview chair. She's quiet as she studies my face with the most peculiar expression—mostly intrigued…just a tiny bit creepy.

"What's wrong?" I ask as I instinctively run my tongue over my front teeth and touch my cheek, trying to find evidence of what she's staring at.

"I always imagined what it'd be like if I had a daughter. Sometimes I dream about what she'd look like. I swear, it's a lot like you." Vesper laughs. "I'm sorry, by the time you are near forty, you just say whatever the hell you want without worrying about how uncomfortable it makes people."

I laugh. "I'm not uncomfortable. I take it as a compliment, and if I'm being honest, you have a likeness to my own mother."

"Passed?" She tilts her chin just a tad.

How did she know? I nod. "When I was very young—right before my third birthday."

She tuts her tongue. "That doesn't leave a lot of memories."

I shake my head. "No, not really. But I distinctly remember how she smelled."

My mom always smelt like her lavender lotion and baked goods. Apparently Mom thought cookies were therapy, and didn't wait for birthdays to bake a cake. Dad told me that my mom used to bake and frost a cake for every random occasion: National Penny Day, Pi Day, Zookeeper Appreciation Day, and sometimes just Thursday afternoons. He'd only let himself have one tiny sliver, but he always said he and Mom vowed to get obnoxiously fat off her baking once he retired from the military…

They never got a chance. Both of my parents died lean.

I change the subject before I have an opportunity to get too lost on memory lane. That path usually ends in tears. "So, logistically speaking, I have a lot of information about the FBI agents, but I still don't know much about the origin of PALADIN. I was hoping you could fill in some blanks for me. But I'm not sure what I'm allowed to ask and allowed to know."

Vesper nods, encouragingly. "I'll walk you through what I can. We trust you, we can be transparent." *Trust.* I love that word. *I miss that word.* I used to be considered trustworthy before I became a whistleblower.

"Thank you for trusting me. What we say here, stays here. I just want to understand so I can help." I take a sip of my coffee, detecting a hint of butterscotch. I give Vesper my most impressed look—this is *delicious.*

"Fire away," Vesper says.

"Okay, so—why does Operation PALADIN exist? How did you get involved with it?"

She scrunches her face and I get the impression I've already stepped too far. "Can I tell you a story?"

"Please." I set my clipboard aside and take another sip of my butterscotch latte.

"Most recruits join the FBI right at twenty-three. They finish their bachelors, have a squeaky clean record, and are prepared to dedicate their lives to the code."

"Fidelity. Bravery. Integrity." That much I understand at least.

"Indeed." Vesper winks at me. "The motto sounds far more glamorous than the reality." She lets out a bitter laugh. "My indoctrination into the FBI was a little different…"

"Meaning?" I ask the question but judging by the menacing look in Vesper's eyes, I don't think I really want the details.

"This is the part where I need to omit a few details, *to protect you.* But, bottom line, I had uncommon knowledge, and a specific skill set so the FBI asked me for help. I was offered a very clear choice." She sighs. "Once I made a decision, the FBI forged a clean record for me. I can't tell you how many names I've had in my life, Eden."

What choice? It's the only question on my mind, but I'm sure if Vesper was willing to answer it, she would've already offered.

"For a while, it was quiet. I was considered more of a consultant"—she gestures to me—"in a way, like you. I was to watch, observe, and assist when they needed me. But eventually, a case came across the FBI's desk—this real piece of shit, Tanner. They called him SGK—the Super Glue Killer. He would glue his victims to..." She trails off, seeming to remember who she's talking to, and probably envisioning my reaction to the gory photo in the meeting room a few weeks ago.

"Anyway, he was a really bad guy. I bet he and The Night Stalker are sharing a prison cell in hell."

I bob my head in understanding. I know of Ramirez, I used to watch true crime when my dad was alive. Not lately though, because hearing stories about serial killers is not a good idea when you live alone, have basically no friends or family, and your paranoia is through the roof.

"But he was so fucking smart. I hate to say anything positive about that shit stain of a human being, but he was highly intelligent. A real sociopath through and through. He was always one step ahead of the FBI. He was slaying people left and right, right under their noses, but he knew exactly what he was doing. Half of his entertainment was watching the FBI spin their wheels, the other half was mutilating his victims. The evidence was shaky at best, there was enough to tie him to the cases, but not enough to make an arrest or hold in court —no witnesses, no slip-ups...he was the cleanest killer they'd ever seen."

I blow out a long breath and just pretend Vesper is telling me fictitious ghost stories.

"Did you get him, eventually?"

"I got a call from... Well, that part I can't say, but let's call this person someone who is allowed to make big decisions. My role with the FBI was to help them understand a killer's mindset and understand their patterns of behavior. This *caller* asked me what the FBI should do. They had no other leads and were no closer to cracking Tanner, so I told him—*they need to handle it.* Tanner is hurting people, he's enjoying it, he won't stop, he doesn't deserve justice... He needs to die."

"What'd the caller say?"

"Do it," Vesper says, turning her lips down. "He told me I had permission to handle it. I left my badge behind and hunted him down at his squeaky-clean home—which the FBI raided twice, and came up short. I sniped him through his bedroom window. It was so quick. All the future victims we feared for were safe in an instant. So, on the official record, the FBI let the SGK cases go cold, but after Tanner died, the slayings stopped. No more signature super glue kills. If there was any doubt in my mind about his culpability, it went away when we finally had peace."

"So the FBI started Operation PALADIN?"

Vesper shakes her head. "No. Tanner was the tip of the iceberg. If you think a serial killer is bad, try terrorists, suicide bombers, human traffickers, warlords, mafias, cults... There are a lot of bad people in this world who don't deserve fair trials and the due process of law. So, a few days after Tanner goes down, I get a call from that person I mentioned, and he asked me if I'd be willing to leave the FBI and join a special operation." An odd smile creeps across Vesper's face. "From there, Operation PALADIN was born. The FBI was a holding pen for me, with PALADIN, I can actually make a difference."

I pinch the bridge of my nose. All this story has done is kick up more questions in my mind, and I try to sift through what is professional and what is personal.

"So why go back to the FBI, now?"

"I'm struggling with recruits. I bring new operatives in, and they let me down. It's becoming harder to find people I can trust."

"You trust Linc," I say, mentally cringing.

It's been almost a week since we kissed. We've been cordial but I think we're both disappointed.

That kiss was everything…

But the blood…

I don't know, I'm having trouble discerning between the feelings I get around Linc. It's not about him, per se. Oddly enough, I feel quite safe around him. I just don't feel *morally* safe around what he does. But as Cricket explained, the operatives and PALADIN are one and the same. There is no Linc outside of killing, and from what I understand, there's no PALADIN without Linc.

"Linc, Lance, and Cricket are a little different. For lack of a better explanation, they are my children. I collected them as teenagers, all from bad situations. I thought maybe PALADIN could protect them where their own families failed. Linc was the youngest—I recruited him at sixteen. Cricket was barely any older, and Linc found Lance around the same time." She smiles as her eyes shift. "They're the family I never let myself have. I worry about them, love them, and would die for them. But I don't want any more of them. I robbed them of their youth. From now on, recruits need to be adults who understand what they are giving up. PALADIN has to figure out a way to stabilize—we're low in numbers and overworked. That's where Callen stepped in."

"Callen's…a good guy."

Vesper raises a brow. "Are you two—"

"*Oh, no.*" She laughs as I shake my head aggressively. "No, no. Callen is… I think the first person to care about what will happen to me in a long time. That's all. Plus, we have the military in common, so it's easy to talk to him."

"You served?"

"My dad. Delta Force—twenty years. I was a dependent."

"He must be impressed you're working with the FBI now," Vesper says, taking a sip from her cup and leaning back into my office sofa. She crosses her legs.

"He passed. Three years ago. Heart failure," I add quickly so I don't have to explain that he wasn't killed in combat.

"*Oh, Eden.* You've been through a lot."

"No more than you guys."

She teeters her head. "We chose this life. And my dad is alive, actually." A peculiar expression crosses her face, like pain mixed with comfort. "I still visit him on occasion. He's blind now, but he can sense when I'm in the room."

I stare at the wall above Vesper's head, getting lost in a memory. My dad used to say the same. Toward the end, when he was so weak he could barely lift his head, he said he could sense when I was near. I used to bring my work into his bedroom when he was sleeping, just to keep him company. He said his dreams would change when I was close—to something more pleasant.

"Are you okay?" Vesper asks.

"Hm? Oh, yes. I'm fine." I flash her a half-baked smile as I take another sip of my latte. I realize we've been talking for a while because the hot drink has cooled to warm.

"Callen said you've had a rough year. He said everything with Empress was a mess. How are you doing?"

I almost tell her I'm fine, but I decide to try honesty instead. "How much do you know about what Empress really did?"

She ducks her head. "Enough to know you're a hero."

"No one back home sees it that way. It's still odd to me that I did the right thing, yet I'm so hated for it. It was to the point that companies were too afraid to give me a job. Why does doing the right thing make people fear you so much?"

"Ignorance often shows up as fear," Vesper wisely adds.

"I think the most difficult part of the whole ordeal is not being able to tell my side of the story. I wasn't trying to be self-righteous, and I didn't want to see Empress fall. But what was I supposed to do? Turn a blind eye? If I would've done nothing, when I had the power to stop it, then I'd have blood on my hands. I hate being seen as some sort of monster when I was only trying to protect people—"

I stop mid-sentence as I taste the hypocrisy on my lips. People have been treating me the same way I've been treating Linc. Scared of what I don't understand. If Linc has the power to stop bad things from happening... Who am I to judge the methods? My dad took lives and I never questioned that. He got his orders from the military. Linc gets his orders from Vesper and now, the FBI. Different handlers, but isn't the war the same? Good versus evil. Right versus wrong.

I eye the book that's still on my desk.

I never got a chance to thank Linc for *War and Peace*. I was distracted when we kissed, and we seemed to keep missing each other—or avoiding each other—ever since. Still, I keep the book on my desk like a souvenir.

I should thank him... *Now.* Or, insert whatever other thinly-veiled excuse I need to go and speak to him. Of course I want a second kiss. A third. A hundred more. *I need to tell him.*

When I hastily rise, Vesper looks at me, concerned.

"I'm sorry," I explain. "Do you mind if we cut this short? I just remembered..."

"Of course, no problem," she replies.

"Um... Is Linc in today?"

Her neat, dark brows raise for just a moment before she neutralizes her expression. "I believe so. I passed Callen on the way to your office and he said he sent Linc to the doctor—his hand is bothering him."

"Okay." I nod and head to the door, already feeling the butterflies in my stomach and the declaration I've prepared myself to make. *Linc...I can do this. I'll stop running and be brave enough to want you.*

But right before I make my exit, another gnawing question creeps to the forefront of my mind and I can't help but pivot at the door and unleash my question from earlier.

"Vesper...off the record. You said the FBI gave you a choice, it was help them, or what?"

When her face flattens, I immediately regret opening my

big mouth. I try to tell her to ignore me, but she must read my mind because she holds up her palm.

"It's okay, Eden. I'm sure you still have a lot of questions. Most I can't answer, but this one... I can trust you, right?"

I nod fervently. "Yes."

"Death row," she says simply, watching my jaw fall open. "I was only eighteen years old, and it was either join the FBI or face my crimes."

"Vesper... I..." *I am lost for words. Crimes? I thought you were the good guy.*

She juts her chin toward the door. "I can see myself out. Go ahead. Whatever you just remembered sounds important," she says with a sly smile.

I rarely venture down the hallway that holds the medical clinic. The word "clinic" may be an exaggeration—it's just two rooms side by side. One sterile room for procedures, and one basic exam room. Our new in-house doctor is a bit of a unicorn. The FBI must be dolling out serious cash for her employment...*and discretion.* From what I understand, she's versatile enough to stitch up a bullet wound but can also perform a gynecological exam. She's a gas station convenience store—a little bit of all the random things you may need.

As I make my way down the hallway, I hear a commotion in the room to the right. Linc must be in the exam room. At any other hospital in the world, interrupting an exam would be completely inappropriate—a sin against HIPAA. But I don't know when I'll run into him again, and right now, I'm desperate to talk to him.

I hold my hand up to knock on the door but the sound of a whimper stops me.

Then, a loud crash.

I'm tempted to barge in. A crash and then a cry means

someone needs help—someone's in danger. But as I place my hand on the doorknob, the doctor's voice sings through clear as day.

"Oh, God. Yes! Just like that. Don't fucking stop."

Another crash, and now the rhythmic banging I'm hearing makes perfect sense. It's the exam table knocking against the wall.

I'm paralyzed as the gnawing discomfort in my stomach expands. The growing pressure of embarrassment renders my whole body immobile, so I have to endure at least another ten seconds of the moaning before my legs are no longer jelly. Once I can feel my legs again, I all but fly back down the hallway.

By the time I return to my office, Vesper is gone, so I sit quietly in my rolling office chair. If I had it, I'd pull out my productivity timer. Ten minutes ought to do it. Ten minutes should be just enough time to curse myself for standing in my own fucking way. *One week.* That's it. One week is all it took to push away the only man I've noticed in the past year of my life. There was something special about Linc, about the way I felt around him…

I blew it.

Apparently, Doctor Hartley did not.

I met her once and I genuinely liked her. Despite the fact that her business clothes were a little promiscuous, she's professional, kind, and intelligent. Funny how quickly she's become my least favorite person at the compound.

I rehearse the truth in my mind over and over: *Linc owes me nothing.* We kissed and he moved on when I basically told him we could never be.

It's probably better this way anyway. I'm day, he's night. I'm rules, he's anarchy. I work with teams, he works alone. We would never make sense together. I don't even know if we'd have the same definition of "together."

I position my metal wastebasket by the side of my desk

and casually as ever, I scoot *War and Peace* to the very edge, hoping gravity causes it to topple right into the trash. But it doesn't budge.

I rub my hand all over my face and think of my dad and this damn book... How I never got to talk to him about it. I should've read it when I had the chance. Picking up the heavy hardback book, I decide against the wastebasket and instead, tuck it into my top drawer.

Sorry, Dad. I'll get to it eventually, I promise.

FIFTEEN

LINC

I DON'T LIKE BEING SUMMONED unless there's someone who needs to die in a hurry. So I'm less than enthused when Callen gathers me, Lance, Cricket, and Vesper in the main meeting room, on a Friday afternoon. It's not because it's Friday—jobs like mine don't get weekends. It's because it's motherfucking Callen, and I still hate that this prick can give me orders.

I stare across the table at Vesper's face... *But look how relaxed she looks lately.* I suppose if my boss is happy, I'm happy.

Lance swivels in his chair like an antsy child, ready to go to the playground. "Does anyone know what the hell we're doing here and how long it's supposed to take?" he asks. "I've got Hot Pockets in the break room, so can we hurry this the fuck up?"

I scowl at him. "Hot Pockets?"

He's still such a child. Lance was barely nineteen when I recruited him for PALADIN. He was—and still is—a goddamn savant with a pistol. I caught him when he was about to put a bullet in his older brother's head, the man who had terrorized him and his mother for more than a decade.

Lance and his mother looked a lot alike—light brown hair, light eyes, high cheekbones, and even matching bruises on their faces and all over their bodies. But Lance's brother favored his deadbeat dad—dark hair, dark eyes, and a frigid cold heart. I stopped Lance in the nick of time—before he committed murder out of anger—and asked if he'd be willing to let this bully go to take down much bigger bullies in the world. We got his mother, Evelyn, to a safe place, and last I heard, Lance's brother was beaten to death in a federal penitentiary. *The irony.*

Lance levels his stare. "I've got two. Ham 'n' Cheese, want one?"

"I've said it before—grow the fuck up, Lancelot."

Lance smirks, unbothered. "A simple 'no, thank you' would have sufficed."

"You're extra grumpy," Cricket states as she pokes me in the shoulder from her seat right next to me at the large meeting table. "Hand still bothering you?"

I flex my hand and then make a tight fist. "It's getting better."

My hand was made worse by the debacle from last week, right before I ran into Eden in the parking garage. Callen's intel was bad, there were supposed to be two targets yet, I walked in on four and it got a little messy. I prevailed...

But it was sloppy.

The bruises and wounds are part of the job. Pain I can handle, but I do need my hand to function. If I can't handle my gun then I'm useful to nobody.

"What'd the doctor say?"

"I wouldn't know." I squint at her in confusion. "I haven't seen the doctor."

"Callen said he sent you—"

"*Cricket.* Callen is not my motherfucking keeper, and he does not decide when I need medical attention," I snarl. And why the fuck is Callen providing my medical details to anyone who will listen?

She lets out a few low whistles. "Toouuchy. You've got too much tension. I think you need to get laid." She winks, and I know who she's talking about. She caught Eden and me kissing in the parking garage.

But that door is closed now.

Did I have hope? *Sure.* Was I interested? *Incredibly so.* But after seeing the look on Eden's face when she saw me covered in blood—a mix between horrified and disgusted—I can't. I don't want to be the reason she looks like that.

Monsters don't get the princesses—that's only in fairytales.

After bursting through the door with unnecessary gusto, Callen holds up a piece of paper with a wide smile on his face. "Look at this shit!"

He proceeds to read us all an email that is basically his superiors praising him for getting PALADIN in shape. There've been no incidents to report, and we've handled twice as many targets than were expected.

Callen stands at the head of the table, blinking at us expectantly. "Get excited. This is really good news. You have no idea how close we were to the chopping block, but you're operating like soldiers instead of thugs. So we're funded, we can keep operating, and the higher-ups are very pleased."

His praise is met with silence.

Lance finally clears his throat. "If you want some tissues for the brown on your nose," he says, nodding to the Kleenex box at the center of the table.

I cover my laugh with a cough, trying not to encourage Lance's immature insult. Callen grumbles and mutters something under his breath. *We listen to you, Callen. But we still don't like you.*

"Our analysts are getting better intel. They're getting a little smarter at prioritizing targets, and the special agents who are field-ready are eager to get their hands dirty and help you guys. I think it's time to start letting them in on some operations. Vesper?"

"As long as you think they're *mentally* ready, too." The way she's pursing her lips tells me she seriously doubts it.

Callen nods enthusiastically. "I do. Things are shaping up quickly and actually, all credit should go to Eden. In fact—"

Callen pushes on the intercom on the back wall and buzzes line three. Eden's honey-sweet voice sounds immediately and Callen beckons her to the meeting room.

"What's up, Callen?" Eden says as she enters a moment later.

I fucking love casual Fridays. I used to think it was a stupid office tradition, but Eden's frayed denim jeans hug her hips just right. She's wearing an FBI athletic t-shirt, which only makes me want to rip it off of her that much more...

I silently curse the stupid, metaphorical closed door. *But what can I do?* I'm pretty sure it's deadbolted shut. Eden's been polite and cordial, but there's no evidence that she's changing her mind about how she feels about me.

"Did you see this email?" Callen asks, holding up the paper.

"Um, yes—and I've read it," she says. "You sent it to me this morning, *twice*."

"Why is no one else ecstatic? Our budget has tripled. What do you want? Company cars? New guns? Some PALADIN merch?" All he gets in return is unimpressed stares. He grumbles like a scorned child as he grips the table and hunches over, hanging his head. "You guys are the worst crowd. Fine, if nothing else, two rounds on me tonight."

Eden steps forward and touches Callen's shoulder sweetly. Every blood cell in my body fills with hot jealousy. It's almost unbearable, so I have to cross my arms over my chest to keep my physical reaction from exploding. I kissed her, I touched her…and now I don't want anyone else touching her, even if she's not mine.

Lance did warn me… *She's Callen's girl.*

"Congratulations, boss," she says playfully then turns to us. "I'm really glad you're getting some credit. You all deserve it."

Callen winks at her and says, "*You* deserve it. You're doing great work, Eden. I think we can all agree this place is that much more tolerable because of you."

She curtsies sarcastically before she addresses the room. "I hope you all have a lovely weekend." Pointing at Cricket she continues, "Stay out of trouble. I'll see you guys on Monday, and as always, my door is open."

"Don't you mean tonight?" I ask, the words spilling out before I can stop them.

Eden makes eye contact with me but her normally enthusiastic smile is lackluster. "Pardon?"

I glance at Callen and then at Eden. "Don't we have the obligatory outing?"

"Right, yes," Callen chimes in. "Drinks tonight at that lounge uptown called Martinis. I reserved a section."

This morning, when Vesper told me to oblige Callen's invitation for drinks with the team, I was close to telling her to shove it up her ass. Then, I remembered the "team" includes Eden. But much to my disappointment, she shakes her head.

"I think I'm going to sit this one out. I'm not feeling so well."

"Is that allowed?" Lance asks, perking up in his chair. "I'm with Eden. I'm also going to sit this one out because I'm not feeling so well."

Vesper points at his forehead. "You're going." She turns a kind gaze on Eden. "We hope you feel better. Let someone know if you need anything. You're one of us now, and we take care of our own."

"Thank you." She nods, and adds with a wink, "You guys will have so much more fun without HR anyway."

"Ha!" Callen laughs. "Even you're saying it now. It's official, Eden's HR."

She sticks her tongue out playfully at Callen, and with that, she leaves the meeting room, taking my enthusiasm for this evening with her.

SIXTEEN

EDEN

I AM spoiled rotten at The Residences—the luxury apartment that Callen set up for me when I first relocated. It's meant to be temporary—until I can find a house—but the real estate market here is a nightmare, and I'm in no rush to leave.

My apartment is on the forty-second floor. The entire back wall of the living room is a giant window, overlooking the cityscape of high rises as far as the eye can see. Yes, the elevator ride up feels like the beginning of the Tower of Terror ride at Disney World, but once you're no longer accelerating at, what seems like, eighty miles an hour, the view from up here is peaceful and astonishing.

I feel like I'm on top of the world—above it all. *Safe from it all.* The monsters can't get me up here.

The apartment itself is tiny. Barely over 800-square-feet, it's a vast difference from my 3,000-square-foot, two-story back in California. But who needs that much space when it's just me? I like this apartment, it suits me well and I'm treated to all the amenities here. I even have weekly housekeeping, not that I leave them much to do.

157

Using my key fob, I unlock the electronically activated door. I step out of my flats in the entry and appreciate the feel of the cool wood floors against my feet. After hanging up my purse, I make my way to the kitchen to put a kettle of water on. My guilty pleasure is instant, decaf coffee with Kahlua and Hershey's syrup and tonight is the night for indulgences.

I try to ignore the image in my head of Linc's wounded expression when I insisted on not attending tonight's outing. I'm sure the doctor will be there, so he should be thoroughly entertained. Judging by the animalistic noises I heard coming out of that office, they—*clearly*—know how to have a good time.

I'm good with being alone… A sweet, decaf coffee paired with a deliciously trashy book has been my routine for months now. There are far worse ways to spend an evening.

The kettle is whistling before I notice the open beer bottle on my kitchen counter. It's dripping with condensation and a small puddle of water surrounds it. *Odd.* I open my fridge door as my heart begins to pound. *Did I miss something?* Checking my fridge, I confirm my discomfort. I don't have beer… Because I don't drink beer.

Someone was in my apartment.

My heart rate rises to the pace of a hummingbird's wings. Breathing in deeply through my nose and exhaling through my mouth, I attempt to ease the panic.

Stay calm.

You are so fucking paranoid.

You have housekeeping, remember?

Rushing to the coat hooks by the entryway, I retrieve my cell phone from my purse and call the apartment building's service line.

"Good evening, this is Georgie."

"Hi Georgie," I begin, forcing myself to speak slowly and clearly. "My name is Eden Abbott. I'm in apartment four-two-eight-nine. I'm calling to check in on the housekeeping schedule this week. Were there any changes? I'm scheduled for Monday afternoons between one and three o'clock but I believe someone's been in my apartment today."

Please, please say there was a swap. My heart is beating so hard, it's impossible to focus on anything else. Georgie asks me to wait one moment as he rustles through papers.

"Ma'am, you're still scheduled for Monday. I don't have any logs for forty-two eighty-nine today." Georgie's tone is lackadaisical. He clearly doesn't understand how important this conversation is to me.

"Were there any maintenance checks today?" I continue almost pleadingly. "I believe I saw an email about fire and carbon monoxide alarm checks."

"Uh," Georgie says, loudly clicking a computer mouse. "Those are supposed to start next week, but it's possible maintenance got started early. We have a couple of guys out for the holiday next week."

Phew. Okay, good. "Georgie, one of the maintenance workers left a beer dripping on my kitchen island counter. All due respect, I'd appreciate it if they'd take their belongings with them."

"*Jesus*, ma'am. I am so sorry. I'll fill out a report. They shouldn't be drinking on the job."

"Oh no, please don't bother. No need to get anyone in trouble, I was just a little startled is all. Thank you for clarifying. Have a good evening."

"You as well, ma'am."

My heart rate finally calms. Never in my life have I been more appreciative of rebellious, sloppy apartment maintenance workers. I dump the beer down the drain and rinse the bottle before dropping it down the apartment's built-in recycling shoot.

Fully dressed in pajama shorts and an oversized t-shirt, I

fix my coffee treat and head to the bedroom. I'd rather read under the covers tonight, and my current contemporary romance novel is already bookmarked on a sexy page and waiting for me on my bedroom nightstand.

Pretend with Me is one of my prized possessions because it's signed by the author. I drove out of my way to San Francisco in the hellish traffic to a local bookstore when I learned Adler Haley was in town. Actually, I believe it's Adler Lewis now. I remember her explaining there was some confusion with her publisher over changing her name on the cover. People were getting confused after she took her husband's last name, but from the sounds of it, she told her publisher to shove it and make the change. She was proud to be a Lewis. I smile at the memory, she had such a big personality for such a petite little thing.

I try to conjure up an image of a suitable male main character in my mind. Adler's book describes him as tall, dark, and handsome. He's intelligent, bookish, and definitely a brunette with dark eyes, but for some reason, all I can picture are Linc's light blue eyes, his thick muscular forearms, and his broad, sculpted shoulders that are always easy to make out through all his thin dress shirts.

Fine. It was a pretty intense crush. It's going to take a little extra time to get over it—

Holy shit.

I nearly choke on my spit when I pull back my duvet cover. The coffee in my mug sloshes over the rim. It's not quite hot enough to burn me, but it makes a mess—down my forearm, onto my clean white sheets, right onto the red envelope lying underneath the covers.

My heart rate accelerates out of control again as I set my mug down like a zombie and confront the reality in front of me.

It wasn't maintenance.

The envelope is unmarked, but the note inside is unmistakable—

Eden, we need to talk.
Visit Hanesville.
- Porky

It was a stupid nickname. On my first day at Empress, when I met the CEO, Pierre Corky, I couldn't help but think what a funny name it was. I had to rehearse our introduction about a hundred times to keep myself from giggling like a loon. When it finally came time to shake his hand, I'd given myself the yips. I accidentally called him, "Mr. Porky." He thought it was so funny, he insisted everyone at the office start calling him Porky.

Pierre and I used to laugh a lot. We genuinely enjoyed each other's company... Until I ruined him and put him behind bars for 25 to life.

He's in prison, so how the hell is he drinking beer in my apartment and stuffing notes between my sheets? I wish I had my timer. Five minutes is all I need to allow the shaking nerves to overwhelm my body. I'd collapse to the floor and cry because I am so fucking tired of living in fear.

But I've got no timer and no time to spare. I allow my rational brain to take over, walking me through the logistics.

I've been home for forty minutes at least. The apartment is small. I'm staring across the bed into my walk-through closet and it's impossible to conceal yourself on either side of the built-ins. I used the bathroom when I got home and saw there was no one in the glass walk-in shower. My bed is on a solid frame. Even the windows have electric blinds, no drapes. There is nowhere to hide. And if someone was waiting for me, they would have presented themselves by now. Whoever was here is long gone.

I'd call the police but I'm not sure what to say. I needed a team of three lawyers to explain the NDAs I agreed to. The public information is that Empress violated basically every single state and federal law, against digital privacy, possible. The whole truth is far more harrowing and I was given a gag order to never share that narrative—not even to local authorities. It's above their pay grade.

I can't go to just anyone with this. I need Callen. If the FBI can't protect me, who can?

After mopping up the spilled coffee as best I can, I hurry to my closet to get dressed. It doesn't matter what I wear, I just need something that won't make me look so out of place at an upscale martini bar lounge. I need to do my best to blend in...

I have no idea who might be watching me.

Martinis is a swanky-looking lounge. The mood lights are vibrant colors and the entire place is covered in a smoky haze, but it doesn't smell offensive. No... It smells like someone is running a Hookah machine in the vents for ambiance. Presently, the entire place smells like cherries, mandarin oranges, and warm vanilla. It's the perfect place for a girls' night, which explains why when I spot the PALADIN team in an enormous curved booth in the back corner, it looks like Cricket is having the most fun. She's sandwiched in the middle of the booth with cards fanned in one of her hands, and cash wadded up in her other fist. She's arguing with one of the Agent Smiths.

"Bambi!" she shouts as I near the table, spotting me first.

Linc, who is sitting at the edge of the booth, whips his head around so fast, there's no masking his surprise. He not-so-subtly eyes me up and down before his brooding stare locks on my face. His brows knit in confusion.

"Hello everyone." I flash a sheepish smile.

"Feeling better?" Linc asks with a flattened tone.

"A bit," I say, quickly remembering my earlier excuse. "Where's Callen?"

To my utter surprise, Linc rolls his eyes. "Of course," he mutters, his agitation unmistakable. *What the hell is that about?* Linc points to the bar where Callen is attempting to flag down a waitress. I don't have time for Linc's sudden attitude, so I turn on my heel and make a beeline for the bar.

I tap Callen on the shoulder. When he turns to face me, I see he's on the phone. "Hey," he mouths distractedly. "You came."

"Yes, um—can we talk in private? Something strange happened tonight. I need to know if Pierre Corky is out of prison, but I don't want to go poking around by myself. Are you able to—"

Callen holds his finger up, interrupting me as he tries to focus on his phone call. His eyes grow wide. "Bring him to the compound," he hisses into the phone. "I'm on my way."

He looks at me and shoots me an overcompensating smile, again, while looking for the bartender. He doesn't have time for me right now, but who else do I have?

"Callen, did you hear what I said? I think I was followed from California. I think I'm being watched."

"Watched?" he parrots, almost incoherently.

I blow out a deep breath, my patience growing thin. *Just listen. For God's sake, someone please take me fucking seriously.* "I think Pierre Corky—"

The bartender suddenly appears in front of us.

"How ya doing, partner?" she asks Callen while she winks at me. Her low auburn ponytail is swept to the side and her teeth are very white, but those are the only distinct features I can make out of hers in the dimly lit lounge.

"I have to go. Keep my tab open for everyone in that corner, okay?"

"Really?" she asks in shock.

Callen's groans. "How bad is it?"

"Honestly?" the bartender asks, glancing over his shoulder. "You don't want to know. You may need to take out a second mortgage."

He snorts. "Buy them whatever they want." Then he turns his attention to me. "Can you sign for me? It's the company card. Give this angel a thirty percent tip of the total. I have to run—emergency."

He's already dialing another number on his phone.

"Callen, wait. Please just one minute—"

But he doesn't hear me as he hustles away toward the back of the lounge. Now, I officially feel stranded. I don't want to go home. Callen is no help. I could get a hotel room for the evening, but whoever could break into my apartment could probably find me at a hotel. *Fuck*. Alone again… I forgot how much this sucks—

"Fisherman's Paradise is pretty good."

A large hand presses against the small of my back. Linc hunches over me from behind and taps the top line of the drink menu in front of me. He whispers in my ear, "But you're so little it'll probably knock you on your ass."

It takes me a moment to realize he's talking about martinis, because quite frankly, Linc touching me still makes my head go fuzzy, and my knees all but liquefy.

"I'm not little." Five foot four is a reasonable height.

He snorts. "Oh yes, Bambi. Yes, you are." I spin around and I'm suddenly in Linc's arms. His hands rest around my hips and his voice goes low and rumbly. "I could scoop you up, hoist you over my shoulder, and carry you right out of here like it was nothing… Maybe I should."

I scowl at him, and yet, I lean forward, resting my hands on his forearms which are exposed. In fact, his arms—all the way up to his protruding bicep—are visible for once. I'm used to seeing him in long sleeves. I fight the temptation to trail my finger over the muscular curves of his arms. I think about

Kryptonite and how helpless Superman could feel at times. *Absolutely powerless in the presence of your weakness.*

Linc circles his thumbs around my hip bone. "Is this okay?"

Yes, don't you dare stop touching me. "You're calling me Bambi now, too?"

The whites of his teeth flash against the dark hue of the lounge as he smiles. "It's just because of your beautiful, big brown eyes."

I scoff, knowing that is *not* the reason Cricket dubbed me Bambi.

"Are you drunk?"

His thumbs freeze in place and I immediately miss the soothing circles. "Why would you say that?"

"You're being so…flirty."

"Two Fishermans," Linc says over my shoulder to the bartender before he grabs my hand and drags me to a small booth on the opposite side of the lounge from the crowd. "Sit," he demands. I slide into the booth and Linc follows, blocking me in with his large frame. Even sitting, he towers over me. Every time I'm alone with Linc I feel like I'm suspended between arousal and fear—the most confusing combination of nerves and hopeful anticipation. Wet from lust, but absolutely dry with anxiety. I still haven't decided if I like it.

"I understand why you ran the other night, but I promise you, Eden, I'm not—"

"You don't owe me explanations, Linc."

"I do…because I still…" His brows cinch, and he pinches the bridge of his nose like he's uncomfortable.

"Do you want to try a lie?" I offer. For some reason, it's easier for us to tell each other how we're *not* feeling, than how we are.

"No." He shakes his head. "I want to tell you the truth, which is I like you and I don't want you to be afraid of me.

How can I show you that there's more to me? I'm trying. I... listen, I thought leaving you that book would show you how I feel about you, but nothing—not even an acknowledgment. Then, we kiss, and you run. Maybe I should let it go, but I can't sleep wondering what the hell is going through your head. How are you feeling, and why?"

"How am I feeling?"

Burying my face in my hands, I let all the pressure in my head swell and I feel dangerously close to exploding. Images flash through my head: the beer bottle, the letter, useless Callen, Porky's laughter, and the visual of the doctor's legs hooked over Linc's shoulders.

"Linc, I don't have time for this, tonight. I just came here because I need Callen's help, but he left."

Linc reaches across me and yanks on a little metal chain dangling from the tabletop lamp. Both of our faces are illuminated and he studies my expression intently.

"You're scared. What's wrong?"

"I..."

There's no one who could protect me like Linc. But what the hell am I allowed to tell him? Explaining how Porky might be stalking me would require telling him what I know about Empress, and why I'm hiding it. The truth ruined my entire life, and I don't know if I want to keep telling it. It's not fair. I did the right thing. *But why me? Why my burden?* I'll never get used to this—stalking, threats, harassment, and worst of all... shame. My neck is sore from constantly looking over my shoulder. I work in a compound crawling with FBI agents with the highest security clearances and their guard dog hitmen.

And I still don't feel safe.

"Scooch!" I growl at Linc. Naturally, he looks confused, so I shoo him with my fingers to further my point. He hesitates for a moment, looking wounded, his normally blue eyes are almost light gray against the black of his polo shirt. But I don't have time to dwell on how stupidly handsome this man is. I'm about to cry, and I want to be alone. "Let me out!" I shriek, and this time he immediately stands.

I take a few paces toward the bathroom before I double back, my hysteric emotions getting the best of me. "And as for the book... I went looking for you to thank you, but you were busy fucking Doctor Hartley. So, I apologize if I'm confused on *how I feel*."

I hurry away before the tears begin to fall.

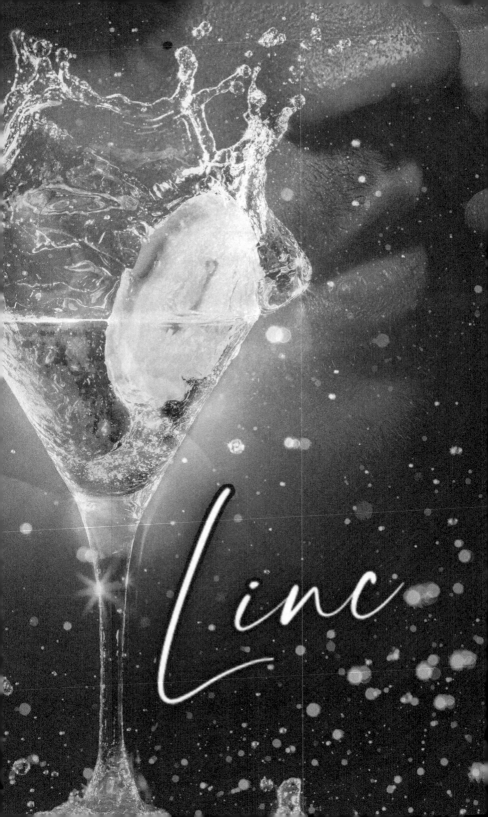

Linc

SEVENTEEN

LINC

CARRYING A MARTINI IS A CHORE—THEY spill easily. I look graceless, walking awkwardly as I carry the drink I ordered for Eden to the bathroom. I can't go back to the obnoxious gang of agents gambling in the corner of the lounge. Not when Eden's having a meltdown. Not when she clearly needs me.

Oddly enough, she went into the men's room. I left her alone for fifteen minutes and she still hasn't come back out. At this point, my patience is gone. I knock firmly on the bathroom door… No answer. I even go as far as pushing against the swinging door—it's locked. I could put a bullet in the damn lock and it'd come free, but I get the impression shooting my way to the girl I want might turn her off.

"Eden," I say, knocking again, softer this time. "Please open the door. Let me help."

"I'm okay. You don't want to see me like this."

"Wrong." I let out a deep sigh. "I *really* want to see you like this."

Silence.

"Eden," I say, lowering my tone. "I'm fully capable of knocking down this door. You'll be saving us both a lot of

169

trouble, and Callen a property damage bill, if you just unlock it."

She debates for a moment but then I hear the lock unlatch.

Upon entering, I find Eden leaning against the bathroom counter, her eyes are still red, and her cheeks flushed, but she fakes a smile. It's obvious she was crying and then composed herself. "Some women would call it predatory, you threatening to break down the door to get to me in the bathroom."

"This is the men's room. I'm more within my right to be here than you are."

Her face twists in confusion. "This isn't the men's room." I point to the urinal in the corner of the private bathroom. *"Oh."* She gasps, just now realizing she's wrong. In Eden's defense, the bathrooms aren't marked "Men" and "Women." There's a martini glass on one door and an upside-down martini glass on the other. That could easily be interpreted either way.

"Here." I hand her the orange-colored drink in my hand which she takes gingerly. "And I'm not a predator." *Not to you, anyway. Not to any woman.* "Now that I know you're okay, just say the word and I'll go. Do you want me to leave you alone?"

She shakes her head before slamming the entire martini back in one gulp. "Someone broke into my apartment today. I'm a little scared to go home." Smacking her lips together, she smiles briefly making her bubbly cheeks bunch up. "That was tasty. I should've sipped that." She's trying to make light of the situation to cover her vulnerability, but I'm in no mood. Every cell in my body is swelling with fury. *Who the fuck was brave enough to break into Eden Abbott's home while I still have a pulse?*

"Judging by your panic, you know who broke in, don't you?"

"Actually, I don't. I think maybe I'm seeing ghosts. Linc… back home I have a reputation… It's not a good one."

Closing the space between us, I rub my thumb against her

cheek, as if I could wipe the splotchy red patches away. "You were an informant."

Her eyes hit the floor as she nods. "So, you know. Callen must've told you."

"No. Even if he did, I don't care. Eden, I've killed four men this week, who am I to judge anyone?"

Her heavy eyelids droop, but she places one hand flat against my chest. "I don't want to talk about that right now."

"Then how about this? I don't know what you think you heard, but I never fucked Doctor Hartley. I've never met her in person."

Eden's eyes light up in curiosity. There we go, that's where all the avoidance was coming from. Poor thing was jealous. I understand more than she knows. I wanted to break Callen's jaw when Eden entered tonight and immediately asked for him.

"Vesper said Callen sent you to get checked out," she explains.

"I don't take everything Callen says as law."

She hangs her head and covers her eyes. I take a moment to soak up the visual of Eden dressed up tonight. She dresses differently at the office. Her clothes are flattering but modest. Tonight, however, she's wearing a skin-tight V-neck, tucked into her high-waisted pants that show off her curves. It's a clever move on a woman's part—subtly seductive. A classy woman makes me weak and I don't think I can keep my hands to myself a moment longer.

"I am so sorry," she mumbles, as she splits her hand and peeks between her fingers at me. "Making assumptions and not communicating is the most disastrous thing you can do in the workplace. I preach this to corporations on my soapbox." She lets out a small huff of laughter. "And now I'm a hypocrite."

"You were upset," I say, wrapping my hands around her waist. She rolls her eyes but then nods. "You thought I got over our kiss that fast? That I want anyone else but you?" I pull her against my body and my cock twitches to life. Eden nods again, this time into my chest. "You had no idea that I've spent every night thinking about you—wondering what you're doing, excited to see you again. I'm not myself lately." I kiss the top of her head and breathe in the floral smell of her shampoo. "And you're the cause."

She lets out a low hum of satisfaction as my hands sink from her waist to her ass, and I grab a fistful. Her dainty hand goes searching too, but instead of my hardening cock, she finds my holstered gun.

She flinches and folds her hands together. Dammit. Stepping backward I unfasten my holster while locking the bathroom door. The safety is on, she has nothing to worry about, but it still scares her. I tuck my weapon behind the toilet, out of sight. Then, I press my body against hers again.

"Better?" I mumble.

"Thank you," she says. "I'm sorry. I know it must be annoying that you have to treat me with kid gloves."

I touch my lips to her forehead, then her left cheek, then her right. I moan as I finally feel her plump lips against mine. "I'm happy to handle you with care because you're precious."

I kiss her again, and I'm trying to taste her tongue but she has more to say.

"Linc?"

"Yes?"

"Am I safe with you?"

"Of course you are."

"You'd never hurt me," she says, not asks.

"Never."

She shudders as I duck my head and rub my lips up and down her neck. I feel her goosebumps rise.

Her lips touch my ear as she speaks. "Then right here, right now, I want you to kiss me like I'm precious, but fuck me like I'm not."

EIGHTEEN

EDEN

LINC LOOKS SHOCKED, but the bulge that's pressed against my lower belly is now a cylindrical rock, so he can't be too turned off by my request. I just want to see what I can handle. Is that so crazy? I haven't known him for long…but I trust Linc. I trust his strength, his tenderness, and his desire to protect me. Right now, I need a distraction. If I can't solve my problems tonight, I want to escape from them.

And if I'm going to dance along this line of fire, I want it to be with Linc.

"You want me to do what?" he asks.

I hop onto the bathroom counter and wrap my legs around him and my arms around his neck. "Until we kissed the other night, it had been over a year and a half since a man had touched me. I've had a lot of time to fantasize about some boundaries I want to test. I'm not asking you to tie me up and hit me or anything…." I take a breath. *How do I explain this?* "I have to be in control all the time—of my reactions, of my emotions. It's exhausting pretending to not be as scared as I feel. So, I just want to give up control of this. If you want me, then take over. *Use me*, however you want."

I can't tell what's going on in his mind, but the gears are

turning. The wrinkling of his forehead and the way his brows are cinched tell me he's furiously debating as his gaze shifts rapidly between my eyes.

"Being controlled turns you on?" he asks me, with a tormented look in his eyes.

I plant my hands on either side of his face. "Opposites attract, Linc. Your *strength* turns me on... Is that okay?"

He doesn't answer and I want to kick myself. *Too far, I went too far.* I think I've been alone too long. I don't know how to read sexual tension anymore. I thought a man like Linc would love it rough and gritty, turns out I spooked him. I drop my hands and try to push against his chest, intent on hopping off this bathroom counter and fleeing from Martinis. But Linc, inhumanly fast, grabs both of my wrists in one of his large hands. His grip is so powerful that I couldn't wiggle out if I tried. I'm not even close to being his match. The only way I could free myself is by telling him to release me; and that's what's making me wet.

The monster... At my command.

Linc tugs me by my wrists so I nearly fall off the bathroom counter. He holds his other arm out to brace me before he spins me around, planting my hands on the counter ledge. His body lines mine from behind, my back to his belly, as he growls a simple command in my ear. "Pick a safe word."

"What?"

"Any word you want to call uncle. I'm not going to hurt you, but I will push your boundaries if you want me to. You need a safe word so you know, no matter what, you're the one who's truly in control."

"You pick one."

"No," he says, rubbing my back, squeezing my ass, and eventually wrapping his hand around my waist, toying with my pants button. "You need to choose." My breathing becomes shallow as the anticipation builds.

Here, Eden?

I don't fucking care. I want him so bad. Let him take me in a public bathroom. Nothing else matters at the moment.

"Martini," I mutter. "Let's use martini."

Linc slips his hand into my pants and strokes along the cotton of my panties. Now I wish I would've put more thought into my undergarments but I did not even consider the possibility of Linc seeing my panties this evening.

"No, that's too generic. We could easily be talking about drinks. You need a word you'd never say in conversation."

"I don't..." My words escape me as I just try to focus on breathing. Linc's slow torture of my most sensitive spot is making me lose focus. I feel the cotton between my legs dampening fast, and if he doesn't stop, I'm going to come from the foreplay.

"Hurry up, Eden. Choose. You're so wet... I want to taste you."

A word... I need a word. A word I'd never take lightly. A word I'd be reluctant to say out loud.

"Whistleblower."

I feel him smile on my neck. "*Good girl.* Whistleblower it is."

He pulls down my pants and pushes up my shirt. I feel his breath on my back as he slowly slides down my body, yanking down my panties like he's angry at them for being in his way. He helps me step out of my pants and underwear and must have thrown them somewhere because I hear a sudden *clank*— the metal button of my pants hitting the wall. He kneels behind me and after an appreciative groan, he sinks his teeth into my bare ass cheek. It's not hard enough to hurt, but just enough pressure to make me yelp in surprise.

My outburst is met with a firm swat to my ass. I melt, I mewl. Linc knows exactly what I want. "Be quiet, Eden," he growls. "You're going to have to take this all very quietly, okay?"

"Okay."

"Tell me when you're about to come," he says as he pushes my thighs further apart so I'm standing with my legs spread. Then he attacks me with his tongue. I'm in a hedonic haze, thoroughly enjoying the feel of his wet tongue teasing my clit, but Linc's not satisfied. He pushes my hips upward and spreads my legs wider until I'm exposed enough for him to slide his tongue across every fold. *Holy shit.* I allow my tears to fall because they aren't from sadness or fear... They are from sinful, delicious fucking pleasure.

Linc suddenly grabs my hips firmly, holding me tightly in place. For a moment, I think he's going to smack my ass again, but then...

"*Ah, fuck, Linc,*" I cry as he plunges into me with his tongue. Over and over until I have to bite back my pleads. I don't even know what I'd beg for. *More. Faster. Wait. Harder.* I close my eyes as if the darkness can silence my thoughts.

I'd keel over if he wasn't holding me securely in place. He devours me without hesitation, eating me like he's hungry, and I'm his very last meal. Toggling from gentle flicks of his tongue against my clit and long lapping strokes across my crease and over my ass, Linc owns me with his mouth. My arousal, or his saliva, or maybe the two combined, drips down the back of my thigh as a swirl of pressure builds between my hips. Oh, sweet memories. It's been so long since a man's given me an orgasm. Then again...no man has ever touched me like Linc is right now. I could black out from the satisfaction. It could all end here, like this, and I'd call my life well-lived.

I try to follow instructions and murmur as audibly as I can, "Linc, I'm getting close. I..." I flex my quads. "Right now, I'm going to—"

I groan when he shoves his wet pinky into my ass. The unexpected intrusion makes me completely explode. I thrash against his grip and can't swallow my cries as I come harder than I ever have before. I'm blinded and deafened by the euphoric sensation. I can't help it if they can hear me up in space, I'm completely overcome—out of control. I have never, ever known pure pleasure like this.

Linc tenderly traces his fingers over my ass cheeks and down my thighs, waiting for my legs to stop shaking. I enjoy the sweet ticklish sensation of his fingertips so much that I take my time before rising.

I spin around and hook my hands underneath Linc's elbows as if I could help pull up his weight. He's been squatting for so long, I bet his legs are numb. "Were you uncomfortable?" I ask with a swoony smile. My eyes lift to meet his as he stands.

"No." He shakes his head. "I could die down there, a happy man. Your pussy is perfection." He licks his lips, tasting my orgasm, with an aching look in his eyes that seems to say, *"Brace yourself. We're not even close to done."*

"No one has ever done that for me before," I admit.

"Licked your pus—"

"No, the other thing." I hold up my pinky.

"You told me to have my way with you." He smirks, a sexy flicker dancing in his eyes. "Did you like it?"

I'd always been curious, but I tried anal sex once in the past and it hurt. He was barely nudged against me before the searing pain took over. I had to forfeit before we even really began. My jerk of a boyfriend at the time made me feel terrible about not having a high enough pain tolerance...but he never offered to start with a pinky. Linc knew how much I could handle at exactly the right moment. I asked him to take control, and he executed perfectly. *A real fucking man.*

"I think I'm going to like everything with you, Linc."

"Sweet girl," Linc says, looking at me like a hunter sizing up his prey. "I am going to make you feel so good." He guides my hand to his hard-on and begins to unbutton his shirt when a heavy pounding at the door makes me jump. Whoever it is tries to push against the locked door to no avail.

Linc presses his finger against my lips. "Ignore it," he whispers to me as he uses his other hand to slide against my still-wet slit. "We're not finished."

But the pounding continues.

"Use the other one," Linc snarls, now irritated.

"Linc!" Lance shouts through the door. "*Spartacus.*"

"*Fuck,*" Linc mumbles before letting out a harsh huff of frustration. He shuts his eyes and hangs his head for a moment before stepping away from me. He retrieves his gun from where he discarded it and collects my pants and panties on the way back to me.

"I'm sorry." He hands me my clothes before reconfiguring his holster. "I'll find you when I'm done. Stay with Cricket tonight. Don't go back to your apartment until I can go with you." He plants a hurried kiss on my lips.

"Okay. Who is Spartacus?"

"Not *who*." Linc shrugs, trying to figure out the best way to explain. "It's PALADIN's safe word. I have to go to work." Linc opens the bathroom door barely wide enough for him to slip through. "Lock this back until you're dressed." I nod at him, crossing my legs just in case Lance is in close enough view to see me half-naked. "Eden, I really am sorry."

I half-smile at him. "Go—go save the world. I'll be here when you get back."

He snorts. "Save the world," he gripes. "I wish that were possible."

And then he's gone, leaving me behind...

But for once, I'm not feeling as alone.

NINETEEN
LINC

AFTER THE SECOND strike he topples, and both he and the chair land with a hard thud on the tile floor.

"Fuck!" I roar in frustration. "Just talk! Do you think I'm enjoying this?"

Our guest whimpers as I grab the chair and set it upright. His wrists, handcuffed behind his back, are chafed and raw. His lip is cut from the impact of my fist. I'm pulling punches but he's still bruising like a peach. *How much more of this can he take?*

I squat down so I'm eye level with him. "When all this shit goes down, they will help you." Pointing to the two-way glass, I continue, "Right outside that window is a very high director in the FBI. He has the authority to relocate you and put you in the witness protection program. They will call you a hero."

I mean to call him by his name but come to think of it, I don't know it. I didn't grab it when Lance and I hauled his ass across state lines in the trunk of a car. I never thought I'd see him again. Callen summoned Lance and me into the compound tonight, saying he needed an interrogation accelerated. While he was chugging coffee, he gave me simple instructions: *"We need an address as soon as possible. A lot of lives are at stake. Use force."*

He's still silent, so I try a different angle. "You don't need to endure any more pain. It's so simple. Just give us the information."

The young man levels a stare and gives me a wicked smile. Even with his face half-swollen, he still looks arrogant as fuck. "Listen," he says, his voice hoarse. He's so worn out, I have hope—maybe he's ready to cave. But the moment is fleeting. He spits in my face. "Fuck you. Kill me if you must, I'm no snitch."

Oh, fucker, I'm tempted.

I wipe his spit from my face before clocking him in the gut, holding nothing back this time. I'll admit that one was out of spite. He groans in agony.

"Don't go anywhere," I say with cruel sarcasm, eyeing his cuffed hands and legs tied to the chair. "I'll be back."

The exit door buzzes allowing me through to the viewing room and I'm met with Callen's unimpressed glare.

"You're less than effective in there," he snarks.

"He's not going to talk. I'm just wailing on him at this point. He needs a break."

"We don't have time for a break," Callen says while rubbing his temples. "Our intel says we're likely a few hours out."

"How much ammunition do you guys think they have?"

Callen hangs his head. "Enough to level a city."

Callen and his team aren't sure if it's a bombing or a mass shooting, but all we know is there is an organization planning a massacre in a few hours and the fucker behind the glass knows who, what, when, and where. The only problem is he won't talk. The FBI tried pleasant tactics over the past few weeks, offering him a pardon for his crimes, giving him the royal—aka humane—treatment. I think they even offered him mental health counseling. A lot of good that did them. After a couple of weeks of getting nowhere, they dumped him back in PALADIN's lap and told us to do whatever was needed, behind closed doors, to get answers.

Stretching out my hand that's still on the mend, I notice his blood on my knuckles. Should I even bother wiping it off? I'm supposed to get right back in there.

"If I beat him to death, he can't talk. What do you want me to do?"

"What the hell is going on?" A small voice behind me sends a shiver up my spine.

We didn't hear her come in—the door is supposed to be locked. Callen and I both whip around to see Eden at the entrance of the viewing room, her eyes locked on the man through the glass. Her long, dark hair is pulled back into a low ponytail, but she's still wearing her clothes from earlier this evening. The pants I pulled off of her, not four hours ago, are a little wrinkled now.

"What are you doing here?" Callen asks, still pressing against his temples. I think he drank at least three of those stupid fruity martinis. In his defense, we didn't expect an emergency tonight. Then again, it's our job to always expect emergencies.

"I couldn't find Cricket…" Eden trails off as she takes a few steps forward, making sense of the scene in front of her. As if on cue, the man grumbles in distress as he coughs, a dribble of blood coming out of his mouth. Eden snaps her head to the side and looks at me accusingly. "You did this to him?"

"Eden, this is a private interrogation," Callen grumbles. "You need to leave. You shouldn't see this."

"*You* shouldn't see this. You shouldn't be *doing* this," she hisses, glaring at me. I'm frozen at the moment. For some reason, I feel like I got caught cheating… I've never been so worried about a woman's opinion of me in my life.

Eden turns on her heel without another word and storms

out of the room. It takes me just a few minutes to decide whether or not to follow her, but by the time I make up my mind, she's back, carrying a plastic bag of snacks from the break room and a few bottles of water.

"What do you need from him?" she asks.

Now I understand where this is going. "Eden, absolutely not—"

"I wasn't talking to you," she shoots haughtily at me. "I don't work for you." Turning to Callen, she asks again, "What do you need from him?"

I'm shocked when Callen takes another sip from the Styrofoam cup of coffee and then actually answers Eden's question. "An address of where he and his buddies are hiding a bunker of explosives and assault weapons. I sent Lance out to chase down more leads, but this asshole is our best chance at stopping this."

Eden clutches the plastic bag close to her chest. "Okay." She draws in a deep breath. "Push the unlock button thingy— I'm ready."

I burst out in laughter which is met with her seething scowl. "Are you out of your goddamn mind? You think I'm going to allow you in there?" I ask incredulously.

"*Allow me?*" she asks, eerily calm, but her normally sparkling eyes are darker and more dangerous than I've ever seen them before.

Fuck. I soften my voice, trying to reason with her. "Eden, I already told you, you're"—I glance awkwardly at Callen, then just bite the bullet—"too precious to me," I finish in a hushed tone. "He's dangerous."

Callen screws up his face at my admission, but Eden relaxes hers. She runs her fingers over my bloodied knuckles as Callen mumbles something I can't hear under his breath.

"You have your superpower...and I have mine," she says. "Trust me."

"We can't do any worse," Callen finally says. "She pretty

much has a doctorate in human behavior. In a way, she's qualified as an interrogator."

I don't like this. But I'm going to lose this battle. "Fine," I grunt.

"May I have the key to his cuffs?" Eden asks.

I lose my temper again. In the most intimidating tone I can muster, I inform her, "No. Non-negotiable." I turn to Callen. "Fight me on this and you lose your best operative right now."

Callen looks between the two of us. He pushes a button and the interrogation room door unlocks. "No key. Don't give him your name, and no personal details about you, PALADIN, or the FBI. Remember that he's violent and—"

"A human being?" Eden interrupts. "Or did we forget that somewhere along the line?"

The nervous energy builds in my veins as she walks through the door. I have to stop myself from ripping her backward and taking her out of the compound.

I don't fucking like this... What is this? *Worry?* I used to never worry...

I might as well be cuffed myself, helplessly watching her walk right into the lion's den that I already rattled. Mostly, I'm pissed, but also a little frightened. Then again, there's a part of me that's excited because it's Eden...

And I know I'm about to be impressed.

Eden

TWENTY

EDEN

I FIGHT the anxious energy flooding through my veins as the door clicks shut behind me. This interrogation room is so bright—it's agitating. I immediately feel uneasy in here, maybe that's intentional. From what I've learned in my experience, people talk faster when they're uncomfortable.

I was so convincing in front of Callen and Linc, I almost fooled myself into thinking I'm equipped for this. *But I couldn't just stand by.* I know Linc was doing what he was ordered to, but when do we draw the line between what we're told is right…and what's *actually* right?

The man looks smaller in person than he did through the glass. His clothes are tattered and raggedy, his dark hair is greasy, and he smells like he's due for a shower. But underneath the swelling in his cheek and the drying blood around his lip, this is just a normal young man. His dark, thick eyelashes give him more of a baby face, and where Callen and Linc see a criminal…I see a prisoner.

I'm so caught up on how I should break the silence that I'm taken aback when he speaks first.

"Please tell me you're 'Bad Cop,'" he sasses, "and that

we're about to get naughty." He forces a laugh, but I recognize the false boldness—it's called fear, and I'm all too familiar.

"I'm not a cop," I say simply. "I'm the one who told the cops they can't touch you anymore. I will make a very big scene if anyone in this compound lays another hand on you."

"Is your *scene* supposed to save me?"

"I can be persuasive." Especially when the big, bad wolf of PALADIN is sweet on me. "Do you want some Doritos?"

I begin to unpack my plastic bag remembering my mantra: free food builds trust. I never thought I'd apply it to an interrogation situation, but I'm trying to see this as a conversation more than anything else. Offering nourishment and a little civility seems like a good way to get him talking.

"What?" he asks, taken off guard by my question.

"Dor-ree-tos," I sound out for him. I scrunch my face, mockingly. "*Chips, man.* I've got Nacho Cheese and Cool Ranch. I also have Goldfish, but they aren't flavor blasted so they're a waste of cracker space if you ask me."

He wriggles his wrists against his handcuffs. "I can't exactly eat at the moment."

I twist the cap off of a water bottle and soak a couple of clean white napkins before I cross the room. I glance over my shoulder to see the silent flashing red light blinking. There's Linc, warning me not to get too close. I continue my mission, ignoring his probably justified concern.

The man flinches when I reach out with the napkin. "Your lip is so swollen. It's just water. You saw me pour it." He stills and lets me press the wet napkin against his broken lip. "Humor me," I say as I lightly pat against his mouth. "It feels a bit better, right?"

He nods, albeit reluctantly.

I head back over to the only table in the room to grab the bag of Nacho Cheese Doritos, remembering that Cool Ranch dust always stings a bit when I have a cut in my mouth. Opening the bag, I return and kneel in front of him.

"Say, 'ah.'" I open my mouth like I'm demonstrating for a toddler.

"You're going to feed me?" I think he means to sound sarcastic but all that comes out is desperation.

"What's your name?"

"Lady, you can play nightingale all you want, I'm not telling you a damn thing."

"Give me a fake one if you must, I just need to call you something."

"Hector," he offers lazily.

"Okay, Hector. I'm—"

I stop myself, remembering Callen's command. If I don't play by his rules, he'll probably yank me out of here and Linc will go right back to assaulting the man in front of me.

"Bambi. My name's Bambi."

"Bambi?" he asks before rolling his eyes.

"Well, come on, is Hector *your* real name?"

He laughs softly and I can already feel it—*rapport*. Slow and steady is how we have to play this. "Now say, 'ah,' Hector —real wide. This is a big chip and I don't want to irritate your lip." He does as I request and I shove an entire Dorito in his mouth. He chews so aggressively I have to tell him to slow down. After six more chips, his manic chomping slows.

"My dad was in a specialized military unit and he went through a lot in his career. He told me when he was in the most dire situations, the pain would go numb, but the hunger wouldn't. He said the hunger pangs were the worst. Enough to make you crazy."

I pop another chip into Hector's mouth before offering him a drink of water. He takes a few greedy swallows. "Why are you being nice to me? Did they tell you who I work for?"

"No, I didn't ask. It doesn't matter who you work for." I plop to my ass and scoot backward on the floor until my back hits the wall.

"Because all you want is info," he says in a sing-song tone, mocking me. "That you're not going to get from me. I'm loyal, lady."

"Do you think they're looking for you?" He narrows his eyes and glares at me, my words obviously striking a chord. "As loyal as you are to them, I hope they are to you as well."

"I'm loyal to a cause," he sneers. "So I make sacrifices."

"What cause?"

He draws in a deep breath as he closes his eyes. "This country needs a wake-up call—a firm message delivered. People here are lawless ingrates who think because of freedom, they are allowed to be disgraceful. Someone needs to remind them that there are consequences for their sins."

Wow. That's a rehearsed speech if I've ever heard one, and Hector delivered the lines perfectly. I'm sure his leader masks violent radicalism as prophetic duty...beautifully. I bet he's even good-looking. A charismatic and persuasive leader is the most dangerous weapon.

"Hector, freedom doesn't make people evil. It just gives them an outlet to express the most shameless sides of themselves. Anger lives in all of us, and those who don't have a proper outlet suppress their agony until the pressure builds so great, they end up hurting other people. Violence is a misguided outlet for pain."

He takes a moment before answering, then finally asks, "Are you a shrink? Is that why they sent you in here?"

No. But maybe close. My doctoral dissertation was about the incredible power—and danger—of social media. If you want to see the true depravity of mankind, look at what people say under the blanket of online obscurity. I've seen starved coyotes act with more kindness and composure than young, bored, women with nothing but time on their hands and jealousy running through their veins. They are triggered by *everything* because they are content with *nothing*. Boredom, laziness, and anonymity mixed together is a concoction for cruelty.

"I'm not a psychiatrist. I'm just...*sensitive*, I suppose. Maybe I should see you as dangerous, but all I see you as is scared. But fear is a really good motivator, Hector. Did you know that?"

"Know what?" he asks, before opening his mouth wide. I scoot back over to him with the bag of chips and deposit another Dorito.

"People do the most incredible, and the most atrocious things when they are scared. Fear gives you adrenaline. It makes you stronger, helps you think more tactfully. Truly, it's our body's secret serum for survival."

He snorts. "Fear makes you radioactive?"

I smile. "Something like that."

He's quiet for a few beats before he speaks again. "I couldn't help you even if I wanted to, Bambi," he admits. "Taking a beating and being imprisoned is far better than what they'll do to me if I talk."

"I get it." I glance nervously at the two-way glass, then decide to chuck Callen's commands right out the window. What choice do I have? "Being a snitch will destroy you." He nods, hanging his head. "I should know," I add.

His eyes snap to mine. "What?"

"Oh yes, I'm a snitch. Or, in professional terms, a whistle-blower." I bite my tongue. *Oh, no.* I sincerely hope my safe word is only applicable to sex with Linc. Otherwise, he's about to barge in here to rescue me. After a few seconds, I determine the coast is clear. "I used to work for a company that created a social media organization system, if you will. It was like nothing else on the market. They secured over half a billion dollars in fundraising for this platform called Empress."

"You're in social media?" Hector asks, obviously confused as to why the hell I'm in this interrogation room with him.

"Me? Oh no, I actually don't have social media. I have very pointed opinions on it—but that's a conversation for another day. I was a leadership consultant at Empress. They went from twelve employees to over three hundred in the span of a year. It was stressful and chaotic. The leaders of the company needed a clear vision, so the very first thing I did was sit the executive team down and ask them to create a mission statement. What was Empress designed to do? What problem was Empress trying to solve?"

I pause, giving Hector the opportunity to say something. If he can follow me through this story, maybe...just maybe I have a chance. Finally, he prods me. "What'd they come up with?"

"Empress was trying to level the playing field. The developers believed that everyone deserved to have their voices heard—not just the lucky, or beautiful, or young, or quirky. Think of it this way—instead of having one mega Powerball lottery, their philosophy was to have thousands of winners, *sharing* the prize. Empress wanted to fight the social algorithms that were causing so much pain and making people feel so desperate, small, and insignificant. They were masters at it. Their tech was astonishingly good at grouping like-minded people. Basically, they were sorting people into the right buckets for societal approval."

"Societal approval?"

"Have you ever used social media?"

He nods. "For a little while."

Dumb it down, Eden. "Likes, Hector. Societal approval in the form of *likes.*"

"Why are you a snitch? Did you sell their tech to a competitor?"

"This next part is confidential. I could be put in jail for sharing this with you. But then again, this conversation is off the record because technically you shouldn't be here, and my current organization doesn't exist. And plus...I fed you Doritos, so..."

He half-smiles. "Secret's safe with me." He looks around the room. "Who would I tell?"

"I like what Empress stood for so much that I took a full-time role with them. The very first day I got executive access I came across a live bidding platform. I think they screwed up the permissions with my login credentials because I was dumped into this sort of online black market. What I eventually realized is that it was an information auction."

"What information?"

"Anonymous avatars were buying groups of data for categories such as highly impressionable, prone to violence, open to conspiracy, racist, has a gun, committed petty crimes, violent felons, interested in radical behavior, politically outspoken, incentivized by money... Do you see where I'm going with this?"

"They were selling recruits to terrorists?"

Hector's quicker to the truth than I was. I studied the database for hours before I understood what they were doing. The only thing scarier than people doing terrible things is people doing terrible things with an army of support behind them. Take the power of mob mentality—like cancel culture—and apply it to terrorism. What do you get? *Civil war.* Maybe even world war.

"We'd call them leads, but yes—same thing. They were buying personal information necessary to build what I can only assume were armies for their causes. They were targeting people...*collecting people*...all via social media."

"Wow. Smart." Hector attempts to stretch his legs, but he's restricted by the rope around his ankles, binding him to the chair. "That's not how I was recruited."

"How?"

His stare lands on the floor. "My older cousin told me we were going to get beer from the gas station... Instead...we ended up at a meeting. They told me they'd kill me if I left." He clears his throat. "So, you told on Empress?"

"I went to the exec team first and they denied everything.

They fired me on the spot and cut off all my access. So, I went to the FBI."

"I'm sure they gave you a medal."

I let out a shrill cackle, like a villainess. "I got a half-assed 'thank you.' My real reward was debt up to my ears from legal fees trying to protect me from a company I helped build. I was basically in hiding during the trial. People threatened my life —they didn't care if war was brewing, as long as they could keep their cushy Silicon Valley paychecks. I lost my job, my friends, my colleagues. I became a pariah. I lost everything and I still live in constant fear for my life. All because I told the truth and tried to prevent something truly evil."

"But you're okay now."

"No…" I shake my head. "I'm not okay. I'll never be okay again. I'm marked. Once a snitch, always a snitch. I'll carry that title to my grave, but you know what I do to make me feel better sometimes?"

"What?" Hector lets out a dry cough. I return to him with the water bottle, offering him another sip. I level my eyes with his before I speak again.

"Lately, I'll see a random person in a restaurant, or in my building, or sometimes just someone on the news, and I tell myself that maybe they get to live because of me. Maybe they won't know true terror, or lose their loved ones to something as tragic as war because I was convicted enough to speak up. Maybe *my* life is ruined, but maybe *theirs* will be okay because of me. And for now, that's enough."

"You sacrificed everything for strangers?"

"Mhm," I say. "The same way I'm pretty positive I just ruined, what could've been a very satisfying relationship, by coming in here to defend you—a criminal I've never met before because, sometimes, being a good person is just as senseless as being a bad one. But I'd rather see people alive and happy and think it's because of me, than see people tortured and dead and *know* it's because of me." I raise my eyebrows right in Hector's face. "The burden of information sucks. I wish I never saw that database. I wish I never knew. But do you know why God, or the universe, or whatever entity you believe in, chose me?"

He matches my gaze. "Why?"

"Because I was powerless not to do the right thing. The same reason you're in this chair, Hector. *You're chosen too.* And the only reason you've been listening to me talk all this time is because you want someone to tell you it's worth it. Right? Or is it just because you want more chips?"

He chuckles, then his face sobers. "I never thought I'd be a person who could hurt somebody, I'm only nineteen."

I knew he had a baby face. I nod. "Nineteen is young. You still have a lot of time left to atone for what you've done—to find a way to forgive yourself. You could start by looking at some of the strangers in this city and thinking maybe they're okay because of you."

"I won't be in the city." Hector nods toward the two-way glass. "They are going to lock me up."

"Then serve your time and do better. Redemption is there for the ones who admit their mistakes and are courageous enough to make a change."

I hold my breath hoping, praying. His eyes start to glisten and if it's not now, it's never. I've thrown every piece of wisdom I have at him...but it still might not be enough.

"Hector, please. What are they planning?"

"To hurt people," he admits.

"How many people?"

His watering eyes meet mine. "As many as they can."

"Hector," I say, placing my palm on his cheek. "In hindsight, I'd do everything with Empress again, the exact same way."

It feels like there's silence for ages as I hold his cheek. The pulse of hope seems to flatline, but then, barely audible, he speaks.

"Huxley's," he whispers. "Huxley's on 48th street. It's an abandoned mechanic shop." The tears begin to stream down his face and I mop them up with the back of my palm. "Chip," he says with a shaky breath. I pop the final chip from the snack-sized bag in his mouth and he can barely chew. He begins to bumble hysterically. "I'm scared."

"You're going to be okay." I use my most comforting voice. *Jesus, he's only nineteen.* Still a kid. "You did a good thing, Hector. It's all going to be okay. You will be protected." *I'll make damn sure of it.*

Suddenly the interrogation door opens and I see a brief flash of fear in Hector's eyes, so I know who it is.

"We confirmed the location. Interview over," Linc says at the door. I rise, feeling the ache in my thighs and calves from squatting for so long. There's a jingling coming from Linc's pocket as he walks over to us. Hector cowers, but Linc is unbothered. Making his way behind the chair, Linc unlocks Hector's cuffs, his eyes on me the entire time. His expression is mixed with anger, fear, and relief. I'm not sure which of those is because of me. *Maybe all of them.*

"Do you understand what I'm capable of if you try to hurt her?" Linc asks coldly before he points to Hector's bound feet.

Hector rubs his freed wrists, moaning in appreciation at the relief. "Calm down, you dick. Bambi might be my only friend in the world now."

I roll my eyes and exhale deeply. *Let's not provoke the man who could kill you with his bare hands, hm?* Regardless, Linc unties Hector's feet and he quickly stands.

"You'll stay here until transport tomorrow. You will be taken to a remote facility where you'll await trial. Your arresting officer will read you your rights. We'll make sure a certain amount of amnesty will be granted for your coopera-tion"—Linc glances at me—"and your discretion. Clear?"

Hector nods as he beats his fists against his thighs, trying to get the blood moving in his legs. "Is that all?"

"What do you want to eat? We'll order something for you." Linc asks like the words taste bad on his tongue.

"The fattest burger you can find. Extra cheese. Lots of fries. And I want a toothbrush and toothpaste." He flashes Linc his teeth. *"Please,"* he adds sarcastically.

"Anything else?" Linc asks.

"I'll let you know," Hector says, pointing to the glass. "I'm assuming I'll be watched?"

Linc nods before he holds his hand out to me. "Come on." Relieved, I lace my fingers between his, feeling his warm bear paw wrap around my hand that feels child-sized in his.

"Bambi?" Hector calls out before I'm through the door. I turn around as Linc lets out an unsubtle exhale of exasperation. "My real name is Roman."

"Thank you, Roman." A warm smile crosses my face as I picture hope for this boy, a second chance for a better life, free from the tyrannical men whose evil plans are about to be foiled and who are about to face justice.

"What's yours?"

"It's Ed—*Ah!*"

Linc yanks me through the door, letting it slam behind me before I can say my name.

Linc

TWENTY-ONE
LINC

CALLEN ASKED me to join the raid at Huxley's, but I told him to fuck off. If nothing else, Eden earned us both a night off. If the FBI can't handle this on their own, what good are they?

It's nearly four in the morning when Eden and I head to her apartment. Parking in her building was full so we had to leave my car four blocks away. I'd never tolerate her walking around alone at this time of night, but I'm with her now. I'll keep her safe. The next person who threatens or harasses her doesn't need to fear the FBI, they need to fear me. I'm much scarier than the law when it comes to something that's precious to me.

The car ride was nearly silent. We're still quiet as we walk, hand in hand, through the bitter cold of night. The only sound is our shoes crunching on the sidewalk. Finally, we both decide to break the silence at the same time.

"I'm sorry—"

"Eden, I—"

Her eyes light up and her cheeks bunch in my favorite way. "*Thank God.* You first, please. I thought you were too upset to talk to me," she says.

"Why would I be upset at you?"

She squeezes my hand. "I've had many boyfriends accuse me of being bullheaded, self-righteous, and overly nice to a fault. I guess I'm prone to doing things like barging in on a top-secret interrogation, accusing you of being a monster, and insisting I know best." She scrunches her nose apologetically. "I'm sorry if it seemed like I was disrespecting you and Callen. It wasn't my intention."

I halt on the sidewalk, accidentally yanking her backward with my hand still wrapped tightly around hers. "Many boyfriends?" I raise my brow.

"Oh..." She's caught off guard and flushes. "Not that many. A reasonable amount"—her eyes suddenly bulge in horror—"and I wasn't implying that you're my boyfriend. I was just explaining why I'd understand if you were upset, but I saw the fear in Roman's eyes. I thought there was a better way."

I bring the back of her hand to my lips and kiss it gently. "Why would you apologize for being right?"

"Because it seems that's all I've been doing for the past year."

Releasing my hand, she continues to walk down the side-walk. I let her lead a few paces as I trail behind. "Do you want a boyfriend?" I call after her.

She stops dead in her tracks before she spins around. "What?"

"Should uh...we go on a date before we go any further?" I ask. I'm not sure how to approach this conversation, I've never had it before.

Her breath is visible in the cold night air and her exposed arms must be freezing, but she acts like she's unbothered—as if adrenaline is keeping her comfortably warm. "Do you date?"

"I never have before," I say honestly. "But I know I like you." I take one step toward Eden. "I know you intrigue the hell out of me because you're this confusing combination of baby bird and badass." She chuckles as I take another step. "I know your pussy tastes delicious."

Turning beet red, she sucks in her lips and looks left and right, and up and down the street like someone could've heard me. "Thank you?"

"You're very welcome." I flash her a smartass smile. "And last but not least, I know that I want to kill every man who gets within a one-foot radius of you. Call it jealousy, I suppose."

She crosses her arms and slightly tilts her head. "From any other man that'd be swoon-worthy, but when it comes from you, I'm scared you mean that literally."

I do.

I take the final step, wrapping my arms around her waist. "Hey now," I murmur into her ear. "Forget what I do... How do you feel around me?" I kiss her soft, cold cheek, then pull her into my body.

"Tempted," she says into my chest as I rub her arms, trying to warm her up. I wish I had a jacket to wrap around her. "But Cricket said you guys can't really do relationships so I don't have any expectations. I know it's complicated."

Fucking Cricket and her big mouth.

"I've never done it like this, I need you to help me out. How does a man go about showing he cares and that I want more than your body?"

She weaves her fingers between mine again and guides me down the sidewalk. Her fingers feel like icicles gently squeezing my hand. "For starters, he'd walk me to my door after one of the longest twenty-four hours of my life. Maybe he'd use all his secret spy tricks to make sure my apartment is safe. And if I was still a little nervous to be alone...maybe he'd stay over tonight?"

"I can do that."

We take a few more steps before we approach the corner

of the block. Instinctively, I pull her back, glancing around the curve of the sidewalk before I let her lead again.

"And how would a woman go about showing you how much she likes you and wants to keep you interested?"

I spend a moment thinking about it, so I can give an honest answer. "All simple things. She'd let me hold her while she slept, fuck her senseless when she wakes up, all rough and rowdy like she wants it, then after, she'd have a meal with me."

"I can do that," Eden says, looking back at me with a playful smile. "I have a Belgian waffle iron still in the box I've been meaning to whip out. The only question is are you a blueberry or chocolate chip waffle kind of guy?" She stares at my peculiar expression, noticing my lack of enthusiasm. "Or...plain?"

I have to nip this in the bud before she forces another muffin on me. "I hate breakfast foods."

"Huh?" Her hand that's not wrapped around mine, finds her hip. "Who says that?"

I shrug. "Me... I hate muffins, pancakes, waffles, French toast, donuts—all of it. I'm not a fan of eggs, bacon, or sausage. I hate breakfast foods, period."

Her jaw drops open. "I was on the fence about you being a monster until right now. Scales did not tip in your favor, buddy."

I let out a throaty laugh and feel the cold air seep into my lungs. "Is that going to be a problem?"

"No. But I have to know... *Why?* What could you possibly hate about a donut?"

This is the first personal detail I'll ever share with Eden, definitely not the last, but the first is always the hardest. I could just lie as an out, but all I see is her big, brown, doe-eyes and her smile that looks like kindness and hope. So, I do something I've never done with a woman.

I share something personal.

"My mom didn't feed me much as a kid. She was too tired

from all the pill-popping to grocery shop or cook. We lived in a small town, right down the road from a breakfast diner and the owner knew what a wreck my mom was. He let me eat as much as I wanted, for free. From age seven to thirteen, before I learned to cook, I ate breakfast diner food, and leftover baked goods for every single fucking meal. All these years later, I'm still burnt out on it."

Eden closes the gap between us and touches her cool lips to mine. How did she know the reward I wanted for my honest admission was her lips on mine?

"Spaghetti and meatballs for breakfast then," she whispers.

TWENTY-TWO

EDEN

LINC CHUCKLES at me when we enter the elevator of my residence building that basically sling-shots passengers up forty-some floors. He watches me take a deep breath and press one fist against my belly while using my other hand to clutch the railing for dear life. He, on the other hand, is completely at ease, wearing a teasing smirk on his beautiful, slightly stubbled face.

"You have to do that every time?" he asks between small, breathy laughs.

Scowling at him, I nod.

After collecting my hands in just one of his, he raises them above my head and traces my stomach with his other fingers. My arousal is urgent and needy, and I can literally feel the apex of my thighs begin to swell. His grumbly low voice doesn't help the matter. If he wasn't pinning my hands in place, I'd let them explore his body.

"Take a deep breath," Linc instructs. I instinctually obey because I'm already breathless from his touch and actually do need air. "Most people combat a fear of heights with pressure. Holding your stomach, clenching the rail… It's normal. But

what you need is to give your breath room. Expand your
diaphragm, breathe deeply, and the nerves will calm."

Maybe his advice works, maybe I'm distracted, but as I
stare at Linc's lips the jitters disappear, replaced by a new
tingling sensation. He's ducking down, hovering over me with
my hands still pinned above my head. All I'd have to do is lean
forward just a little bit to kiss him. Seeing the ravenous look in
my eyes, Linc trails his hand below my belly button. He
powerfully cups my sex over my pants with his palm, making
me grunt in response.

"Eden, I really like that I can touch you whenever I want
now because I've been suppressing the urge for weeks. We
have a lot of lost time to make up for." He grinds the heel of
his palm against my sex and something between a moan and
whimper escapes my lips as my head knocks against the
elevator wall. How long is this ride? I hope it never ends. Send
me to space, as long as Linc can come with me. There's something extra exciting about the way I'm trapped underneath his
grip. Whatever happens next... All I can do is let it happen.

I buck my hips, pressing myself deeper into his palm.
"Please touch me."

"I am," he says with a soft laugh.

"You know what I mean." I want his hands beneath my
underwear. I want his fingers in me.

He whispers in my ear, "Needy girl, there are cameras in
here."

Are there? My eyes dart around the elevator walls, but I
don't see cameras. And actually...

"I don't care—"

Ding! And just like that the spell is broken.

"You'd care later. You're just all worked up right now," he
says. He kisses my forehead before pulling me through the
elevator doors right as they open. "I have some work to do
first. Which is yours?" he asks, looking left, then right down
hallways that lead in opposite directions.

208

"Eighty-nine," I reply, nodding toward the left. "Four-two-eight-nine."

I'm still ticklish between my thighs but it's clear Linc no longer has sex on his mind. It's fascinating to see him like this. Sometimes I forget that Linc's not just a killer, not just a brute —he's got a skill set. He sees everything. His eyes scour the hallway as we cover the short distance, but he's looking at things I never notice anymore, like the decorative hallway table topped with potted plants and classic books. He opens each of the books and to my great surprise the middle one is hollow. Inside, there's a small copper key.

Linc looks at me and raises his eyebrow. "Eden——"

"That's not mine," I assure him.

"Good. It's an incredibly stupid thing to do. Don't ever hide your keys in a public area like this, and I better not find a key above your door frame. Don't make yourself an easy target."

Pursing my lips, I blink at him. "Save your lecture. I *just said* it's not mine." While our apartments have electronic locks, I believe there's a manual key override. Likely, someone's fob has been giving them trouble and they planted that little copper key in case of technical difficulties. "And there's nothing above my door." *Not here anyway.* Back home in California though, not only did I have a spare key above my entry door frame, but there was also a ceramic toad in my garden that contained the key to my patio door and my car. *Whoops.*

Reaching my door, I pull out my fob and press it against the sensor. Linc reaches over my head and places something above the door frame that I don't see. He's too quick. "Don't ever touch that."

"Touch what?"

He doesn't answer. Instead, he gently presses my back against the hallway wall. "Stay right here. I need two minutes then I'll come get you."

"Okay," I say, nodding. *I'll behave.*

With his hand on the handle, he turns to me once more. "Eden, as a general rule, moving forward, if I ever tell you to run, you run. Okay?"

"Okay."

"I'm serious," he says, locking in on me with his light blue eyes that look like ice the way he's staring at me. "No playing the hero. No trying to be brave to prove a point. *You. Run.* Do you understand?"

"Yes. Fine, Linc. I hear you."

"Good girl," he says, causing a tingly little twitch well beneath my navel. I wish he'd stop saying that. I'm starting to develop a bit of a praise kink because of him. With that, he disappears behind the door and I begin to count to one hundred and twenty.

I'm on ninety-nine when Linc returns. He wordlessly pulls me to the bathroom, closes the toilet lid, and sits me down.

"Your apartment is small."

I stick out my tongue. "Well don't be a jerk about it."

He laughs and his all-business demeanor briefly disappears. "I meant it's ideal. I wasn't sure I brought enough equipment. Let me show you something."

He squats down and grabs my hand, guiding my finger to what feels like a small vinyl sticker hidden behind the toilet paper holder. "Do you feel it?" he asks and I nod.

"What is this?"

"It's a panic button. It's heat sensitive, so an object brushing against it won't make it go off, but if you flatten your finger against it for one second, the entirety of PALADIN will get an emergency alert. If someone left a note for you, they likely want information, which means they'd need time. The first thing they'll do in a hostage situation is collect your phone and scan for any obvious modes of communication. They'll shut the blinds, cut your internet lines, and threaten you if you scream. Discretion is everything, so, if you find yourself in a precarious situation, first put them at ease by complying. Give up your phone, your wallet, whatever they want. Then make an excuse to use the toilet."

"It's so subtle," I say, examining the tiny black sticker that easily looks like...*nothing*. Like remnants of packaging that didn't make it into the trash. I would've never noticed it.

He winks at me. "That's the point, Bambi."

"Wait—the entirety of PALADIN? I don't want to worry *everybody*. Can it just alert you?"

"Vesper, Cricket, and Lance are my family. They care about what I care about—which now includes you. If you are in harm's way, what matters is who can get here fastest, I don't care who it is."

I place my hands on the top of his thighs, then kiss his forehead. "Thank you."

"You're welcome, Precious." Linc fishes in his pants pocket and pulls out what looks like a mini marble cut in half. He holds it in his palm patiently while I examine it. "This is surveillance. I'm going to put these all around your apartment except in the bathroom. I need you to stay here while I place them. You can't know where they are."

"What? Why?"

"Because if someone broke in, it's the very first place your eyes will go. It's natural for every victim in an intimidating situation. You can't control it. But you'll give away the fact that you're under surveillance. An intruder is far more likely to pull a trigger and cut a loss if they feel they've been made."

"Jesus," I whisper, my arousal fading and the reality of the break-in settling in. Linc makes me feel so safe, I almost forgot how serious and dangerous this all could be. "Maybe I should—"

"Stay with me?" He cocks his head to the side, trying to find my eyes. "I'd feel better if you did."

I shake my head. "No, Linc. I don't want to be babysat. I'm an adult, I should be able to live alone and take care of myself. What I meant to say is, perhaps I should get over my fear of guns. Maybe I should get a firearm and learn how to use it."

"If that's what you want, I'll teach you. But if I'm being honest, I like that you don't like guns. It's refreshing that you flinch even when someone else gets hurt. Eden, it's okay to be tender and soft. I really like that about you."

When I first met Linc, he was hardly a talker. Fast forward a few weeks, now he's speaking in poetic soliloquies, telling me what he *really likes* about me. "I don't want a gun. I just don't want to feel so weak."

He tilts his head to the side, showing off the elegant cut angles of his jawline. "I watched you in that interrogation room, and I can't for the life of me understand why you think you're weak, Eden."

Standing upright, he pats the pocket where he pulled out the little camera. "Stay here until I'm done."

"Wait!" I squeal. He turns around as his eyes pop in surprise. "So, you're going to put cameras all over my home that I won't know about?"

"It's for security. If someone breaks in again…I'll know who to hunt." The way his jaw clenches makes me nervous for whoever dropped that note off. By intruding on my personal space, they've made an enemy of Linc.

"It seems awfully invasive."

"I'm not putting cameras in here, Eden. You'll have privacy in the bathroom. The surveillance is for my eyes only. Neither PALADIN nor anyone in the FBI will have access to it."

"But they'll be in the bedroom, right? You'll be sitting around watching me?"

He chuckles again and my cheeks begin to burn with red-hot embarrassment. "The tapes are for *review* if something happens...like you find another letter. I won't be sitting around watching you." The sexiest smile curls at the corner of his lips as he lifts his brows. "Unless you put on a good show." Before I can respond, he's out the door, closing it behind him.

The minute he's out of sight, I leap up off the toilet seat and look in the mirror. *Holy shit, Eden!* Bad, this is bad. I realize I haven't looked at myself since Linc's tongue was between my thighs at Martinis, but I look beyond ragged. My hair is frizzy, my cheeks look blotchy. My eye makeup is so smeared I look like a raccoon.

I quickly go to work, the way every single woman is equipped to in an *I wasn't expecting to get laid* emergency situation. I squeeze a dollop of toothpaste on my tongue and swash it around furiously before quickly rinsing. Pumping a few drops of smoothing serum in my palm, I try to calm my flyaway hairs and cover up my dry ends. *Screw it—there's no time to fix my eye makeup.* I grab a cleansing wipe and clean the smudges under my eyes. I settle for a quick brush of finishing powder all over my face—my fancy one which smells faintly like sweet roses. Looking in the mirror, the finished product really isn't that much better. *Geez.* I just look so tired, my cheeks are sunken in. I probably have less than two minutes before Linc comes back. What the hell can I—*oh.*

I open the smallest drawer of the bathroom vanity where I store all the makeup I never use. I find the cherry red lipstick that Vesper's picture reminded me of all those weeks ago at the diner with Callen. *Bold.* I want to be bold right now. Twisting the silver tube, the bright red lipstick emerges looking like a neon police siren. I snort at myself. There's no way I can pull this color off, but I force myself to drag the balm over my bottom lip, then my top. When I'm finished, I have to resist the urge to immediately wipe it off.

It's not that it looks bad, I just look...noticeable. For the past year, I've been trying to slip under the radar, but Linc makes me want to be seen. *No, don't take it off. Another coat.*

I'm lifting the lipstick back to my mouth when Linc startles me, abruptly busting back through the bathroom door. I toss the tube out of surprise and with near perfect accuracy it flies right to him. Linc snatches it out of the air before it drops to the floor, unintentionally showing off his superior reflexes.

"What are you doing?" he asks, looking at me through the mirror.

Dammit. I exhale. *He just installed cameras in your home, what do you honestly think you can hide from him now?* "I was trying to fix up a bit for you."

"Really?" he asks as he swaggers over to me and sets the lipstick upright on the bathroom counter. "Well, I'm finished."

"Are you staying?"

"Of course. Unless you changed your mind?"

Instead of answering, I spin around and cup the space beneath his belt. Immediately I feel his erection grow. Just a touch, that's all it takes.

"Mmm," he moans. "Okay, let's talk."

"*Talk?* No, thank you," I sass, rubbing my hand along his growing length, getting a little nervous I may have bitten off more than I can chew. I copped a feel at Martinis, but I'm realizing now I barely scratched the surface. Of course a sexy, brooding, manly man, who's only sweet to me, and calls me things like "precious" while holding my hand, has a mammoth-sized dick—because obviously I've fallen into Wonderland and dreams must be real.

"Eden," he growls, collecting my hand and handing it back. "Let's talk."

Pouting, I cross my arms and lean back against the vanity. "About what?"

"What you said at Martinis. How you like it rough—"

"I said I like you in control."

"Whatever you want to call it, I need to make some things clear. Rule number one—I refuse to hurt you. Nothing that bruises you, marks your skin or makes you bleed. Do you understand? I know the impression you have of me, but I don't get pleasure from inflicting pain on anyone. And the thought of you hurting is the biggest turn-off in the world to me."

"Okay," I whisper, swallowing back my tongue before something crazy like *I think I love you*, accidentally slips through.

"That being said, explain this control thing to me. What do you like?"

The ache immediately awakens. The idea of sex with Linc? *So damn hot.* Talking about sex with Linc? *Someone save me, I'm already gone.*

"I know it's weird."

He shakes his head determinedly and lifts my chin with his finger so I'm staring at the icy fire in his eyes. "No, don't be embarrassed, it's not weird. Quite the opposite—so sexy. Just tell me what you like, *specifically*, and I'll tell you if it's on the table."

"I like it when you pin me down, and I'd actually be okay with being tied up with something soft. Just my hands, and feet. I don't want to be hogtied like a calf at a rodeo or anything."

"Okay."

"I like denial."

"As in…?"

"I want you to make me wait. Tell me when I can come."

"*Fucking hell*, Eden," he groans in what I think is delight. I glance down and because he's so damn big, I can literally see his cock twitch against his pants. "I can do that. Do you like dirty talk?"

"I like *filthy* talk."

"You're going to ruin me, woman. Anything else?"

"Anal is fine, but you have to be gentle. I'm not experienced."

He shakes his head. "Rule number one, remember? I'd split you in half and it would hurt a lot."

"We have a safe word. We can work up to it."

"Why?"

The truth is that I've spent a lot of time, by myself, thinking about things I was too scared to try. I've had moments over the past months where I felt my life was in danger and all I could think about was how disciplined I'd been. I'm always so tidy, structured, and by the book. Where did it get me?

I promised myself, with the next man I trusted, I'd try everything. I'd be a different kind of person—brave, bold, and daring. I'd find a way to make what's dangerous, *pleasurable.* Maybe that'll help me conquer the fear that lives in me. But I'm not telling Linc that. I'm dripping for him at the moment and confessing that my default is more cowardly than the damn lion from *The Wizard of Oz* is not sexy.

"Have you done it before?" I ask, avoiding his question. He rolls his eyes but refuses to answer. It's a gentlemanly move not to talk about the other women he's been with, but I'm curious. *What kind of girls does the assassin like?* "Can you honestly say you didn't like it?"

"Let's not worry about that tonight. Maybe in time. Is there anything else you want?"

I show him a shy smile. "Sex aside, I still like dates, flowers, cuddling, good morning texts, and all that so-called girl stuff. Oh, and…um, I prefer exclusivity."

Linc returns my smile. "I'm on board with most of that."

My heart pounds audibly in my chest. It's so loud, a normal man would hear it, but Linc with all his seemingly heightened senses must be able to hear my nerves clear as day. *Shit.* Cricket warned me. Is this too much too fast? Exclusivity might be asking too much from the man they call a ghost.

"Which part is the problem?" I bravely ask.

"Do you really need a good morning text if I'm right there lying next to you?"

There's a tickle running up my arms, it swirls around my neck and drops to my chest, filling my heart with pressure. This feeling is a little different than lust. It's far more dramatic. This is how it starts...the beginning of hope. It's been so long, but the feeling is a flood of warmth and comfort, reminding me that my life is over as I knew it, but maybe that's not such a bad thing.

Here, there are new possibilities.

"Linc. Wreck me. Now."

Stepping back, he pops the top button of his polo, giving him enough room around the neck to pull his shirt off. I can sit on my hands to control them, but there's nothing I can do about the gawking. Linc's chest and abs are inhuman, like a Grecian sculpture of a mythical creature. The cut grooves of his six-pack could trap my fingers, they are so deep...so tight. His torso is perfect, outside of the healed-over scars. The one just to the left of his belly button still shows the teeth of the staples that were used to close him up. It's the kind of patch-work they do in emergencies to rapidly close a bullet wound. Looking at his body, I'm torn between lust and concern.

"I like that lipstick on you," he says as he unbuckles his belt. I don't know where he stashed it, but I'm just now noticing Linc's holster and gun are missing. He continues to unbutton his pants and lets them droop just a little so I can see the waistband of his briefs and the hearty bulge they are trying to contain.

First, he turns on my shower, pulling the handle to the hottest setting. Then, he makes his way back over to me, but before I can put my hands on his beckoning hard-on, he grabs my wrists.

With his other hand, he collects the silver tube, and pops off the lid with his thumb. While dragging the lipstick across my top lip and then the bottom, he releases a sexy low grumble.

"Eden?"

"Yes?" I gasp. I'm regretting the denial request already. I want him and judging by the wicked smile on his face, I'm not sure if relief for the ache I have is on the way.

"It's been a very long night."

"I'm not tired," I insist.

"Good. Then I want you to use your lips to paint my cock red."

Linc

TWENTY-THREE

LINC

"WHAT'S THE SAFE WORD, EDEN?"

She's getting drenched on her knees in the steamy shower. She's been sucking me for so long that the water has gone from scalding to barely warm, but neither of us cares. She slowly pulls her mouth away from my throbbing dick to answer me.

"You're going to have to remember all by yourself, Linc. Because I'm not going to say it." She doesn't wait for a response. Immediately, she engulfs me again, twirling her tongue around my tip like it's her favorite flavored lollipop.

I asked her to paint my cock, and she did. Just for good measure, she planted kisses up and down my shaft so I could see the imprint of her lips in red all over. But the lipstick marks have long since washed away under her fancy shower head with the powerful stream.

For such a small apartment, it's an enormous shower. My arm span is barely wide enough to brace myself against the tile and glass door, but I stretch to hold myself steady as Eden expertly sucks me into submission. *Fuck, it's amazing.* I inhale and exhale deeply whenever my balls clench, trying to calm my brewing orgasm because we're in a battle of endurance. She knows it, I know it. One of us will cave first. Either her knees will give out on the hard floor, or I'm going to spill all over her pretty tits.

Hunching over, I weave my hands through her soaked hair and guide her away from my cock. Her eyes lift to meet mine. "If you can't speak to say the safe word, tap my arm. I'll stop immediately. Understand?"

She nods enthusiastically, understanding exactly what I'm about to do. "You can come in my mouth, by the way."

I raise my brows. "You swallow?"

"Not for any other man."

I smirk. When she talks like that I feel like a starving shark in the middle of a feeding frenzy. I can only focus on one thing. *All mine. She's all fucking mine.* "Is this a first-time thing, or are you always so generous with your mouth?"

"For you, I'll be generous with everything." She opens her mouth and sticks out her tongue. I have to fist my tip tightly, to control the pounding.

"This won't take me much longer," I admit. "Is that what you want?" She nods wordlessly. "Good girl. Open wider."

Tightening my grip on her hair, I slide into her mouth, inching slowly until I feel her adjust her breathing comfortably to her nose. She cups and strokes my sack gently like she's admiring me.

Once she's steady, I fuck her mouth, *hard.* Touching the back of her throat with every thrust, I'm half thrashing into her, half pulling her mouth over my cock by my fist in her hair. She's trying so hard not to gag and sputter, but her eyes begin to water. Everything is wet. Her saliva pools and drips, mixing with the beads of water still raining over us.

"Let me know, Precious," I grunt, as I pick up the pace, "if you can't handle it." Her mouth is slick and warm, making a mess out of my throbbing cock. *She wins.* Her tolerance rules over mine. "Fuck, Eden. You're too good, baby."

Releasing her hair, I step back, gripping myself firmly.

"Push your perfect tits together. Now," I growl, as I feel the swell of pressure hurricane in my balls.

She does as she's told, and with one quick thrust in between her soft supple fleshy breasts, I shoot into her hair, her chin, all over her chest, coat her pink nipples, and dribble down her belly.

I step back and admire her for a moment, looking as vulnerable as a woman can. She's on her knees, completely naked, wet, and close to shivering. It's right now, in this very moment that I realize what I'm so attracted to. Her openness. She's vulnerable enough to cry for strangers, intelligent enough to teach kindness, and she shows mercy to those who don't deserve it. Yet, she's also brave enough to demand from me all her depraved desires.

She's everything.

From now on, I'm the only man she kneels for like this. Because she's safe with me. I respect her. I appreciate her. I revel in this gift. I'll take care of her if she lets me. Eden's words from earlier, in the interrogation room, knock around my head. The burden she carries… She doesn't have to do it alone anymore. Not while I still have a pulse.

"Linc?"

"Yes?"

"Are you finished? I want to get up."

Lifting her up by the elbows, I pull her off her reddened knees, slightly cursing myself for bending rule number one. I press her into my body and spin us around so she's under the last remnants of the warm water. Grabbing a bar of soap from a nook in the tile wall, I begin to rub it over her shoulders. The pleasant smell of something sweet and minty fills the shower.

She turns around so her firm ass is against my softening cock. Playfully jiggling her hips against me, she says over her shoulder, "That soap bar is for hair too." I lather up her long hair before rubbing the soap over her tits and stomach, washing away the last remnants of my cum.

"You are incredible." I plant light kisses on the back of her neck and across her shoulders.

"Was that good?"

"The best I've ever had," I assure her. And, not that I'd tell her, I've had quite a few. But no woman has ever made me feel like Dr. Eden Abbott does.

"Good, I'm glad." The little vixen that lives inside of Eden is at peace for the evening. Her regular tone has returned and she sounds soft and weary. I think the excitement of the last twenty-four hours is finally catching up to her. She doesn't need more sex, she needs rest.

I step out of the shower and fetch a towel we can share. I pat myself dry just so I'm not dripping before I cover her with the fluffy towel. These towels are too big for Eden, I could wrap her up once and then some, like a burrito.

"Put your arms around my neck." I duck my head so she can reach. As soon as her hands lock together behind my head, I scoop her up, one arm under her thighs and the other beneath her shoulders. When we reach her bedroom, she points to the top dresser where I find her a pair of simple black underwear. She rustles the towel against her hair as I retrieve my briefs from the bathroom, and then we both tuck into bed, topless.

Moaning softly, she shifts backward, tightly into my embrace. "I haven't slept next to someone in so long," she murmurs. "I forgot how good this feels."

I wrap my arm around her, enjoying the feel of her tits against my forearm and her soft skin against my chest.

"It does feel good," I say into the crook of her neck. I listen as her breathing goes rhythmic and her body relaxes. Sleeping with a warm body beside me is indeed comforting.

It's just the first time in my life I've ever done it.

TWENTY-FOUR

EDEN

I WAKE UP ALONE, next to another note.

Well, a note of sorts. It's my phone, lying on the unoccupied pillow next to me with an orange sticky note that reads: *Call me when you wake up*, with a phone number I don't recognize.

I reach for my phone and quickly dial the number.

"Good morning, sleepy," Linc answers on the first ring. His voice sounds echoey wherever he is.

"Good morning." I sit up, feeling the cool air on my bare chest. I forgot I slept without a bra or shirt because I wasn't chilly. Linc was my personal space heater last night, not to mention he spent the entire night cupping my breasts. Judging by his behavior in the bathroom at Martinis, I really thought he was an ass man…I stand corrected. "You ran out on me," I tease.

"I'm sorry," he says. "Emergency." He doesn't offer a further explanation.

"You know it's funny, I didn't really picture you with a cell phone."

"What?"

"Yeah, I sort of thought you'd be completely untraceable.

227

Life in the shadows. Maybe you'd sleep with one eye open. Actually, I'm surprised you sleep, period."

He laughs. "Do you think I'm a vampire?"

Maybe a little. A very sexy vampire. "Where are you?"

"Can't say specifically, but I'm very high up."

Suddenly the aroma of coffee hits my nose. I sniff around for a bit before I find the source—a traveler's mug of coffee sitting on my nightstand. Peering through the lid, I see it's light in color, fixed with cream and likely sugar.

"Did you make me coffee, Linc?" I press the speakerphone button and put the phone on the pillow beside me before collecting the mug in both hands before I take a sip. *Mmmm, perfect. Still hot.*

"I had every intention of being there when you woke up. I'm sorry, something came up—"

"Linc, if you say it's an emergency, *it's an emergency.* I appreciate the morning call though, and the coffee. Thank you."

"You're welcome, but it's not morning, Bambi."

"Hm?" I check the time on the top bar of my phone and am shocked when I see it's four o' clock in the afternoon. *Holy shit.* I slept an entire day away.

"I waited as long as I could, but I didn't want to wake you. I'm with Vesper and Lance. But when we're done, how about I take you to dinner tonight?"

"Out?"

"Yes, why are you surprised? You asked last night and I told you I'm fine with dates."

I grin into my coffee mug, remembering our antics. Linc was sexy, needy, and caring. He ripped apart every single assumption I'd ever made about him.

"It was more the 'out' part. Can you be seen in public?"

"*Jesus*, Eden, as I said—I'm not a vampire. We can go to dinner."

I giggle. "All right. That sounds great." I hear mumbling in the distance, maybe the sounds of radio static.

"I have to go. I'll call you soon." He doesn't wait for me to respond. The line goes silent and it's just me and my mug of coffee. I dawdle in bed for a while, enjoying the non-anxiety ridden occasion. Finishing my cup of coffee, I read a chapter from my book on the nightstand. I thought I'd be embarrassed if Linc saw my smutty romance book, but we broke a lot of barriers last night. I slept half naked next to him all night. I know what his precum tastes like. I wore his actual cum like war paint last night, right before he washed me, towel-dried me, and tucked me into bed. There's nothing left to hide from him.

Not to mention, he could be watching me as we speak. I still have no idea where the cameras are. I'm not remotely put off by Linc's extreme measures. I've reported break-ins and suspicious situations so many times to the police in the past year and they've always shrugged it off. They called me paranoid and unnecessarily hysteric. I'd officially become a nuisance to them and before Callen showed up, I wasn't a priority for the FBI either. No one took me seriously until Linc. So he can watch me all he wants, I'm grateful.

Finally pulling off the covers, I set my coffee cup aside and make my way to the bathroom. I laugh out loud in utter glee when I see orange sticky notes everywhere.

On the mirror is another note right above my sink: *You're so beautiful.* Next to the toilet paper: *Don't forget your button.* On the back of the bathroom door: *Remember, no cameras in here.* On the glass of the shower door: *You make me fucking crazy.* On the shower handle: *I already miss your tits.* I collect them all before entering the kitchen where I find one more orange note next to a plate of Belgian waffles. It reads: *I guessed chocolate chips.*

I grab the fork Linc laid out for me and help myself to a big bite of the fluffy waffles with melted chocolate chips. I don't care that they're no longer warm, they're still perfect. I must've been in a deep sleep for him to pull all this off without me noticing. I look at the sink embedded in my kitchen island counter to see a bowl, measuring cup, and a spatula washed and drying on the dish rack.

Linc might be the perfect man…job aside. I was expecting a really good fuck. I was not expecting…*dreamy.* Is this finally karma? I've tried so hard to be a good person. Is Linc finally my reward?

I whip out my phone to send a quick text, hoping it goes unread for a while. I don't know what Linc's doing, but I can't imagine it's the kind of thing that should be interrupted by a text message.

ME

> You guessed right. Always chocolate chips for waffles.

I set my phone down but scoop it right back up when the soft chime tells me I have an instant response.

LINC

> *kissy face*

I gawk at my phone. *Stop.* Was that an emoji? Did the cold-blooded assassin who has FBI agents shaking in their boots just send me a kissy-face emoji?

ME

> *heart on fire emoji*

LINC

The wet concrete is starting to dampen my shirt and agitate my stomach, but I don't get up. I don't want to risk missing my window, so I stay low, on top of this high rise, my eye on the scope and one hand on the trigger of the sniper rifle.

I've been lying here for over an hour, even through the

brief rainstorm, but at least I have company. Vesper impatiently paces. "Lance, what the fuck is he doing?" she whispers.

Lance, who is pretending to smoke at the back of the building across the street, is our ground operative, because while he's better with a pistol, my long-range aim far exceeds his. Cricket's our best sniper, but Vesper sent her out of the country for something I'm not privy to, nor do I care to be. There's enough bullshit here to worry about. Plus, Cricket can handle herself. Everyone thinks I'm the fearsome one, little do they know that when provoked, Cricket's the most terrifying of us all.

Through my scope, I see Lance put his phone to his ear, pretending to make a call. We can hear each other through our hidden earpieces, but he's trying to act natural. We don't normally complete hits in public where witnesses could see, but this is a special case.

"Hey, Mom," Lance says into his phone, sarcasm lining his tone. He only calls Vesper "Mom" when he's annoyed. He's still pissed off he got ground detail for this job. "Lunch is going to take a little while longer. He just ordered another round of drinks...and dessert."

"Fat fuck," Vesper grumbles.

"He's stalling," I say.

"It's out of character. He's such a flight risk. He usually doesn't like to be in the U.S. for more than a few hours."

"Who the fuck cares, Vesper? He's a trafficker, mass murderer, rapist, and degenerate. As soon as I pull this trigger, he won't have a character to worry about."

We're here for Paris, or that's what we call him anyway. Who knows what his real name is—he's had so many. He bounces around continents so much the FBI and CIA can never find him to extradite him. Even if they did, it's impossible to pin him to his crimes. This is the problem when warlords and criminals outsmart our legal systems. Enter

PALADIN. We don't need the paperwork to put a war-hungry menace in the ground. I've never known someone to enjoy evil as much as this piece of shit. I'm bothered he gets such a satisfying last meal at this swanky lunch locale we're watching.

My phone vibrates on the ground and I see Eden's reply. It's a little heart with flames around it. I can't help but smile to myself. I made the girl waffles this morning. *Who am I? I don't care. I think I like it.*

"Lance," I say, "in your experience, what should I say back to a woman who sent a fire-heart emoji thing?"

"Hold on," he mumbles, barely moving his lips as he whips out his phone. My phone pings again almost immediately.

LANCELOT

> *peach emoji* *eggplant emoji* *splash emoji* *umbrella emoji*

"Does that help?" Lance asks. "Send it in *exactly* that order. It tells a story."

"You need serious help." I try not to laugh at his perversion.

"Who are you texting?" Vesper asks but I don't hear her through my earpiece, I glance up to see her hovering over my phone. There's no point in lying. Vesper knows everything.

"Eden," I admit, pulling out my earpiece which automatically mutes my radio so I can momentarily shut Lance out. "I set up surveillance at her place last night."

"Why?"

"Someone broke in."

"Something to do with Empress?"

"How'd you know about that?" I furrow my brows, but I'm still looking through the scope. I don't have time to check Vesper's reaction.

"I knew about Empress before I knew who Dr. Eden Abbott

was. The FBI made a huge fuss about it, then the whole case went dark—and I mean black-out dark. I asked a few people on the inside, including Callen. No one has any information besides a violation of civil rights and the dissolution of a tech company."

"But you suspect there's more?"

"Of course I do. But when do I not? Always expect for there to be more and pray you're wrong, Linc."

"I don't care about the company," I say, pinching my shoulder blades together, trying to relieve the discomfort of laying on a concrete roof top for so long. "As long as Eden's safe."

Vesper sits in front of me, resting her back against the ledge so I can see her out of my peripherals. "Linc, be careful."

"About what?"

"Getting involved with her."

"Since when do you care who I'm sleeping with?" I ask, trying to sound nonchalant. I don't know who I'm kidding, Vesper knows me better than anyone—she raised me since I was sixteen.

"I care when there's a woman who makes you smile like an idiot when she texts you."

I blow out a breath. "I'm still well aware of the rules, Vesper." It's not like I'm planning to propose. I doubt Eden would ever be interested in marrying someone like me anyway, she's still jumpy every time my pistol is in view. Little does she know, it's the tamest weapon I operate.

"Do you know why we have the rule of no families?"

"Because you don't want us kissing anyone's ass except yours?" I snark. She kicks my shoulder with the heel of her boot, hard. I try not to wince but she's freakishly strong.

"I was married once."

For the first time in an hour, I pull my eyes away from the scope. Vesper's brows are raised at me expectantly. She has her earpiece in her hand as well. Whatever she's about to say, she doesn't want Lance to hear.

"You never told me that."

"It was before I found you. While I was working with the FBI, the first time around, I thought I'd try my hand at a normal life."

"Was he an agent?"

Vesper snorts. "No. Not even close. He was a high school math teacher. He had the muscular integrity of a teddy bear. But he had these really sexy glasses…" She trails off as she gets lost in a memory. Shaking the thought away, she continues, "We were chasing this thug, Marlin. A few bank robberies, a couple of drive-by shootings, but the amount of cocaine he was pedaling was unrivaled. We planned a big raid, we got his drugs and a couple of his goons, but he slipped away. It still pissed him off to no end."

"I get a call a couple of days later to get to the hospital and I find my husband lying in a bed with his face and body so swollen and bruised he was unrecognizable. He stayed in the hospital for two weeks. Another teacher found him in his classroom after school let out. He was unconscious and had a note taped to his back from Marlin."

I keep my eye locked on the scope. Lance is on his third fake cigarette in ten minutes and if Paris doesn't come out soon, we're going to have to blow his brains out through the restaurant window. The FBI wouldn't be thrilled about that, but better we make this look like a rival gang retaliation than a government-approved hit.

"Was your husband okay?"

"Physically, yes. But he was traumatized."

"Who wouldn't be?"

"We eventually got Marlin, but my husband was never the same. He was skittish and depressed. He quit teaching. He wouldn't leave the house. I know he tried to put on a brave face for me, but he lost something that day. He never looked at people the same way again. His blissful ignorance was lost, all he saw were monsters. *I did that.* My job did that. I didn't want to put him in harm's way ever again, so I left him. I set him free so that maybe he wouldn't have to live in fear for the rest of his life. The rules aren't for you, Linc, *they're for her.* Evil likes easy targets. The best way to get to you is through someone you love."

Fuck. I know she's right. I'm quiet because there's no valid argument against it. I can swear to protect Eden, but I'm the threat. I'm the thing that could put her in harm's way.

I pop my earpiece back in as I see Lance swipe at his nose. "Go time. He's on the move. North door."

I draw in a breath and hold it. I picture Eden's panicked eyes at Martinis after someone had broken into her home.

"Less than ten seconds. His car is pulling around the corner. It's our last chance." I hear Lance in my ear one more time before he disappears behind the building. Paris can't get into that car. There's no doubt in my mind it's bulletproof. *No.* This slippery coward is done living...*today.*

I feel the tension build in my lungs. I am so sick of the assholes of the world. I am so sick of all these fuckers that make my existence necessary. I am so tired of the kind, worthy people being easy targets. We need change. I don't know how, but until then I'll be here, taking out the trash, piece by piece.

The back door of the building opens and I yank the rifle's trigger in one fluid motion. The vehicle peels away and leaves the motionless body behind. I wait to ensure he's not moving before I let out my breath.

"Clean shot," Lance says through my earpiece.

"Well done, Linc," Vesper says in front of me. "The FBI will take it from here."

"Who will they pin it on?" I ask. Paris is a high-profile target, this won't go unnoticed.

"Don't worry about it. Get out of here and enjoy your evening, just—"

"I hear you, Vesper. I understand." No longer needing to stare down the rifle's scope, I'm able to see her cloudy eyes, the aftermath of dredging up something extremely painful. I stand and stretch feeling the stiffness in my back slowly dissipate. "Do you ever look him up? Your ex-husband?"

I hold out my hand and Vesper takes it, hoisting herself off the ground as well. "I do, often. He's re-married. Beautiful woman. Three kids. And he's teaching again. So, all in all—a happy ending."

I look at Vesper's sad eyes.

For who?

Linc

TWENTY-FIVE

LINC

EDEN HAS THANKED me countless times this evening. She thanked me on the phone when she learned I made reservations for dinner at an upscale Italian restaurant. She thanked me when I arrived at her door on time with flowers to pick her up for our date. When I told her she looked like a goddess in the silky dark green dress that hugged her body like a glove, she thanked me again. Another time, when I opened the car door for her and helped her out of my bulletproof sedan with the blacked-out license plate. And yet again when I helped her shuffle into our private booth by the window with a view overlooking the city.

"Linc, have I thanked you yet for such a lovely evening?"

I laugh to myself. "Yes, Bambi. Several times." I squeeze her thigh through her thin dress. "In fact, you only get one more for the entire evening. One more 'thank you,' and that's it. You can't say it again, so make it a good one."

Her eyes hit the ceiling as she taps her fingertips together, contemplating. Then, she eyes me up and down. "Thank you for dressing up, you look so handsome."

Confused, I say, "You're welcome, but that was an odd one

239

to waste it on. I plan on paying tonight, and I have a little present for you back at my place."

She eyes my lap and gives me a naughty smile as I burst into laughter.

"Well, that too...but I mean a literal present. Nothing fancy, although I did put it in a small gift box." I rotate my fingers around each other. "There's even a bow."

She leans over and kisses my cheek, the smell of her rich perfume lingering between us. "Do other women know about you?" I let out a breathy chuckle. *More than I care to admit.*

"Not this version of me," I say honestly.

"Good," she responds matter-of-factly. "Let's not tell them. I'd have to go to war to keep you."

After taking in a panoramic view of the dimly lit restaurant, Eden scoots out of the booth. "I need to visit the restroom." Tapping her clutch on the table she adds, "My license is in the clear flap. If this waiter ever decides to return, would you show him my ID and order me a drink?"

"Of course. What would you like? Or do you want me to control that too?" I ask with a wicked smile. I'm half-distracted by her breasts which look unbelievably tempting in her low-cut dress. I have to keep reminding myself to keep my eyes on hers when she's speaking. I'm suddenly very annoyed at this tardy waiter, delaying dinner...and my after-dinner plans.

Her tongue darts out quickly before she winks. "Prosecco, please." She takes a few steps, then returns to the table and furrows her neatly trimmed eyebrows at me. "Do you have an ID if you get carded?"

My forehead wrinkles from my perplexed expression. "Do you think I'm underage, Eden?"

She snorts. "No, I'm just curious."

Leaning to the side, I pull my wallet out of my back pocket and retrieve my driver's license. I hand it to her. "I'm twenty-eight, like I told you."

She grabs it from me and scours the little lines of text, looking for something. "You're shitting me."

"What?"

"Lincoln. Abraham. That's what is on your driver's license?" Her eyes widen to startling proportions. "*Lincoln Abraham?* And no one suspects that's a fake name?"

Laughing, I scold her. "Are you trying to announce that to the entire restaurant?"

She exhales in cute frustration and heads toward the ladies' room. In perfect timing, the waiter arrives shortly after she leaves. He's dressed up in a three-piece suit and my irritation is quickly replaced by pity. It must be hot and uncomfortable to wait tables in that monkey suit all night.

"Would you like to start with a drink?"

Yes, thirty minutes ago. "Your nicest bottle of Prosecco for the lady, and a mid-tier whiskey for me. I don't care about the brand."

"May I see your IDs?"

I shuffle through Eden's purse, finding her license in a clear flap. As I pull it free, a notecard slips out and onto the table.

"Would your girlfriend like strawberries for her Prosecco?"

I don't correct him. *Do I need to? Is Eden my girlfriend now?* "I'm not sure. How about on a plate to the side?"

He nods and saunters off. I stuff Eden's belongings back into her purse until I notice the title on the card and my curiosity takes over. I have to swallow down my laughter. Across the top of the notecard, underlined, reads: *Questions to Ask Linc.*

EDEN

Sometimes I wonder if I'm attracted to Linc because, in a way, he's elite. From the moment Callen spoke about him at the diner nearly a month ago, he's had a spotlight on him in my mind. I got goosebumps the very first time I laid eyes on him in that meeting room and realized who he was because he has a magnificence about him.

Am I so hot for him because of his job, even though I claim it's the only off-putting aspect of him? Do I like the power he holds? The way he takes what he wants and executes justice as he sees fit?

But, as I cross the restaurant floor, eyes locked on his burly frame, looking fine as hell in a baby blue dress shirt that matches his eyes, it's obvious... I would've dropped my panties for this man even if he scooped elephant shit at the zoo. Damn, he's hot. And sweet. And such a gentleman. It's like he studied a first-date playbook before this evening. He's executed every single part flawlessly.

When I return, there's a bottle of Prosecco chilling in an ice bucket and a small plate of halved strawberries.

"Oh, that's a nice touch," I say, nodding at the strawber- ries as I glide back into the booth. My smile is replaced with utter mortification when I see the pink notecard, face down on the table in front of my spot. I realize instantly what Linc has unearthed and my stomach twists. *Shit.* I completely forgot I stuffed those stupid questions into my purse.

"Ah, dammit," I huff, hanging my head.

Linc shoots me a teasing smile. "If I knew this date had homework, I might've studied."

"You weren't supposed to see that," I groan. "I could die of embarrassment right now."

"Oh hey, now." He nudges me with his arm, but when I won't look up from the table, he hooks his finger under my chin. He has to tilt my chin to the ceiling before I'll meet his gaze. "Everything you do is either sexy, endearing, or inspiring. You can do no wrong in my eyes."

"No wrong?" I ask, skeptically.

He lifts the bottle out of the ice bath and fills my empty glass flute. "None. But why the questions, may I ask?" He taps the notecard.

My cheeks puff up as I blow out a slow breath. "Because I'm a little confused."

"About what?"

"If we're on a date…and we're sleeping together…and you stay over at my place… Does that mean we're together? Is *together* even something you're interested in?" I don't care how gentlemanly Linc is, or how kind he's being, every woman in the world gets a flood of nervous energy when she asks a man if he's willing to claim her. I hold my breath, anxiously waiting for a response.

"One or two?" Confused at first, I realize Linc's asking about the strawberries. I hold up one finger, and he plops a strawberry half into the glass. I watch as the golden liquid bubbles furiously as the fruit sinks to the bottom. He slides the glass closer to me. "You asked for exclusivity. Doesn't that mean we're together?"

"Sexually, sure. But there are a lot of things I'd want to know about my boyfriend that I don't know about you. I brought these notes along just in case, but I don't want to put you on the spot. I like you, but by now I also know PALADIN a little better, so, I didn't expect dating you to be conventional." I slide the notecard off the table and attempt to shove it back into the deepest corner of my silver clutch but Linc grabs my hand. He carefully wrestles the notecard from my grip.

"I answer these questions right and then I'm your boyfriend?"

I scrunch my face at him. "Well, it's not a pass or fail kind of thing. It's more like a get-to-know-you kind of thing. I just feel like this is moving a little fast."

"I see lives end almost every day, Eden. When I want something, I move fast. If you wait, you might miss it forever."

Linc's full of these profound truths. It always catches me off guard because he's so casually conversational with them. He reminds me of an old philosophy professor that I couldn't get rid of all through my undergrad and on to my doctorate. Professor Ross was a total ass, but he was so intelligent. He taught me how to navigate this world. His opinion was that right versus wrong was a concept that was so overly simple, it was borderline idiotic.

Surviving amongst each other takes a very high pain tolerance. We have to forgive far more often than is comfortable, and our entire existence is a life lesson about upending the biases and assumptions we create ourselves.

Professor Ross was a walking contradiction, and he wanted it that way. My teacher would spend the first few weeks of the semester convincing us he was Nietzsche's biggest supporter, only to pivot and preach Kantian ethics before midterms. By the time I had my diploma in hand, I only knew one thing—that I knew absolutely nothing... Well, that and studying any more philosophy might drive me to the brink of madness. How do you unify that which is vehemently divided? How do you marry two polar opposites?

How does a woman, who hates violence and guns, fall for a professional killer?

"These are the answers you need to feel comfortable being with me?" Linc waves the card side to side, and I nod. He hands back the questions. "All right, ask away."

Knowing Linc, he's already read through all of these. "You're going to answer these honestly?"

"Yes."

"Every single one?"

"All eight of them." *Knew it.* But if the opportunity is here to get answers from the ghost, I'd be crazy not to take it. Taking a little swig of my drink, I start the impromptu boyfriend interview. The first question is easy.

"Do you have any pets?"

Linc smiles. "Lance is loyal like a dog, and if you spend some time training him he'll fetch you things, but outside of that—I've never had a pet."

I snort. "Okay, fair enough."

"How about you? Why don't you have a pet?"

"I love dogs. I had a Malinois who passed a couple of years ago. She's impossible to replace and I haven't had the heart to try."

"What happened?"

"My dad bought Mickey for me right before his fifth tour. He told her to look after me, but that girl was obsessed with her Daddy Jorey, she'd get mopey whenever he was gone." I chuckle to myself thinking about how she was supposed to cheer me up during the times Dad was away, but I always ended up taking care of her instead. "She was such a good dog though—so smart, patient, and sweet. After my dad retired and his health really started declining, I thought I'd have Mickey to help me through the aftermath, but the day he died, she crawled up into his empty bed, closed her eyes, and never opened them again. I guess…she wanted to go with him."

Linc presses his lips to my temple and wraps his arms around my shoulders. I want to bathe in the clean soap smell he's always wearing. It's a smell I'm starting to miss whenever it isn't around. "That's a shame," he murmurs.

"It's okay," I assure him. "She went peacefully. They both did."

"Good. Next question."

I glance down at the card as if I don't have all these questions memorized in order. "Where do you see yourself in five years? Jobwise." I cringe. That sounded more like an *actual*

KAY COVE

interview question. *Geez.* It's official, I no longer know how to date.

Linc chuckles lightly. "Dead."

My expression flattens. It's the first and only thing he's said to upset me this evening. I have a hard time seeing the humor in it. "That's not funny."

"Bambi, I'm kidding."

"Okay, let's try a different question," I say, wiggling away from his grip and angling my body so I'm facing him head-on in the curved booth. "How many times a week are you in mortal danger because of PALADIN?"

Linc folds his hands together and taps his knuckles against his lips. "If it helps, I am very good at what I do. Disturbingly good. You don't need to worry about me."

Something dangerous flashes in his eyes. Linc's so normal around me, sometimes I forget who he is, and how I met him in the first place.

"Okay." I flash him a half-hearted smile. "But maybe work on your secondary skills, you know, in case you ever want a career change." I wink and click my jaw, but he doesn't return my playfulness.

Linc's expression hardens. "Eden, there's only one way out of PALADIN, and it's not a happy ever after. Do you understand what I'm saying?"

A small lump lodges in my throat that I can't swallow down. *Surely, he doesn't mean...death?* "I think so."

Grabbing my hand, he pulls it to his lips. "Next question," he says before planting a quick kiss on the back of my hand.

"How many prior relationships have you had?"

"Zero. Next question." Linc answers in a hurry, eager to move on but I'm too clever for that.

I narrow my eyes. "How many women have you slept with before me?"

"Technically we haven't slept together yet." He pumps his eyebrows.

246

"Oral sex is still sex," I say, sounding like a sexual harassment seminar I've delivered on several occasions. "Which means I'm a little late in asking but are you, um...clean...you know, health-wise, are you in the clear?" I pinch one eye shut. I don't care if you're a nurse who hands out condoms for a living, asking someone you like to see naked about their sexual health is uncomfortable. Not even I know how to handle this gracefully.

A teasing smirk spreads over Linc's face. "Are you asking me if I could potentially have an STD?"

He's enjoying the flush of embarrassment reddening my cheeks. I don't think Linc gets embarrassed because he acts like he doesn't understand it. Every time I'm humiliated, he looks at me like I'm the most fascinating creature in the world.

"I'm asking if maybe the last time you got a bullet wound stitched up, they asked you to pee in a cup...and then later sent you the results?"

He's full-on laughing now. "Thanks to Callen's protocol, I actually do have to piss in a cup every time I cross country borders, so yes, Eden—I can assure you, I'm clean."

"Good, me too."

"Does that mean we can omit the condom tonight?"

I flash him my teeth. "Whether or not you're having sex tonight is highly dependent on your answer to that other question," I tease.

He presses his lips together. "You're asking a question you don't really want an answer to. What does it matter how many if they all pale in comparison to you?"

I stare at him and try to keep my mouth from falling open. "I'm going to need a copy of that playbook," I whisper.

"What?"

"Nothing, sorry. But anyway, the condom is probably best. I didn't have insurance for a long time, so I haven't had a chance to get a new IUD. I'm not on birth control right now."

I must've said something wrong. Linc pulls down on his

face with both hands. When I finally see his eyes, they look tormented. He looks like he's debating whether or not to ask the question on his mind. Finally, he gives in. "Do you want children one day?" he asks.

I don't like the panicked look in his eyes, but I refuse to lie about this. Not to any man, not to anyone. "Yes. But not necessarily right now. And I'm not dead set on how many. But overall, yes. I always figured I'd be a mother eventually. I take it you don't want children?"

"I can't."

"You're sterile?"

"By choice," he admits, no longer looking me in the eyes. Linc glances toward the bar, across the restaurant, toward the kitchen…pretty much everywhere but at me.

"What does that mean?"

"I had a vasectomy a very long time ago."

Oh. "A very long time ago? You're only twenty-eight."

Inhaling sharply, he lets out a harsh breath. "I joined PALADIN at sixteen. They gave me a gun, a new name, and a vasectomy."

I tent my hands over my mouth to cover my gasp. Of course our very tardy waiter returns during the most shocking revelation of the evening.

"Would you like to hear the specials?" he asks as he spreads a napkin over his forearm, pulls the bottle of Prosecco from its melting ice bath, and refills my flute.

My mouth is still covered and my eyes are wide with shock, so Linc collects our menus and hands them to the waiter. "Surprise us." Linc turns to me. "Do you like pasta?" I nod, but I can't find my appetite at the moment. Speaking to the waiter again, Linc's tone is clipped. "Whatever you'd recommend. If it's good, I promise your tip will be triple the bill."

The waiter nods enthusiastically. "Thank you, sir, I know just the thing. Any allergies?"

248

Linc shakes his head, and I follow suit, eager for this waiter to leave the table. The second he's out of earshot I reach up to stroke Linc's cheek.

"They castrated you at sixteen? You were just a boy. That's disgusting. What doctor would do that?"

"Castrate?" Linc reels in response. "No, no—you saw. It still works." He winks.

I give him a pity laugh. "Poor word choice. I meant *neutered*. Linc, who makes a sixteen-year-old boy do that? It was too soon to make a decision that'd mark the rest of your life. Vesper asked this of you?"

He cups his hand over mine that's resting on his cheek. He leans further into my palm. "If it wasn't for Vesper, I probably would've ended up just like the men I rid the world of today. I didn't have a good childhood, Eden. PALADIN gave me a new life."

"Well, it certainly asks for a lot in exchange. You can't get out. You put your life in danger daily. You'll never have kids, even if you want them? It seems cruel."

"It'd be cruel for a child to have me as a father." Pulling my hand away from his face, Linc tucks it back into my lap. He finally grabs his drink, something amber-colored and strong-smelling. He throws it back in one glug.

"Jorey and I aren't the same," Linc continues. "Your dad was honor and duty—he was a hero. Do you understand that's not me? I'm in the shadows because our governments have deemed the things I do to be evil and unacceptable. There's no medal coming for me, Eden. I'm different, and I thought because of everything you'd gone through with Empress and working off-the-books for the FBI, maybe you would end up a little different too. I thought we had some common ground... But I see now, your life is still promising, while mine's unsalvageable. Maybe whatever this is between us...will only trap you." He kisses my forehead. "I don't want to trap you. I don't want to hurt you."

Does he really believe that? Is it true?

I had plans. I planned to be married by twenty-six and have my first baby by twenty-eight. Maybe my second two years later. I planned to have my house paid off by forty and have a million dollars in the bank not too long after. I promised myself I'd start a charity—there were so many causes I wanted to support, I wasn't sure which direction I'd go, but I was determined to help someone, somehow. I signed up for a golden life but I missed all the fine print.

I didn't expect to lose my dad *after* he retired from one of the most dangerous jobs in the world. I never planned to be a whistleblower. Bankruptcy, debt, fear... I didn't plan for any of that. And I definitely didn't plan to fall for an assassin who is charming and tender. Linc and I make no sense on paper. But right now, looking into his beautiful icy, hot eyes—it's clear as day.

Fuck the plan.

Grabbing the notecard, I rip it straight down the center. I line up the pieces and do it again. I don't stop until I have pink confetti on the table. I act nonchalant as I brush the pieces to the edge of the table.

"I hope the waiter picks the lobster ravioli. It sounds divine."

"Eden," Linc says.

I dump the confetti pieces on an empty bread plate and push it to the edge of the table so the waiter can collect it and dispose of it.

"Would you be open to sharing dessert? Because if we want the chocolate soufflé, we have to order it now. I'm assuming they make it from scratch, which will take a while."

"Eden?" Linc asks again, nodding toward the bread plate littered with pink notecard scraps. "What are you saying?"

"I'm saying, it doesn't matter what the answers are—I'm in. If you want to be with me, I want to be with you too. No conditions."

"It's not just kids. I'm not allowed to get married, either."

I shrug. "Changing my name always seemed like such a hassle anyway."

"I'll have to leave a lot."

"As long as you come back."

"I'd have to move you sometimes, for my peace of mind. A new home every few months."

"I'm good with travel."

He shakes his head at me, seemingly in amazement. *Bring it on, Linc. I've got an answer for everything.*

"Your life with me wouldn't be normal."

"I'm an organizational leadership consultant for an off-the-record division of the FBI that unofficially employs assassins. Yesterday, I conducted a very illegal interrogation and helped stop a massacre by hand-feeding a criminal Doritos. My home is riddled with hidden cameras to catch a stalker in the wind who likely wants information about a terrorist scheme I helped uncover. And last but not least, last night, I let you fuck my cleavage until you came on my chest. I don't think I do normal anymore."

Without his gaze leaving mine, Linc raises two fingers in the air. Our waiter appears out of nowhere, likely more motivated by the promise of a very large tip.

"Yes, sir?" He's sweating while holding a large tray in one hand filled with plates for another table. Linc smiles at me wide, his perfect teeth gleaming against the dim lights of the very romantic Italian restaurant.

"Will you please put in an order for a chocolate soufflé? My girlfriend wants dessert."

TWENTY-SIX

EDEN

LINC'S HOME is like a mausoleum. It's eerily minimalist, and that's coming from a minimalist myself. He has so little furniture that my words are echoing off his dark gray walls. Outside of the barren, drafty ambiance, his place is magnificent. I shouldn't be so surprised at the grandeur of the interior, seeing as the drive from the privacy gate to his front door was a good quarter mile of beautiful, hand-laid cobblestone, curving in a roundabout at the front of the entry.

Being from Silicon Valley, I am no stranger to men who are incredibly proud of their over-the-top homes. On my past dates, the walk from the car to the front door was a boring lecture on all the lawn and security upgrades they made to the property. We'd get through the door and I'd spend another ten minutes covering my yawn as I was informed that the kitchen marble is incredibly rare and was imported from Venice on a tugboat.

Linc's home is brag worthy, but he's not interested in peacocking. The only thing he keeps bragging about is how beautiful his new girlfriend is and how he's going to rip her dress to shreds.

I'm torn. I want his raw, animalistic passion...but I also really like this dress. It's a perfect mix of sexy and classy, and of course I brought out the showstopper for my first date with Linc. He's A-game worthy.

Passing the foyer, we enter Linc's kitchen, which is the size of my entire apartment.

"White or red, Bambi?" he asks, examining bottles on a metal wine rack.

"White, please," I say distractedly, taking in the luxurious kitchen. Linc abandons the rack and opens a tall cabinet which turns out to be a hidden fridge. "Linc, are you rich?" I ask with my brows cinched in curiosity.

Uncorking a bottle of what looks like White Zinfandel, he pours two glasses and then points to the living room area behind me, silently instructing me to take a seat and get comfortable.

After handing me a glass, he sits down next to me on his oversized black leather sectional. His knee is touching my thigh, sending glorious anticipatory jitters up my leg. The kind of jitters you get when you know you're about to have the best sex of your entire life. Nothing will match this night for the rest of my life, I'm sure of it. Not even another night with Linc, because this is the first time. It's lust mixed with the tantalizing unknown. It's the most seductive combination in the world and we'll only have it once. *No pressure.*

"What's rich to you?" he asks before taking a sip from his glass.

"Before my fall from grace, I thought I was doing pretty well for myself, but I could never afford a place like this, especially in this city."

"How much were you making?"

Instinctively, I flinch. I used to lie about my salary to men I dated. Even my boyfriend of eight months never knew I out earned him tenfold. I didn't want to be taken advantage of or start a pissing competition, so it was easier to omit the truth. But Linc's a different breed of man.

"At my peak? A little north of a quarter million, annually."

Linc takes another long sip from his glass. "Then yes, in comparison, I'm rich," he says before a sexy smile takes over his face. "Why? Are you looking for a sugar daddy? Because I'm open to it. I'll buy you all the pretty things you want. Just keep wearing dresses like this and doing that thing with your mouth that I like." He chuckles at his joke before setting his wine glass down on the leather-top coffee table. His hand creeps up my thigh, pushing the hem of my dress upward. I'm undecided amidst the growing heat between my thighs and my inescapable curiosity. I should just shut up and kiss him…

"I was just wondering what the going rate is for taking someone's life?"

Linc's hand freezes in place. *Dammit, Eden. You and your big mouth.* Removing his hand from my thigh, he sits back on the couch. He's silent. I sip from my glass just to have something to do. I swirl around the tart, crisp white wine in my mouth until it goes warm and I have to swallow. It's not until I take another sip, that he speaks.

"It depends on the benefactor. But it's more complicated than getting paid for a hit. The money goes through the house first—it gets pooled for family needs."

"I'm sorry, what? Family needs...? Like groceries?" I can't help but smirk at his bizarre response.

"No, Eden." Linc sighs in exasperation. "I mean like the time we had to pay a foreign dictator over forty million dollars to release Lance from torture after he fucked his wife. 'Supposedly,' he didn't know who she was." Linc's pointed stare tells me he doesn't believe that for one second.

"I want to say I'm surprised…but it's Lance, so…"

"Right," he says, chuckling. "Anyway, all the money logistics go through Vesper. I don't make deals, so I can't give you a dollar amount. Something's changed since the FBI took over, but again, I don't handle the money outside of recovering funds from closed accounts."

"Closed accounts?" I bring the glass to my lips, but I don't sip. I'm too transfixed with anticipation.

"Deceased colleagues. Usually, they keep emergency reserves somewhere in their residences."

I sputter, choking briefly on my own spit that went down the wrong pipe. My blood begins to bubble in agitation and I can't control my outburst. "You rob your dead cohorts? Are you kidding me?"

"Rob?" Linc asks, looking offended.

Slamming my glass on the table, I stare Linc dead in the eyes. "After I exposed Empress, the company sued me, threatening to put me in jail for breach of confidentiality. The FBI was building their case and couldn't help me in the interim. The whistleblower association couldn't do anything because they protect against intracompany retaliation. Empress was no longer a company, so there was nothing they could do.

"I had to lawyer up immediately. And I'm not talking about public defenders. I needed the best defense to go up against their corporate lawyers and they were not cheap. The money my dad left me when he passed paid for the top legal minds of Silicon Valley, and I owe him everything for it. To think you're depriving the families of your comrades of—"

"Eden," Linc interrupts me. He squeezes my knee gently, which is what catches me off guard—every time. When I cross the line I expect to be met with anger, instead all he shows is…tenderness. "We don't have next of kin. Our parents have either passed or think we're dead. PALADIN is the only family we have. Are we supposed to be buried with our cash?"

My stomach cramps as if someone is grabbing a handful of my intestines and twisting their fist. I drop my head in shame. "I'm sorry. I'm such an idiot. I'll shut up now." Pouting at my own insensitivity, I swivel the wine in my glass. I can feel his eyes on me but I don't look up.

Linc grabs my glass and sets it aside. Leaning into me, he finds my lips with his, but I can hardly commit to the kiss.

"Don't ask me questions you don't want answers to, Bambi, because I'm not going to lie to you," he says, softly. "But you have nothing to apologize for."

"Thank you for—"

He interrupts me by shoving his thumb into my mouth. "What did I tell you about saying thank you for the rest of the evening?" I'd tell him that I'd used my last one at the restaurant, but his thumb still fills my mouth, making it impossible to talk. "Suck," he commands. I do, and when he pulls his thumb back out it's wet with my saliva.

Grabbing my hips, Linc pulls me into a lying position on his couch. He pushes the hem of my dress all the way up and yanks my lacy thong to the side. My pretty black underwear is an overcompensation from my plain comfort cotton panties he saw at our last encounter.

I groan in pleasure as he begins to rub small circles against my clit with his wet thumb. I clamp my eyes shut, and grasp my bottom lip with my top teeth, enjoying the pressure that begins to build.

"You're going to *want* to thank me all night long." He slides his thumb down my crease and teases my entrance. His thumb easily slicks over my slit. I'm already wet. Lately, I'm always wet and wanting. I wait, then buck my hips with perfect timing, forcing the tip of his thumb to barely penetrate me. I groan like I'm in agony as I open my eyes and see his sly smile. "But try to resist."

"Please, just this once, don't make me wait," I beg. "Then, the rest of the night is yours."

He kisses me while he trades fingers, and slinks his longest finger into me. I cry into his mouth as his tongue dances over mine. When his knuckle presses against my clit, everything inside me is jolted awake. He pumps his finger slowly, purposely toying with me. I beg for my release but judging from the wet sloshing sounds as his finger slides in and out, I'm really enjoying the teasing. My nipples are hard and aching, barely shielded by my lace bra and thin dress. I press them into Linc's warm chest as I arch my back, trying to withstand the slow torment he's unleashing upon me. I want his thick cock so bad, but I also could die happy in this anticipatory torture. It's so damn good. I don't know which way to go —suspending in pleasure as long as I can or exploding in relief.

This…

This is why I want Linc in control.

I can't decide.

"What makes you come fastest?" Linc asks with his eyes on my mouth. "Can you come from this?"

"You want this to go fast?" My breath hitches, making a coherent response difficult.

"No. I just need you soaking wet so it's not uncomfortable when you take every single inch of my cock." I don't respond, I just breathe, staying focused on his fingers, trying to clench around them. "Eden," he says warningly, "answer me."

"Your tongue," I grumble, annoyed he's making me think and speak when I want to float away in the pleasure. "Or rub my clit. That's the only way I can have an orgasm."

His finger slows, then stops. He pulls away completely. "You've never had one from penetration?"

I shake my head. "I don't think I can. It takes too long. None of my exes had the patience."

The corners of Linc's lips turn down as he bobs his head slowly. I see the challenge in his eyes. *Dammit.* The blinding ecstasy from his fingers was more than satisfying. I just want to go back to when he was touching me.

"Linc, please don't."

"Don't what?"

I waggle my finger in his face. "Whatever is going through your head. I know men take it as a challenge, but I've tried before and it never works. I end up rubbed raw and sore. Then I just fake an orgasm anyway. I'm twenty-nine, I know my body by now. Trust me. Just give me your fingers again."

He lets out a low hum and for a moment I think I'm about to get my way. But then he smiles...*that wicked smile*. "Wish I could, Bambi, but that sounds like a boundary to me, and we both know you want those pushed."

I gripe in protest. "Linc—"

"What's the safe word?"

I roll my eyes, both annoyed at my admission but also intrigued to find out if Linc's the one to challenge what I know about myself. "You're going to have to do more than ask if you want me to say it."

"Good girl," he says, drawing out the syllables. He wraps his hand gently around my throat and my heartbeat begins to race. I can literally feel the power in his large hand, all he'd have to do is squeeze. He could crush my windpipe with minimal effort. Linc could end my life right now.

In a moment of panic, I push his hand away. "Sorry, I like it. I just wasn't expec—"

"Don't be sorry." He bites his lip, something hazy claiming his face. "It's sexy when you fight back. Let her out tonight."

"Who?" I ask.

He moans, his voice dropping to a low, rumbling growl. "That naughty little freak inside you who wants to come all over my cock."

My world goes blurry when his sweet breath, filled with wine and mint, is so close I can taste it. I tap my throat. "Try it again, I'm ready now."

"Later. I have another idea."

Linc grabs my hand and pulls me off the couch before leading me down a long hallway. We enter the double doors to his bedroom, which, in line with what I've already seen of his home, is minimally furnished. No matter, there's only one thing we need right now and it's King-sized, plush-looking, and neatly made up. I suspect that's about to change.

"I need to get something," Linc says, before heading toward what I'm sure is his walk-in closet. He pauses and smirks at me over his shoulder. "If you want that pretty dress to stay in one piece, you better have it off before I get back."

TWENTY-SEVEN

LINC

EDEN LOOKS ALARMED when I return with two sets of handcuffs. I hardly notice because she's down to her see-through thong and bra. A tornado could come through my bedroom and I wouldn't notice while she's in the room, almost naked, looking like *this*. I might be overestimating my self-restraint with what I'm about to suggest.

She nods to her dress that she draped neatly over my reading chair. "It's my favorite dress."

I lift one brow. "Well, it's off your body, so I guess it gets to live another day."

She doesn't laugh at my joke because she's staring at the cuffs in my hand. Looking nervous, she holds her elbows and rubs her bare feet anxiously against the wooden floor. *I'm scaring her.*

"What's wrong?"

"I said you could tie me up with something soft," she murmurs. "Those could hurt."

I strut over to her, expecting her to back away, but she plants her feet, her big honey-brown eyes are steadfast. What I've learned quickly about Eden is that a little danger turns her on. Maybe just with me, because deep down she feels safe, but the truth is, the nerves make her all kinds of wet.

She jumps at the loud clunking when I drop the cuffs by her feet. I strip my shirt off and toss it to the side. "They're not for you." Making two fists, I hold my wrists out and nod to the cuffs on the floor. She bends down and picks up one set, questions flickering in her eyes. "One set on me, and one set to cuff me to the bed."

She eyes me cautiously but proceeds to handcuff me like an expert. She even tucks her two little fingers through the metal ring to make sure I'm comfortable before stepping back to examine her work. "Do you have a key for the double lock?"

"Right pocket."

She digs in my pants pocket and finds a key ring with several little tools. Using a flat pick, she slides the bar of the double lock to the right and mumbles under her breath. "These are old school."

"You know your stuff, Bambi. Have you done this before?"

"Done what, exactly?"

I smirk. "Put the keys on the nightstand so you don't lose them." She plays my game, padding over to the nightstand and dropping the keys with a clank against the hard surface. She returns to me a little antsy.

"Now what?"

"Take off my pants."

She rips off my belt hastily, more out of nerves than anything else it seems, then yanks down my pants and briefs. *All right. I'm naked.* I was planning on drawing that out a little longer, but I carefully step out of my clothes that are bunched around my ankles and kick them to the side. I don't love being cuffed, it throws my balance off kilter, but for the moment it's necessary.

"*Ah*," I groan when I feel the most enticing warm, wet sensation at the end of my erection. I was expecting Eden to ask another question, not sink to her knees and swallow the tip of my rock-hard cock.

"Eden, wait." I reluctantly step back.

"What's wrong?"

I lie flat on the bed and roll once so I'm positioned in the middle of the mattress. She takes my unspoken cue and straddles me, the other set of cuffs in her hands. "Are you sure about this?"

"Yes."

I raise my arms above my head and she exhales deeply before clamping one cuff around the iron rail of the headboard and the other around the center chain of the pair on me. I tug in the air, making sure they're secure. "Good work, Bambi."

She narrows her eyes at me. "I'm lost. What's your game here? Do you want me to tease you or something?"

"My hands are occupied and it'd be hard to get your sweet pussy in my mouth in this position. So, I guess the only way you're coming tonight is by riding me until you're satisfied."

"Linc, it's not going to work."

I smile innocently. "I hope it does because you're not going to free me until you come on my cock, Eden. I don't care how long it takes." I jerk my hands, making the cuffs clank against the headboard. "I've got all night and then some."

"What if you don't last?" she asks with a torturously teasing smile. I pump my hips, making her ass pop off of me briefly. She squeals, then giggles.

"Don't underestimate me, baby."

Eden presses her soft lips against mine while placing her palms on both of my cheeks. She kisses me affectionately, with just a light trace of her tongue, sending an uncomfortable tremor down my back. The way she touches me is so intimate. I like it…I just need more time to get used to it, because when she looks at me, it's like she's *really* seeing me…

And I pray that she sees more good than bad.

Pressing her body against mine so I feel her firm nipples through her lace bra against my bare chest, she plants a final kiss on my cheek and whispers in my ear. "I've made a lot of mistakes in my life, Linc. Underestimating you...*underestimating us*...won't be one of them."

Eden

TWENTY-EIGHT

EDEN

STARING at Linc who is completely naked, cuffed to this massive bed, is intimidating for so many reasons. For starters, I never thought I'd look at a man's penis and wish it was a little smaller. Either because of, or in spite of, his massive dick, he really is the perfect male specimen. Every groove and ridge of his body is cut deep, showing off his toned muscles. They aren't the kind of muscles that are simply for show from hours at the gym. Linc's muscles are beautifully forged from his strength and agility.

My eyes land on his eager erection again, watching the tip begin to glisten. He must see me leering, because he suddenly says, "Don't even think about putting it in your mouth, Bambi. I'll come too fast and then good luck getting off when I'm soft."

This whole thing is ridiculous. It's not going to work and it's too much pressure.

Then again…isn't that what you asked him for? Pressure?

"I don't know where to start," I confess.

"Do you want me to tell you?"

It's not that I'm suddenly sheepish in the bedroom. It's just all moving so fast. I had a dirty dream about Linc shortly after meeting him. I woke up that night sweating, flushed, and damp between the legs. What we're doing in real life just a few weeks later is ten times more erotic than my literal dreams.

"Yes," I say firmly. "Please."

He lifts his head off the pillow to get a better visual of me. "Climb off of me and take off your panties."

Once my bare ass is on the comforter next to him, I trace my finger down the wall of his chest, rustling the scant blond chest hair. "Why this game?" I ask. "I'm going to disappoint you. It'll be awkward when it doesn't work."

He reaches for me, forgetting for a second that he's bound, making a ruckus with the metal clanking. He groans, already annoyed with his own game.

"There's no disappointing me, Bambi. You'll see. What was, can change. It'll feel different with me."

I kiss his pec before straddling him again. As I slide back down his body, I purposely rub my crease against his cock. He groans miserably, reminding me of the power I currently hold. We're both counting on me to find relief tonight.

Positioning his tip at my entrance, I wiggle a bit, coating his tip with my wetness. His arousal and mine work together as an inviting cocktail, and I slide over the first half of his erection with ease. Between the two of us there's a grunt, a groan, a plea, and a whimper. I'm not entirely sure which of us is making which noises.

I take another inch and feel the resistance. He's too much —too big. This is the worst position for his colossal proportions, but at the same time, *fuck*, does it feel good. I'm so full and tight and swollen with Linc burrowing into me that it validates his earlier sentiment—this is different. This is new.

I sink down another inch, gasping as I stretch my limits.

"Holy shit, Eden. Your pussy has a death grip. You feel so fucking good, baby. *Go slow.*"

One more inch and my eyes are watering. I feel stuffed to the brim, ready to burst, but not from pain, just from the pressure. It's already way too much, but I still want more. It's like standing in the middle of the ocean, staring below into the dark depths, unable to see a damn thing from up here. Below the surface, it could be peaceful...it could be war. I don't know. But curiosity is king...

I have to dive in.

"*Fuck,*" Linc groans as I sink down, swallowing the remainder of his dick. When the backs of my thighs land on the tops of his, I feel Linc's balls jostling against my bare ass. He's trying hard to stay still and let me run the show.

He grunts between shallow breaths. "Take your time."

"Are you okay?" I ask. My words sound garbled in my mind like I'm somewhere far away, watching this unfold.

"I'm in heaven, baby. How's my whole cock feel?"

I dig my fingers into his chest hard. My nails, manicured short and rounded, are far too tame to do any damage to his skin. "You're so big, Linc. I can feel you in my throat."

"*Good girl.* Use it, get yourself off."

Beginning slowly, I bounce on top of him with my knees on either side of his obliques that feel like they were cut from marble. For a while, it's perfect. His length and girth are beyond satiating and I enjoy myself for a long time, listening to his moans of gratitude. I get drunk off of his praise. I love the words coming out of his mouth—*you're so beautiful...so tight...such a fucking angel...you're ruining me, woman...you're mine, Eden.*

But eventually, as it always does, the chatter in my mind starts. *How much longer? If this isn't enough, nothing is. Stop thinking so much. He's bored.* My thighs start to burn and fatigue. My arousal fades. Lust is replaced by worry. What was deliciously gratifying starts to become uncomfortable as his erection drags against my walls. The last part is the worst...

Because of course Linc notices.

He's *in* the well, he can tell when it's dried up.

"Are you okay?" His eyes are open now, no longer closed in pure delight.

"I'm sorry, Linc. I told you… Just let me uncuff you. You must be so uncomfortable."

I reach for the keys on the nightstand but he growls at me, "Stop. Don't you dare touch those," he hisses before softening his tone. "Come here, kiss me."

He can't hold me, so he sucks hard on my lips, trying to keep me close. He kisses me deeply like he hasn't given up. Linc's stubborn and determined…and apparently he meant what he said that it's not over until it's over. Maybe he knows this is my Kryptonite. This is why Linc is tied up and I'm free as a bird. He knew what would motivate me more. *Pleasing him.*

"Give me your fingers," he says before opening his mouth. I pop my pointer and middle finger into his mouth and he coats them with his tongue. "Relax, sweet girl. Touch yourself."

Rising onto my knees, with his erection still lodged inside me, I drag my wet fingers across my most sensitive button. At first, I'm cringing because it feels forced. I feel too on display, but Linc starts manipulating me with his words. He tells me everything I've been longing to hear for years. He says he's wanted me from the first moment he laid eyes on me. That he's completely under my spell. He tells me he's enraptured by my body, but humbled by my heart. Who knew Linc was holding on to so many beautiful, intimate words?

All his smooth talking begins to work. I like the praise, I like the attention, I love how powerful I feel from him wanting me. Worshiping me. Needing to please me. Refusing to give up.

I start to lose my breath as I get worked up again.

"Lean back, baby, hold my knees," Linc commands. "Now just grind on it. Don't wear yourself out." He runs the entire operation like a coach, as if he knows my body better than I do. I rock on top of him instead of bouncing around, and it's far more comfortable.

"Is this good for you?"

"It's perfect, but don't worry about me. Find that spot you like."

I almost ask him what he means until I lean a little further back and he nudges me *there*. A tender spot that feels like lightning striking inside of me. I whimper when he nudges against it again and again making my legs tremble. It's an addicting sensation, one I've never felt before. It's so fucking powerful that I lose all my goddamn sense and begin grinding on Linc like I have no manners, mewling like an animal in heat.

He continues to coax me along, his sweet nothings morphing into dirty talk. What dried up is flooding now as my orgasm brews from the deepest chasms of my body. The pressure swells from a place I didn't know existed in me as I writhe on top of him, shamelessly.

"Linc, it's so good. *You feel so good.* I'm going to—"

"Not yet," he says.

"I can't help it."

"*Not yet,*" he growls this time. "I'll tell you when. Unless of course, you want to use the safe word?"

"No." But I feel myself losing control, so I try to pull off of his dick.

"Don't you dare climb off," Linc says with authority. "Breathe, baby. Like I showed you in the elevator." I sit back down, feeling his full length again. I inhale deeply, stretching my diaphragm, giving my breath some room. "That's my good girl. Slow it down. I'm not like the ones before." His jaw clenches like the thought of me with another man is repulsive to him. "I'm patient."

I barely rock my hips, letting my almost orgasm simmer, enjoying the blissful ups and downs of pleasure. I dove into the ocean, and what I found were still, peaceful waters.

It's not too long before another orgasm builds in a slow

crescendo. It's sneaky. It subtly lulled me to the point I didn't even realize my toes were curling so hard that they could snap off. "Oh my God, Linc—"

"There it is," he says, a satisfied smile on his face. "You're so fucking wet for me. Give me those lips." He lifts his head hungrily.

I lean forward to put my lips on his.

"Now ask me for what you want, Eden," he murmurs into my mouth.

"I want…" I have to inhale again to prevent my implosion. "I want… Please tell me I can come, Linc."

The satisfaction on his face is everything I need. *"Good girl.* Come hard for me."

I close my eyes right before I implode. I scream at the eruption that's so deep and debilitating that my legs go numb and my vision blurs. I fall forward, barely catching myself against Linc's chest as I tremble from the aftershocks of pleasure. This feeling is so all-encompassing, it makes me feel like I've never really come before in my life, until tonight.

I'm instantly worn. I could yank a blanket over myself right now with Linc still nestled in me and rest for the evening, but the sound of clanking metal reminds me Linc is still chained up. Willing my heavy body to move, I grab the keys and fumble with the cuff locks. Even my hands are weak. The shockwave that ripped through me stripped me of my energy.

The minute Linc's hands are free he scoops me up and flips me on the bed. He's not done. Unclasping my bra, he sucks on my tender nipples, grazing them with his teeth. I have the urge to arch my back, but I'm still too tired.

"I don't think I can come again," I murmur.

"Hush," he growls. "This part is for me." He positions himself, spreading apart my thighs. I gasp when he pummels into me. "Drove me fucking crazy how I couldn't touch you." His voice is gravelly and breathy. He grips my breasts hard, using them as handles as he ruts into me like a madman. My swollen walls grip him like they're holding on for dear life.

"*Fuuuck,*" he roars as he spills inside of me, pumping furiously until the very end, collapsing on top of me. We lay there for a while as his twitching calms. Eventually he joins me in the post-orgasmic euphoria. His bed might as well be a cloud in the sky. I've never felt so satiated, like there's nothing else in the world that matters.

He falls to the side of me, smirking, but he omits the, "*I told you so.*" Propped up by his elbow, he uses his finger to trail the space between my breasts, down my belly button, and the thin strip of trimmed hair that leads to my still sensitive clit.

I feel his cum seeping down the inside of my thighs but I stay still, unmotivated to get cleaned up at the moment. I'm comfortable here, under his embrace. I must look high off happiness, but Linc's brows are furrowed in distress. His eyes are glazed over like there's a storm brewing. It's obvious he's lost in a troublesome thought.

"What's on your mind?" Even my voice is worn and cracking.

"We're in so much trouble, Bambi." Linc's eyes lock onto mine.

"Why?"

"Vesper warned me… I'm not allowed to keep you." He touches my lips and then brushes his thumb against my cheek. "But now there's no fucking way I can let you go."

TWENTY-NINE
LINC

I WOKE UP ALONE.

In the past it would've relieved me knowing my date excused herself before I needed to ask, but this morning I was less than thrilled to be by myself, in bed. My disappointment quickly dissipated when I heard a ruckus in the kitchen—some clanking, something metal rolling around, and then Eden hissing, "Shit! *Shhhh.*" I assume she's talking to the pots and pans because no one else is here.

After the third crash, I pull myself out of bed and make my way to the kitchen. She swivels around in surprise when I enter. Eden's long hair is wavy and loose, spilling over her back and shoulders. She's wearing one of my button-down shirts, the tail covering her ass but leaving her silky thighs on display. Judging by the little pebbles poking through the shirt, she's not wearing her bra and she's removed the last remnants of her makeup.

Her hand lands on the curve of her hip. "Why are you staring at me like that?"

"This is a good look on you," I say with a smirk.

She shrugs. "I was unprepared for a sleepover. I thought

we'd be going back to my place last night. I wasn't entirely sure if you had a place, or slept upside down in a basement."

"Really? More vampire jokes this morning?"

Closing the space between us, I wrap my arms around her then trail my hands up her thighs and over her bare ass until I'm disappointed to feel the lace band of her thong. No bra, but underwear, nonetheless.

"I just mean you look comfortable here, and by comfortable I mean stunning. I want you barefoot, in my shirt, and looking this relaxed all the time."

Tilting her chin up, she finds my eyes. For a moment she stares at me, her eyes nearly glowing in satisfaction. She melts when I speak to her like this. It makes me sad when Eden drinks up my adoration like she's been dying of thirst. Who's been treating her so poorly that she doesn't expect kindness?

"I need to tell you something." She parts her lips and pauses. I'm almost expecting a declaration of love, but instead she whispers, "I borrowed your toothbrush this morning. It's a pretty invasive move, so I felt the need to fess up."

I duck down to kiss her forehead. "You've had more intimate things of mine in your mouth, Bambi. I think we'll find a way past the toothbrush."

Giggling, she spins out of my arms to attend to the pot filled that's beginning to boil noisily. Eyeing my kitchen in total disarray, it's clear Eden's been busy.

"That smells good. What is that?"

"That," she says over her shoulder, "is breakfast, that is *not* breakfast—bolognese." A timer dings and she quickly pops a pan of buttered, sliced bread into the oven. "Or are you sick of Italian food after last night?"

"Not at all," I say, sliding out a bar-height chair tucked under my kitchen island. I don't have a dining table—I don't usually have guests. I eat at this massive kitchen island that Eden has prepared a feast on. *Good, I've been in and out of town so much, the groceries would've gone to waste.* "Italian is my favorite."

"I've always wanted to go," she says, stirring the sauce on the stove with a wooden spoon. "My dad told me one time when he was in Italy, he had an affogato that was a religious experience. He told me he seriously considered going AWOL and hiding us in Italy where we could drown ourselves in espresso-soaked gelato. I mean I was twelve, so I really shouldn't have been drinking espresso anyway, but…"

I'm quiet for a moment but when she doesn't respond, I prod. "But what?"

"It was one of a million things we didn't get to do together." Eden fills a mug with freshly brewed coffee and sets it in front of me. "How do you take it?"

"Black is fine." I grab the mug by the handle and take a sip. "How long was he sick?"

"It wasn't too noticeable until the last six months. Or maybe it was for longer, and he hid it." She grabs her half-empty mug and touches her lips to the rim. With her eyes down in shame, she speaks into the cup. "Sometimes I wish I would've put off my doctorate. I don't know why I was in such a rush. I was building my portfolio and always had a big project, or an exam, or presentation. Looking back, I should've *just lived* instead of working so hard to set myself up to live. Does that make sense?"

I nod. "Seize the moment, if you will."

"Right. When I look back on the past few years of my life and think about what I've lost… I'd handle Empress just the same. But I wish I could turn back time and go with Dad to Italy and eat some damn gelato. I wish I would've read *War and Peace* and talked to him about why he likes that boring-ass book so much. I should've asked him more questions about my mom before it was too late."

"Your mother?" Eden hasn't mentioned her mother before. I assumed, like with my own mom, it was a less than pleasant memory.

"She died when I was little. I was barely two when they

279

told her she had Stage IV ovarian cancer." She shrugs quickly. "We had a little time after that…but not enough."

"Eden, this is too fucking much."

Her eyes widen, then freeze in alarm. "Sorry, I didn't mean to unload on you."

I spin in my chair and pull her between my legs. "No, sweet girl, I mean you've gone through far too much. How are you still standing? Why do you still smile all the time?"

She rolls her eyes. "I'm not that impressive, Linc. I cry in private. I have a timer…it's a whole thing." She tries to wave me off.

"Give yourself credit. I've seen people turn bad because of far less than what you've gone through." I stare into her eyes until she looks uncomfortable but I don't break my gaze. I have a question I desperately need answered—a truth that needs uncovering before we go any further. "What's the secret? Why are you so good, kind, and forgiving in the midst of this fucked up world?"

"Am I?"

"Also humble," I add. Squeezing her hip bones gently, I wait for her answer. I'm not letting go until she helps me understand the *Eden Essence*—the very reason I am obsessed with this unicorn of a human being.

"You want a lie?" she asks.

"Sure."

"It's all a cover. I'm a hardened assassin. You've met your match, Lincoln Abraham, and I've got you right where I want you."

I blink at her ridiculous statement. Although, I do feel like I've finally met my match. She just happens to be my polar opposite. "Great. Now, the truth."

"I don't know, Linc. I am who I am…who I've always been," she whispers. "If I have to choose between anger and sadness, I prefer sadness. If I have to choose between hurting and hurting someone else, the first is less burdensome to me.

I'm trying to lead by example I suppose. We should go through life being mindful of each other, not by validating our pain and insecurities by criticizing and terrorizing others. We have to stop acting like starting war is easier than starting conversations. I want to live in a world where——"

She stops abruptly, her eyes landing on her toes.

"Where what?" I ask.

"Where your job isn't necessary. Where people who don't like guns and violence...people who don't want to fight... don't have to be so goddamn scared."

Me too.

"Speaking of which," I say, hopping up to retrieve the little box I left on the TV stand. "I forgot to give you your present last night." I didn't forget, I *never* forget. I knew this present would start a conversation, and there were more pressing matters last night to attend to.

By the time I'm back, Eden has stolen my chair. I hand her the little box.

"What's this for?"

"Because you're pretty, and because I'm your sugar daddy and like to buy you nice things." *Was that sarcasm? Since when am I sarcastic?*

She rolls her eyes. "We'll call it an early birthday gift then."

"When's your birthday?"

"The fifth. So, Thursday."

I feel my brows furrow and she notices my face pull in concern. Setting the box aside, Eden peers at me quizzically. She must misunderstand my confused expression. "What's the problem, Linc? Is thirty too old for you?" She shoots me a playfully daring smile that tells me she's joking...but I should also choose my words carefully.

"I've never been a boyfriend before, let alone during a birthday. Should I... What should I do?"

"Oh." She laughs and exhales in relief. "With me, it's easy.

As my boyfriend, all you need to do is leave me alone." She scrunches her nose, trying to be adorable.

"Seriously?"

"Yes. I prefer to spend the day by myself. I already told Callen I won't be at work. In fact, he gave me Friday off as well."

"You want to be alone?" I ask and she nods in response. "On your birthday?" She nods, again. "Is it because you're...sad?"

She shakes her head emphatically, her long hair whipping both of us in the face. "Not at all. On my birthday, I don't want any obligatory surprise parties or fancy dinners I have to get dressed up for. I want to be lazy, lounge around in my underwear all day, and eat dry cereal right from the box while watching trashy reality TV. You wouldn't want to see me like that, it's not a pretty sight."

Trailing my fingers over her chest, I pop open the top button of my shirt and trace the top of her full tits. "Says you."

Snatching the box off the counter again, she shakes it playfully, as if it should rattle. She snorts in laughter when she opens the lid and sees a pink tube of lipstick. "Is this for more artwork on your dick?"

"Flip it over. Feel that button?... Two taps." She does as I instruct and flinches when the low buzzing sound of electricity surrounds us. "Anywhere will do the trick but aim for the throat if you can."

"This is a lipstick taser gun?" she asks, admiring the little device.

"Essentially, but I had it...*upgraded*."

"This won't kill someone right?" She sets it back in the box and I grab her hand, bringing her fingertips to my lips and planting soft kisses on each one.

"No." *It'll hurt like hell, though.* "This is so you can feel a little safer, without feeling less like yourself. You don't need to kill anyone, Eden." I nod toward the pink tube. "That'll slow them down until I arrive." It's hypothetical, but my jaw still clenches at the thought of anyone threatening Eden.

"You must really not want me to get a gun," she muses softly.

"I don't want you to change—not a goddamn thing about yourself. You be the light in this dark, depressing world. Let me be the big, bad wolf."

She touches my cheek, her fingertips warm and soft. "You wouldn't really kill someone because of me, right?"

"No, Precious," I murmur. Pulling her off the chair, I hoist her onto the kitchen island, wedging myself between her smooth thighs. I trail slow kisses down her neck as she moans in appreciation and instinctively spreads her legs and pushes against the growing bulge in my pants. I can't get enough of the way she smells...tastes...feels. *Fuck, I need this woman like I need air.* "If someone tried to hurt you, what I'd do is so much worse. I'd make them fucking beg for death."

Eden pulls away and her eyes grow wide. "Linc, no. I don't want—"

I swallow her protests when I cover her mouth with mine, ending all her objections with a demanding kiss. I yank the rest of the shirt buttons free, exposing her plump tits and slim waist.

"*Hush.* You're mine now, Eden."

And no one who wants to live, threatens what's mine.

THIRTY

EDEN

THE ENTIRE WEEKEND WAS A HAZE. A sexy, satiating, blur of orgasmic overload. I more than made up for my dry spell. Linc has more endurance than any man should, so when he got called away Sunday afternoon for a job, I was slightly relieved. I returned to my own apartment, took a scalding shower, and slept for twelve hours straight.

I've been in enough relationships to know to really lean into the honeymoon phase because it's fleeting. You need all the sweet memories to survive the bullshit that follows. At least with Linc, I have a lot of material. It's more than a honeymoon, it's the entire beehive and the whole fucking cosmos.

This man… I couldn't have conjured him up any better in a dream. He's thoughtful, patient, so intelligent, and so gruff exactly when I need him to be. I like him so much in fact that I'm trying very hard to ignore what he's out in the world doing at the present moment.

I don't want to know. It's easier that way.

Walking into my office on Monday, I make my way to my desk and pull out my gifted copy of *War and Peace* from the desk drawer. I return it to its rightful place on the top of my desk, front and center—my favorite souvenir.

"Knock, knock," Callen says instead of actually knocking, seeing my door, *as usual*, is wide open.

"Hey, Callen, come on in. How was your—*Oh*. Hello." I greet the woman in a smart suit trailing right behind. She's wearing a badge, identical to Callen's, but I immediately recognize the extra authority in her. It's in the way she walks—directive, with a purpose and no tolerance for distractions. She sidesteps Callen and makes her way across the office, her hand outstretched and aimed at me.

She shakes my hand firmly as she introduces herself. "Dr. Abbott, it is an absolute pleasure to meet you. I've heard so many impressive things."

I correct almost everyone who calls me "Doctor." But for some reason, I don't correct her. Maybe because she's already wildly intimidating with her thick manicured brows, angled features, and thin lips pressed firmly together that still somehow scream, "I don't have time to fuck around."

"I'm Director Mierna Ravshervesky, but that's a mouthful so everyone just calls me Ravi."

"This is my boss," Callen adds, plopping into a chair by my desk. He looks a little shrunken, like his suit is a size too big and he's playing dress up. His demeanor is docile today.

"Actually," Ravi says with a playful smile, "I'm his boss's boss." That was a blatant power move if I've ever seen one.

"It's very nice to meet you."

Use her name, it shows you're paying attention.

"Director Ravi," I continue, "Would you like to sit down?" I look at the only other movable chair in my office right in front of my computer. "It rolls, I can pull it around."

She shakes her head. "No thank you. I had a long flight and I'd prefer to stand."

"Did you just get in?" I ask, eyeing her wrinkle-free suit.

"A half hour ago. Callen has been showing me around the compound. So, you're the one who insisted on the *very expensive* in-house doctor?"

Her tone feels accusing, so I nod sheepishly.

It was justified, Eden. Speak up. Explain yourself.

"Sometimes preventative medicine can save companies in the way of insurance long term, and I just figured—"

I abruptly stop speaking when she holds up her hand. "Dr. Abbott, it was a good suggestion. Last week the doctor identified early onset cancer in one of our agents due to a mandatory physical. He has a good chance at total remission because of you."

My jaw drops. "Wow. That's incredible…um…and also a HIPAA violation, I believe?" My brows cinch in disbelief. This woman is not a killer. She's in a suit, obviously a major authority at the FBI. I'm sure her concern is more politics than logistics. She should know the rules.

"I didn't give you the agent's name," she smoothly replies. "At any rate, I like what you're doing around here and I also wanted to personally thank you for cracking Roman Broder. That little shit has been giving us problems for weeks."

"Hector," Callen clarifies for me. *Yes, I remember the informant you and Linc had tied up and tortured a couple days ago.* I have sex fatigue…not amnesia.

"How is Roman?" My overly enthusiastic tone triggers Ravi to raise her eyebrows at my nosey question. I immediately backtrack. "Sorry, I probably don't have clearance for that."

She lets out a harsh, breathy laugh. "You don't. But you also didn't have clearance to be in that interrogation room. In fact, this entire compound, including PALADIN, doesn't have clearance because it technically doesn't exist. Therefore, I don't think it's problematic to inform you that Roman Broder agreed to a plea for unlawful possession of a deadly firearm. He'll serve a minimum sentence and be offered parole with mandatory rehabilitation counseling. He was indoctrinated into a gang—apparently against his will—so prosecutors have agreed to be lenient."

I nod while closing my eyes and picturing Roman's tears when he finally gave up the address. I promised him hope and I'm so glad I didn't lie.

"Good."

The conversation is at what I feel is a natural close, but Ravi crosses her arms and very unsubtly examines me, up and down.

She's sizing you up, Eden. Stand tall. Straighten your shoulders.

"What exactly is your role here, Dr. Abbott?"

By the third time I've heard it, it's enough. "I prefer Eden, please."

"Okay, Eden—what exactly do you do?"

I look at Callen for an assist but he sits silently. "In the past, I'd help mostly tech companies in their early infancy scale by training their leadership teams and guiding them in the establishment of employee-centric corporate directives."

She narrows her eyes. "How long does that usually take?"

"Three to six months, depending on the shape of the company. I usually need a few weeks of evaluation, a few more for personnel interviews, and then I build a training program based on the information I gather. After implementation, I usually stick around for an evaluation period."

"And you've been at PALADIN for about a month now?"

"Correct...but...well PALADIN is a much smaller team, and additionally..." I trail off glancing at Callen again but he's staring at his shoes. I blow out a deep breath. "Director Ravi, I'll just be honest, I'm making this up as I go. I'm doing what I can and applying what I know, but yes... It does seem a little farfetched to complete performance evaluations on undercover assassins. So, I completely understand if you feel my salary is overly generous, but in my defense, I was *offered* this position and I'm adapting as I go. I'm open to discussion—"

"Eden." Ravi holds up both hands as if in surrender, with

a tongue-in-cheek smile. "Who do you think told Callen to offer you a job?"

"Pardon?"

Ravi clasps her hands together and the hollow clapping sound echoes off the walls. "I was in charge of the Empress case. There were so many moving pieces that dragged out over almost a year. We were so busy building an iron clad case that we foolishly overlooked the sacrifice you made. You were dealing with repercussions we weren't even aware of until long after the fact, and for that—on behalf of the entire FBI—I want to apologize. We should've done more, sooner, to make you feel safe."

My eyes widen to the point they begin to feel dry. "Thank you," I choke out.

She continues, "When I got word that you were seeking employment and couldn't find anything, I instructed Callen to create a position for you. I figured a decent salary and being under the protection of the FBI moving forward might be the first step to making amends."

Amends? Too little, too late.

But I tell my brain to shut up because I truly appreciate the sentiment. After all this time…an apology is welcome.

"Thank you," I say again. "I really do appreciate it."

"If you're interested, we could use your insight at head-quarters."

"Headquarters?" My question comes out as a squeak. Even Callen raises his eyebrows in surprise.

"Keep an eye on your email. Once this place is in order, I have some bigger fish for you to fry." She winks before tossing her head over her shoulder. "Callen, let's finish the tour. I have exactly forty minutes before I'm needed on the tarmac."

"Yes, ma'am." Callen hops out of his chair and waits until Ravi is a few paces down the hallway. He turns to me and presses his hands together in prayer and mouths, "Thank you," dramatically, before disappearing down the hallway.

A job with the actual FBI...not tucked underground and hiding all these illegalities. Fidelity, bravery and integrity are all along the things I already teach, so it wouldn't be a bad match.

I'm here supposedly to get PALADIN in line, but the joke is on Callen. I've studied enough companies to know there are kings, queens, and pawns. Right now, Callen thinks he's in control but it's only because Vesper *allows him* to think so. PALADIN is already in line and it has nothing to do with me or my so-called "magic touch."

Graceful, calculating and patient... Vesper is the king, queen, knight, and bishop of this entire operation.

Now alone in my office, I run my fingers over *War and Peace*, reflecting on Linc's words from the other night. My stomach flits at Vesper's warning to Linc, telling him not to get invested. At the present moment, I'm not worried about Empress or break-ins. I'm worried about the only woman who Linc is more loyal to than me...

Vesper doesn't need me, soon, she'll realize that. At the end of the day, when she, Linc and PALADIN are done with me, where will I go? What will I do?

Maybe Ravi's introduction is in perfect timing.

Linc

THIRTY-ONE

LINC

I FIND TOTAL DARKNESS COMFORTING. I can enjoy the silence without closing my eyes.

I took the liberty of dragging a chair into this shipping container because God knows how long it'll take before these fuckers show up to collect the contents of this oversized, dry cargo container. They are unaware that it was already unloaded a few hours ago.

I was warned there would be a handful of men coming.

Good, I'm especially angry right now. I don't mind unloading a few bullets.

It took six months of intel to intercept this illegal ship-ment. The authorities were expecting the criminal ammuni-tion. The guns, the grenades, the missiles—not remotely surprising.

The women, however, were very unexpected. Chained together like dogs, they didn't even look scared when we opened the damn door. They were past fear, well into the realm of defeat. They hung their heads, accepting their dreary fate, probably wishing for death over the harrowing sentence awaiting them when they arrived.

Some of them got their wish. Apparently the ship was

unexpectedly delayed off the coast. Of course, the ship captain wouldn't know to relieve the prisoners he had no idea he was transporting. The women had just enough food, water, and waste buckets for a four-day journey… The trip took more than eight.

This is why Vesper asked me to handle it. Anyone could've easily ambushed these assholes and put a few body bags in the ocean, but Vesper knew what this scene would do to me. She wanted a vengeance-fueled bloodbath as payment for what these poor women were put through…

And I'm here to deliver.

The women who survived were quickly tended to by trauma teams. I watched as they barely nodded or shook their heads in responses to questions that they probably didn't understand. They don't speak English, and even if they did, who the hell would be in the mood to be questioned after that ordeal? It took everything in me not to interfere with the authorities, tell them to shut the hell up, and get these women to safety. Let them wash themselves, drink some water, eat, sleep in a safe place—then ask the fucking questions in the morning.

The container was emptied at record speed, then lightly bleached to help with the smell. Afterward, I took my place inside, to wait…

And wait.

I used to enjoy the calm before the storm. My job is very calculated, and it's far more planning than action. There are long periods of calm, followed by short bursts of excitement. I can imagine what Eden assumes about the side of my life I try to hide from her. It's not nearly as eventful as she probably thinks it is. Most of my time is spent waiting and wasting time. I never used to mind…but those were the days before I had something I was eager to return home to.

I was reluctant to leave Eden behind, unable to tell her where I was going and when I'd be back. I'm not even sure if she's aware I left the state. But she's incredible that way. She didn't ask for details or whine that she'd miss me, and she didn't beg me to stay. She kissed me goodbye and told me to be safe. While she doesn't approve of what I do, she certainly seems forgiving.

Forgiving is good. With forgiveness, is hope.

I hear the low murmur of voices approaching, so I rise, abandoning my chair and positioning myself in the corner, away from the light. I don't have a visual as the loading door opens, but I count the footsteps.

"Ey, yo—it's empty. Is this the right one?" the first voice asks.

"Fucking 'course it is. The key worked right?"

Another voice. Another pair of footsteps trailing behind.

"This ain't good. Why is it fucking empty?" the first voice asks again.

"There's supposed to be three girls going to one house and five going to the other. All I see is a chair." There's one more new voice as they all stomp like idiots into the dark container, still completely unaware of my presence in the back corner. This is the difference between thugs and professionals. Never walk into a dark enclosure, especially when what you were supposed to find, is missing. To anyone with some fucking sense, this is obviously a trap.

Hand on my pistol, I almost make my move, but something in my gut tells me to wait.

Just wait.

"Who goes to who?" *There it is*—a final new voice, the last set of footsteps. I can leave no witnesses behind tonight.

"Doesn't matter, a bitch is a bitch. But it's no good if we can't find them."

I've heard enough. I inhale and hold my breath.

It's so quick.

One step forward, three pulls on the trigger, and then, by the time I exhale, the tip of my gun is pressed against the head of the only man left standing. The rest of my guests are lying motionless on the ground, beginning to bathe in their blood.

I pull down on the dangling metal chain above my head, turning on an overhead light so he can see the hot fury in my eyes. His eyes fill with fear in response as he assesses the scene of his associates dead on the ground. He's a burly piece of shit, that's for sure. His size alone would've terrified those women…but not me. All that extra weight just means he'll hit the ground harder when my bullet wedges between his eyes.

"Wait," he pleads. I recognize him as the one who delicately explained that *a bitch is a bitch.* "Stop, please. I have information."

Ah fuck. Those are the magic words. "Then speak quickly," I snarl.

"D-don't kill me," he stammers. "I'll…I'll tell you if you don't kill me."

"Tell me what?" I ask as I press my gun harder against his forehead.

"There are more… More containers are coming." He sucks his breath in short gasps. "More guns. More women."

"Sit down." I nod toward the chair. "Now."

He must be eager to live, because he's very obedient. He whimpers when he slips in a puddle of blood that's pooling from his friends. For someone who treats other people's lives so carelessly, he certainly seems horrified to see one taken away.

"Sit still," I hiss. With him shifting uncomfortably in the small chair, I'm convinced the metal legs are going to snap under his weight. "Are you armed?" I ask, more for curiosity than anything. He nods and holds his hands up in surrender.

"Left pocket. Just take it."

I snort. "Keep it for all I care. But I warn you, you're outmatched in speed and skill. You'd be dead before finishing the thought of pulling a gun on me."

"Who are you?"

"Someone curious about your information," I respond flatly, narrowing my eyes. "Now talk, before I lose interest."

PALADIN's compound is quiet today. I checked Vesper's office but it was empty. *Odd.* She told me to meet her here after I messaged her that business at the dock was handled and I was on my way home.

Just for good measure, I peek into Eden's office. The door is open like it usually is, but it's empty. It's been four days since I've seen her, and I have to wait one more. Today is her birthday, and she gave me strict instructions to leave her alone.

I resolve to head home, take a shower, get some rest, and deal with Vesper later until I hear a ruckus coming from the medical wing. I rush down the hallway and barrel through the door of the exam room.

Vesper's standing in the corner, her arms folded with a scowl on her face. Cricket sits on the exam table, one leg bent and tucked into her chest as the doctor fusses over her bleeding arm. She's sporting quite the shiner but she flashes me a big smile.

"Well, hey sunshine," she says.

"Damn Cricket," I tease. "Losing your touch?"

She barely flinches as the doctor douses her open wound with some type of antiseptic.

Scoffing, she flips me off.

"Will you stay still?" The doctor scolds Cricket. I give her a once over, somewhat curious about the woman that Eden was jealous of. *Not even a comparison, Precious.*

"What happened?" I'm not concerned... It's Cricket. She might be tougher than I am.

"I rushed a job. I did not see the arsehole with the machete behind me. It's just a scratch," she says, shrugging off

297

the deep gash in her arm. "Mom made me go to the nurse's office." She shoots a dirty look Vesper's way.

"How's the other guy look?" I ask.

Cricket beams, her smile spreading ear to ear. "He looks like a corpse."

"Atta girl."

"Hey, where's Eden by the way? She didn't show up for work today. We all figured you were out somewhere screwing."

I texted Eden when I got back into town, but the message remains undelivered. She warned me she turns her phone off on her birthday which is the only reason I didn't immediately go banging on her door, demanding proof of life.

"It's her birthday, today. She likes to spend it by herself. I'll see her tomorrow."

"What?" Cricket asks, screwing up her face and jutting her palm to the ceiling. "No, Linc. No woman wants to spend her birthday alone. Are you stupid?"

"Stay still," the doctor scolds Cricket again who grumbles in irritation.

I nod to the door, silently requesting a word with Vesper. She follows me into the hallway and I pull a key out of my pocket before dropping it in her palm.

"Tell port authority there's a clean-up in container 41B-2A."

Vesper looks worn. Her normally bright red lips look faded and her low ponytail is loose—the exhausting aftermath of babysitting her wild child for the evening. "How many dead bodies?"

"Depends."

"What?" She furrows her brows in confusion.

"Three and a prisoner if they go tonight. If they wait a few days...*four*."

"You let one go?" Vesper's eyes grow wide with anger. "You had direct instructions to clear the scene, Linc."

Rubbing my jawline, I feel the stubble softening. It's been

two days too many since I've shaved. "He had information about more shipments."

Vesper shakes her head, crossing her arms again. "What information? The FBI has been hunting the source for years. It took a tremendous amount of luck to intercept that shipment."

"What do you want me to say, Vesper?" My tone is hushed, not wanting to accidentally pique Cricket's curiosity. Like Vesper, she has ears like a bat. "I have coordinates that lead to a little village in the Sahel. The only thing left for you to decide is what you want to do about it."

She matches my steady gaze. "What do *you* want to do about it?"

Picturing the tormented women in chains, my answer is easy. "I want the head of the snake."

"It's the Sahel. The threat out there is like a Hydra. Cut off one head, there's a million more, Linc. Anyway, Africa is outside the FBI's jurisdiction. Callen won't agree to that."

"Fuck Callen. Fuck the FBI." I feel my adrenaline rise. *Don't bite the hand that feeds you, Linc.* "You've lost your way. PALADIN's jurisdiction is wherever there's bad people doing evil things. Or have you forgotten that, buried behind all your paperwork?"

Vesper's pointer finger lands an inch from my face. Her eyes grow cold and menacing. "Don't question me. You don't understand the burden I bear because I intend it that way. You aren't responsible for any of the bodies you've put in the ground, *I am.* I sic the dogs, not you. Until you're willing to wear the crown and accept that you're the cause of thousands of sons and daughters rotting six feet under, don't you dare fucking question my choices. The FBI and I—"

"You left the FBI, Vesper. Isn't that how PALADIN was established? Then, for what?" I growl, matching her combativeness.

"Not because they were bad, because they were ineffec-

299

tive!" She buries her head in her hands as soon as the words leave her lips and she hears the irony clear as day.

Pulling her hands from her face, I stare into her dark eyes. "If you were struggling, you should've come to me. You didn't have to run back to the badge."

She lets out a low hum and I can almost hear the guilt in her response. "You were only sixteen, Linc. Maybe if I'd left you alone, you would've ended up with a normal life. That's what I want for you—to find something that grounds you, so you don't end up floating away, like me. It's very lonely. There's nothing up here except—"

"Monsters and ghosts," I finish for her. The first time I heard Vesper's metaphor about how she chased monsters and ghosts, it sounded so badass to a sixteen-year-old kid. Now, it just sounds tragic.

We stand in the hallway for a while, hearing nothing but Cricket's occasional protests through the door as the doctor argues back in a low murmur.

Vesper's the one to break the silence. "I'll give Callen my strong recommendation for a visit to the Sahel. But we need more intel."

"Well then, check container 41B-2A. There's a canary in there that'll sing for you."

Vesper exhales in exasperation. "I have enough to deal with between Cricket and Lance's theatrics. Please don't become a problem child for me. Keep your jobs clean from now on."

"Yes, ma'am." I salute her mockingly before turning down the hallway, already salivating over the idea of a hot shower and a decent meal.

"Oh, and Linc," Vesper calls after me.

I throw my head back and grumble before turning around. "What?"

"Cricket's right."

"About?"

"Eden's birthday. No woman wants to spend it alone."

"But she told me—"

"I know what she told you," Vesper says, her tone condescending like she's talking to a toddler. "But I'm telling you to at least pick up a card, some flowers, and go wish her a happy birthday in person. Believe me, I'm a woman... You'll have hell to pay if you don't."

I rub the back of my neck trying to soothe the ache. "Aren't I supposed to respect her privacy? Why would she say she wants to be alone if she didn't mean it?"

"Hm... Why would a woman say what she doesn't mean? That's a question for whatever god you pray to, right after 'Why did the dinosaurs die?' and 'Do you actually exist?'"

I snort at her sarcasm, then ask in all seriousness, "Is that your way of giving me your blessing?"

Vesper purses her lips and slowly bobs her head. "I can't say I want you grounded and then rip you away from the only person that's ever made you smile like that. Just remember, if she's next to you, the target on her back will always be bigger than the one on yours."

I nod in understanding. "Bye, Vesper," I say before I turn back around and head down the hall, mentally debating where the hell I'm supposed to buy birthday cards and flowers.

THIRTY-TWO

EDEN

I GROWL AT MY STUBBORN, ancient VCR. *Please, please. Just work.*

The numerous converters I have to use to get my TV to hook up to the old-school VHS player make the floor by my entertainment center look like a snake pit. It's a hassle, but I have no choice—the video is stuck *inside* the player. I'm lucky that it still plays and rewinds, but the thing hasn't ejected for years. The VHS player stubbornly holds on to my most prized possession, knowing it has made itself completely irreplaceable. *Clever bitch.* I'll have to keep the damn thing and all its accompanying cords, forever.

I curse myself for not converting the tape long ago. This message from my mother should be preserved on the air cloud, a backup drive, and maybe copied to a USB and stored in a top-secret safe. It's by far the most valuable thing I own.

Flattening myself on my living room floor, I drop down to eye level with the VCR. I push open the video flap and send a final plea as I hit rewind on the player once more. There's a feeble clicking sound, but the tape doesn't budge.

"Fuck!" I howl.

Outside of my current technical difficulties, it's really been a birthday for the books. My phone has been off all day, tucked into some corner of my bedroom. I have a rule about not using my phone on my birthday. It really wasn't an issue for my twenty-ninth, but in the past, I'd spend my entire day crafting thank you messages to every single person and their mother who texted me a happy birthday GIF or left a funny birthday song on my voicemail. By the time I'd come up for air, my birthday was over, spent catering to everyone else but myself. *Hence, my rule.*

But last year it wasn't necessary, which I'll admit, *sucked.* No one texted, no one called. I spent the evening at the police station begging for an overnight detail after finding a threatening note on my car windshield. The police told me I was overreacting, but the note said—*Stupid bitch, you better run, hide, or die.* So, honestly, I was just following directions.

This year there are no menacing notes, just the loneliness. Which would feel a touch less lonely if this damn player would just…

"Do your job!" I growl as I get up. Doubling back, I run two fingers over the top of the player, petting it kindly and softening my tone. "I'm sorry, please don't ruin my tape. *Please.* It's all I have left of her."

Knock, knock.

Ah, sustenance is here. I'm in my underwear and a very thin t-shirt with no bra, so I call through the door to the delivery person who is bringing my dinner, "Just leave it at the door, please!" Once they're in the elevator, I'll retrieve my Chinese food like a scavenger. It's a perfect plan… Except they won't stop knocking.

Ugh. What good is contactless delivery if they *insist on contact?* Maybe they need a signature on the receipt, or maybe they want to personally thank me for the forty-percent tip. Either way, I scurry to the bedroom and pull on a cotton robe that's thick enough to cover my nipples.

Ripping open the door, I see my takeout food on the doormat, and my boyfriend with a thick bouquet of roses in one hand and a grocery bag in the other. His small smile widens into a teasing smirk when he sees me in a state of disarray.

"You're back!" I chirp. "I wasn't expecting you."

"Clearly." *That smile...* It still gives me the most delicious chills.

"You were gone for a while. Is everything okay?" I eye him up and down. Outside of the paper grocery bag and flowers in his arms, he looks much the same. He's in a black suit, with no tie. The top button of his collared shirt is undone. The smell of his soap is stronger than normal, like he just showered.

"I was out of the state," he says, avoiding any more detail. "I know you said you wanted to be alone on your birthday, so I won't bother you, I just came by to drop this off."

"What's in the bag?" I glance at the brown paper grocery bag that's damp at the bottom.

"The best gelato I could find at a Walmart—which is not great. Instant espresso. Various toppings."

Holy shit. A man who surprises you on your birthday is a winner. But a man who listens to you and remembers the little details... I don't stand a chance. I scoop up my takeout bag by the plastic handles before shaking my head at him. "Are you just perfect, then?"

He laughs. "You know about my more unsavory habits by now."

"Right now, they don't seem so bad." I hold up the bag. "This is definitely enough food for two."

"Bambi, are you inviting me to your private birthday party?"

"Unless you have plans?"

He plants a tender kiss on my lips, before squeezing by me through the door.

"I do now."

I barely poked my dinner. After Linc's arrival, I simply wasn't that hungry... Except for dessert, of course. I watch Linc compose my birthday surprise at my meager kitchen island. After spending a couple of nights at his place, my entire apartment seems doll-sized.

"So, that's it?" I ask, watching him pour the dark espresso over the scoops of chocolate gelato. He drops a few raspberries on the side and sprinkles shavings of dark chocolate on top.

"That's it," he responds, sliding the glass bowl over to me.

I take a hearty bite, and I'll admit, the combination of the piping hot espresso mixed with the melting chocolatey gelato is pleasant. I pop a dripping raspberry in my mouth—whole —to complete the experience. But it's not the religious experience my dad claimed it to be.

"I just thought it'd be more mind-blowing the way Dad talked about it." I compose another spoonful and hold it out to Linc. Like the gentleman he is, he swallows before responding. I don't think I've ever seen him speak with his mouth full.

"Your dad was referring to homemade gelato and freshly ground espresso *in Italy*. It's a little different from store-brand. All the food in Italy is superior."

"You've been?"

"Mhm."

"France?" I ask and he nods. "Greece?" He nods again. "Spain, India, Thailand?"

"Yes, to all three, Bambi. It'd be easier to tell you where I haven't been. Before PALADIN got into bed with the FBI, I spent more time out of this country than in it."

"Huh."

"What?" he asks, finding my eyes. "What's wrong?"

"Nothing. There's just still so much I don't know about you."

Taking the spoon, he stabs it into the melting gelato once more and pops another bite into his mouth. He then pulls out the remaining items from his grocery bag. A nice bottle of prosecco and a card in a cream envelope. He grabs my hand, bringing the card along and tossing it onto the coffee table before he pulls us onto my living room couch. Draping my legs over his, he rubs the arches of my feet.

"Okay, best birthday ever." I groan in appreciation at my unexpected foot massage.

"What do you want to know?"

"Hm?"

"About me. What do you want to know?"

"Linc, I don't want to pry. I understand your life needs to be as private as possible."

"But there are things you're curious about?"

My mouth falls open. "Obviously."

"Then ask." He stops the concentric circles he's drawing with his thumbs against my arches. Gazing at me with those panty-droppers he calls eyes, he elaborates. "I think the fewer secrets between us, the better. I want you to know me. As I said, I won't lie to you, so just be careful what you ask because I don't want to tell you something that will end this."

"No passes?" I ask.

"None. No conditions. No lies."

I rub my hands together wickedly and for the briefest moment, he looks nervous.

"When's your birthday? And, I mean your *actual* birthday, not what's on your fictitious driver's license."

He chuckles. "April ninth. But I really am twenty-eight."

"I believed you," I say, wiggling my toes, encouraging him to continue with the foot rub. "How come you've never been a boyfriend before?" He arches his brows, so I add, "Besides the obvious. I mean, you offered with me, so it's not impossible."

He blows out a breath slowly as he contemplates his response. "I'm not interested in having multiple women if that's what you're asking. It's simply that when I'd see a woman I'd picture how much simpler and safer her life would be without me in it, so it'd be easy to keep our interactions...*minimal.* I felt like I was doing the kinder thing. But with you..." He runs his thumb over his eyebrow, his expression straining. "I... I'm having a little trouble picturing your life without me in it. I know you think I'm being gallant by wanting to be with you, but it's actually incredibly selfish and reckless."

"Well, good," I respond and he cocks his head in confusion. "I needed something to knock you off that pedestal I put you on."

He lets out a hearty laugh. "You're something else, Bambi. Anything else you want to know?"

"How many people have you killed?" His smile immediately disappears and there's silence between us again. "You said no passes," I remind him as his grip tightens around my foot. His gaze falls to the floor and I hate the way his expression looks tormented. Suddenly the pressure on my foot hurtles past uncomfortable into outright pain.

"Linc! Ow!"

"Shit," he grunts and immediately loosens his grip as he brings my foot to his lips and plants soft kisses all over my toes. "I'm sorry. Are you okay?"

"I'm fine," I assure him. The "ow" was a warning before he accidentally snapped my foot in half. I knew Linc was very careful around me, but I didn't know he was strong enough to snap a bone when he was simply lost in thought.

"One thousand, one hundred and eighty-three...possibly eighty-four...depending on how the FBI handles a pending situation."

I am powerless to control my reaction. My eyes bulge to uncomfortable proportions. My jaw drops, and my mouth dries as I try to stomach the number. *"What the fuck?"*

Clamping his eyes shut, he grumbles, "Over the course of a decade, Bambi."

"Still! You've killed well over a thousand people?"

"Men," he says matter-of-factly. "I don't kill women."

"PALADIN doesn't deal with women criminals?"

Linc widens his eyes. "That's not a PALADIN rule, that's a personal covenant."

"That's oddly...chivalrous of you."

Linc shakes his head. "Not really. If the target's a woman, it goes to Cricket. Better they would've died at my hands. I don't play games. Cricket gets *emotional* during her jobs, and please, I beg you, don't ask. Let me leave it at that."

I don't ask further, respecting his wishes. I wriggle my toes that are still resting gingerly in his hands.

"What are the PALADIN rules?"

He hesitates, but staying true to his promise, he answers. "No family, no side jobs, and no one takes a life without Vesper's approval."

"Vesper? Don't you mean Callen?"

Linc shakes his head. "No. I mean Vesper. I don't care what Callen thinks. She's PALADIN's commanding officer and that's all I care about. Her word is everything to me. She's the only person in this world I trust."

"Oh." I don't know why that hurts my feelings. Linc's known me barely a month, why would he trust me?

"Do you still want to be the girlfriend of a monster?" he asks with a humorless laugh.

"I'm just..."

He looks at me pleadingly. His question was a joke, but he looks afraid I may have a very real answer for him. "You're what?"

"*Sad.* I'm sad that there are so many evil people in the world. I'm sad that your job is even necessary. I'm terrified that right now humanity would rather have money and war than peace and love."

"I know, me too. Except, you're sad, while I'm angry. I've been angry for a really long time." Suddenly, his expression softens, like he's enjoying warm sunshine on his face.

"But I've been less angry lately." Flashing him a goofy smile, I pretend to be bewildered and point to my chest. Chuckling, he says, "Of course because of you, Precious."

"Not too precious, Linc. I can handle it. You. PALADIN. All of it."

"Okay." He nods. "No one said you couldn't."

"I just don't want you to worry or see me as some damsel in distress. My life's been complicated lately but I'm figuring it out, or at least… I'm *capable* of figuring it out." I try to sound light-hearted, but Linc's expression flattens.

"Is that why you didn't contact me over the past few days? To prove you don't need me?"

"What?"

"I was gone for four days. I thought I'd hear from you at least once."

"Well, side-stepping the fact that you could've called me too, I was trying to help keep you safe."

"Safe? How so?"

Yanking my feet back, I sit upright, suddenly aware of how bulky my robe is. *For fuck's sake.* Linc's been looking at me like I'm gorgeous since he arrived, so I completely forgot what a train wreck I am at the moment.

"You know how Delta Force works. My dad would leave"—I snap my fingers—"like that. Most of the time without warning. My aunt would stay with me when I was too young to stay by myself. I'd worry sick that my dad might not come back and all I'd want to do is call, even if he couldn't answer. In those moments, my aunt told me the best way to keep him safe was to let him focus. My job was to be good, trustworthy, and always be where I was supposed to be, *on time*. If my dad wasn't preoccupied worrying about me, he could do his job better, and get home faster."

"This was your reasoning as a child?" Linc asks, sadness coating his face.

"I was coping, Linc. I didn't have my mom. My dad was always gone. I didn't know what to do, but I wanted to help my family. So I'd pack carrot sticks instead of cookies for lunch. I would always make sure my pigtails were neat. I was early for the school bus every day. I colored carefully in the lines...like all that could keep my dad alive."

"Oh, Bambi—you didn't stand a chance. You were always destined for HR, weren't you?" Linc clutches his chest as he laughs lightly with me.

"Point is, I don't want you watching surveillance footage of my apartment, worrying about me, and then getting yourself hurt. When you're away—doing the things we don't talk about—I don't want to be a distraction. I need you to stay safe and come back to me in one piece."

"I told you I don't watch you. The surveillance is just for review if something happens."

I crawl onto his lap, tucking my legs on either side of his hips. I give him my most serious expression. "Really? You're honestly telling me you didn't see what I did in bed this morning when I was *really* missing you?"

"No," he murmurs as he scours the part of my chest that has become visible due to my loosening robe. "What did you do, bad girl?"

The delicious swirl of excitement flurries between my thighs. Apparently calling me a *bad girl* works just as well as calling me a good girl.

"Let's just say I was all kinds of wet thinking about those handcuffs and—"

Linc sits up in a hurry, holding my back so I'm forced to straighten up with him. "Okay, I see where we're headed fast. I want to give you your birthday gift, first."

I grind against the bulge in his pants playfully, really not interested in opening presents at the moment. He grabs my hips, forcing me to sit still.

Linc reaches for the card and hands it over. "This is your present. I wanted it to be special and you don't strike me as a diamonds and purses kind of girl. So, I went with sentimental."

Now my curiosity has peaked. With a little more angst than intended, I snatch the card from his hands and rip it open. It's a pretty card. There's a beautiful basket of flowers on the front. The card's wording is a little basic—*Wishing a beautiful girl a beautiful birthday*. But that's okay, the thought is sweet. The affogato dessert is sweet. Linc knowing that I really didn't want to be alone tonight *is sweet*. This man can do no wrong in my eyes. I'll treasure this simple card, forever.

"Thank you," I say, before pecking him on the lips.

He looks disappointed. "Thank you? That's it?"

I shrug. "What? It's a nice card—"

His lips turn down. "I thought you were good with details. Who is the card from, Eden?"

I check it again, wondering if I missed the entire compound signing the back and wishing me a happy birthday. Instead, I just find one signature. "It says from Chandler Jan—"

I catch my breath as the realization hits me.

"There it is," he says, tracing my shocked expression with his finger. "There are exactly three people alive who know that Chandler Janey is my given name. Now, you're one of them. I hope that tells you how I feel about you."

All I can do is blink at him. The rest of my body is paralyzed.

Chandler.

Chandler Janey.

So, he didn't lie about his name the first time we met after all.

This is a new kind of intimacy, which means I'm nervous

all over again…but it's the good kind of nervous. The kind of nervousness that makes me realize what I have in front of me is so much more than I realized. My heart pounds demandingly like it's been called to the stage and it's time to perform.

Placing the card back on the table, I wrap both hands around his cheeks. "Thank you so much," I mumble between kisses. "For trusting me." Another kiss. "For chasing me." I use my teeth to tug on his earlobe with barely any pressure. "For wanting me, Linc."

Our soft touches change. I taste his tongue and suck in his breath as he wrenches me against his growing erection.

"Happy birthday, Precious." He cups my ass with both hands, making an audible clap. "Now you can have me however you want," he says against my ear.

The urgent neediness I feel is hard to understand. Everything with Linc has moved at warp speed, but that's what happens when you fall for a man who looks at the world through the barrel of a gun. When he leaves, I won't know when he's coming back. What he's doing while he's away—I can't ask. The danger. The unknown. It's become a temptress.

Now we're both scrambling, bumping into each other as we try to accomplish our separate agendas. He grabs at the front tie of my robe. I lunge for his belt. We only pause to kiss and press our bodies so hard against each other that it almost hurts.

"Mmm," he moans, "I missed you." He groans in delight when I find my destination and wrap my hand firmly around his cock. "Tell me you missed me too."

"I missed you," I breathe against his ear before biting his earlobe, this time with more pressure. But he's entirely unfazed. "Tell me you touched yourself while you were thinking about me this morning."

"I touched myself thinking about you *every morning* while you were away."

He lets out a satisfied grumble and pushes the robe off my

KAY COVE

shoulders. Smiling, he gently pinches my hard nipples through my top. His touch leaves me wanting—it's not enough force. I can't do gentle tonight. I'm brimming with guttural need and all I want is pressure, perhaps a touch of pain. *I just want to feel.*

"Linc," I whisper against his ear, "I have a birthday wish." I tighten my grip around his erection, my fist barely covering a third of his length.

"Whatever you want, birthday girl."

"You promise?"

"Yes," he says surely, his eyes fixated on my breasts, visible through my thin white tank top.

Holding his cheeks, I tilt his chin upward so he can see the hot flames dancing in my eyes. "Tonight, *I want the monster.* Don't hold back."

He doesn't waste time pretending like he doesn't understand. Instead, he licks his lips. "Are you sure?"

"Yes," I answer in a breathy plea.

He flashes me a wicked half-smile and I'm convinced it's the last time I'll see him smile tonight. Linc rips the tie free of my robe and holds the fabric in front of me, dangling it menacingly. I pull my hand out of his pants and hold my wrists out in surrender.

"I didn't ask you to do that," he says, his tone growing cool, sending a shiver up my spine. His eyes go glacial and I feel the tickle of nerves dotting my lower back, exactly like I wished for. He looks so dangerous at the moment, yet I feel so safe. "I haven't decided, Eden. I could tie you up with this and handle you like a toy. I could bend you over and whip your perfect ass with it. I could shove it in your mouth, so you can't beg me to come while I fuck your tight pussy in whatever way I want. So many options... *What do you want?*"

I know he can feel me trembling on his lap, coming undone from the painfully delicious anticipation. His filthy talk turns my flames up well past high. I'm about to boil over.

"I want all of it," I whisper.

"Good girl."

Linc scoops me up, hoists me over his shoulder, and carries me to my bedroom. He sets me down and pulls my tank top over my head. He rips my panties off with minimal effort, the sound of fabric tearing turning me on even more. After tossing the cotton scraps aside he pushes me so hard onto the plush bed that I bounce like a skipping stone right into the middle.

He pounces on top of me, pinning me down under his thighs. Hovering over me, he takes in my nakedness as he slowly unbuttons his shirt.

"What's the safe word, Eden? I want to hear you say it."

I narrow my eyes and shoot him a defiant look. "Then you'll have to make me."

Linc

THIRTY-THREE

LINC

SMACK!

Eden squeals so loud, I have to reach around her body and cover her mouth. Hunching over so my chest presses against her naked back, I growl in her ear, "Hush, Bambi. You have neighbors above you and below."

"I don't care," she pants out.

I smack her other ass cheek and this time her cry is muffled against my hand. "Do as I say," I whisper in her ear.

I actually love to hear her scream as I spank her ass and drive her to the brink with just my fingers playing in her tight, wet pussy, but the way she's screaming, someone's going to think I'm hurting her.

Bunching up the tie of her robe, I hold it to her mouth and she immediately clamps down with her teeth. "There you go," I say. This time it's a wet smack between her thighs, and she whimpers into the cloth when my fingers contact her clit. "Too much? Say the word."

She spits out the gag. "What word?"

"You know the word, baby," I say with a smile on my face because I know without a doubt, Eden's not even close to calling, "*Whistleblower.*"

"*Oh, that word,*" she moans. "Again."

"Stubborn girl," I say as I smack her pussy again, this time I follow up by slipping my finger into her dripping slit. Throwing her hips backward, she tries to pull me deeper. She's unsatisfied, so I give her another finger and fuck her with my hand with primal aggression. I can feel her walls clenching around my fingers trying to hold them tightly in place.

"I'm so close... *Please.*"

There it is—my favorite part. I could take or leave the spanking and the angsty fucking, but the begging gets me. *Fuck, I love her begging for me.* Her pleasure is mine now. It comes from me—*only me. Only when I give the command.*

Facing her headboard on her hands and knees, she can't see me shake my head. Her overflowing arousal causes a squelching sound as I rip my hand away. "Not yet."

"Liiiiinc," she whines as she slams her fist against the mattress.

Grabbing her by the hips, I flip her over and spread her thighs, allowing my tip to slide across her swollen clit. Sick of the teasing, she tries to grab my cock but I'm too quick. I grab her wrists in one hand and pin them over her head before dragging my tongue all the way from her neck, over her left tit and nipple, down the divot in her abdomen. "All you have to do is say the safe word and I'll make you explode." I blow on the wet trail I left, enjoying how she shudders.

She brushes her hair out of her face. Her long hair is wild and frayed, damp from sweat. I'm really impressed, for nearly an hour now, Eden's let me drive her to the edge and dangle there. She's a feisty little thing, forfeiting her relief because she refuses to throw in the towel. She's stronger than I am. If the roles were reversed, I'd be bellowing "whistleblower" at the top of my lungs while drenching her chest with my cum.

She shakes her head at me with a sexy smile, but I know I'm slowly wearing her down. Releasing her wrists and hooking my hands under her knees, I push her hips up so I can wedge my tongue between her ass cheeks and drag my saliva all the way to her clit. I suck on her little button until she's writhing like she's in agony.

"Just say it. Say the word and you can come all over my tongue, baby."

"I don't need the safe word," she wails. "Just your permission."

Trailing kisses up her belly, then nibbling at her nipples one at a time, I finally make it to her lips. I stare at her, my eyes level with hers.

"Why are we doing this, Eden? Why do you like when men are rough and controlling with you?"

Wrapping her small hand around the back of my neck, she pulls me closer. "Not men, just you."

"Why?"

"Am I safe with you?"

"Of course you are." I stroke the top of her hair with a tender touch. "I wouldn't just kill for you, Precious, I'd die for you too."

Grabbing my hand, she places it against her chest so I can feel the rough thuds of her heartbeat. "That's why. Because it's easy to be brave when I feel safe." She bridges her hips so I feel her wetness along my length. "Now, I'm not saying the safe word. But I want to come, so tell me what you want in exchange."

She tries to wedge her hand between our sweaty sandwiched bodies, headed for my cock again, but I stop her. I pull her hand to my chest so she can feel that our hearts are beating the same way—wild and erratic. She's still as I stare into her glossy brown eyes, feeling a medley of emotions that shouldn't mix together.

Rage-inducing jealousy over every man who had her before me.

A possessive ache for her to fully belong to me.

A desperate need to come already, and yet, a more urgent need to please her first.

"Eden, the closer we get, the more you'll learn about me. I want to know that when you see the worst in me, you're not going to run. I want you to stay with me." *Kiss.* "Let me keep you safe." *Kiss.* "Miss me when I'm gone." *Kiss.* "Need me."

She dodges my next kiss, her wide eyes unblinking. "Are you asking me to fall in love with you, Linc?"

"Maybe," I admit, as the vulnerability washes over me like a blanket of worries. *Is that what this feeling is? Love?* This woman has no idea the power she holds because I'm completely at her mercy.

She shakes her head against the pillow and it tears me apart. I wish I could say that her flawless naked body, at my beck and call, is enough to satiate my craving. But it's not. *Fuck.* Honestly? For the first time in my life, I wanted a woman's heart too.

But what did I expect? I don't have a heart to give her. How can I ask for hers?

"Okay, turn over," I say, dead set on fucking her from behind until she finds her release. But instead of following instructions obediently as she's done for the past hour, she grabs my cheeks and forces me to look at her again.

"You're a terrible negotiator." Her honey-sweet tone does not match the urgent clamp she has around my jaw. I'm beginning to understand why she likes it rough. Her demanding grip causes my cock to twitch against her belly. "Why ask for what you already have?"

I'm lost for words as I study every inch of her face, trying to memorize this moment. Either Eden is my reward for a life dedicated to a worthy crusade. Or she is my punishment for a life of killing—just a teasing taste to show me what I turned my back on all those years ago. I can't explain why suddenly a normal life next to this woman who is the most luminous light, seems far more heroic than chasing monsters in the shadows.

"I think I—"

"Shh, Linc." She strokes my cheek. "Don't rush it. We have time. Right now, just fuck me and make me feel good. You're the only one who's ever done it right."

Scooping the underside of her knee, I trap her bent leg against my forearm, putting her pink, needy, dripping-for-me pussy on display. I can't help but stare at the perfection. She closes her eyes, scrunching her face like she's uncomfortable.

"What's wrong?"

"Nothing." But she tries to close her legs as her cheeks redden with embarrassment.

I smile as I use the pointer and middle finger of my free hand to spread her crease. She melts in mortification over the attention. "Eden, don't be embarrassed. They should write poetry and ballads about your pussy. It is the fucking most beautiful thing in the world. It feels…" I blow out a breath and pinch my eyes shut like I'm lost for words as I try to describe the eighth wonder of the world to a blind man. "*Perfect* doesn't do it justice, baby."

Maneuvering my hips, I position my cock and nudge against her entrance, letting the slickness from her crease coat me. She's so wet. *For me. All for me.*

"It's almost a shame no man besides me will ever get to feel this pussy again."

She screams as I plunge into her and this time I don't stop her. *Sing for me.* With her pinned in this position, I know I'm in so deep, bumping against that place that makes her go feral. A few thrusts and I feel her clenching again so I hold my hand up against her throat.

"Is this what you want?"

She's gasping too hard to respond with words, so she nods eagerly instead.

"Show me your hands," I command and she wiggles her fingers in the air. "What do you do if it gets to be too much and you can't talk?"

"Tap your arm."

"Good girl." I wrap my hand around her throat firmly but not with near enough pressure to actually starve her of air. She knows the rules, I won't cause her pain but I'll play all her kinky games for fun.

I bury into her with uncontrollable, animalistic need until her thighs begin to tremble. "Eden you're mine." I pump my hips harder. *"Say it."*

She continues to gasp and pant but ignores me, so I pull out and let go of her throat.

"No. What are you doing? *Don't stop,"* she whines as she arches her back and bridges her hips, trying to guide me back in.

"You want my dick?"

She narrows her eyes as she nods at me. "Yes."

"Then say you're mine now. *Only mine."*

She quickly snatches up my cock in her fist and pulls me back toward her entrance. "I've always been yours, Linc. Since the day we met. Now, it's *my* birthday so *fuck me."*

"I want to hear it when you come," I growl. Freeing her leg, I wrap my arms around her back, entangling her before I drive us both into the mattress until I feel her toes curl as she wraps her legs around my waist. She screams, obediently. It's an ear-splitting, glass-shattering wail as she explodes for me. After a few moments of riding the wild waves of her orgasm, I feel the familiar storm in my balls brew to fruition. I groan as I empty into her.

There's no space between our bodies. We're glued together with tears, sweat, and cum, feeling every twitch, jerk, spasm, and then, finally, the deep breaths of relief.

I roll us over to the side, our stomachs still locked together. I grab a handful of her fleshy ass as I kiss her hot, cherry-red lips—she's wearing that lipstick that I like.

"How was that? Birthday worthy?"

"Beyond worthy. By far the best I've ever had," she says,

pairing it with a low hum of satisfaction. "In fact, you earned this."

I nuzzle the tip of her nose with mine. "Earned what, Precious?"

She flashes me a teasing smile, trying hard to hold back her laughter.

"Good boy."

THIRTY-FOUR

EDEN

A SLEEPY-LOOKING Linc joins me in the kitchen well past sunrise. I smile to myself, knowing I wore him out last night—hardly letting him sleep. I am a greedy girlfriend indeed.

"Good morning, you." I blow him a kiss that's pointless because it takes him about two seconds to cross my tiny kitchen and wrap me in his arms.

"I borrowed your toothbrush," he says playfully.

"You monster." I try to keep a straight face but fail. Chuckling, I continue, "Maybe… I could keep a toothbrush at your place…and you could keep one at mine?" I eye his ensemble. He's wearing his collared shirt from the night before, halfway buttoned up, and his suit pants. "And possibly some comfy clothes," I add.

Linc kisses my forehead before fetching a mug from my cabinet. "Or you could just move in with me," he says over his shoulder.

"*What?*" My high-pitched shriek makes him turn around.

"What?" he asks, bewildered. "We're spending every night together anyway."

"Yeah…but…it's…I…"

I rack my brain trying to come up with a better excuse for my dramatic reaction. Pinching the bridge of my nose, I remind myself that Linc has never been in a relationship before. Calling me his girlfriend is probably equivalent to taking a blood oath in his eyes. I may need to walk him through this.

"In a normal relationship, you date for a long time, get to know each other, and then, just when things are going great, you fight about something really stupid and break up. You spend a couple of weeks apart, heartbroken, and when you realize that nothing is more important than the two of you being together, you ditch all your problems, make up, declare your love, and *then* you take the plunge, move in together, and live happily ever after."

It's incredibly bizarre how Linc's eyes are locked on me as he pours coffee into his mug. I'm convinced it'll spill over, but even without looking, he knows exactly when to stop. "Isn't that a lot of extra steps to get to the same result?"

"Well, yes," I say, sipping from my mug. "But—"

"And don't you get to know someone by spending *more* time with them?"

"Technically." I draw out the syllables, suspecting that I'm headed into a trap.

"Do you want to date other people?" he asks.

"No."

"Do you feel like you can talk to me?"

"Yes."

"Is the sex up to your standards?"

I scowl. "Exceeds expectations." *Aka exceeds my wildest, dirtiest dreams.*

"Mhm, okay." He lifts his brows, a knowing smirk taking over his face. "Do you like sleeping next to me, and waking up with me around?" I nod in annoyance, seeing where he's going with this. "And you feel safer when I'm with you?"

"*Yes,*" I grumble.

"Hm." He shrugs casually before taking a sip of his black coffee. "Well then, you're right. Moving in together sounds ludicrous."

I glower at him. "This glib side of you is new. Where's all the brooding?"

Linc winks at me, with a cheeky smile. "Something last night must've put me in a good mood," he says over his shoulder as he settles into my couch.

Me...living with Linc. *Is that so crazy?* I try to remember when I would begin to think about moving in with past boyfriends, but the funny thing is, at the moment I can't even remember their names. Linc's cast such a huge shadow over every man I've ever been with, I guess I'm officially in uncharted territory. It's not like I have any friends or family left to tell me I'm being crazy and moving too fast. And even if I did... Would I listen?

"What's this?" Linc points to the coils of cables and the silver VHS player lying on my living room floor.

"My old VCR."

"I see that, Bambi. Isn't a VCR a little old school?"

"I was trying to watch an old movie for my birthday, but my tape is stuck and it won't play."

"Ah," he says, setting down his coffee mug on the table and sitting on the floor amidst the cords. Linc may have a unique job but he's still a man, nonetheless. A broken electronic is basically a siren's call, singing *fix me, fix me.* "Is this a dirty birthday movie?" He glances at me with a grin.

"The furthest from it," I reply. "I watch it every year. It's a video my mom made for me before she died. I was only two when she recorded it. She knew when I grew up, I'd like to know more about her. She spends an hour on the tape just telling me about all her favorite things, about my grandparents, how she met my dad. She apologizes that she was too sick and couldn't be here. That's why I like to be alone on my birthday... I spend it with my mom."

"If I would've known, I wouldn't have—"

"*No.*" I nearly shout from the kitchen, again—unnecessarily. My kitchen and living room are basically one open space. "I am so glad you surprised me yesterday. And anyway, the tape has been stuck for about four years, but this is the first year it wouldn't even play. Had you not shown up, I would've truly been by myself."

Linc balls up a fist and I see everything play out in slow motion. "Usually these just need a good pound when they get stuck." His words come out garbled as I slam my mug on the counter.

"*Linc! Wait!* That's my only copy—"

His fist lands with a hard thud on top of the player and my heart stops. The VCR whirs and grumbles to life. The obnoxious clicking and clanking inside the machine makes my stomach churn. *Oh no.* I picture the tape tangling and unraveling inside the out-of-date VHS player, my only memory of my mom, being ripped to shreds. Goosebumps bubble to the surface of my skin and I bury my face in my hands to hide my look of horror. I know it's not Linc's fault, but *fuck! Why?*

Why do men always think the solution is to slam their fists into things? I could've had it carefully disassembled by a professional and saved my only remaining memory—

"Bambi?"

I peek between my hands to see Linc standing right in front of me, holding out a fully intact VHS tape. "It's rewound." He kisses my cheek nonchalantly before he makes his way to the coffee pot to refill his cup.

I stand, mouth ajar, but speechless as I hold the tape tightly against my chest. It's the first time I've touched it in nearly half a decade.

"If it's that important, maybe you should make a backup,"

Linc says. "The compound has a digital lab that could convert that in a heartbeat. Do you want my help?"

His question sinks to the bottom of my heart. Linc is completely unaware of its weight. It's been the longest year of my life. I don't have my mom, my dad, or my dog. I learned that my friends were all fair-weather, and not even a doctorate in business could give me job security. All I've known for so long is anxiety, stress, and betrayal. I've made peace with being alone. I'm learning to make peace with fear. But now... Am I ready for it to change? *Do I want his help?* I know how to convert a VHS tape and I would've, long ago, if I could've freed the damn thing myself.

I turn around to see Linc handing me a paper towel to wipe up where my coffee spilled on the clean white granite. His light blue eyes are gleaming, so sweet and tender.

The killer has the kindest eyes when he looks at me.

I nod. "I'd love your help."

"Okay, then. I'll get it done." When I don't move fast enough in taking the paper towel, Linc proceeds to clean up my coffee spill on his own accord.

"Hey, Linc?"

"Yes?"

"Um...maybe you can also help me move some clothes, and my pillow, and my toothbrush to your place, for a little while... Just to see?"

He smiles, pulling me against his muscular chest. "Maybe some shoes, too."

"Good thinking." With a sly smile on my face, I add, "And maybe we go shopping for some breakfast foods, just for my benefit? I promise I won't force cereal on you."

He laughs. "Actually, cereal and oatmeal I'm okay with. The diner never served those."

"And fruit?"

"I like fruit. Look at us—already more in common than

we thought." He swats my ass playfully on his way to the trash can.

Holy shit. Did I just agree to move in with Linc? I don't even—

Pound! Pound!

Two loud knocks at my front door makes me jump.

"Did you order breakfast?" Linc asks me. When I shake my head, his face flattens. "Are you expecting anyone?" When I shake my head again, his eyes narrow. "Stay here," he commands, before he heads to the front door.

After a short silent pause, I hear my front door open and close, and Linc returns to the kitchen with Vesper in tow.

"Good morning, Eden."

Looking at Vesper's neat ensemble—her navy pantsuit, slick ponytail and subtle, yet clean makeup, I immediately feel embarrassed at the sloppy, just-rolled-out-of-bed-after-a-marathon-of-sex look I'm sporting. I hastily smooth my loose hair and tuck it behind my ears.

"Good morning, Vesper."

"Please pardon me, I didn't mean to interrupt. I figured Linc would be here. We have a work emergency."

I almost ask her why she knows where *here* is, but how stupid of me to assume that the real commander of PALADIN doesn't know exactly where we all sleep, eat…and fuck. Vesper has an ethereal, all-knowing presence.

"Do you guys want a private word?" Not that I can really oblige. My apartment is quaint. The only way they are getting a truly private word is if I shut the bathroom door, turn on the shower full force, and blast some music.

"No need, and no time," Vesper says calmly. She turns to Linc. "Your coordinates panned out, we've got your guy. We found out a private jet was chartered right after the shipment was intercepted."

"Mhm," Linc says, understanding the context I clearly don't. "I bet he wants to know what happened to over a million dollars worth of ammo and other"—Linc eyes dart quickly in my direction—"*valuables.*"

"I'm assuming he thinks he's being toyed with. He's coming into town to deal with the arms dealers himself. There's no better way to send a message than a bloodbath. Money's gone, meaning—"

"Someone has to pay," Linc finishes for Vesper.

"Right."

It's uncomfortable how they continue to talk shop as if I'm not even in the room. I down half my mug of coffee just to have something to do.

"If he has no idea he's being watched and now he's crossing country borders, why wouldn't the FBI just arrest him?"

"They intend to," Vesper says, giving Linc a knowing look. "But you asked for the head of the snake—I'm giving it to you on a silver platter. We need to go, *now.* Oh, and we're driving. If we board a flight, Callen will know you're headed back to New York and he'll intervene."

Linc wraps his arm around my shoulder and roughly yanks me into his chest. "I'm sorry, I have to take a quick trip." He adds in a whisper against my ear, "When I get back, we'll move your pillows, okay?"

"Okay."

"Bye, Bambi." Linc presses his lips against mine, distract-edly. He's saying goodbye, but his mind is already long gone, thinking about…*work.*

"Goodbye, Eden. We'll be back soon," Vesper adds politely.

I hold my palm in the air in a stoic wave.

"Drive safe," I say, immediately wishing I could suck the words back in. *Damn, that sounded stupid.* But what's the alternative? *Don't die!*

The front door shuts with a loud bang. I'm suddenly alone and very aware of how quickly my boyfriend jumped at the command of another woman. I thought this weekend would be full of all the cliché couple crap I've been craving. Linc *just* got back and now he's gone again. It seems life with Linc is very similar to the lifestyle I had growing up. My dad was gone constantly at the drop of a hat with no explanation— Linc is much the same. The only question is whether or not that means I'm well-prepared for this relationship...or if this is my early red flag to go running in the opposite direction.

Linc

THIRTY-FIVE

LINC

WITH PERFECT TIMING, Eden texts me right before I have to shut my phone off. We're close to the tarmac and expecting the flight to land in less than ten minutes. We can't risk giving off any accidental signals that will tip off our target.

EDEN

Here's your peace of mind text. And in case you're wondering...

I miss you.

ME

Are your pigtails in order?

EDEN

Neat and tidy. Don't you worry about a thing.

ME

Good. Now all we need is a naughty schoolgirl skirt.

EDEN

Oh, Professor! That can be arranged.

I laugh out loud and try to cover it with a cough when Vesper shoots me a disapproving look from the passenger seat.

ME

I have to go. Miss you more.

I'll admit the text is out of character for me but I've never been the type to care about anyone's opinion of me, which is ideal because I don't know how to justify over a thousand dead bodies in the ground. That number will continue to grow. The worst of humanity is becoming braver, more prevalent, and far more stupid. *Easy targets.* They're so motivated by blind hate and power trips that they're getting careless about who might be watching to deliver their swift justice…in the form of death.

Humans. We will, without a doubt, be the cause of our own extinction… It's just a matter of when. I used to hope it'd be in my lifetime so I could watch the flames as I walked right through them. But since Eden came into the picture, I'm a little less motivated to face my own end.

EDEN

Be safe.

Normally my departing commands are along the lines of, *"keep it clean,"* and, *"no witnesses." Be safe* is a much sweeter send-off.

Vesper and I both shut off our phones and tuck them into the glove box. "They're stalling," Vesper huffs in annoyance. "If they take much longer I'll have to switch to a night vision scope."

I snort. "Cataracts getting to you, Grandma?"

She punches me in the thigh, hard. *Shit!* Vesper is under five-foot-seven and can't weigh more than a buck twenty-five, so sometimes I forget how fucking unnaturally strong she is. "You're not *that* far behind me buddy." Age-wise Vesper isn't old enough to be my mom. But based on how haunted she is, she might as well have lived a hundred lifetimes. I know who Lance and Cricket were before PALADIN. I still don't know what motivated Vesper to become a killer.

I never asked.

She never offered.

Vesper taps the side of her assault rifle, a subtle tell of her nerves. Nobody else in the world would notice except me. I clear my throat, breaking the silence between us.

"Do you miss the field? Callen keeps you stuck behind that desk."

"He likes to keep his captains well behind the front lines. Callen's ex-military, did you know that? Navy SEAL."

"Why the hell is he working for the FBI?"

"He took a slug in the gut during a Black Ops mission. He won't talk about it, but they med-boarded him. I guess he missed the action and joined the FBI."

Letting out a snarky laugh, I raise my brow at Vesper. "Action and FBI?"

"Listen cocky-ass, I saw some shit during my time with the FBI. You underestimate the agents. You speak to Cricket and Lance, but no one else. They're all afraid of you, Linc. PALADIN under the FBI's direction was supposed to help unify us."

Turning my head, I glance at her with wide eyes. "Unify us? They're glorified cops. If our targets weren't on their most wanted list, they'd be hunting *us*, Vesper. What unity?"

Running her hand up and down the rifle's barrel, she closes her eyes. "There's a difference between a soldier and a killer."

I grumble, "I wonder if that defense would hold up in court."

She laughs. "Fair point."

"What's with your guilty conscience lately? You've been at this for how many years? Why Callen? Why now?"

She reaches across the console and holds my shoulder.

"Because you're all grown up now, and I'm starting to see what I created. What I took from you…from all of you. I thought I was saving you when I—"

"You did," I growl, unwilling to hear her spinning this ridiculous narrative of how I would've been better off without her.

"You could've had a different life. I should've given you a college scholarship instead of a .22. Maybe you could've become an FBI agent the right way."

I cover her hand on my shoulder and pat it tenderly. "Don't insult me, Vesper."

She snorts in laughter as we hear the roar of the jet nearing the runway. I nod at her rifle. "You sure you don't want me to hang back for support?"

"Don't forget who taught you how to shoot. I could hit my marks blindfolded. Now grab your hat."

The plan is more comical than anything else. We commandeered the chauffeur's vehicle to get access to the tarmac. After ridding ourselves of the driver and his security, Vesper insisted I keep the hat as a disguise. Really, she just wanted to see me in a stupid-ass chauffeur's hat. Eden is constantly reminding everyone to find a way to laugh at work. I'll probably omit sharing this particular joke seeing as the warlord's driver is growing cold in the trunk as we speak.

Once the plane touches down, the stairs drop almost immediately and an assembly line of armed thugs begin shuffling out of the plane. Vesper rolls her window down barely an inch. Just enough for the barrel of her gun to poke through.

I shout a greeting as a distraction when I open my driver's side door. Waving as I cross the pavement, I hustle towards the plane as if I'm here to eagerly welcome them. By the time they recognize I'm not who they're expecting, it's far too late.

Pop, pop, pop, pop.

I slow my pace and watch the men fall one by one off the stairs, dropping from alternating sides like a synchronized dance. Plummeting to the pavement, they begin to stain the clean ground red. I'm at the bottom of the stairs when a man in a tan suit with a rifle strapped around his back pauses in terror. He opens his mouth to shout a warning, but I don't bother reaching for my pistol.

Wait for it.

I can sense the bullet whizzing above my shoulder before it buries into the center of his forehead. I step aside on the stairs so he can topple down. Tapping my earpiece, I speak to Vesper. "A little close for comfort."

She ignores me. "Be quick about it," Vesper says. "But I'd like a confession."

"Are you asking me to play with my food?" I mutter under my breath as I take the stairs quickly.

"Don't touch the pilot. He thought he was moving an ambassador—his jet was hijacked."

If Vesper's command wasn't enough, when I look left, I see a man in the cockpit in a pilot's uniform with his hands tied and duct tape around his mouth. His eyes look bloodshot and he's sporting a shiner on his left cheek. I shut the door to the cockpit after assuring him rescue is on the way.

When I turn my attention to the back of the luxury jet, I find my target. The arrogant piece of shit in a tan suit with his hands in the air and a cocky smile on his face. It becomes instantly apparent that he's not a local of Africa.

"You're American?" I ask.

"Are you surprised?" he responds clearly, with no trace of an accent. He speaks calmly even though there are sweat beads dripping down his bald head.

"So, you're not a terrorist, you're just a corrupted fuck who takes advantage of a war-torn region?"

I slide into the captain's chair opposite of him with my pistol pointed at his head. The smell of his overbearing cologne makes me nauseous as I eye the gold rings around his hands that match his gold teeth. Even if he wasn't a vile excuse of a human being I think I'd hate him.

I watch his eyes dart down to his weapon.

"Oh *please* reach for it," I snarl, nodding toward his gun sitting on the table between us. "Give me an excuse to put a hole in your head right now."

Keeping his hands in the air, he snickers. "Take it. There's no need for such theatrics." After sliding his gun off the table, I remove the bullets in front of him so he can watch them fall on the carpeted floor.

"How many of my men are dead?" he asks with a cruel smirk.

"All of them."

"The pilot's not with me," he explains.

"We're aware."

"I'm going to put my arms down now because they are tired," he says, far too calmly, "but you're free to check my pockets."

"I'm not concerned. One flinch in the wrong direction and this interview is over."

"Interview? I'm flattered." He chuckles like he's unworried for his life. *Foolish.* But I'll admit, I'm annoyed. I wanted terror. I wanted to do to him what he did to all those innocent women, but this asshole seems oddly comfortable staring down the barrel of the gun…as if it's a dance he knows well.

"Let's talk. You're FBI or DIA?"

"I'm just a man who can't fathom how you could chain up human beings like dogs in a crate, and leave them to die."

He shrugs. "It was not my intention for them to die. That was a…shipping mishap."

"But you were okay with the chains?"

Watching his smug smile, it takes everything within me not to drop my gun and finish the job with a pocketknife, so I can hear him howl in agony.

"They were a *precaution.* Listen, I'm not the villain. They

340

were headed to a better life. Do you know where they come from? America is the dreamland."

"Sexual slavery is your understanding of *the dreamland?*"

"Not slavery," he balks before tutting his tongue. "There's food, protection, a roof over their heads, and wages. I *help* people—"

My anger takes over and suddenly I'm standing, the tip of my gun touching his lips. "Keep giving me reasons to make this incredibly messy," I threaten. For the first time, I see fear flicker in his eyes.

His arms are immediately in the air again. Leaning back, so his lips have a little room to move, he begins to plead. *There it is.* This is what I'm here for. Go ahead and beg for something I can't give you. *Mercy.*

"What do you want?" he asks. "I'm no stranger to negotiation. Whatever you want. *Name it.* I have money, information, and connections."

I lower my gun and take a step back as he continues to speak. He relaxes now that he has my attention.

"What're they paying you to do this, hm? Surely not enough. I can get you more. Help me, and I'll more than help you. Whatever you want, full discretion, I can be very generous." His tone drops to a warm tenor, like he's conducting a sales pitch and I'm already interested in purchasing.

His lips keep moving but all I can picture are the victim's eyes. So full of defeat, like they'd seen the devil and they'd never be the same. *And this?* This sniveling, pathetic piece of shit was the source? I wonder if Eden could look at this man and show mercy.

"Do you have what you need?" I ask and Vesper responds with a quick "yes" in my earpiece.

"What do *I* need?" he responds, thinking I was speaking to him. "I don't require much—just my life. And stay out of my way, that's all. In exchange, I'm capable of granting you more than you could ever dream of. I've been doing this a very long time and I know by now that every cop has a price."

"Here's the problem," I say, letting out a deep breath. "I'm no cop." He furrows his brows in confusion. "And all I want is for you to stop breathing."

Without another word, I raise my pistol and pull the trigger. Standing this close, I catch the back spray of blood on my jaw and neck. He slumps, then falls out of his chair with a heavy thud.

I can't help but feel disappointed. I normally take pride in a clean execution, but the monster in me wanted him to suffer.

To really suffer.

THIRTY-SIX

EDEN

THE DAY after Linc's abrupt departure, I asked Callen to meet me for breakfast. Watching him eat waffles is like watching a hippo smash a whole watermelon in its jaws… It's not graceful. He's eating like it's a competition and the clock is ticking down.

"Callen do you always eat like you're——"

"Starving?" he asks with his mouth full.

I cringe. What's worse, is this time we're not at a backwoods diner on the outskirts of town. This is a fancy brunch restaurant, the kind where they lay a cloth napkin in your lap.

"Sorry," he mumbles. "My wife used to complain about it all the time. Residuals from the military. I'm used to eating in a hurry."

"You're married?"

"Sorry—ex-wife. We were married *very* briefly," he grumbles, wiping his mouth with the napkin.

"Good to know," I say, sipping my second blood orange mimosa. These things are so tasty, I'm relieved my apartment is within walking distance from this downtown restaurant.

"Why is that good to know? Is this supposed to be a date that you've asked me on?"

345

I raise my brows at him. "Seriously? A date? Would you like Linc to *actually* break your hand this time?" *Or worse.* I don't get the impression Linc would be comfortable with me dating anyone else behind his back. I also don't think I'd be the one to pay the consequences.

Callen chuckles before taking a long sip from his orange juice. "I'm kidding, Eden. I'm almost ten years your senior. I didn't think you were asking me out. But since we're on the subject, to what do I owe the pleasure of your company this lovely Saturday morning?"

"Ah, yes—well, Director Ravi emailed me like she said she would," I explain.

"I'm not surprised. She's one to follow through with her word."

"She offered me an interview. Something akin to an organizational strategist...at Pennsylvania Avenue."

"I see," Callen says, folding his arms and leaning back in his chair. "You'd get a badge and everything." There's something peculiar about his expression.

"What's that look for? Tell me, what's your honest impression of her?"

He shrugs noncommittally. "She's a very powerful person."

"Callen." I flatten a stare. "Come on. I'm asking you as a friend. I'd be working for her, directly. What's she like as a boss? As a person?"

He lets out an exasperated breath. "She's got better stats than anyone in the bureau. She's a legend. The first in the office, the last to leave. Nobody is dedicated like Ravi is. She's a tough boss, but you can learn a lot."

"And as a person?"

He pops his empty fork back into his mouth and shrugs. "She's a mean bitch. I avoid her like the plague."

I cross my arms and scowl. "Whenever a woman holds a

powerful position and has expectations for her subordinates, she's always marked as a bitch. It's not right."

"I agree, it's not right. But this isn't sexism. There are plenty of respectable women in the FBI who don't breathe fire when they speak. Director Ravi is mean because she wants to be. She was on her best behavior with you the other day. She must've really wanted you to take this interview."

"Oh, I see." I figured Ravi's clipped tone in her email was because she was busy, not because she was less than friendly.

"Are you going to take it?"

Tilting my glass to the ceiling, I steal a moment to debate internally. "I'm used to being a bit nomadic with my work. PALADIN never really needed me to begin with. You certainly don't need me now. I'm not trying to be self-important here, but once upon a time, I was doing big things. I used to make a significant difference in a lot of powerful companies. I miss...*mattering*."

"Eden," Callen says, clicking his tongue. "You matter. Maybe not in the way you expected. But you're making a huge difference, *here*. With us."

I squint one eye. "Because I'm sleeping with Linc and he's being nice to you now?"

"I wouldn't say he's being *nice*," Callen says with a nervous chuckle. "He's tolerating me at best. But no, what I mean is you are bringing a sense of normalcy to PALADIN. Think about your past roles, how did people feel if they were treated like shit because they were feared and hated? Even *assassins* have feelings. You're the first person to treat them with kindness and not because you're afraid or have a hidden agenda. You're a good person, Eden. Never underestimate what a big difference a *good* person can make."

Warmth spreads from the top of my head all the way to my toes as Callen smiles at me. It reminds me of how Dad used to smile at me when he was proud and I'm lost in the past, remembering what having a family feels like—it's the best feeling in the world. The best people I've ever known, even if Callen inhales waffles and eggs like a ravenous hyena.

I think about Lance's cackle when he nudges my shoulder after laughing at his own pervy jokes. The afghan in my office always smells like Cricket these days from her daily couch naps and our daily chats. Even Vesper's been kind to me at every turn. Every time she looks my way, there's a comforting smile or an assuring shoulder squeeze. And Linc...

Linc lit my world up, so bright, so fast, I feel blinded by it all. But didn't I pray for a new beginning? A fresh start. And didn't I get it? Why am I so eager to start over, again, when this place is starting to feel a whole lot like home?

"Thank you, Callen."

"You're welcome," he says. "But for what?"

"For helping me decide. I'm with PALADIN as long as you guys will have me. I won't bother with that interview."

Callen lifts his glass to me. "Good girl. Glad to hear it."

I flinch slightly and wrinkle my nose in discomfort. *Oh no. No, no. Good girl?* That only sounds good when Linc says it.

Thanks to the brisk walk home, my mimosa buzz has dissipated. They were by far the best mimosas I've ever had. Callen talked me into the chicken and waffles, and for that alone he will go down as a hero in my book. They were divine. The drinks, the food, the atmosphere... It was all superb and I really wanted to share it with Linc. Mark my words, if it's the last thing I do, I'll find a way to make him love breakfast foods again.

I lackadaisically tap my fob against the sensor to unlock my door, still in such a blissful mood. So blissful in fact I almost miss the hairs rising on the back of my neck when I enter my apartment.

I'm like a bloodhound as I sniff the air, catching a whiff of something foreign. It's not a bad smell, just...new? Like a man's deodorant or aftershave, mixed with a musk that is definitely not Linc's. I mentally rack my brain for the housekeeping and maintenance schedule this week as I shut my front door and begin flipping on my apartment lights.

The smell is all throughout the apartment. I set my purse on the kitchen island and fish out my phone. Someone was definitely here—

I hear the gun cock the very same second that I register the cool metal brushing against my temple.

No, Eden, someone is still here.

"I'm going to need you to put that down." The smell is stronger than ever as the bone-chilling, crackly voice of my intruder sounds from behind me. His hand, covered in a leather glove, wraps around my throat, but he doesn't squeeze. It's a warning.

I'm completely still as the terror washes through me. The fear is like taking a straight shot of whiskey. The burn begins on my tongue then slips down my throat. It brews a fire in my chest cavity before melting in my stomach. All I can do is wait it out. Wait for the bitter swell of agonizing dread to slowly permeate into my blood.

Just when I feel like my knees could give out, *she* enters the scene—my rational brain. I step back to whimper in the corner while she takes the reins.

Calm down, Eden. Calm is what will get you through. Breathe. Deep breaths. If he wanted you dead, you'd already be dead.

Ignoring my hammering heartbeat, I follow directions and speak as calmly as possible. "I'm putting it down." I place my phone on my kitchen island face down and slowly put my hands in the air.

He lowers the gun from my temple and takes a step back. I turn around slowly, *so slowly*, like I'm trying not to provoke an agitated blood-thirsty bear. My heart drops another floor when I see his tall, thick frame. There's no chance I'd survive a physical struggle. He's literally twice my size. I'm not fast enough either. He could shoot me at least three times before I got to my lipstick taser in my purse.

But what's encouraging is that he's in a ski mask. All I can see are his dark brown eyes.

A mask is good, Eden. He doesn't want you to see what he looks like. He doesn't plan on killing you.

Trying to control my shaky breath, I say slowly, "I have to pee."

"What?" he grunts out.

"I just had several drinks and you have a gun pointed at my face. I'm scared," I explain. "Unless you want us both to be standing in my urine, you need to let me use the bathroom."

I press my lips together so they don't tremble.

"Fine," he grumbles and then points toward the bathroom with his gun.

I take the ten paces down the hallway, hyperaware that his gun is pointed at my spine. He doesn't have to kill me to paralyze me. After following me into the bathroom, he closes the door, cutting off my escape. "Be quick about it," he barks.

Fuck.

"I need privacy. I can't pee with you—"

He turns and glares at me. "I'm not leaving you alone, so figure it out." I clasp my hands together to control the shaking.

Breathe, Eden. Calm. Calm is survival.

He looks me up and down. "I'm not here for any *funny* business, so just piss already. I won't watch." At the very least he turns around and faces the door.

"Talk me through this," I plead silently to my rational brain. I beg the strong, logical side of my mind to get me through this.

Sit down on the toilet and just try. He has to hear the trickle so he doesn't suspect a trick. He's not looking at you, he doesn't want anything of that sort. But you do have something he wants. You wouldn't be alive if you didn't. So be smart.

One step at a time.

Just pee, Eden.

And push the motherfucking panic button.

It's incredibly hard to pee with an audience, but not impossible. His eyes are still fixed on the door, but, like a skilled actor, I pull the toilet paper down slowly, ensuring my warm finger touches the black flat sticker beneath the roll. Linc said it'd only take one second. I hold it for at least five.

I don't know if I was expecting an alarm of some sort, but nothing happens. I have no choice except to stand, flush, and be escorted by a pistol back into my living room.

I wish I could see the time. Surely I've been held at gunpoint for several days and nights at this point. Or at least, that's how it feels. Time stops for fear, so it can slowly swallow you whole while you futilely try to paddle against its powerful current.

"Sit down."

I slump onto my couch obediently as he rummages through a black duffel bag on the ground with one hand. I nearly puke in my mouth when I see zip ties in his hands.

"What do you want?" I whisper.

"To talk."

"Are those really necessary?" I nod at the ties in his hand. "Please."

He smiles at me cruelly. "There's a lot in this bag that isn't *necessary* until it's necessary. It depends on how quickly you're willing to talk."

"About what?"

"Empress."

Of course, this is about Empress. *Of course.* It brings me great relief and another layer of panic. "What about Empress?"

"Don't play stupid. Where is it?" he snarls.

"Where is *what?*"

Now, for the first time, I suspect I've pissed him off.

"Fucking stupid girl," he bellows. "Let's do this the hard way then." Pointing his gun at my head again he tells me to hold out my wrists and I have no choice but to oblige. He loops the tie over both of my wrists and pulls so tight the plastic nearly cuts into my skin. He does the same with another set around my ankles, and once he is satisfied with his handiwork—

Slap!

I whimper as his palm collides hard with my cheek, disorienting me. The room spins as I see blurry specs against my watering eyes. The entire left side of my face is burning.

"Porky says it's with you. So *where is it?*" he barks at me again.

I have no fucking clue what he's talking about, but I'm scared to admit it.

Keep him talking. Say whatever you need to. Help is on the way.

"It's not here, with me. It's...back home. My home in California."

"Where?"

How can I tell him *where* when I don't even know what it is we're talking about? I take my best guess.

"My office. My home office, in my desk."

He blinks at me for a moment that feels like a century. "Be careful with your words. I have someone who can corroborate that right now. If you're lying to me, I will pull out everything in that bag. Do you understand?"

I nod as my body goes numb. I'm suddenly tired and worn, like I could lie down to nap. It's odd, I always thought adrenaline would keep me alert in a situation like this, but instead it has wiped me out entirely. Everything is foggy and hazy. I'm using every last shred of energy to not fall apart into a bumbling, panicked mess.

With me tied up and helpless, he pulls his phone out of the

menacing black duffel bag and dials a number. Something must go wrong because he squints his eyes and dials again, but apparently to no avail.

Suddenly, the lights start shutting off, room by room. The power goes dead in my apartment. With the blackout shades drawn, even in the middle of the day, my apartment is pitch dark.

"What the fuck did you do?" I hear him hiss right before I hear the front door open. So quick that I can't comprehend the sequence of events, there's the sound of multiple footsteps, something cracking, and then a loud howl of agony.

"He's down. Get the lights, Lance. She's scared." I'd recognize that Irish accent anywhere. Cricket's voice rings through like a fucking angelic symphony.

You did it, Eden. You survived.

One by one, the overhead lighting and the lamps flicker back to life and I see Cricket standing over the intruder with his pistol in her hand. He's writhing on the floor in agony and I notice his hands are displaced. All of his fingers are pointing in different directions. The cracking I heard…

It was bones breaking.

Lance is kneeling in front of me in an instant. "Oh, Bambi." He strokes my face with the back of his knuckle where it's still hot and tender. "He hit you."

I suck in a breath, trying to hold back my tears. "Just once. I'm okay."

"I'm so sorry. We got here as soon as we could."

"Thank you. *I'm okay*," I reiterate. The momentary sense of relief is fading and my voice begins to crack and squeak. Burning tears begin to coat my face.

Lance checks his pockets for something and comes up short. He scours the black duffel bag the intruder brought with him.

"Do you know this arsehole, love?" Cricket asks me.

I shake my head, but my eyes are fixed on the bag as

353

Lance pulls out items one by one. A wrench. Handcuffs. A bottle of clear liquid that I'm positive isn't water. A hammer. Pliers. Duct tape. What looks like a cattle prod.

"He's the perfect serial killer but doesn't have a pocketknife?" Lance mutters to himself. "Hang on, Bambi. I'll get you free."

"I have kitchen shears," I say. "In the island drawer to the left."

"Fuck!" Lance suddenly shouts, making me jump. "Cuff him, Cricket. Don't kill him. We need to talk to Vesper."

"Oh, I'm going to hurt him a lot more before I kill him," she says with a sinister smile on her face.

Lance tosses a black leather wallet her way before he retrieves my kitchen shears and returns to me. "There you go," he says as he frees my wrists. I instantly rub them together, flinching where the ties dug into my skin and broke the surface. He frees my ankles next, right before Cricket rips the intruder's ski mask off.

He looks so...normal. A fresh military-style haircut with a clean-shaven face. His eyes are cinched closed as he tries to stomach the pain from his disfigured hands.

"You filthy fucking piece of shit," Cricket growls. "There's nothing I hate more than a dirty cop."

"Cop?" I ask, looking into Lance's light eyes.

"The dumbass brought his badge." Lance pulls me into a tight hug and when his body starts to jostle, I realize it's me who is shaking out of control. "He's FBI."

The news upends me, even more than the pliers and the hammer. There's nothing scarier than the people you're supposed to trust, hunting you, stalking you, waiting for the perfect moment until you're alone and most vulnerable...

FBI? But then what does this have to do with Porky?

"Shut up," I silently scold my rational brain. I'm tired. I've done enough. *I survived.* Now leave me alone. I don't want to think any more.

"Eden," Lance says, as he snaps his finger in my face. "Don't pass out. Stay with me, okay? Linc is on the way." My ears begin to ring, and Lance's words sound distant and distorted. "Do you hear me? Linc is coming."

The wooziness is too strong...

I'm far too warm and nauseous...

My vision goes blurry...

The world goes black.

THIRTY-SEVEN

LINC

I DON'T like Callen in my home. Right now, I don't want *anyone* in my home. And I certainly don't want anyone within a stone's throw of my girlfriend.

Callen's watching the surveillance footage on my laptop at my kitchen counter while I glare at him as if he's culpable. He shares the same badge as that piece of shit, so right now, in my mind—*he is*.

I sip the neat whiskey in my hand. A slight buzz has been the only thing keeping me somewhat calm over the past few days. My head hurts from all the unwelcome emotions flooding my body, and the thoughts bouncing around in my head.

I'm mad at myself that I wasn't there and Cricket and Lance had to rescue my girl.

I'm frustrated that I was so busy chasing some thug that I left her vulnerable. I wanted the kill, and therefore I nearly got her killed.

I'm seething to the point I want to rip that fucker's heart out and feed it to him. I saw what was in that bag. He was going to torture her.

I'm so angry, but I'm also confused.

357

Eden is…fine. Cheery. Chirpy as usual. No tears. No trauma. Nothing. Lance said she passed out when they rescued her three days ago. I drove one hundred and twenty miles an hour home while Vesper hung on to the passenger handle for her dear life. But she knew better than to protest. I expected to come home to a fear-stricken Eden who'd be clinging on to me, begging me never to leave her again.

Not even close.

She didn't argue when I told her she'd be staying with me, she wouldn't be returning to work for a while, and I wouldn't be letting her out of my sight. She told me if it made me feel better, she understood. *Only Eden.* Only this unicorn of a woman could go through a violent hostage situation and be concerned about what makes *me* feel safe.

"Christ," Callen grumbles. "He slipped in literally the moment she left to meet me."

"Meet you? On a Saturday? For what?"

"May I have one of those?" He nods toward the drink in my hand.

I fetch a crystal glass and pour him a generous drink. When he reaches for the cup, I pull back my hand. *"Met you for what?"*

"Breakfast," he snaps and snatches the glass from my hand before taking a hearty sip. "Will you please stop treating me like the enemy? I am just as disturbed by this as you are."

Not likely. Are you fantasizing about ripping his limbs off one by one until he's just a torso I can use as a punching bag?

"Did you find out who he is?" I try to warm up my icy demeanor. Everyone has been tiptoeing around me lately. Even Cricket has been jumpy when she's come by to check on Eden. My moodiness may be a little out of control.

"He's *ex*-FBI, but the badge is legitimate. I'm thinking he brought it in case he could use it to coax her into a confession, or information, or whatever it is he wanted. He still won't talk. Have you asked her what he was after?"

"I have. She doesn't know. She said it's related to her old boss. If you would just let me——"

"No."

I'm not allowed to know where they are holding the intruder. I had Lance check the compound for me. He's not there, or Lance was instructed to lie to me. I can't check myself because I refuse to leave Eden's side, and she's not leaving my home until this is sorted out. It's probably best. If I saw him, I don't know if I could control my outrage, and dead men can't give up information.

Callen takes another swig of his whiskey. "That's the thing. This Porky guy—Pierre Corky—he was the CEO of Empress. He's in a minimum-security prison."

"You think he could've slipped out?"

"No." Callen shakes his head, looking at me like I'm missing something. "I've already had local law enforcement check into it. He's a textbook prisoner. Compliant. He works in the chapel for god sake. They are able to account for every single one of his eye blinks over the past year. He didn't send any notes, he didn't make any calls, his only visitors are his wife and daughter, who are both squeaky clean. His name is being used, but he didn't do this."

Tipping my glass to the ceiling, I debate another round that will surely push my buzz to drunkenness. I hold my empty cup out at Callen. "Callen, get to the point. What are you saying?"

"You don't see it?"

"See what?"

Callen scoffs and I'm tempted to smack the smug look off his stubbled face. He looks tired. We all look tired. We're all angry for Eden. We're all worried for her, too. "Linc you're unrivaled as an operative, but you don't think like a detective."

"Because I'm not one."

He taps his temple twice. "Why, oh why is a man, who was accused of intentionally inciting terrorism and trying to provoke a civil war, serving out a life sentence in a cushy minimum-security prison?"

"It's still a life sentence, isn't it?"

"He's at Hanesville. They don't even have guards at the front doors. Everyone there has less than ten years, and most get out on parole within a fraction of their sentence. He'll be back in his McMansion with his Barbie doll wife in less than a year, I guarantee you."

"*So what, Callen?*" I bite out. "What the hell does this have to do with Eden? You think worse is coming for her? Because I won't work another fucking job for you until I'm sure she's safe. If my entire life purpose is to lock her behind a door and gun down anyone who approaches it, so be it. This won't happen to her again, mark my words."

"Linc!" Callen thunders. "*Think. About. It.* Pierre's sentence isn't just leniency, it's a cover-up. Look at all the pieces. Eden went to the FBI about Empress. The FBI gives her a job. An FBI agent attacks her. Are you seeing a trend?"

I let his words sink in as I finish debating and pour another drink. "Well, wouldn't you know what's going on then?"

"That's what I'm trying to figure out," he responds distractedly, "but I have to be careful about who I ask. I don't want to flip on the wrong switch and put her in danger. Just because I'm not sleeping with Eden doesn't mean I don't care about her. I care about all of you guys. You're my team now."

Ah, fuck. All this camaraderie bullshit Vesper's been preaching about... It's kind of nice. I haven't been scared of anything since I was a teenager, but then again, I didn't have anything to lose, until now.

When the alarm went off letting me know Eden pushed the panic button, the world stopped spinning. I froze. My instincts, my reflexes, and my quick reaction is everything when it comes to my job... *And I fucking froze.* It was jarring to realize my life's not my own anymore. Eden has quickly become the nucleus of everything important to me, and I almost lost her. I almost lost everything. I can't let that happen again, and I'm desperate enough to accept all the help I can get. Even if it's from Callen.

"I know you're not sleeping with her, Callen," I say with a dark chuckle. "Because you'd be dead." He rolls his eyes as he lets out an awkward forced chuckle. "But thank you," I add, trying to remedy my threatening joke. "I only want to help."

"Then be patient, sit tight, and don't do anything stupid. I will figure this out. I'm going to—"

"*Ahem.*" Callen and I both whip around to see Eden standing behind us with her arms crossed. She wrinkles her nose as she laughs lightly. "It's a little concerning how unobservant you both are."

Callen laughs and hastily shuts the laptop.

Eden throws her hands up and scoffs. "No need to tiptoe around me, I've already seen it." She makes her way past us and over to the coffee maker, then spins around to watch us both staring at her. She's in sweatpants and a loose t-shirt, but her hair is curled and her makeup is done. The light scent of her sweet-smelling perfume lingers as she walks by. She's making a point.

"*I'm fine,*" she insists.

"Eden," Callen says, hopping off his seat at the island. "I didn't get a chance to tell you that you did really well. You stayed calm, you kept your head. I am incredibly impressed with how you handled that situation. And I'm also very sorry."

"Thank you. And, for what?" she asks over her shoulder, filling a coffee mug.

Callen rubs the back of his neck awkwardly. "I should've walked you home after breakfast. I just... I was trying to be respectful of..." he trails off after glancing my way. *You were trying not to get your ass kicked by me.*

Eden breathes out heavily. "All right, I'm just going to say it for the record. I was held at gunpoint, and it's not your fault"—she points at Callen—"for not walking me home after a breakfast meeting. And it's not your fault"—she points right at my chest—"for being away on a job. And someone please tell Lance to stop texting me and apologizing for the fact that he was so late. It was less than ten minutes from when I pushed the button to when they showed up. It was well before he would've..."

For the tiniest moment, she trips up. Her whole façade is nearly over as her eyes grow wide and almost fill with tears. But she recovers so quickly.

Eden continues. "The only person at fault is the man who broke into my home and threatened me. And he's gone now. Everything is okay. So, everyone *stop* apologizing. I'm grateful for you all."

She flashes us both an overenthusiastic smile as she disappears into my walk-in pantry. Callen raises his shoulders at me and I shrug mine in response. *I don't know.* I can't figure out why she's acting so nonchalant.

Eden reappears with a box of cereal in her hand and a pout on her face. "I'm so sick of cereal."

"What do you want to eat?"

"Can we go out? To a restaurant. I want to speak to other human beings even if it's just to order something."

Closing the space between us, I pull her into my arms and rub her back sweetly, like it can soften the blow. "No."

"Linc—"

"Eden, in time. Right now, it's safer to keep a low profile. I don't know who's watching you. We can order something. Callen will go pick it up, right?" I glance his way and he nods in agreement.

"Sure. Happy to."

Eden nuzzles into me and puckers her bottom lip out even further. "I'm tired of being your prisoner. I'm bored." She pops her lips, emphasizing the b of her last word.

I whisper in her ear, "There are things we can do to pass the time." I'm mostly kidding. Sex has been the last thing on my mind over the past few days, but Eden enthusiastically tugs on my belt.

"Interesting," she mumbles with a seductive undertone. I feel the familiar stirring in my pants.

"Callen, leave my home. Now," I bark.

"Roger that," he says, basically flying out of the room. "I'll call with developments," he shouts from down the hall. I wait until the front door slams and the security system beeps before I slide my hand down Eden's stretchy pants. I feel the heat before I stroke the damp cotton of her panties.

"You get ready fast, don't you?"

She bats at me with her thick eyelashes. "I've *been* ready. You haven't touched me in days. I've been really patient...like a *good girl*." She clicks her jaw as she winks.

Chuckling, I run my finger over the left side of her face where that fucker struck her. My stomach twists when I think of what I saw on the surveillance tapes. "I didn't want to rush you if you needed time to process—"

"*Liiinc*," she pleads. "I'm *fine*. Let's forget about it, just for an hour. Please." She unbuckles my belt and pops my pants button free. "I'm due for a reward."

"That you are." I follow her to the bedroom. I expect her to get naked and crawl on to my bed, but instead she disappears into the en suite bathroom and returns with a little bottle of lubricant.

"Look what I found in your bathroom while I was snooping." *Fuck.* My stomach sinks and I'm hoping she doesn't ask me why I have that.

"You were snooping in my bathroom? I thought you were sleeping while you were alone in here."

"You have hidden surveillance cameras in my apartment. Pot...kettle? Plus, I told you, I'm *bored*."

"It was from a long time ago—"

She holds up her palm to interrupt me. "No, no. I don't want to hear about your past women." She dangles the little

363

bottle playfully in the air, as she bites her bottom lip. "I want you to take my ass."

Every single alarm in my mind is going off. This can't be good. Eden just had her life threatened, she's acting unfazed, and now she's begging me for anal sex. This is a downward spiral if I've ever seen one.

She sinks to her knees and unzips me, pulling my pants and briefs to the ground. She tickles my hard tip gently with her teeth before engulfing as much of my cock as she can.

"*Oooh, fuck*, baby," I groan.

"Please?" she begs when she comes back up for air. Eden's so strategic. All the blood in my brain has flooded South, and all I can think about now is giving her exactly what she wants.

"Get yourself comfortable on the bed," I command before I pick up the lube she set on the nightstand. "We're going to go really slow."

THIRTY-EIGHT

EDEN

I'M. *Not. Fine.*

I want to be, but I'm not. I keep saying the words over and over again, hoping they'll ring true, but at this point, I flinch at my own shadow. I hate myself for it. I want to be brave, but right now I'll have to settle for *pretending* to be brave.

It wasn't just about having my life threatened. It was all the questions. All the *unanswered* questions. *Who? Why? And why me?* What if I'd died and the mystery was never solved? Would my soul be able to rest?

The fear that had slowly been fading since I got to PALADIN has returned, tenfold. I can't stop thinking about it. I can't sleep. This has been too much for too long. I wish I'd never set foot inside of Empress. I'm so tired of it all and I just want to feel something *different.*

Something new.

I'm face down on the mattress, my head comfortably resting on a pillow that smells like Linc—clean soap and a tiny hint of sandalwood from the shampoo he uses.

I fidget in anticipation. The truth is I'm nervous. I've never really done this before, and from what I know, it's not exactly a pleasant walk in the park the first time. But a six-foot-two, probably two-hundred-thirty-pound man struck me as hard as he could across my face. It can't hurt much worse than that, right?

Linc drips the lube on my back first and I giggle when I smell the sweet cherry scent fill the air. I want to ask if he used this on a stripper but I bite my tongue. He's already apprehensive about all this, best not to push my luck.

The sensation is incredible as he rubs the oil into my skin. With perfect pressure from his warm, large hands, the massage is pure ecstasy.

"Screw anal," I moan. "Just keep doing this."

He laughs. "We can. I'm fine with that." More oil dribbles down the divot of my back. It's cool when he pours it, but he instantly warms it up as he works it into my skin. He massages my shoulders, my back, my ass, and the back of my thighs. "I'll do this as long as you want."

"I'm kidding," I say, popping my hips up off the bed. "Don't chicken out on me."

Linc presses against the small of my back, flattening me again. "You have to relax, Eden. Or it could be excruciating. I don't want to hurt you."

"I'm relaxed. I'm ready."

I can't see his face, but I hear his exasperated breath as he straddles the backs of my thighs. His hard length rests against my ass cheek, reminding me how big he is. I let out a deep shaky breath.

Relax, just relax. It's going to feel amazing.

He spreads my ass cheeks this time, letting the oil drip into my crease. All my apprehension melts away. *Damn, that feels good.* With a lubricant coated finger, he enters me slowly, and just like the time at Martinis, the sensation in such a different erogenous zone makes my stomach twist with forbidden delight.

"How's that?" he whispers.

"So good," I moan. "I love it."

"Good girl." He drags out his praise, savoring the words before switching to his thickest finger. "How's this?"

"*Ah*, it's good, Linc. Just fuck me, *please*."

With one more squirt of the little bottle, he tosses it aside, so it lands by my head. "Talk to me, Eden. Tell me how you're feeling."

"Okay," I say then gasp as I feel his tip nudge against my smallest hole. At first, it feels sinfully, deliciously arousing. It's so provocative and freeing that I'm cursing myself for not trying this sooner. *At first—*

Then, all I feel is red hot rage.

It's like I'm splitting at my seams and someone has lit me on fire. I gasp, the pain is so grotesque, I feel paralyzed. I can barely move—my body trying to absorb the shock.

"Are you okay? Talk to me."

"Yes," I whimper. "It feels good."

I convince myself that every inch further I get closer to nirvana. I had friends in college who vehemently swore that anal sex is a religious experience, you just have to get past the first sixty seconds. So, I start to count, while I lie to Linc and tell him I like this.

Sixty, fifty-nine, fifty-eight...

I try to relax, but instead I brace myself against the invasive pressure as he pushes in a little further, slow as molasses. *Slow freaking torture.*

"Are you sure?"

"Yes," I say between clenched teeth. "I can take it."

Forty-two, forty-one, forty...

"Baby, if you don't like it—"

"Keep going," I demand. "*I can take it.*"

I clench my fists underneath the pillow, so Linc can't see. If he could see my strained expression, it'd ruin everything.

Twenty-eight, twenty-seven, twenty-six...

"Oh fuck, Eden," Linc groans as he pushes in deeper. "Your ass is... *oh God.*" His groans of delight are almost

KAY COVE

enough to keep me going. I love the sound of his pleasure. It's comforting and motivating—all I want to do is make him feel good. And maybe I could've made it…except I shut my eyes.

Against the back of my lids, all I see is that black ski mask. The pliers. The hammer. The zip ties. I can still feel the cool metal of the gun pressed against my head. The tears begin to rush down my face, absorbing into the pillow when I think about the shock and disappointment I felt when I pushed my panic button and nothing happened. I really thought I was going to die. I thought I'd see my mom, my dad, Linc…all the people in my life I treasured, but my mind blanked.

I saw nothing except the malice in his eyes.

Seventeen, sixteen, fifteen…

I'm in agony as Linc fills me way too full. The pain isn't alleviating, only compounding. I feel so invaded. My mind, my heart, body… I'm well past overwhelmed. It's too fucking much.

"I'm all the way in. Are you okay? I won't move until you're ready."

Three, two, one…

But there's no pleasure… Just the searing hot, rageful pain.

I can't. I give up.

"Stop," I sob. "*Please stop.* No more."

Linc rips out of me, causing the painful sensation to spike, then dispel. Grabbing me by my hips, he flips me around and winces when he sees my tear-drenched face.

"Oh, Eden," he says so somberly. "I'm sorry. I'm so sorry."

I reluctantly meet his panicked stare before my lip begins to tremble, thinking about how much I've lied over the past few days.

I'm. Not. Fine.

I can barely choke out one word before I completely lose it.

"Whistleblower."

The warm water soothes all the ache. The tension in my neck slowly loosens as the pain in my rear dissipates as well. I slosh the water back and forth in Linc's deep claw-foot tub, feeling relieved, embarrassed, and relaxed but also anxious like I'm waiting for the other shoe to drop. All in all, I'm feeling way too much.

"*Sensitive*," I mumble quietly to myself. "So freaking sensitive."

I smash my lips together, making a popping sound when Linc returns to the bathroom holding a glass of bubbly white wine.

He hands me the glass before dragging a teak wood stool to the side of the tub and taking a seat. Dipping his finger in the water, he asks, "Is it getting cold? You've been in here a while."

"No, it's still warm. Thank you," I say as I take a little sip of the crisp, sweet wine. "*Oh*, what is this?"

"A Moscato d'Asti."

"Ah, a drink and dessert all in one." I take another big sip.

"Do you like it?" Linc gives me a questioning look.

"Very much."

He slants his eyes. "Are you sure you like it? Or are you just saying that to appease me?" He pumps his eyebrows twice.

"I'm sorry," I apologize in a muffle, my embarrassment rising to my cheeks seeing as we're definitely not talking about the wine. "I really tried."

"Why? I don't need that to be content."

"But I think I do," I whisper.

"Eden." Linc hunches over so his face is level with mine and it takes everything in me not to look away from his ghostly blue eyes. "It's time to be honest. You don't have to be a masochist in the bedroom to prove you're strong." He strokes my forehead and traces my wet cheek. "What you went through... You must've been so scared."

I glower at him as he sings my insecurities out loud, but I'm finally honest nonetheless. "Terrified."

"Why are you so embarrassed of that?"

"I'm not embarrassed, Linc. I'm a prisoner. Don't you understand that? Before Empress, I was a very normal woman. *Normal.* I didn't check for the exit signs when I first entered a building. I hate guns, and now for some reason, I see them daily. I am trapped by my fear. I thought this was a fresh new beginning and yet, I'm right back where I was a year ago. *Actually worse.* Before it was threats, now we've escalated to attacks."

"Bambi—"

"See? Exactly," I grumble. Linc tilts his head like he's confused. "Bambi is a baby deer who is skittish, and clumsy. He watched his mom die and his home burn down. He constantly had to run away or be rescued. It's by far the most depressing Disney movie."

Linc's mouth opens and closes like he's struggling with what to say next. "I haven't seen enough Disney movies to refute that."

"I've done the research. Trust me."

Setting the stool aside, Linc fetches a towel and holds it out to me. After helping me out of the tub, he wraps me up tightly and rubs my shoulders.

"Do you know what being scared means?"

I shrug my shoulders.

"Being scared means you still have a conscience. And before I met you—I never got scared. I was apathetic about my own life. Live or die, I didn't care. But when you were in danger, I was *scared.*" Linc holds me at arm's length so I can see the seriousness in his eyes. "I was fucking terrified."

Hanging my head, I see my tears splashing on the floor. So much for my rule of no one seeing me cry.

"Eden, you think fear is a weakness, but I see it as beautiful. Being scared lets me know that now I have something worth living for."

I burrow into his chest, letting him hold me as I weep. When my knees begin to buckle, he scoops me up and carries me into the bedroom, tucking me in, towel and all. He lies down behind me and holds me close so I can feel his breath on my neck.

"What made you feel better?" I ask.

"What do you mean?"

Spinning in his arms, I wrestle against the prison of the sheets so I can face him. I plant a quick kiss on his lips.

Linc's hair looks a little longer than normal. His face is clean-shaven, but he needs a haircut. If he continues the way he's been going, he'll look like Tarzan before he lets me out of his sight and goes to a salon. It dawns on me that this amazing, protective, beautiful man who only *thinks* he's a monster, is so devoted to me, that if I don't find a way to put Empress in the past, it'll trap *both* of us.

"When you were scared, what made it okay?" I ask.

"I had to see you were okay with my own eyes. Once I held you, I felt much better."

"So, once you faced your fear, you felt better?"

"Something like that," he murmurs into the back of my neck. "Now, get some rest, Eden." I feel him shuffling behind me.

"Where are you going?"

"To order us some real food, and maybe get you a bag of ice to sit on." He very lightly pats my ass.

"Hey, Linc," I call after him, causing him to turn at the door. "I know you're new to this boyfriend thing, but you should know, you're doing a wonderful job."

He blows me a kiss at the door which is bizarre coming from a man who could snap your neck with minimal effort.

"Thank you, Bambi. That's sweet."

Waiting until the door clicks shut behind him, I lunge for my phone and pull up my preferred flight search engine. A last-minute ticket to California will cost a small fortune, but thanks to my new job, I have a little money in the bank—untouched and ready for me to put it to good use.

Linc faced his fear, now it's time for me to face mine...

Enough is enough. I can't continue to live like this... because it's not living. It's time to get to the bottom of this mess and put Empress behind me for good. Getting to Hanesville won't be particularly troublesome. The real difficulty will be escaping Linc's home, unnoticed.

Closing my browsers, I send a quick message before Linc has a chance to return.

ME

I have to get to the bottom of this, and I need your help.

Don't tell Linc.

THIRTY-NINE

EDEN

A LIGHT TAPPING on my shoulder wakes me from my slumber. I wipe the bottom of my chin and try to hide the evidence. I must be exhausted if I'm drooling from a plane nap.

The agent next to me wears his FBI badge proudly around his neck, right on top of his neat tie. I secretly used to call him Agent Smith number three when I'd seen him at the compound, but his actual name is Harmon.

Agent Harmon loves Mexican food, has two handsome blond haired, blue-eyed little boys, and his wife makes the best cinnamon coffee cake on the planet. We had a little time to get to know each other over the past eight hours. From the moment Harmon picked me up in the middle of the night from Linc's place, through the drive to the airport, and our nearly four-hour flight to California, he's been my shadow.

These were Callen's conditions. He'd help me get to Hanesville to talk to Porky, but with an agent escort. Callen assured me Agent Harmon is his best, most trusted, in-house resource. Outside of him, I'm to tell no one what I'm doing, where I'm going, or why. Callen arranged my visit to Hanesville and by now Porky should be expecting me.

Our hope was, by the time Linc realizes that I'm not actually out having a "girls' day" with Cricket, I'll be home safe and sound with some answers, all before his rage has time to boil over. By now, he must've found my note, so the clock is ticking. I'm sure he's calling my phone in a panic, but Callen instructed me to keep it off. Linc's outrage at the fact I slipped out will only be a distraction. We'll deal with the fallout when I get back. Callen will probably face it the worst. My master plan is to strip down naked the minute I'm home to calm Linc's fury.

"Ma'am, wheels down in less than thirty. How are you feeling?"

"*Dear God*, Harmon, for the last time, stop calling me ma'am."

His thick blond eyebrows furrow. "I don't think I can. Force of habit."

I scoff dramatically. "Well, I'm feeling fine."

"Do you want to go over your questions again?"

"I think I'm set," I say assuredly. Once upon a time, Porky was a friend. I adored him actually. He was one of the deciding factors for me taking a full-time role with Empress. I was impressed and inspired by Pierre and his vision. Or the vision I thought he had anyway.

"Just make sure you—"

"Don't say too much. I know. We want *him* to lead with the details."

"Good," Harmon says, nodding once. "I can still go in with you if that would make you more comfortable."

"No." I shake my head. "This is between me and him. He won't talk if you're with me."

Actually, I'm not sure if he'll even talk to me. I just need to look him in the eye, so he can see me and remember the person he's terrorizing is an actual human being. I've done nothing wrong, and I'm tired of paying for mistakes I didn't make. There's still good in him, deep down. *I know it.*

No more guns, no more violence.

I'm solving this with a goddamn conversation.

"Just so you're aware, he won't be cuffed at a minimum-security facility, but you'll have guards nearby if you need anything, and I'll be waiting right outside the front doors. If at any point you feel uncomfortable—"

"I know. Thank you. I'm ready."

I've been ready. It's time to end this once and for all and put the past in the fucking past.

They patted me down at the front gates. My purse was searched and I had to sign in on a clipboard. Other than that, there is absolutely no indication that this is a correctional facility. I certainly didn't think I'd find a cushioned, wicker patio set at a prison, but here we are, enjoying the light breeze on what can only be described as a terrace in the middle of a quaint garden.

I stare at Porky, who looks well-rested and far more fit. It's been over a year since I've seen him in person, but I remember a slight beer belly that he would strategically hide underneath his dress shirts, one size too big. Either he's been getting a lot of exercise, or his khaki prison uniform flatters his figure.

"You look well, Eden," he says, a sheepish smile on his face as he glances at the guard who is pretending not to listen to our conversation.

"Do I?" I ask, my eyes narrowing. "Because I've been through hell. You, however, look like prison is treating you well." *If we can call this "prison."*

Folding his hands together, Porky ducks his head. He used to keep his blond locks a little long, just grazing the tops of his shoulder. His previous California look has been replaced with a neat, short do. "The strain here is more psychological than physical." He gives me a small smile and I'm immediately furious at his casual attitude. I wanted him to look in my eyes and feel guilt, not...*joy*.

"I don't have a lot of time," I say matter-of-factly.

He nods in agreement. "I'm just happy you visited at all. I wish I could give you a hug, but physical contact is against the visitation rules."

"*What the hell is wrong with you?*" I hiss in a cruel tone I don't even recognize. Porky's eyes pop into wide circles as he assesses the outrage in my expression. "You tried to have me beaten and tortured, and you're *happy* to see me? What kind of sick, twisted fucking mind games are you—"

"Eden. *What?*" Porky interrupts.

"You're one of the most intelligent people I've ever met. You can't fool me by playing dumb. Just tell me what you want. I need this to stop. I'm done living in constant worry. I'm done looking over my shoulder. Right here, right now— tell me what the fuck you want, so I can explain how *I don't have it.*"

He shakes his head at me, perplexed and startled. "Who tortured you? What don't you have?"

"Here's what I know." Holding up my hand, I extend one finger. "After you tried to sue me for corporate espionage, I was harassed and threatened for an entire year. *You* filled the employees' heads with all that awful bullshit about how I stole their futures. The very bullshit that started a witch hunt for me. I waited out the storm—scared shitless for a year—until I was driven away from the only place I've ever called home... but that still wasn't enough for you." I hold up another finger. "You had a note delivered in the most facetious way asking me to come *here*. I'm embarrassed to say it, but it spooked me. I didn't like the fact that you were *still* pulling puppet strings from prison." I hold up a third finger. "And when the note wasn't enough to get my attention and pull me back into the fray, you hired someone to hold me a gunpoint, tie me up, and hit me—"

"Eden, I don't—"

"No!" I shout. *"Let me finish.* What you did not account for is my ability to adapt. I made new friends even after Empress stole my whole fucking life. You got in bed with the most evil and depraved criminals to try and light our country on fire. You forced my hand. I got no joy from tearing apart the company I helped grow. *You tricked me.* I believed in you. I thought you wanted to help people and instead you were just teeing them up for the slaughter. Aren't you the one who was preaching across all of Silicon Valley the dangerous influence of social media on world issues? Yet, you manipulated it and jumped right past bullying, straight into terrorism. How could I stand by, Porky? How could you turn out to be so evil? *What the hell do you still want from me?*"

He's silent now, his eyes shifting back and forth like he's thinking way too hard. The only sound between us is our loud breathing until Porky finally breaks the silence.

"The lawsuit was just to buy time," he calmly explains. "You shouldn't have lawyered up, Eden. It was never going to go through. It was a defensive move, so I could figure out how to build my case."

"You didn't deserve to have a case—"

He holds up his palm. "It's my turn to speak." Raising his brows, he continues, "I had nothing to do with the harassment after Empress went down in flames. That's just *people* for you. They needed an easy target to blame because a lot of money was lost. I'm sorry you bore that burden. And yes, I did have Abby find a way to contact someone at your building who had access to your apartment to leave a *subtle* note."

"You had your wife bribe the maintenance workers at my apartment?" I ask.

He cringes and nods. "Just to leave a message. Neither

Abby nor I could call you directly. All of our phone conversations are tapped."

"They tucked the note in my *bed sheets*," I growl. "Do you know how menacing that is?"

Porky presses his fingers against his closed eyelids. "These aren't rocket scientists, Eden. I'm sorry. They might've misunderstood what we meant by *subtle*."

"That still doesn't explain—"

"No." Porky's eyes begin to redden, then water. "I never hired anyone to hurt you. I never would. *Never.* I only wanted to talk to you to warn you. You never gave me a chance to explain my side. Although... I couldn't have even if I wanted to. I'm not the villain you think I am. I've been um..." He trails off as he tries to choke back tears.

"You've been what?" I soften my voice to a whisper as I get closer to the answer I need most. "What Pierre?"

"*Scared, too.* Not just for me, for my family." He looks over his shoulder again at the guard who is fidgeting like he needs to pee. "And for you. I dragged you into this."

"Dragged me into what?" I plead.

The words are on the tip of his tongue but he's holding back for some reason. I have to think on my feet.

"Excuse me, sir?" The guard paces toward me. "We're almost done. If you need to relieve yourself, I'll be ready to go in five. I don't know my way back to the entrance, I'll need an escort."

The guard squints between me and Porky. "You'll be okay for a moment?"

I smile warmly. "We're amicable."

"All right then, I'll be right back. Just holler if you need anything." He hustles off toward a small building about fifty yards in front of us. I watch him walk away in absolute shock and horror that it actually worked.

"So security around here..."

"Is a joke," Porky finishes for me.

"Okay, you have five minutes of as much privacy as we'll ever have. *Warn me of what?*"

Porky glances over his shoulder one more time before lowering his voice to the point I almost can't hear him. "Right when I brought you on board to Empress, the government contacted me about *collaborating*. I wasn't surprised they wanted Empress's technology. It wouldn't be the first time an authoritative agency was interested in illegal surveillance. When I initially refused, I was bribed, then blackmailed…then forced. They did the same to my partner. We both had secrets we wanted to stay buried and we were scared. Eventually we gave in. Everything would've stayed under the radar and they would've gotten their way, except they didn't account for *you*, Eden."

I push two fingers against my temple, trying to make sense of all the loose puzzle pieces. "That's why you offered me a full-time role. I found that marketplace because you *wanted* me to."

Porky nods. "It had to look like an accident, but I *knew*, Eden. I knew you'd do the right thing. You were stronger than I was." Holding his head, he solemnly shakes it from side to side. "They threatened my wife…my daughter. I had to play the game their way."

"Who, Porky? Who is *they*?" I see the guard in the distance heading back to us. "Quickly," I urge. Although I have a sneaking suspicion that I already know who. The hairs rising on the back of my neck tells me I can answer this just the same as Porky.

"Who do you think? The very people you ran to."

Shit. I feel nearly nauseas as the truth washes over me. I'm working for the people who are trying to hurt me. There's a mole and I have no idea who it is. He could be waiting for me right outside of this compound, eager for me to spill every detail Porky just gave me. Or maybe he's back at the compound, waiting for the report.

Is this why Callen didn't want Linc to know where I was going? Is he using me too? But Empress is gone. *What do they still want?*

Porky rises, and I follow suit. "I'm sorry, Eden. I wish I would've never involved you in this. I wish I would've never invented Empress's tech. We'd all be better off."

His tears are pouring now, and I realize why he's in shambles. Porky is serving time for a crime he was forced to commit. The very people who prosecuted him are the true guilty party. Leaning over the little table between us, I wrap my arms around his neck and pull him into a tight hug.

"No contact!" the guard shouts from a few yards away.

"When this is all sorted, I'm going to come back to help you too," I whisper in his ear before releasing him and holding my hands in the air. "Sorry!" I say back to the guard who has finally reached us. "I didn't realize. My fault. It won't happen again."

"Are you finished here, ma'am?"

I nod enthusiastically. "Yes, sir."

I rehearse my game plan as I follow the guard back to the main entrance. I only know one person I can trust, and I have to get back to Linc as quickly as possible. PALADIN is not afraid of the FBI. If there is anyone safe to share this secret with, it's them. I won't say much to Agent Harmon, I'll simply tell him that Porky had no information and denied everything, *unhelpfully.* Callen will know I'm on the way back, there's no stopping that, but I'll secretly call Linc to come meet me at the airport as soon as my flight lands.

As promised, Harmon is waiting for me just outside of the entrance.

"How'd it go?" he asks, looking relieved to see me. But now, everything feels layered. His question sends an uncomfortable chill down my spine and I am very aware of how alone I am. I didn't ask her to budge in, but my rational brain leaps to the forefront of my mind anyway.

Lie, Eden. Stay calm and act casual. You can't afford to tip him off.

"He was unhelpful to say the least," I say with a little shrug. "He denied everything."

"Damn. That's a shame," Harmon says, striding right beside me. When I get a length ahead of him, he grabs my elbow pulling me back. "Whoops, this one, ma'am."

He points to a black sedan with windows so darkly tinted that they blend with the trim color. I try to gulp down the lump in my throat.

"That's not the car we came in."

"I made a switch, just to be inconspicuous," Harmon says. It's a lazy lie, that makes no sense at all.

Run, Eden. Now you should run and scream.

But I'm frozen, curiosity gluing me in place as the side window rolls down and I see who's driving the vehicle. It all hits me in an instant, like the storm clouds parting, making way for the truth to shine through.

"Hello, Dr. Abbott—or apologies, *Eden*."

Trying to control my shaky breath, I return her greeting. "Good afternoon, Director Ravi."

With that I pivot, fully intent on running back to the front doors of the correctional facility while screaming for the guards, but for the second time in a week now, I hear a pistol cock. Harmon presses the gun against my back.

"Don't run," he commands, grabbing my purse from my shoulders, relieving me of all my personal items. "Please just get in the car."

"Come along, Eden," Ravi says in a menacing, sing-song voice. "We need to talk."

She rolls up her driver's side window as Harmon escorts me into the back seat, gun still pressed against my back in broad daylight. There's no one here to help me, what's the point in screaming?

And this time I see it.

Mom, Dad, Mickey…Linc. I see them all flash before my eyes as the car door shuts and the vehicle peels away from the curb.

Linc

FORTY

LINC

SOMEONE'S HEAD needs to come off.

It certainly won't be Eden's. Watching my security tapes, I don't know who the agent was that picked up Eden from outside my gate in the dead of night, but I do have a sneaking suspicion as to who helped orchestrate all this bullshit.

Callen has some fucking explaining to do.

Barreling into the PALADIN compound like a shark who smells blood, I check his office first. *Nothing.*

I check the medical wing. *Nothing.*

I check Vesper's office. *Empty.*

When I burst into the break room, Lance jumps about two feet away from Cricket. They are both panting and flushed.

"What the—"

"It's nothing," Cricket grumbles and brushes past me as she leaves the room in a hurry.

Pulling down on his face in anguish, Lance looks at me. "Hey, didn't know you were coming in today. Where's Eden?"

"Great question," I growl. "Where's Callen?"

"Meeting room, I think?"

I don't bother to respond as I turn on my heel and head to the meeting room where Eden made us play that remote island game over a month ago now. It seems like such a short time frame for everything in my world to change so drastically.

Ripping open the door, I slam the note in my hand down in front of Callen, who is seated at the head of the table.

"Please tell me I'm wrong," I snarl. "Tell me you had nothing to do with this." I unfold Eden's note that informed me she needed some space, she was out with Cricket, and to please trust her. She said she'd be back within twenty-four hours. *She promised*.

And time is up.

"I just saw Cricket, who is *obviously* not with Eden. Where is she? Explain. *Now*," I roar.

"Linc," Callen begins, looking nervously at Vesper, like he wants the master to chain up her dog. "Eden was the only one he'd talk to—"

I lose control.

My hand is around his throat, squeezing as hard as I can.

"Linc!" Vesper screams in my ear as Callen's eyes begin to bulge. "So help me God," she says, her tone dropping so low and cold that it snaps me out of my rage-induced blackout of a reaction. *"Let. Him. Go."*

Releasing him, I step away as Callen paws at his throat, coughing and choking. *"Jesus!"* he sputters.

Slumping into the closest office chair, I hold my head in anguish. There's a pressure between my ears, thumping at my temples—maybe panic and worry. Maybe paranoia. But all I know is it's not going to go away until I see Eden's okay.

"She said twenty-four hours. It's been more than thirty-six."

Glaring at me, Callen taps his phone. "She *was* at Hanesville. But she's back. Her flight landed ten minutes ago. I bet she's still on the tarmac now," he seethes. "Your temper tantrum is *highly* unnecessary."

"Why is her phone off, then?"

"She probably forgot to turn it back on," Callen explains. "I talked to Harmon a few hours ago. They were just about to board their flight. I have the itinerary on my phone." He taps his phone, pulls up an app, then slides it my way. "See? Landed."

The green checkmark and "on time" symbol mean nothing to me. *Why haven't I heard from her?* I called. I texted. I begged. I told her I wasn't upset but to please just let me know she was okay.

"You shouldn't have been this careless, Callen," I say. "It was too risky."

"Linc," Vesper chimes in, shuffling around the table to sit right next to me. "Eden is not a doll that you can dress up and put on a shelf. She's haunted and hurting. You can't protect her from her own mind. She needs closure and you need to give her the space to find it, otherwise, you're trapping her in her own trauma. Do you understand that?"

I hang my head, unable to answer because my more primitive side disagrees. When you find something so precious to you, you lock it in a box and protect it with your life. On the other hand, Eden has a strength that escapes me. An unfamiliar force to reckon with—so powerful. It's her kindness and forgiveness, and it's why I fell in love with her so fast in the first—

Oh.

The tightening in my chest. The pounding in my head. Sick with worry, desperate for the relief of knowing she's okay. Rageful at anyone who stands in my way. This out of sorts feeling of trying to balance on a rolling ball… *Is this love?*

"I'm sorry," I say to Callen, barely above a whisper, "for putting my hands on you."

Callen's jaw drops open and he turns to Vesper with a stupid smile on his face. "Did you hear that?" Vesper chuckles. "Seriously? Did I imagine that or did Linc just apologize to me?"

"I could choke you again if you need to hear the apology once more," I threaten, unamused at his playfulness.

He laughs and shakes his head. "I'll pass. But look, let me give you peace of mind. I'll call Harmon right now on speakerphone."

The phone rings three times before he answers. "Callen."

"Hey, what's your ETA? I saw your flight landed."

"Ah, we missed it. Got caught up going through airport security. We're on standby right now waiting for another flight."

I roll my eyes, but Callen places his finger to his lips.

"Where's Eden?"

"She went to the restroom."

"Where are you?"

"In the food court. I've got eyes on her. Surely you didn't expect me to follow her into a public ladies' room did you?" He laughs awkwardly.

"Can you put her on? I'll wait."

"Ehhh," Harmon grumbles, "it's a long line. It's wrapping outside the door. I'll have her call you when she's back."

Callen's face falls. He opens his mouth, then shuts it. "Okay, no worries. Don't bother her. Just let me know when you get another flight, okay?"

"Yeah, I will. Hey, uh—did Linc ever figure out where she is?"

Callen squints his eyes shut and beats his fist against his head silently. He looks anguished, but his response comes out cool and casual. "Nope. He still thinks she's at a spa day with Cricket, but he's getting suspicious. So I'd be mighty grateful if you guys can get another flight, *soon*." Callen chuckles humorlessly, his eyes remain narrowed.

Harmon laughs on the other line. "Roger that. I'll be in touch."

Once the call disconnects, Vesper and Callen are immediately on their feet, exchanging panicked glances.

"Linc," Vesper says, steadying her eyes on me, "Eden's in trouble. We have to go."

"Because they missed their flight?"

Vesper and Callen are the detectives in the room. Clearly, they both understand something I don't.

"What?" I ask, standing. "How do you know?"

"He wouldn't let us talk to her. Red flag," Callen says.

"He's in an airport food court, yet there's no background noise? He's lying," Vesper adds.

"He asked about *you*, Linc. He wanted to know how much time he has before you start hunting him down."

My instincts told me. I felt it. I couldn't make sense of it, *but I sensed it.*

"Do you have any idea where they are?"

"I have a hunch," Callen says. "I need to call in a quick favor. We can't use FBI resources to get to her." Callen holds his head and shakes it side to side. "*Fuck!* I don't know who I can trust anymore."

"Callen," I roar. "Have your pity party when Eden's safe. Go make your call, *now*," I demand.

With just Vesper and I left in the meeting room, I feel the need to give her a warning as the gnawing ache of anger and worry seeps through my skin and poisons my blood.

"I won't ask your permission," I mutter.

Vesper places her hands over mine to steady their shaking. "Breathe, Linc."

"If anyone has hurt her, they will die. Cop, not a cop, I don't care. I won't ask your permission to end their life. Do with that what you must."

Vesper puts her hand on my shoulder as I threaten to break PALADIN's most prominent rule. The rule that put Frankie in the ground.

"You don't need to ask for my permission," Vesper responds, "you already have it."

FORTY-ONE

EDEN

WHEN I WAKE UP, the first thing I see is the view from my home office window—I recognize it immediately. Looking around, I see my cranberry-colored drapes, the clean white executive desk, and my matching built-in bookshelves. I used to love this room. It's a little dusty, seeing as my home in California hasn't been occupied in over a month. It's so dusty in fact, my throat catches as I inhale, and I fall victim to a coughing fit. Instinctively, I try to cover my mouth, and that's when I remember I'm tied down.

The zip ties cut into my skin as I try to lift my arms, but the arm supports of my office chair don't budge. My feet are free, and I can roll and shuffle around, but between Harmon, Ravi, and two guns pointed at me, I find it safer to sit still. Escape isn't an option—I'd be dead before I made it to the door.

Coughing, sputtering, and gasping for breath, Harmon finally approaches me with a bottle of water. He tilts my chin back and pours a little sip into my mouth which calms my irritated throat.

He can't even look me in the eye.

Clearly, he's having a hard time stomaching what he did to

me. My mouth is hot and swollen. Running my tongue over my bottom lip, I taste the open wound. He wiped the blood from my chin at least. He hit me three times before my ears were ringing so loud, I couldn't count any more. I remember Ravi screaming at both of us in the background. She screamed at me to give up the information. She screamed at Harmon to hit me harder.

Harmon was holding back, I know that for sure. He's quite large. He could have broken my jaw or my nose if he wanted to, but he still had to follow orders. I don't know what Ravi is holding over him, but I imagine beating me to a pulp is the safer alternative to seeing his wife and kids in the same condition.

But still, his attack was shocking. My intruder from the other day struck me with an open palm. Harmon...did not. Eventually I just succumbed to the stars swirling in my head, welcoming the darkness that eventually cloaked me. I thought it was death, apparently it was just a nap. I shudder realizing the bastards probably let me sleep it off so I'd be alert enough to *really* feel round two.

"How long have I been out?" I ask when I glance around the room and notice Ravi is missing.

"A couple hours. Eden—please just tell her what she wants to know. How much more of this can you take?"

I clear my throat. "What she's after, I don't have. You're hurting me for no reason."

As I shift, I feel a twinge in my ribs, where earlier Harmon's fist collided with my midsection so hard, I was certain one of my internal organs busted. Opening my mouth, I wordlessly ask for another sip of water. This time he gives me enough to gulp. The cool liquid washes over my empty stomach, making it growl.

Funny. Dad was right...the hunger hurts. My face is numb. My headache is dull. My ribs ache, but it's not too bad if I don't move. Even the stinging from my wrists rubbed raw against the ties is starting to fade, but the hunger is *loud*. It's been over twenty-four hours since I've eaten, and there's no one here to rescue me and feed me Doritos.

Harmon opens his mouth to say something but shuts it quickly when Ravi reenters the room. I hang my head in defeat when I see the small silver tube in her hand.

"It took me a minute to realize what this was when I found it in your purse." I simply blink at her cold, angular face that's twisted up in a wicked smile. "Are you going to talk, Eden, or are we about to figure out what this does?"

My entire body preemptively braces. My tone is more pleading than I intend it to be, but at this point what's left to hide? Yes, I'm scared. Yes, I want to live. Should I be ashamed of that?

No, Eden. We're going to get through this. Keep her talking.

My rational brain wakes up and I suppress the urge to ask her, out loud, where the fuck she's been for the past few hours.

"Ravi, for a moment, humor me. What if I really don't know what you're talking about? Have you considered that? How can I give you what you want if I don't know what it is? Please."

She angles her head and blinks at me a few times. "I don't like my time wasted."

"I'm not trying to waste your time."

"Pierre Corky, or Porky as you call him, already told us that there's only one remaining copy of the data Empress collected for us. The user names, the categories, the groups— all of it. The entire digital marketplace was backed up, and we know you have it. *He told us* you have it."

Dammit, Porky. Liar.

"Why?"

"You want to know *why* I'm looking for the resource *I* commissioned? Are you that fucking stupid?" Ravi snarls at me.

"Why did you want the data in the first place? I keep

397

thinking about it and thinking about it and I can't figure it out. The marketplace would've allowed known terrorists to recruit a lot of impressionable social media users to do awful, evil things. There would've been mobs storming the streets. They would've called on law enforcement, the FBI, and DIA, to clean up the mess. Why would you want to create such chaos in our country? I don't understand."

"But you understand how performance and funding works, right? Isn't that part of HR?" I level a blank stare at her. I'm going to die today, and the worst part is that HR will be carved on my tombstone because still—nobody understands what my actual job is. *Good grief.*

Ravi ignores my reaction and continues, "Corporate and government agencies are much the same. You give funding to your most successful departments."

"Okay," I say. *Just keep her talking, Eden.* "I still don't understand."

"Between the war, election, international threats, and cyber warfare, the CIA, DIA, and homeland security are the highest priority. The FBI is starving. Our recruits are lackluster. We're being picked to the bones. I was tasked to demonstrate the true value of the FBI. We needed more cases—easy cases. It's as simple as that."

I let out a deep breath, understanding finally washing over me.

It's clever. It's fucking evil, but it's clever.

And scary. Because it would've worked.

Never underestimate the influence of social media. You can take a perfectly sane person and drive them to extremes by anonymous bullying, public humiliation, and harassment. But starting with someone who already craves chaos and violence and feeding them the most enticing bait—we would've been in a state of war... *In need of heroes.*

"You were trying to provoke crimes, so you could be the first to stop them. All to build your number of successful cases closed... That's what this is all about, isn't it? That's also why you wanted PALADIN under your command. You were basically raising pigs for the slaughter, and they were your suicide squad. You wouldn't even have to lift a finger."

Ravi chuckles. "It's not that wicked. The wretched lowlifes that Empress singled out are bound to do something stupid in their lifetime. Why not draw them out now and put them in the ground? Let's call it, *preventative justice.*"

I glance at Harmon, whose jaw is dropped. Apparently, we're both just learning of Ravi's malicious overarching plan for agency dominance.

"Eden, I'll let you go," Ravi says, softening her demeanor. "Just hand it over and walk away—it's that simple."

"I don't have it. Why do you—"

"You are wearing my patience thin," she says, cutting me off while uncapping the silver tube. "You said yourself it was in your office. I checked all the drawers. *Where is it?*"

I shouldn't be surprised that Ravi was behind my intruder, too, but it still makes my stomach churn. How long has she been watching me? Stalking me? This only ends one way...

"You're not going to let me go," I say softly.

"Excuse me?" Ravi asks.

"Porky lied to you. The data was wiped." There's only one reason Porky would throw me under the bus like this. I was the only one who could fight back. The only one who could get to the bottom of the truth... Because I have no family, and no friends for Ravi to threaten. Her normal manipulation tactics won't work on me.

I was alone and somehow that made me powerful.

She underestimated the whistleblower.

"I don't believe you."

I sniffle, as the tears paint my cheeks. "Then beat me to death and keep searching for the rest of your life."

"You're a fucking idiot," she growls as she taps the taser twice, just like Linc showed me. The sound of electricity buzzes and my heart begins to pound. I brace myself for more pain.

I close my eyes as she lunges, but I don't feel the searing sting of an electric shock. Instead, I hear a thud and Ravi shouting profanities. Opening my eyes, I see Harmon on top of Ravi trying to wrestle the taser out of her hand.

"Run!" he yells. "Eden, go now!"

"I can't!" I shriek, tugging against the zip ties.

"Shit," he grumbles before he shouts in pain. He jerks and writhes on the floor, like his entire body is vibrating. Ravi pulls the taser from his neck and kicks him in the side. His eyes look blank and his mouth begins to foam. As far as I can tell, now it's just me and Ravi alone in this room. She smiles as she pulls her gun from its holster.

"*Ah,*" I wail in agony when the butt of her gun finds my cheekbone. I can almost feel the crack as hot pressure balloons on the right side of my face.

"Last chance, Eden," she says, cocking her gun and pressing it against my fractured cheek bone.

"Ravi, I told you—"

The door kicks open and of course the first thing I see is the barrel of yet another gun. "*Jesus,* Callen," Ravi says, relieved. "Call first, hm?"

I feel nauseous when I see him smile. *Fuck. Now, it's over.* No wonder Ravi knew where I was. No wonder he picked Harmon to accompany me. *It's really over.*

"You alone?" she asks.

"Of course. Tweedle-dee and dumbass are searching for her at the correctional facility. But it won't be long before they clue in. Let's hurry this up."

How could I be so wrong? There's no way.

"Check Harmon's pulse. He lost his fucking mind a moment ago."

Callen does as he's instructed. "He's fine. Let him sleep it off." He nods in my direction but doesn't look at me. "Do you have what you need?"

"Nope. You two are chummy, want to take a stab at it?"

He snorts. "Is a pawn chummy with the chess player?" Now his cocky smile spreads, and his slanted eyes meet mine. "She's more of a honey than vinegar girl though. Put that down."

Ravi rolls her eyes and lowers the gun. As soon as the metal is no longer touching my face, Callen lunges. Ripping the gun from her hand, it goes off amidst the struggle putting a hole in my ceiling fan.

"Linc! She's alive!" Callen shouts right before he groans and shrivels when Ravi knees him hard between the legs.

Oh, thank God.

Linc storms in and the entire room drops a few degrees. I shouldn't be so relieved when I see the malice in his eyes. I have never seen such putrid hate before. It's pouring out of his expression as he assesses the scene and then sets his sights on Ravi. She makes a feeble attempt to grab her gun, but she's no match. Surpassing her in speed and agility, Linc slides the gun away and wraps his hand around her neck.

He picks her up by the throat and I watch her entire face turn purple as she gasps futilely for air. "I have never killed a woman or a cop before," he snarls. "Clearly today is a day for exceptions."

He chucks her with such force that she hurtles into my desk before crumpling on the ground. There's a loud crack. Maybe my desk, maybe her back, but all I know is that the only man who makes me feel safe is scaring the shit out of me at the present moment.

"Linc, please."

Hearing my voice breaks the rageful spell. He stops his attack immediately, crosses the room, and squats down in front of me. He doesn't bother turning around as Vesper enters, he's busy examining me head to toe.

"Oh, Eden," she murmurs, then proceeds to collect the gun on the ground, Harmon's weapon, and helps Callen stand. "Do you need an ambulance?"

I shake my head.

"Your cheek…your lip…your wrists." Linc names off body parts softly as he pulls a pocketknife from his pants and cuts the zip ties. I moan in relief as I rub my freed wrists. "Does anything else hurt?"

"My stomach," I say. Helping me stand, he yanks up my shirt and grits his teeth. Perhaps my ribs look a bit worse than they feel at the moment. Pulling my shirt back down, I smile, ignoring my aching lip. "I mean I'm hungry."

He begins to laugh and then tears well in his eyes.

Holy shit. Is he crying?

He's so silent and still, I reach up to touch his tears, just to ensure they're real. "You can't do this to me again," he says softly. He nuzzles into my hand before grabbing it and kissing all over the marks on my wrists. "You have to be careful, Eden, because you're responsible for both of our lives now. Do you understand? I can't live without you."

Sucking in a deep breath, I nod, before I fumble for his holster and free his gun. Linc lets me take his weapon, knowing exactly where I'm headed. He doesn't intervene. Standing over Ravi, I nudge her shoulder with my toe. She rolls over and looks up at me. I'm sure she'd lunge if she could, but it's quite apparent her back is broken.

"I said I didn't have it." I cock the gun. "You should've listened." She looks scared. The same way the last prisoner in the photo did. The same way Roman did. The same way I must've for the past year of my life. But for some reason, I don't feel sympathy for Ravi, just rage. For the first time in my life, I want to pull this trigger.

I want to hurt her.

I want to kill her.

Extending my arms, I hold the gun closer to her face.

"Watch the recoil, Eden. The force on my pistol could snap your wrists," Linc says from behind me.

"Does it change you?" I ask, briefly looking over my shoulder before I return to Ravi's twitching eyes. "Killing someone?"

"Yes," Vesper answers. "Forever."

"From the moment you pull the trigger," Callen adds.

Linc takes a few paces and puts his hand against the small of my back. "Do what you need to do to be free. I'll love you either way."

My lips spread wide as I look into his steely light blue eyes. It's not the time or place, but I can't help but smile. "Love?" I ask him.

"Yes," he says. "*Love.*"

"Fucking do it already," Ravi growls from the ground, but her angry bravado comes out shaky and unconvincing. For someone who was so willing to inflict death and destruction, she sure is terrified to meet her end.

"You're a special kind of evil, do you know that? *The cowardly kind.* The kind that hides behind a smokescreen while you invoke terror on the unsuspecting. You risked other people's lives for work accolades. You're careless with consequences, as long as they aren't yours. People are numbers to you—to be manipulated and cheated. What you've put me through over the past year should've changed me for the worse."

My hands begin to tremble, causing the gun to shake in my hands. Linc notices.

"Eden, you don't have to do this. Let me," he says, reaching for the gun. I jerk away from his grip.

"No. She'll live," I say firmly. I look into Linc's eyes so he registers my command clearly. "Do not kill her."

Looking back down at Ravi, she looks confused. I'm still glaring at her but I feel the relief in my chest. The tight hold that fear and shame has had over me for far too long releases as I realize the truth. I'm not violent, cruel, hateful—but that doesn't mean I'm not strong.

"I take a lot of pride in being your opposite," I say the words while looking down at her, rightfully so. "I'm good, merciful, kind...*sensitive*." I chuckle as I say the word I once thought was an insult. "The world needs *more of me* and *less of you*. And I won't let you go to your grave not knowing what you really are. I have a feeling that, for a coward like you, exposure is worse than death."

Callen laughs, still cupping his balls through his slacks. "Prison for a dirty agent is worse than hell."

"That's your business," I say with a shrug. I look at Ravi for, what I promise, will be the last time. It ends here. It stops now. Yes, I was afraid, there's no shame in that. I know fear because I have a lot to live for—I have a lot to be proud of. "You may not deserve my mercy, but I deserve to keep my hands clean. I won't change because of you."

I nod my head, confident in my resolve as I toss Linc's gun to the ground.

Bang!

I jump as everyone else freezes as the bullet lodges into the wall. Grimacing, I wince when I feel the agony of my injured cheek. Holding my face, I mumble, "I'm sorry."

Linc presses his lips together and tries to find a safe place to kiss me. Come to think of it, even my eyes are throbbing. I'm so glad I don't have a mirror right now. I don't want to see whatever is making his face pull in pity like that. He settles for lightly kissing the top of my head as he gently pulls me into his body and rubs my aching back.

"Oh, Bambi," he murmurs as I breathe in his familiar scent, feeling like I'm home. "You're not getting a gun, but you're definitely getting a run down on gun safety."

"I love you too, by the way," I mumble. "I really do."

"Yeah? Not too soon for me to say it?"

"Mmm," I mumble into his chest, not even caring that we

have an audience. I'm so cozy and safe now. I did it. I survived. I more than survived. *I overcame.* "I've nearly been killed twice in one week...so in my mind, you're actually a little late in saying it."

He chuckles. "I love you, Eden. I never thought I'd say that to anyone, but *I love you.* Now, I want to take you home and take care of you, but I think we should go to the hospital."

"Okay," I agree. I feel a sharp pain with every breath I take in. I most definitely have a cracked rib. At this point, there are too many broken pieces. A doctor is necessary and I'll probably need something stronger than Motrin when the pain really begins to register. But first...

"I'm starving. I need to eat something before going to the emergency room. I just *know* the bastards will admit me and then put me on a liquid diet."

"Can you even chew?" Linc asks, worry lines painting his expression as he examines my injured face.

"Oh, believe me, I'll make it work," I say, trying to keep a straight face.

He laughs and looks over my shoulder to Callen and Vesper. "Can you believe this woman? Chirpy as usual." He returns his gaze to me. "You're so fucking brave, Eden. You blow me away—everything is going to be okay."

Little does he know, in his arms like this, everything *is* already okay.

Callen steps on Ravi's shoulder before cuffing her, clearly holding a grudge about her assault on his manhood. "I'll make some calls to pick up the trash, then we can get out of here."

"Harmon was under duress. In the end, he did try to save me," I say to Callen, a little relieved my rage has calmed and my more empathetic attitude has returned.

"Did he help do this?" Linc asks, his eyes narrowing at the sleeping heap on the floor.

I grab his chin and pull his eyes to mine. "I don't want your vengeance." I widen my eyes. "I want you to feed me. Now."

"What do you want to eat, Bambi? We'll all go," he says, with Vesper and Callen nodding over his shoulder.

I slump in Linc's arms, letting him support my weight. I'm bold with my request because looking this pitiful, there's no way he could turn me down.

I smile at him innocently. "Waffles—"

"Ah, fuck."

"Muffins...donuts—"

"Mhm."

"Eggs, bacon, pancakes...basically anything a diner serves for breakfast."

Linc scoops me up in his arms with ease, holding me so carefully, like I'm his precious treasure. I snuggle into his arms as we leave my office with my new friends...no, *family*, in tow.

"Come on, Bambi," Linc says. "Breakfast doesn't sound too bad."

EPILOGUE
LINC

3 MONTHS LATER

I OPEN my eyelids reluctantly as the sun peeks through the cracks of the blinds. Reaching over to the other side of the bed, I search for Eden's soft, warm tit to squeeze, but instead, all I feel is a hairy round belly.

"Dammit, Mouse," I grumble.

This dog ignores the fact that he's not even allowed on the bed and finds every opportunity to tuck himself in the sheets. Eden says she doesn't allow him on the furniture when I'm away, but seeing as Mouse likes to spoon, I'm going to call bullshit.

"Bad dog. Down," I growl at him, pushing against his back, but he only pushes back. He's exceptionally strong for only six months old and is not intimidated by me in the slightest. He only listens to his mother. I ask the one thing that can coax him out of my bed. "You want food?"

He leaps up in a hurry and barrels off the bed, taking the comforter with him, and leaving me exposed. *"Mouse!"*

I thought a protection dog would make Eden feel safe after

the ordeal she went through three months ago. So, I bought her a Malinois. There's no dog that's more loyal, smart, and brave, not to mention Eden is already very familiar with the breed.

I was expecting obedience and poise from such a revered pedigree, but for some reason what I got was a rebellious, clumsy goof of a puppy that Eden loves with her whole heart. We were going to name the pup Minnie, in honor of her childhood dog, Mickey. I requested a female, but the minute he was delivered, he rolled on his back for belly scratches and it was clear he had different equipment than we were expecting. I wanted to return him because I felt a female was a better companion for Eden, but he strategically curled up in her arms so fast. Eden gave me the look of death, daring me to try and take him away.

Therefore, we settled on Mouse.

Dragging myself out of bed, I find Eden's note on the kitchen island tucked under a traveler's mug of coffee. I blink away my irritation. It's been months since the whole ordeal in California, but Eden gone in the morning with just a note left behind, is still triggering for me…

PALADIN stuff was delivered.
I'll be at the compound all day if you want to help.
Don't feed Mouse. He's already eaten twice this
morning.
I love you.

Mouse nudges me, wagging his tail in anticipation.

"Sorry, man, spoke too soon," I say and bend down to pat his head. His tongue lolls out of his mouth as he cocks his head to the side. "Your mom told on you, you'll have to wait for dinner." Pulling his tongue back into his mouth, he looks at me with what can only be interpreted as a dog pout.

I take a big gulp of the coffee that is still warm. Eden must've left not too long ago. The last thing I want to do is spend today at the PALADIN compound. Vesper and I just got back last night. Interestingly enough, now that we're no longer working for the FBI, our workload has tripled. Vesper told me on the way home yesterday that it's time to recruit.

We have an empty compound...

It's time to fill it.

Looking at Mouse's sad eyes, I offer his next favorite activity, second only to eating. "Want to go for a ride?"

Entering the compound with Mouse trailing me, I see that I'm late. Lance and Cricket are holding paintbrushes, dripping black paint over their ridiculous denim overalls. They are standing too close, and I'm really starting to doubt the siblingship that I, for so long, thought they shared. Not to mention, I'm almost certain I caught them kissing at the compound a few months ago, but after finding my girlfriend in perilous danger, the thought slipped my mind for a few weeks. When I finally asked if they were fucking, of course they denied it. But would anyone be surprised if killers were also liars?

"Why doesn't it smell in here?" They are painting underground where there are no windows. It should reek of fumes.

"Because your girl is a genius," Lance says, pointing to each corner of the main entry where tall ventilators are positioned. They are quiet but clearly powerful. "Want to do the honors?" Lance nods at the FBI emblem that was painted on the back wall.

I let out a short laugh. "All yours."

Lance eagerly drags his black paintbrush across the blue and gold seal. "That's better, much better."

"*Hey, Mousey,*" Cricket coos and Mouse trots eagerly to her side, sitting patiently while she rubs his giant ears. "Down,"

411

she commands and he lays immediately. "Show me your tummy, love." He rolls on his back, his four paws in the air. Mouse wriggles with glee as Cricket gives him belly scratches.

"Does he listen to you?" I ask Lance, with a scowl on my face. Mouse spends most of his time at the PALADIN compound. There's a dog bed in almost every office for him.

"Fuck no. I'm pretty sure he flipped me off with his tail the other day. Vesper can get him to do tricks though."

All right, it's official. My dog is pussy whipped.

"Eden's in her office," Cricket says to me. "She's buried under a mountain of boxes."

"Stay he—" I say to Mouse, then change my mind halfway through. "Cricket, tell Mouse to stay here."

She laughs as I make my way down the hallway, headed to the office with the door that's always open. I knock on the door frame, grabbing her attention first. No one blames her, but Eden's still a little skittish these days. I've learned to announce myself before I enter a room.

"Hey, baby," I say.

She whips around, her long hair fanning out before falling across her shoulders. "*Hi, you.* What're you doing here so early? You should've slept in. You got home so late."

I take a moment to admire her. I snuck in so late last night that she was already in bed, so it's like I'm seeing her for the first time this morning. After nearly five months of knowing Eden, she still makes me catch my breath. She finally looks like herself again. Her face was bruised for weeks after what happened with Ravi. Luckily it was just hairline fractures in her cheek, so she didn't need surgery. Her ribs were bruised, but not broken. Her busted lip healed quickly. And she smiled through her entire recovery because my girl is resilient as all hell—a fucking warrior.

Crossing the room, I wrap my arms around her and pull her small frame between my legs, as I lean against her new white, wooden desk. "I missed you, Precious."

"This was a longer trip."

"Five days."

"Where'd you go?"

I grimace. "Italy."

"Aw, come on!" she whines, pushing against my shoulder. "Not fair. I would've gone."

"There wasn't much leisure time."

It was two full days traveling, almost two days waiting in an abandoned cathedral, twenty minutes gunning down a herd of Italian mobsters, and another day dumping bodies. I don't think Eden would've enjoyed that vacation at all.

"Well, one day," she says with a shrug.

"Next week," I say determinedly.

"What?"

"Let's go next week. Just you and me. We'll get real Italian Margherita pizza and find that gelato shop your dad loved. What do you think?"

"Really?" Her smile is so big her teeth show. "You can just drop everything and go? What about work?"

I laugh. "I think I'm due for some vacation time. Or have you written that policy yet?"

She snorts. "For the last time, I'm not HR! My official title with PALADIN is organizational operations manager," she says with a fake, fancy accent and a sarcastic roll of her wrist.

"What does that mean?"

She pops her shoulders cutely. "It means... I don't know. Vesper just told me to purge this place of all things FBI, so that's my current plight. Look," she says pointing to the stacks of boxes in her office. "That's new merch and new desks that need to be built. We've got new furniture being delivered. We're converting some of the empty rooms into more offices. Vesper is trying to build a small army."

"Did she tell you how she's paying for this?" I wrap my hands around Eden's hips, letting them wander across her backside.

"The FBI still has a generous budget for us. Let's just say my silence was *very* expensive."

Those found guilty were punished severely, and in my opinion, it still isn't enough. Eden's testimony buried Ravi, and Pierre Corky's testimony sealed her fate. In exchange for Eden's silence in the media, they promised full exoneration for Empress. In addition, the FBI let PALADIN keep the compound along with our independence while still funding our *activities* as long as Vesper stays at the helm.

A few months ago, I would've been thrilled to be relieved of Jeffrey Callen. Now, I'm glad he's one of us. Officially abandoning the badge, Callen is second in command at PALADIN. I say that to be polite, but I still don't listen to a goddamn thing he tells me to do.

They also promised the most severe punishment for Director Ravshervesky. She was stripped of her title, awards, and money, and was thrown into solitary confinement in a maximum-security prison. I don't know which one, and it's probably best that way. I close my eyes and still see Eden beaten and bruised and it's enough to provoke the monster. If I ever cross paths with her again, only one of us will survive the encounter, I can promise that.

"So?" I ask. "Italy?"

She nods enthusiastically. "I just have to find someone to watch Mouse."

"Look how far we've come, baby. We officially have baggage now," I say, laughing.

Vesper never liked us to have pets. Now I have a dog. We're not supposed to get married. When the time is right, Dr. Eden Abbott *will* become my wife. We can't have kids, but from everything the doctor has told me, my sterility might not be as permanent as I thought. If Eden wants children, we'll find a way to open that door.

It's time for new rules. A new PALADIN. A new way to live.

"Well, if we're going on vacation next week, I need to get this mess in order in a hurry then." Wiggling out of my arms, she collects a box cutter from her desk. She begins opening the brown packages one by one.

"Eden?"

"Yes?" She spins around and matches my stare.

"I know you like to work, but it doesn't have to be here. The dust has settled and you can have your old life back. If you want to work in San Francisco, we can move. Vesper can deal if I don't report to the compound every day."

Eden makes her way back over to me and grabs my hands, weaving her delicate fingers in mind. "She needs me."

"What?"

"Vesper…she says she needs me. I want to be here, Linc, because somehow I matter here. I think I can do more good with PALADIN than I've done at any job before. I want to stay." She squeezes my hand.

I look around the room filled with office supplies. "So, Vesper needs you to be her little errand girl, huh?"

Eden laughs. "No. She says… Never mind." She tries to pull away but I yank her back.

"Vesper says what?"

"That I'm her canary. That I'll keep PALADIN from losing its way. She trusts my conscience more than her own. She doesn't need me to hold a gun. Vesper needs…my heart."

That makes two of us, then. I press my lips against Eden's forehead and breathe her in. "Okay, baby. How can I help?"

"Umm," she mumbles absentmindedly, "I just need to start unpacking everything to see what we have." She hands me the box cutter. "Here. You open them, I'll do inventory." She grabs a pen and clipboard off of her desk.

"What is all this?" I move towards the small box on top of her desk to start.

"Just office stuff."

"What is 'office stuff' exactly?" I cut through the thick

tape of the flat square box and see a small silver case of some sort.

"Um," Eden says over her shoulder, distracted, as she mentally counts the contents of a box, "mugs...t-shirts... pens...mouse pads...that sort of thing. Vesper is working on having a more face-forward division of PALADIN. I think we're calling it a private investigation agency as a cover. Ha!"

"Mugs? Mouse pads?" I ask with a big teasing smile that she can't see behind her back.

"Yes—"

"So not butt plugs and lube?" I try to hold in my cackle as I pop the lid on the flat silver case and find three butt plugs of different sizes with little gemstones on the base. The freebie gift from her order is apparently a small bottle of scented lubricant.

Eden freezes and lets out a loud, deep exhale before she spins around to face me. She looks mildly horrified. "Did you get that off my desk?"

"Yes."

"That was a *personal package*. I meant for you to open those," she says pointing with her pen to a large stack of heavy-looking boxes. Her cheeks are growing even redder and more flushed if that's possible.

"Well, I didn't," I say, unable to hold in my laughter. "You're caught red-handed, Bambi."

Covering her eyes, she ducks her head. "I just thought if we wanted to try *that* again, it'd be better to work our way up."

Our sex life has been tame over the past few months. Eden was healing, so we didn't fuck. We had careful, tender sex which was just as gratifying for me. But now that my girl is fully healed and feeling more like herself, I see that familiar flicker in her eyes.

I pick up the smallest plug with the light pink gemstone at the end and examine it. It's really not that much bigger than a finger. "I thought all your *requests* were just an expression of your anxiety, but now that the Empress mess is behind you…"

She smiles wide, her cheeks bunching into perfect spheres. "Secret's out. It had nothing to do with Empress, babe. It's you Linc—you're my kink."

"Seems a little cheap. You're my heart, and I'm just your kink?" I swivel the plug in my hand as she cocks her head to the side and blows me a kiss.

"You're my heart, too."

I shoot her a sexy smile. "*Good girl.* Glad to hear it." I shut her office door, then lock it. After yanking on the cord to close her office blinds, I spin around and raise my eyebrows at Eden who is biting on her bottom lip.

"Did I wake up the monster?" she asks teasingly.

"Hush," I growl. "Strip. Now." Tossing the clipboard aside, she peels off her blue jeans that hug her like a glove. I wait until she pulls off her t-shirt to give her the next command. "Bend over and put your hands on the desk."

When she's in the right position, I hunch over her, tracing her clit over her cotton panties. She shudders in delight, right before I lightly smack her panty-covered ass.

"Oh, come on, Linc," she grumbles. "Harder."

Whirling her around, I hook my finger under her chin and tilt it upward until she meets my eyes. "Do you feel safe?" She nods. "Do you promise to tell me if you're hurt or unhappy?" She nods again. "Do you know I love you?"

She kisses me tenderly. "Yes. I love you too."

Turning her back around, I force her head down so her cheek rests on the desk and her ass is poking out. I swat her again, this time much harder and she groans in delight.

"*Yes,*" she mewls. "Like that."

I hope Lance and Cricket have left the building because there's no way this is going to be quiet. The things I'm going to do to her…*for her,* Eden's going to be screaming at the top of her lungs.

"Eden?" I ask, yanking her panties to the side. I pop the plug in my mouth, getting it as wet as possible.

"Yes?" She wiggles her hips in anticipation.

"What's the safe word?"

THANK YOU FOR READING!

I had so much fun writing this story and I hope you enjoyed reading Eden and Linc's journey to happily ever after! Please see the next page for access to the bonus epilogue.

To stay up to date with my new releases click here to join my newsletter or visit the link below.

JOIN KAY'S NEWSLETTER

www.kaycove.com/newsletter

BONUS EPILOGUE

For a peek three years into the future, Eden and Linc's happily ever after, and the future of PALADIN, click here or scan the code below.

BONUS EPILOGUE

THE PALADIN SERIES

"I DON'T WANT FREEDOM...
I WANT REVENGE."

Tattle Tale

CRICKET & LANCE - 2024

KAY COVE

ABOUT THE AUTHOR

Kay, a former HR professional (survivor), startup junkie, and former CEO of the teeniest, tiniest virtual assistant company, has been writing pretty much forever. She finally decided at age thirty to start writing the stories she loves to read and to actually share novels she poured countless hours, tears, sweat, and coffee into.

Kay writes sweet and steamy contemporary romance novels as well as scorching romantic suspense. Her favorite writing tool? Banter.

ALSO BY KAY COVE

PALADIN SERIES

WHISTLEBLOWER
TATTLETALE (2024)
SNITCH (TBA)
CANARY (TBA)

LOVE, ME & THE 303 SERIES

PAINT ME PERFECT
REWRITE THE RULES
OWE ME ONE
SING YOUR SECRETS
FIRST COMES FOREVER (2024)

STANDALONES

CAMERA SHY
SNAPSHOT (2024)

ACKNOWLEDGMENTS

To my husband—thank you for letting me have "Paladin." Thank you for growing *with* me instead of changing on me. I love you.

To Ashley—look, I'm just going to say it... Thank you for making me put on my big girl britches. When my heart was broken and I wanted to quit, you told me to go into the cave and write down everything I was feeling. This book started the very moment you told me I was stronger than I realized.

To Sara—almost everything I write about loyalty, friendship, and overcoming impossible odds is inspired by you. Thank you for being the source material for all of my favorite characters.

To Matt—for being team PALADIN from the very beginning, and for breaking your reading slump for this story. I am completely honored and your support means so much to me.

To Caitlin—thank you for loving my stories, but *loving* WB. When I felt a little out of place, you informed me that I was exactly where I needed to be. Thank you for every single emoji and double-explanation point in your editing comments, and for going a little feral after you edited the bonus epilogue. I wrote from my heart, and you helped me translate it.

To Kristin—where do I even begin? When I lose sight of the beauty and excitement, your enthusiasm pulls me right back into the place I want to stay forever. Thank you for your beautiful designs, our chats, and our friendship.

To Laura—thank you for working so hard to help me share my stories with the world in as many different formats as they'll take 'em. I appreciate you so much!

To my squad and hype team—thank you for not panicking when I shared the trigger warnings. You trusted me when I wanted to show you my true colors, and for every single one of you who gave me a chance as I entered into a new subgenre, I am forever grateful.

To that "reader," who I'm not going to name—girl, you almost had me. I won't lie, it *hurt*. You almost got your way and I was ready to quit. But in the end, I want to thank you. I've become the strongest, most resilient version of myself because of people like you. I hope you're out there working on your best self, too.

Last, but never least—to all my repeat readers who have spent so much of their time with my stories, and to all my new readers who have given me a chance, I am *so* grateful. Thank you for reading and loving books. You're keeping the magic of words and stories alive and giving little authors like me the chance to pursue their dreams.